Straight to Heaven

Christine Young

Published by Rogue Phoenix Press
Copyright © 2015

ISBN: 978-1-62420-286-5

Credits
Cover Artist: Designs by Ms G
Editor: Christie Kraemer

The Beginning

We not only live among men, but there are airy hosts, blessed spectators, sympathetic lookers-on, that see and know and appreciate our thoughts and feelings and acts.

Henry Ward Beecher, Royal Truths

Jacksonville, Oregon 1868

Midnight...the witching hour, a time to ease one's conscience and look to the next world for answers. Wild tales of a vortex told by the Native Americans where up was down and large was small, intrigued the valley settlers. One had only to expect the unexpected and it would occur. A ball could roll up hill but not down. No one ventured through the vortex unchanged, simply because the site defied the human mind. Here there were no limits set and no boundaries defined.

Mysterious tales ran rampant among the Native Americans. Fantastical stories portrayed visitors from other ages, other worlds, and even other dimensions passing through time and stopping here for a moment of rest before continuing their journey. Difficult to comprehend, impossible to believe unless one met his fate head on at the appropriate hour. Midnight. When spirits roamed the earth, anything could occur and anyone could vanish.

Midnight...an hour to be wary of, to remain at home and hope it passed by without illusions floating on the stairway, of distinctive flickering in the candlelight, or a hesitant knock on the door from some invisible apparition. No one would wander out at this hour or challenge another, unless faced with no other choice.

Captain James Lawrence had sworn to uphold the law. Tonight, he might have to venture into the unknown; meet any challenge. He might stumble upon an innocent unsuspecting traveler, perhaps encounter a miracle and find a path straight to heaven.

The deserted countryside lay as a freshly painted picture bathed in the moonlight, and the crystal ice that coated the laurel trees shimmered, sending prisms of light toward the heavens. Even February's freezing rains paused as if paying homage to the hour.

Midnight.

James watched the moisture hover in a mindless drizzle of mist; low lying clouds floated and swirled in gossamer veils near the earth, entwining themselves in the manzanita and laurel, around the blackberry bushes, and the fields of grasses and weeds that dotted the hillside.

"Not tonight. Not again..." He pounded his fist against the railing, hoping he heard wrong.

From the west, James Lawrence could hear the low baying of hounds and the steady beat of horses as he stood on the porch of his home surveying his land. Charles Majors would bring his hounds, six of them, merciless in their intent, and trained to hunt man. They did not give up and he'd never known them to fail.

"Son of a bitch!" he said fiercely, "not tonight!" His fist landed squarely on the wooden beam holding up the roof. He stared into the night, cursing the situation. Duty and honor in the forefront of his mind, he knew he would join the posse.

Soon the men would stand at his porch expecting him to mount and ride with them. They were law-abiding men from town. A couple of them owned stores, some panned for gold. One was the saloon owner and another owned the town newspaper. He owed the community, knew he couldn't avoid this responsibility. If they would only come without the dogs, the nightmares might stop.

He rubbed his temples and wished the hammering within would vanish, but the pounding hooves grew louder, the hammering worse. His muscles flexed and as a brittle tension radiated through him, he held his breath, purposely waiting.

Staring into the cold night, he reflected on another time. A time during the war when the dogs had hunted him and they had come so perilously close to his heels. Now, on this moonlit night, even his home offered him no protection, no safe retreat. They came to him for his help— for his expertise. James shivered, yet the sensation wasn't caused by the cold.

He had hoped they wouldn't call on him again, but now it seemed as if the trail lay fresh and in his direction. He hated the look in a man's eye when cornered with nowhere to go; loathed the utter despair that accompanied it.

And the fear.

"Poor wretched soul," he said. "He'll know what hell feels like before the morning sun rises."

James turned and entered the warmth of his home. The blast of hot air from the well-tended fire hit him squarely in the face. After standing in the cold for so long, the sudden change in temperature raised goose bumps on his arms and sent chills up and down his spine. He stopped. A log crackled and hissed in the fireplace. In the following silence he heard a creak from the bed directly above him as Jessie turned over in her sleep. His gaze traveled to the ceiling and he smiled. Thoughts of Miss Jessica erased the hollow feeling that so often tormented him. His dead sister's six-year-old child. Family, his family.

The little girl had made him whole again and taught him to love and laugh, even when the War Between the States had taken so much from her. She always had a warm smile for him.

And at this moment, he wanted nothing more than to forget his commitments to the town. But he couldn't. Civic duty or pride—he wasn't sure which—obligated him to join the party hurtling this way. His muscles, stiff from the cold, hindered his movements up the stairs to check on the little lady.

"Sugar plum," he said softly.

From inside the house, he could hear the stamping of the horses' hoofs and the men shuffling in their saddles. A shrill whinny pierced the night. The dogs barked and he knew they strained at their leashes fighting the hand that held them back. Above the din he heard his frightened tabby cat hiss, knew the cat would seek protection from the horses with his old basset hound.

"Crazy old cat," he said to no one in particular. "Rupert can't protect you." James heard the old dog groan. He chuckled then forced his mind back to the job that waited.

"Jessie." A moment later he was in Jessie's room gazing into her doll-like face. Coal black hair framed the tiny head, and if she raised her lashes, he'd gaze into deep blue eyes that held a subtle hint of mauve, Lawrence eyes, eyes the color of his own.

"Miss Jessica, my little mischief maker," he grinned, reaching for the portrait by her bedside. Just two weeks ago today he'd had the picture taken. The precocious child had refused to look solemn and austere. Instead, her bright smile lit up the daguerreotype. He remembered how hard Peter Britt, the photographer in Jacksonville, worked to coax her to sit still. Nothing had helped until he'd offered a peppermint stick as a reward.

Watching Jessie had long been a favorite hobby of his. She was a paradox of contrasting values. Jessie was every inch a girl, feminine to the tips of her little toes, yet at times when she forgot herself, she managed to turn his household upside down. He watched her because he loved her so very much. The child appeared in ruffles and lace, and the moment he turned his back, he'd find her covered in dirt. She found mischief everywhere, keeping him eternally on edge.

After placing a chaste fatherly kiss on the little girl's forehead, James strode to his room. He picked up his hat and gloves then walked down the back servant staircase. Headed for the laundry and the slicker he'd tossed over the huge sink, he moved with a determined purpose.

The little girl's clothes, all lace and ribbons, dotted the area. With concern and a tender look, he bent over to pick up a doll Jessie had dropped inadvertently then forgot. Jessie would want the treasure, and she wouldn't remember where she left it. Her little face would pucker up in a pretty sob and copious tears would run down her cheeks until someone found the lost possession.

4

James pulled the slicker and his heavy coat close in an attempt to ward off the tremors that threatened. The cold held so many reminders of a past he'd rather forget. Nothing would ever cleanse his mind of the long sleepless nights spent huddling in ditches, waiting the dawn of the next battle; the days on end without food, shelter, or a warm jacket to fend off the icy hands that ripped at him. Nor could he forget the winters that greeted him with soleless boots and tattered clothing, only to turn to the sweltering heat of summer and a staggering need for a cold drink or a pleasant swim in a long forgotten pond. So many times his mind had returned to the waterfall at his ancestral home then he'd wake finding only a dry dusty road.

"James! Get your lazy carcass here before they get away!" Charles bellowed. James could picture Charles sitting on the horse; pushing his hat back, waiting impatiently for him, his smile stretching from ear to ear.

Silence followed Charles's loud greeting. James, in no mood to answer, ignored the man and continued his preparations, peeking his head into Kim's apartment located near the kitchen. Already she'd set dough to rising for the meals tomorrow and the odor of cinnamon and cloves permeated the air. He pushed a bundle of dried lavender hanging from the ceiling away from his eyes and ducked into the room.

Jessie's doll, he still held next to his heart.

"Kim, wake up." Even to him, his voice sounded weary. Kim would have to sleep in Jessie's room until he returned, but he knew she didn't mind. Plagued with nightmares Jessie would, at times, wake in a cold sweat, in tears, and crying out for her mother.

"Mr. James?" Kim sat up in bed. After brushing her long black hair out of her eyes, Kim stared at the doorway where he stood watching. Light filtered into the room. She looked tired, exhausted from chasing Miss Jessica around the pasture. Lines, age lines, he hadn't noticed before crinkled around her eyes.

"God, Kim, I..."

"They've come again?" she cut in. "One minute, I'll be with her. Go on and don't worry, I'll see to Miss Jessica." Reaching quickly for a wrap, she put it on. Without hesitating, Kim stood swiftly then looked his way and nodded. She pushed him away, gesturing. "Go now."

"I owe you, Kim," he said quietly, because there was more truth in those words than he liked to admit. Oh, he wished he didn't take such horrible advantage of her warm heart, prayed also he could find a way to give her back all she'd lost.

"Oh, no." She laughed, but her eyes glistened with the hint of unshed tears, "You've given me the daughter I lost. You know that...Miss Jessica." Her small hand, wrinkled and so very fragile rested on his arm; he gathered it in his, kissing the top.

"Give this to Jessie," he said and placed the doll at the end of Kim's bed. "She'll want her baby when she wakes up."

"Of course," Kim promised.

James had turned from Kim's room, leaving without another word. Determined to get this over, he strode to the front of the house listening to Charles bellow his name.

"James! Time to rise and ride. We've got two criminals on the loose," he yelled from his horse, and the animal danced skittishly on the front lawn, pawing the grass.

As he opened the door and stepped on the porch, rain pounded against the roof. Fog gave way to more rain that froze as it hit the earth or whatever lay in its furious path, thundering against the mud in a never-ending torrent. Gusts of wind shook the naked branches of an ancient oak tree that stood sentinel over his house. Shards of ice exploded from the branches and shot to the ground.

His voice was wary. "Two?" James studied Charles. Handsome, his blond good looks enhanced deep set blue eyes the color of a summer sky, but the blue eyes were cold and hard.

"One's a lady, James, but she's dressed like a man. Just as bold too. She shot a man in cold-blood tonight."

"Was the lady defending herself?"

"No." Charles pushed his hat back. "That's why she's coming in for a trial. After she pulled the gun on Skinner, her partner shot up a couple of people in the Eldorado Saloon, and they took off before anyone could stop them. Old Harvey Skinner doesn't look as if he'll make it through the night. Took a bullet in the gut, not much the doctor—"

"Where are they headed? I assume you have some idea." He cut into

Charles's dialogue impatiently.

"Sure do. Folks say he talked about a little cabin up near Gold Hill, just off Sardine Creek. Tracks led that way too. At least one set does. The tracks separate about a mile up the road. The lady is on foot."

"Is that so?" James moved casually. His strides carried him swiftly down the steps of his house.

"Folks here want to string the pair of them up soon as we catch them." Charles' hand raked his hair and the lead hound bayed.

"Not if I ride," James voice carried to the posse and they all heard the subtle threat. "When we find the killers, they will come back for a trial, a fair trial. And keep your hounds off because I want the man and the woman in one piece. Everyone knows what those dogs can do to a person." James was determined that every man understood.

The posse stilled, horses and riders froze.

The silence following sent chills to every bone in his body and scared the hell out of him, if the truth meant anything. Charles held his hands up in supplication. "Whatever you say."

"I mean it, Charles!"

"That's a bad fix, but there'll be no lynching if you don't stand behind the hanging." He turned for confirmation, "All right, men?"

They answered in unison. James heard the disappointment in their voices and understood it was only because the thirst for blood had grown strong on the ride to his home. James appreciated they'd rallied around each other convincing themselves the pair deserved to hang. But James also comprehended the power he held over them. His voice was strong, and his influence powerful.

James studied the men. Twelve in all and he could name each one, their families, and children. Some had marriageable daughters they had thrown at him.

Just this morning Belinda Parker and her mother had cornered him outside the Wells Fargo Station. Belinda flirted with her large brown eyes, batting her heavy lashes at him, assuming a pose meant to entice. She had looked up at him, her face delicately tipped so her best side showed to advantage. Her stance did bring his gaze directly in line with her large bosom. When he looked up, she'd turned the conversation to her favorite topic—herself. "Do you like my new hat?" It was a flirtatious, inviting question, whispered in a seductive tone when her mother's back was turned.

"Son of a bitch." James reflected on the incident. He loved women but he didn't want Belinda Parker batting anything at him. He'd seen enough of her, enough to last a lifetime—perhaps two; besides he never saw women for any length of time. Jessie needed him and she would always come first.

"What?" Charles looked confused.

"Do you have a description, in case we run across some poor fool who is innocent?"

"Yes," Charles spoke ever so slowly in his deep southern accent. "Red hair, bushy red mustache, quite the lady's man I hear tell. One of the tavern whores...a, ladies of the evening, helped them out the back door or they'd never made it past the deputy. Average height, green eyes, and slender build, fast with his colt too. Some who know of him say he's dangerous."

"They're all dangerous, Charles," he scoffed. "What about the lady?"

"No one remembered much. One of the other gals said she was new around these parts. No one recognized her." Charles hesitated a moment, his clear blue gaze hard and unrelenting. "It's best if you go after the lady."

"You're sure."

Charles nodded. "And James—don't take any chances."

Resigned to his fate now and his task, his steps turned to the stables. "I'll saddle General Lee and meet you by the front gate." He moved swiftly across the yard. Entering the stable, he waited a moment, letting his eyes adjust to the darkness.

He heard the men in the posse turn their horses. Excitement, the thrill of the chase, and the hounds baying set up a ruckus the town could probably hear. Horses pranced and he knew the men tensed and readied themselves for action.

~ * ~

General Lee nickered and took the sweet offered him, nuzzling the desired coat pocket for more. James' laughter echoed around the stall. After that moment, silence prevailed once more and James leaned against the wood watching his horse, wishing he could forget.

"Greedy devil aren't you?"

The animal answered with a swish of his well-groomed tail and a friendly whinny.

"We've got work to do so best get on with it." He spoke to the stallion softly and let his hand roam the horse's flanks, checking out the hooves, legs, and finally coming back to scratch General Lee behind the ears.

"Midnight," he crooned, "but you're not afraid of goblins. I have it from the best authority they don't exist."

General Lee nodded twice as if to agree with his owner. James laughed again. When he finished saddling the horse, he led him from the stall. Fastening his coat then the tin star on its collar, he mounted. Feeling a strange calmness surround him, he approached the posse waiting at his front gate. Crisp cold air stung his nose. He wrapped the scarf around his neck higher for protection. As they travelled east, the rain gradually changed to snow and white flakes drifted gently to the ground sticking on impact.

As if beckoned by an unseen force, he looked to the North. A golden light in the foothills glimmered, growing in intensity before the high piercing cry of a cougar echoed through the night, catching every man's attention. Electrified, the men gazed at the strange light as an eerie glow hovered against the horizon. General Lee shook his head then reared, his forelegs pawing the air. Fear saturated the ethereal black night, encased in the freezing rain and snow. It inundated him, seeping into his soul. The fear wasn't for himself yet it haunted his memories. The light remained, calling to him, beckoning. Releasing his breath he nodded to Charles.

Suddenly, James Lawrence was eager to begin the search.

Chapter One

Oh mistress mine! where are you roaming?
Oh! stay and hear; your true love's coming...

William Shakespeare, Oh Mistress Mine

She was lost. Frantic. So close to hysteria she tasted the fear bubbling up inside her and threatened to consume every coherent thought.

Lies. Everything he said was a lie. Tears welled in her eyes yet she quickly brushed them away, refusing to give in to the possibility his words were true.

Everything Sean Cassidy said was a lie.

Alexandra's father went missing and was presumed dead after the Gulf War. He was not alive somewhere in the South Pacific like Sean said. He had not abandoned her. He couldn't have because Alexandra's mother had told her that her father loved them more than life itself.

Cold air and needle thin branches stung her face as she raced through a thicket and away from Sean Cassidy. "No way..." she said aloud. She held her breath, stiffening then straining to see past the curious shadows that flickered and danced around her. A sudden snap of a twig startled her.

"It's not true. My father loved me. My mother was not his wealthy whore," she cried out suddenly. "Damn you. You're not going to touch me—not again. Not ever!" Furious with her stupidity and determined to get away, she fought the surge of fear and humiliation engulfing her, prayed Sean was somewhere else, prayed, too, that he'd lost her trail. She ran faster, her heart pounding.

Terrified, she knew her prayers would never be answered. He would chase after her, would never willingly let her go. A man like Sean Cassidy would never quit. He'd pursue her until he caught her and exacted his revenge.

Alexandra's determination and stubborn pride surfaced, and she tried to forget what Sean Cassidy had done; the awful lies he'd told her. She stiffened, bracing herself against the memory and the revulsion that refused to leave her. Sean and his groping hands. His refusal to stop. She knew about date rape, seen videos, but she'd never expected to be a victim. Damn him. An icy chill swept through her again.

Terror and dread returned two-fold, insinuating and compelling every thought, every breath, every beat of her heart. Alexandra stopped and tried to find her bearings before wrapping her arms around herself for warmth, making sure her fingers slid beneath the jacket she wore. Resting against a tree, she closed her eyes, and her breath tore from her in ragged little spurts. Her breathing was all she could hear now. The rest of the forest was cloaked in silence and with the sudden peace and stillness, her nightmare returned.

"One letter. A lost letter found in an old trunk..." Sean had thought he had unequivocal rights to her body. He thought because the letter said her mother was bought and paid for, it gave him the right to use her anyway he wished. But his insinuations were all lies and he'd found out how wrong he was about her.

She told him no when he first tried to kiss her, had wrenched her hand from his when he tried to hold it. There had never been a question. But he ignored her adamant "no" and she resorted to begging and pleading with him to stop, yet he'd kept at her, tearing at her clothes. Shivers started once again, horrible teeth rattling shivers.

"So where are you, Sean Cassidy? And where am I?"

Alex ran again. She glanced at the sky then down the road, her feet beating against the earth, trembling, wishing for a nice warm car.

Tonight both the weather and men were intolerable. She'd never forget this night nor would she forgive Sean. Family friend or not, she hated him, despised him now.

Suddenly, the forest was no longer quiet. Sean's steps pounded behind her, closer—closer still and with each passing moment, they grew louder. She leapt forward, running with renewed determination. She stumbled to the fence at the House of Mystery, the site of the Oregon Vortex.

"Please," she said, desperately. "Please, God, let me find a place to hide. If I can only get inside."

Alex searched the barrier for an opening, tugging frantically on each board, her fingers ripped and bloody. One old wooden board unexpectedly creaked away from the others. She quickly squeezed through the small hole. Leaning against the fence, she paused for breath, and after a moment, dashed madly across a clearing.

The little shack in front of her offered shelter and safety from prying eyes and groping fingers. Alexandra ran toward it, muscles burning. Finally, after gasping one more breath of air, she entered and steadied herself against the doorframe. When she turned around, she looked into Sean Cassidy's eyes.

They were green eyes. Repulsively, hatefully green.

Suddenly the earth began to shake.

Midnight—blackness—deathly silence.

Air, heavy and thick, enveloped her, and the ground fell away. For a scant second she felt suspended in time.

She heard herself scream but the sound vanished and was followed by a relentless silence that lasted a lifetime.

Blackness surrounded her, stillness encompassed her, and she held her breath, listening to blood thunder alarmingly in her veins. The witching hour. It was midnight and suddenly she felt as though she understood the meaning of the words. She groped blindly with her hands and met nothing, nothing except a cold black emptiness.

No light penetrated the dense cloud cover surrounding her. She couldn't see her fingers. The cabin had vanished or had it ever existed?

She couldn't remember.

Alexandra couldn't begin to guess what had happened, and she'd seen Sean, if only for a moment, but now he was gone too.

She was alone once again, completely alone and lost.

Alexandra was afraid to move, afraid if she did move she'd fall and spin through the darkness once more. She gritted her teeth hard, fighting the trembling that seized her. She had only herself to rely on, only her courage and strength.

A golden thread of moonlight found its way through the thick canopy of blackness surrounding her, beckoning and perhaps leading the way. The light gave her hope in what seemed like an impossible situation. She had never succumbed to her fear before, and she promised herself she would not do so now.

"So, Alex, you have a potential rapist and liar behind you and the forest in front of you. What now? Do you intend to give up or march down the mountain as if you owned it?" She challenged herself with every ounce of courage she could summon. Then she looked back to the heavens, tempted to shake a fist but her fingers were too numb. "Send your worst at me, Mother Nature. Snow. Wind. Sleet. But I'm going to beat you."

Dismayed, she rubbed her arms and looked at her shredded clothes fingering the bits of material helplessly. Then as if to give credence to her nightmare, a cougar screamed in the night and chills twisted up her spine. Alexandra shuddered, looking toward the eerie sound.

More determined than ever, Alexandra pressed forward, wandering through the night and the forest in a puzzled daze. She stumbled over huge roots and climbed over fallen trees.

Another glance to the sky showed the barest hint of a moon. The North Star, the Big and Little Dipper, Orion, and even Taurus the Bull, for a fraction in time, shone brightly. Peace settled around her, giving her a reason to believe in her sanity and perhaps the truth of her past. Suddenly, the clouds covered the stars and she found herself alone on the mountain again. Snow began to fall. Soft flakes floated down from the sky, drifting in a lazy pattern eventually landing on the frozen earth.

Without stopping, she pushed her wet, tangled hair from her face and strained to see farther into the forest. The dense brush on either side of her appeared as a solid impenetrable wall. She saw no one, only darkness and shadows and the barest hint there might be a path she could follow.

The trail in front of her was rough and winding. It would lead to town and someone would offer a phone. Except she remembered a road that was smoothly paved, not a tiny strip of dirt covered with large ruts and oozing mud.

The narrow road curved downward, bending in and out, sometimes wide enough for two cars to pass but most often not. Then it narrowed perceptibly, cutting through a thicket of manzanita. The going was difficult here and Alex's feet slid precariously before she rested in a muddy, almost frozen bog. She sat for a moment in the mud and licked a flake of ice from her trembling lips.

"You didn't have to be so agreeable," she muttered. "The snow would have sufficed."

Alexandra pulled what was left of her jacket together, and with a resigned sigh, she pushed herself from the frigid earth and kept walking.

Down the road the cougar screamed once more, its cry plaintive in the chilled night air. The pelting snow melted when it hit her skin then soaked through her denim jacket and the silk blouse she wore underneath. She hesitated mid-stride, searching for some landmark she could trust, believing that by now she should see city lights.

She felt as if she were Persephone and Pluto had come from Hades to drag her back to the underworld. Alexandra wrapped her arms around herself, rocking back and forth, fighting the hysteria and the chilling numbness. Afraid Sean Cassidy would loom in front of her and attack her again, she swung wildly around yet saw nothing.

Still she shrank back against an old, moss-covered log and waited a second before regaining her courage. Determined, she dropped to her knees and scrambled on all fours, looking through the thick undergrowth for something to protect herself with. Her fingers closed over a rock.

Alexandra paused—unsure. In the distance she heard the barking howl of dogs and the terrifying thunder of hooves. Warily, Alex crawled to the edge of the narrow road ready to throw herself into the bushes to escape this new terror if necessary.

Confused, she inched cautiously another few feet and peered into the darkness. Still she saw nothing but the sound of a horse grew steadily closer.

"Friend or foe?" she whispered, once again frightened by the images her mind conceived and the irrevocable terror of the unknown. For a transient moment, her horrible fear turned to anger and she rallied with renewed determination. The anger vanished as quickly as it appeared, replaced once more by the vivid and immediate danger surrounding her.

"I will survive."

She told herself to stand up, that the ground was wet and cold, but suddenly she no longer cared. She wanted to sleep. The thought floated in her mind and she closed her eyes, dreaming of a crackling fire and a hot cup of mulled cider. She felt warm for the first time that night. All she wanted was sleep, blessed sleep—sleep—sleep.

"No!" She shook herself awake, forcing her eyes to open and her mind to work.

She had to keep moving, couldn't stop. Yet no matter how hard she tried, she couldn't pull herself to her feet.

"Dear, Lord," she said, "what has happened to me?"

Exhaustion finally claiming her, Alexandra McMurdie crumpled to the forest floor, tears freezing instantly against her cheeks. Snow still fell from the sky, freezing on impact and fear still twisted up her spine offering no respite. For a second, her blood felt very cold. Ice within her.

Floating in the warmth of her dreams, she forgot the cold. As her breaths slowed, she closed her eyes and quietly surrendered to the elements.

"Whoa!"

Surprisingly she found herself jerked off the ground. Even as she blinked and tried to focus, she saw the man and he wasn't Sean Cassidy. Still, she cried out. The sound of her frenzied voice struck terror deep within and her breath rushed from her lungs. She didn't dare stop to analyze what was happening. With all her strength, she wrenched herself from the man and ran. She wouldn't let him touch her, not without fighting, not without trying to get away.

His fingers wound about her waist and she lashed out at him as she was determinedly pulled back against his chest. Without conscious thought, she struggled fiercely, grabbing hold of his arm yet unable to free it from around her waist. Even as she kicked and flailed at her assailant, she found herself rudely spun around, plucked up by the waist and tossed to the ground. She thought, fighting hysteria, that her lot this night had not improved.

This man was dangerous. Far more intimidating than Sean Cassidy and much stronger. Her assailant straddled her, capturing her wrists, pinning them to the ground. Fighting him brought the relentless pressure of his thighs tighter about her hips. She opened her mouth to scream, yet at almost the same time, she felt him relax his hold upon her.

As Alexandra looked at him, he appeared a phantom in the dark, silhouetted against the sky by the finest of moonbeams. The light reflected off the snow revealed the most handsomely cavalier man she had ever set eyes upon. Moonglow touched his face, and for the longest time, she stared open-mouthed at him. As she watched him, he appeared frozen like the night, in time and in her mind, forever a dream. His features were perfectly crafted, his face registering grim determination. He reminded her of the picture of her father resting by her mother's bed, the same picture she'd placed lovingly in her locket. For a few breathtaking moments, fearless moments, moments in which she could feel nothing, she gazed into eyes that seemed to pierce into her, pinning her to the ground as easily as the arms and legs that held her so completely.

~ * ~

James had lost the trail hours before. Dawn was swiftly approaching and Charles would expect him to have the lady locked away by now—safe in the Jacksonville jail. Exasperated and bone-weary, he wanted to turn General Lee around. Until a few minutes ago, the sky had been infinitely cold and endlessly black. A blast of polar air chafing against his skin had reminded him of the cozy warm room he'd left behind. The weather hindered his efforts and if it weren't for his promise to Charles, he would have turned back hours ago. The trail had led north, into the hills, miles away from Jacksonville, and the old rutted out road he followed snaked alongside Sardine Creek.

Snow seldom fell in the Rogue Valley, but now they had snow on top of freezing rain in February. Even the horses had trouble, slipping and sliding on the frozen surface.

"All-fired," James spoke fiercely and pulled his coat tight around his neck before pushing the collar up to cover his nose.

When he first saw her, strangely still in the moonlight, he wondered how on earth any man, even a hunted one, could have left her to fend for herself. Her hair lay all around her, a curtain of fire. A perfectly formed face, he thought, surprised to find himself at a loss for words. Her slim form apparent in the tight fitting pants she wore. The tattered material left nothing to his imagination, giving him an unobstructed view of pale ivory flesh. Even covered with mud and tinged blue from the cold he had never seen a woman so perfect.

Wherever she'd been or whatever she'd done, it appeared she'd been to hell and back this night.

General was sidestepping nervously. James wrenched back on his horse's reins, doing his best to avoid trampling the woman sprawled on the icy ground. His horse whinnied then sidestepped one more time, coming to a halt inches away from the body.

James dismounted, keeping his gaze focused on the girl. He wondered what had driven her to the life she led now. She was beautiful. "Heaven sent."

After a slight hesitation, he crouched beside her and touched her cheek with the back of his fingers. Her flesh was cold, her lips outlined in blue. When he traced the column of her throat, he found a faint thready pulse. He only meant to set her on his horse, but when he pulled her from the ground, her lashes fluttered open; a wild panic swept across her delicate features and she struggled within his hold, lashing out at him. Nothing he tried calmed her. Fighting like a wildcat, she drew blood.

He was straddling her now, her eyes flashing crystal blue daggers at him. If he loosened his hold for only a moment he was sure she'd continue the fight. But even as that thought crossed his mind, he felt her strength giving out.

"Don't touch me."

"I don't mean you harm but I'm not about to let you go," he warned. "You've got a hard right cross."

"You deserved it."

He closed his eyes in frustration. "You needn't fear. I mean only to bring you back for a trial. A fair trial," he added, trying to reassure, yet he hesitated, knowing she wouldn't like what he told her.

"A trial? I've done nothing wrong."

He arched a brow and leaned down closer to her. "Killing a man is wrong and from what I've heard, you killed him in cold blood. After that you helped your partner shoot up the saloon."

Her face paled with his accusations and she began to tremble. Yet even as he thought she'd surrender, she surprised him. "I've killed no one," she told him, her voice wavering as if she didn't have the strength to speak.

It didn't matter what she told him. "Everyone claims they're innocent. This will be a lot easier if you come along peaceably."

"All right," she told him.

Under the circumstances, that seemed a little too easy. He arched a brow again and he thought he saw anger and pain before her eyes clouded over, shutting him out. Yes, she'd been running away, probably been running for a very long time. She had no choice now. Like it or not, he was bringing her back. She'd never be able to sway him from his duty, not even when she lowered her lashes so sweetly, so seductively and with the intent to charm.

Disgusted with himself and the direction of his thoughts, James pulled the lady off the ground. "Do you need help mounting the horse," he asked her, expecting her complete obedience.

She slipped her hands inside her coat and backed up a step. "I can't ride a horse and I'm not going anywhere with you."

He held his ground, waiting for her to run again. "I'll help you up. Then all you have to do is sit. You do know how to sit?"

She turned, a bit unsteady, and staggered down the mountain, giving a good impression of a drunken sailor.

He mounted and followed along behind. "Have it your way, but you'll freeze to death."

He thought he heard a reply but wasn't sure.

James was silent, anxious to find a way to get her on his horse. He watched as a tremor swept through her then she stumbled. If left to her own strength, she'd falter soon but he didn't intend to wait that long. He swiftly dismounted and saw to it she was upon his horse, riding in front of him. He felt the cold from her body penetrate his clothes and he shivered, fear for her life instantly paramount as she slumped against him.

~ * ~

Alex felt ill as they rode, the sights and sounds and memories of the strange night she'd experienced, haunting her. She tried desperately to sit up straight and keep her back away from this man who'd taken her prisoner, but she couldn't.

The man didn't talk at all, silent and resigned; it seemed, to ride hard. The forest swept by her and she couldn't begin to tell in which direction they traveled. At first she thought he was an escapee from some asylum but she changed her mind. He was too serious and way too sure of himself. He moved with a stubborn determination and every gesture cried out to her that he knew what he was about. She fought the cold, fought, too the need to surrender to this man's will.

But Alex's lashes lowered and she gave the up fight, snuggling deeper into the form that enveloped her freezing body. She drifted in and out of a deep all encompassing sleep. The back of her head rested on a solid wall of heat and occasionally she'd move against it, searching for warmth but nothing penetrated the cold. Even in her half conscious state, she felt an arm tighten in a protective vise around her.

"C'mon General." The horse picked up speed and its hooves pounded across the fields and through the snow covered hills. Alexandra sensed his presence as she drifted in-and-out of a comforting haze, her mind registering neither fear nor concern. She clung to that mindless state, because it allowed her to forget the terror and the mysterious unanswered questions nagging in the far recesses of her mind. Slowly she stirred once then decided she liked it right where she was. "Umm." She rubbed her cheek on soft fabric. A groan rumbled in her ear, and she nestled her bottom to fit more solidly into the space it rested in. The groan sounded again, this time causing her eyes to flicker once before closing. Again, she settled comfortably into the protective shelter surrounding her.

It was early morning before Alex opened her eyes and feeling more alert peered into the sunlight. Cautiously, she turned and when she looked up, she not only saw daylight, but also eyes the color of a deep blue lake. Stunned by the gentleness there, she touched her hand to the man's chin then closed her eyes again in an attempt to gain time and the equilibrium she knew she'd lost the previous night.

A second later Alex pushed herself away, but the man pulled her back. She relaxed a moment before she looked to the east where the light was beginning to spill above the rugged Cascade Range. Mt. McLaughlin stood guard over the valley and the newly fallen snow glistened in the dawn. A few wispy clouds hovered in ribbons near a horizon the color of ripe peaches. Where the sun hit the ground, the snow shimmered and sparkled in all the colors of the rainbow but nothing melted. She squinted her eyes against the bright glare then blinked, trying to focus. She looked back at the man who even now resembled the picture of her father, her fingers slowly tightening around the locket she wore.

"How do you feel, Miss?" he queried, interrupting her thoughts. His voice was very near her ear, strong and gentle.

He was speaking to her and she didn't know how to answer. So, instead she stared at him blankly.

"Never mind. Are you warm enough?" The stranger smiled at her.

"I…" she began.

The man laughed before brushing the hair from her face in a very protective way. "Can't make up your mind?"

Alex buried her face in the cape he'd wrapped around her for warmth.

"Can't talk?" he asked softly the warmth of his breath feathering across her cheek.

"No," she blinked again and now she was staring back. "Too cold."

"How cold?"

She pulled his cape tighter but couldn't find the strength to answer.

"Perhaps you shouldn't wander around in the middle of the night." His mood changed and he gazed at her with clear blue eyes. "Can you wiggle your toes?"

She tried to do what he said and was appalled that she couldn't move them. "No," she said, feeling very cautious and weak.

"Next you'll tell me you were defending yourself," he said wryly.

"Yes." Alex wondered how he knew, and she wanted to ask him all the unanswered questions in her head. She tried. She really did. "Where?" Her voice croaked, so she licked her chapped lips and tried to talk again.

"You're safe. Hush now, it doesn't matter," he said. "You need rest."

She wanted to yell at him that it did matter, but when she tried to speak, all that came out was, "Rest." Everything about this man confused and baffled her. His clothes. His manner of speaking. She wanted to know where he was taking her, and she didn't like the way she felt. Helpless. Lost.

"Angel." He looked at her, concern paramount in his eyes. He tightened his arms around her. As if he could read her mind, "I'm taking you to my own home. It's close and you're cold and wet," he said patiently. "I think it would be best until the posse comes back with your partner."

"Partner?" Dear God, but she couldn't think straight. This man thought she was a criminal of some sort. Finally, she managed a weak defense. "Whatever you think I've done, you're wrong. I'm innocent. You have to believe—"

"You're a wonderful actress," he told her. "You should turn your talents to the stage—something honest. A life of crime is no place for a young lady. Or do you sell yourself to the highest bidder, too?"

Highest bidder? She held her breath for a moment and listened to the beat of the man's heart, to the crunch of snow under his horse's hooves.

"You're lucky they didn't send the dogs after you."

Lucky? Dogs? A mysterious feeling, a sixth sense told her she was somewhere she didn't belong, somewhere she wasn't supposed to be. Accused of a crime, held by a strange man...

Exhausted and thoroughly puzzled, she closed her eyes trying to think. Yet the rigid and unrelenting tension in her body refused to let that happen. She wanted to sleep, but she was too afraid. She needed to understand, but nothing made sense, least of all this man who seemed so gentle one minute but so very condescending the next.

"Yes. You're fortunate. I doubt if your partner is faring so well," he told her patiently. "You should have known better. That little stunt in the saloon could cost you your life," he said, his voice strangely tender.

She opened her eyes, completely baffled. "I've never been in a saloon."

He nudged his horse to a faster pace. "So you say."

He doesn't believe me?

"You played for high stakes. And lost. Now you'll have to pay. I'll take you to my home. You can wash up and I'll find something decent for you to wear. Then I'll take you into town to the jail."

Jail?

"As I was saying, we're 'most there." He went on smoothly. "Kim, my housekeeper and cook, will see to you and I'm sure you'll find your brief stay pleasant."

Alexandra's heart filled with fear; all the while her mind swirled with questions she had no answers for. She was desperately tired and so very cold. Even though this man had rescued her, he was also her jailer. She looked at him again, this time seeing only the harsh angles and planes of his face.

"You will stay with me and you will behave yourself," he went on.

She heard his voice but it sounded distant as if he spoke to her from far away. She wanted to tell him he'd have to lock her away because she was going home. And she was not going to stand trial for a crime she didn't commit. But she couldn't quite form the words.

He kept talking to her even though she didn't respond. His drawl was deep, confident and incredibly sexy, and she thought for a moment he was very charming. Too bad he was the enemy.

It took a great effort but she managed to open her eyes long enough to speak. "I'm not staying," she said, but she wasn't sure he heard until after a slight hesitation.

"Would you escape me and a chance at something better only to meet another man who would lead you astray?"

She shook her head, fighting to sit up, to explain all that had happened to her.

He sensed her distraction, pulling her closer to his chest, to his warmth. "Hush. Now just relax and enjoy the ride because you're not going anywhere."

I don't want to relax. She tried to ignore the tangled emotions sweeping through her, tried to push away from him.

Then he told her softly. "Enough. Now be a good girl and do as I say."

Alex blinked several times before her body shuddered, too stunned by his patronizing and ridiculous words to argue the mute point. *Good girl? Do as I say? Doesn't he know this is the twenty first century?*

A moment later, she felt his arm tighten around her again, felt him pull her closer. The cape he'd draped around her and the wall of his chest created a warm barrier against the cold.

Enough for now, perhaps he was right. She had started the evening hoping to reach an understanding with Sean Cassidy. The lies about her father had gone on long enough, and she was ready to let the truth be told. She closed her eyes tightly. So she had accepted a date with Sean and he'd turned into a wild man.

Now she was in the arms of a stranger and accused of shooting someone. She was his prisoner, yet he'd saved her life. She knew no matter what she was willing to admit, she would have died on the mountain if he hadn't come along. Now—if she understood him correctly, she was about to stand trial for murder.

Dear God, how could she fight this and how was it possible she suddenly had no future?

Yet, as she reflected on all that occurred, she felt the hot sting of tears well up inside her. To hold on to the future, to defend herself, she had to make sense of all that had happened to her since she first stepped inside the vortex.

And she would have to confront Sean Cassidy again, if only to prove herself. Ironically, his testimony could set her free or condemn her. She might very well need this man's protection.

She didn't know how long they rode, didn't care. She was gathering strength for a confrontation she knew was inevitable. The silence surrounding them was more unnerving than his quiet banter. After a while she turned in his arms once more, staring into his clear blue eyes, and unable to account for her sudden show of strength, "A girl should know who her executioner is."

"James..." he said, "Captain James Lawrence at your service. And I'm not an executioner." He tipped his hat to her and pulled her closer. A gesture so protective and so masculine Alexandra felt instantly fragile and feminine.

A protective gesture, she told herself, nothing more, but her strange emotions unnerved and frightened her. It was all she could do to maintain the tenuous grip she had on her sanity and stifle her mounting apprehension. "Where are we?"

"Ah..." he said and stared at her. "Let's see, we are, as the eagle flies, about four miles due north from Jacksonville, and my home is over that rise, two miles at the most. That's where we're going. I'm taking you home."

Chapter Two

As James rode down the long road toward his home, he felt a welcome lifting of his heart. He'd built this home for Jessie and for himself; to this day, he loved it.

Yet, as he approached, he also felt tension sweep through the young woman's body, and shivers travel up her spine. Her fingers shook against his arm and she shrank back against his chest. Protective feelings he didn't understand, surfaced again.

"No..." she whispered, the catch in her voice surprising him. She was trembling, her nails digging into his arm. He pulled back on the reins then crooned to his skittish horse and the frightened woman, trying to calm them both.

His prisoner looked at the house then the grounds and the outbuildings. "It's all so different," she said, "yet so very much the same. Yesterday, I could have sworn there was a highway in front of this house. And my grandfather played here when he was a little boy. He told me so."

James watched as tears rose in her eyes, watched her brush them away. He was stunned by her strange reaction to his home.

"A what? Your grandfather? I built this house."

"You did?"

Her voice sounded like a thready whisper in the cold, and her face turned a deathly shade of white. James tightened his hold, trying to reassure her.

"It's my imagination...I'm dreaming..."

The words were so quiet, he wasn't sure at first if he heard them. He pulled her closer and searched the grounds for something that might have frightened her.

But there was nothing he could see. The valley floor spread out in panoramic splendor below his house. When he stood in front of the large window in his parlor, he could see Table Rock and Mt. Pitt. His home was due north from Jacksonville, and it was everything he'd ever wanted for himself and Miss Jessica. The outbuildings were all new and located behind the main house. At the carriage house an old wagon sat off to the side. The stable doors stood open and the soft nickers of his horses floated out on the chilled breeze.

"You're not dreaming," he said. A soft moan interrupted James, but he didn't have time to question her.

Jessie catapulted across the veranda and down the dozen steps to the ground. The little girl ran, waving her arms wildly. "Papa! Papa!" Kim emerged from the house to stand on the balcony directly above the veranda on the second floor then turned, disappearing into the house.

Jessie's mad dash across the frozen earth lasted little more than a few seconds. She appeared all black pigtails, calico arms, and white petticoats. Every loose part flapping in the wake of the breeze she created.

Quickly James jumped from his horse, and tried to steady the woman and General Lee, the horse prancing nervously. Before James could calm the powerful stallion, Jessie dashed into his arms. The flying bundle firmly wrapped herself around his large body. Her childish laughter and impetuous grin filled his heart.

Jessie clung to him and giggled excitedly.

"Bear hug, Papa!"

"Behave yourself, sugar plum. This lady's near frozen to death, and I have to see to her. C'mon, now, let's get her off the horse and inside." He placed a loud kissing smack on Jessie's forehead and hugged her back. General Lee snorted and pawed the ground, moving restlessly once more. "Whoa, there, General."

As James looked up, the woman's eyes grew huge and her white knuckled fingers tore at General's mane.

James didn't have time to grab for the reins before she slipped from the horse with a cry so shrill the sound sent chills down his spine. Instantly, he dropped everything, including Jessie, and lunged for the lady.

Jessie giggled again.

The woman landed half in his arms and half out, shaking like a cornered animal. She clung to him as if she were afraid of more than just the fall. At the same time, he felt her softness as his chest cradled her breasts and the length of her molded against him. His protective feelings warred with desire as he fought the urge that came to mind. James groaned and pried her fingers lose. Gently swinging her into his arms, he started for the house.

"Mr. James," Kim greeted him. Her gaze rested briefly on the young lady he held so close.

"James." Charles was behind Kim. "Well I'll be hornswoggled. What did you find on the trail?"

"What does it look like? The prisoner. Get a warm bath ready for her, but not hot, lots of warm towels too. She needs to thaw out a bit," he called over his shoulder to Kim. His long booted strides took the stairs leading to his house two at a time.

Charles slapped the brim of his hat against his thigh. "That's where you're wrong. We got the real killers locked up tight as you please. I dropped by to give you the good news. Seems that extra set of tracks was a decoy."

"I told you I was innocent," her voice was a mere whisper against his cheek.

He paused long enough to hold her away from him. "That remains to be seen. So tell me, why were you on the mountain by yourself?"

"I don't think you'd believe me." Her eyes flashed defiantly.

Well, she wasn't as weak as he thought. "Try me," he challenged.

"Who is she, Mr. James?" Kim interrupted, sputtering Chinese and English behind him.

He felt Kim's look of concern bite into his back.

James stopped at the front door before slowly turning to confront his audience. "I don't know. I found her on the mountain nearly frozen to death. And if she's not the lady we searched, for I don't have any idea who she is."

Alex opened her mouth to tell them. "I..."

Without a moment's hesitation and not giving Alex a chance to finish a sentence, James carried her into the house and up the main stairs to his room. He had only seconds to place her on the bed before Kim had the huge copper tub set behind privacy screens and water steaming on the stove.

Decidedly masculine, the dark paneling and large bed in his room overwhelmed the young woman. Her red hair stood out vividly against the forest-green quilt beneath her, and her skin appeared virgin white, innocently reminding him that he'd assumed she was guilty the moment he'd seen her. He liked the way she looked on his bed.

Kim ignored the situation and went about filling the tub. Jessie was in the doorway, grinning and hopping on one foot.

"Who is she, Papa? Is she nice? Did you bring her to be my new mommy?" The questions continued non-stop. She didn't seem to want an answer. And he didn't have one. At least not yet, but he intended to find out soon. New mommy? His gaze shifted back to the girl on his bed, and he wondered what on earth could have given Jessie that idea. His prisoner was sitting up now, her knees tucked into a tight little ball against her chest, her face flushed with anger, her eyes shimmering.

"Run along, sugar plum. I'll talk to you later. Right now she needs to warm up some. Maybe when she feels better she can answer our questions. What do you think?" He winked at Jessie then turned his attention to Kim.

"Can I help her warm up?" Jessie asked.

"Not this time. Kim will take care of her. Oh, and Kim, keep the warm water coming. I'll check on her when she gets out of the bath." Kim was bustling around the room, casting curious glances his way. He was just as curious, perhaps more so. Yet now Kim stood in the doorway, hands clasped together in front of her, a strange look on her face and a curious light in her eye. He didn't know what to think.

Kim finally spoke, "I've known you since you were knee high to a grasshopper, and Mr. James, I don't think, well, you never brought a lady home before. Have you thought about Jessie?"

"It's not what it looks like, Kim, and I didn't have a choice." He cut off further argument. "A jail is no place for a lady. Besides she's suffering from a mild case of hypothermia, and her body temperature has dropped dangerously low." With clinical detachment James touched the lady's forehead before skimming his hand down her arm. "She needed a doctor."

Kim stepped forward. "I'll take care of her. You go on down and talk to Charles. Find out who she is."

He frowned at Kim. "I don't think he knows any more than I do."

"I'll call you as soon as she's through with the bath," Kim said. "Go downstairs, please. And bring up more water. Hurry. Send something warm to drink too."

"Some of that tea you brew with those dried leaves you've got hanging from the kitchen ceiling?"

"Of course. Now shoo."

James frowned at being dismissed so casually, but he strode downstairs. He never did understand why Kim followed him west, never understood why he'd always been her favorite. Among all his brothers and sisters, Kim had always held a tender spot for him.

James returned and emptied another kettle of hot water into the tub then stepped outside the door. He leaned against the wall, listening, waiting for the women to finish. The girl really did need to be checked out.

Life was so very fragile. He closed his eyes, remembering so many things he'd rather forget. At times no matter how much he hated the senseless killing, he could see the good that had come from the war. Yet, in the end he saw the endless stream of bodies on his operating table, and he knew it would be a long time before the pain and suffering would stop. He didn't want this lady to suffer.

He could hear Kim shuffling about. "I'll help you with your clothes," she told the woman quietly. Kim's earnest concern caused James to feel a moment's guilt at the way he had treated the lady, but it vanished. No real lady would have been alone on that mountain in the middle of a snowstorm. She had something to hide, and he meant to find out her secrets.

"Mr. James, come quickly."

Kim hurried through the door, almost running into him on her mad dash.

"Something's wrong."

When he stepped into the room, Kim behind him, the lady in question was curled in a ball, softly moaning, her cheeks flushed and her forehead creased. He crouched beside her, gently touching her, searching for a pulse. "Can you tell me what hurts?"

"My toes, my fingers, I can't..." The pain so evident in her voice, he cursed himself for not realizing sooner.

"They feel like a hundred bees are stinging them?" he asked softly.

"A million," she choked out.

"Can you walk?" He picked up her hand and warmed the fingers gently in his. "Can you?" Her hand felt cold and small, so fragile encompassed in his.

"I don't know." He helped her from the bed only to find she couldn't stand, couldn't move her fingers to undress herself, and he knew there was no other choice. James swept her into his arms, carried her to the tub, and very gently put her in, clothes and all.

Water molded the silk blouse to her form, exposing everything to him, all he'd tried to avoid. Without thinking, his gaze touched every part of her. She was exquisite. For a second, all thoughts of professionalism vanished. It was impossible for him to turn his head away.

"Call for Kim if you need anything," he told her while he backed up slowly. After a few brittle moments, he shouted more directions to Kim.

Alex cried out softly.

"Are you all right?" He hesitated before he stepped forward once more to help. Taking in the long line of her leg, the soft curve of her breast beneath the water, James backed up again. He had to walk away. She was extraordinary in her dramatic beauty, a loveliness that didn't compare to the courage she'd graphically shown him. Until this moment he didn't think he'd really looked at her, at least not as a woman. Until now she'd been his prisoner. Framed by the extraordinary color of auburn, her features, as delicate as a flower, perfect. Then again her eyes had a life and fire all their own, dancing and sizzling, so blue they rivaled the deep hues of the summer sky. The full rise of her breasts just below the level of the water was unbearably evocative, and he found himself thinking of all the possibilities, realizing he wanted her. Not just any woman. But her.

Long moments ticked by as he watched entranced by her poetic beauty. Passion and stubborn pride shimmered reminding him of a halo circling around her. He wanted to touch the silk of her hair and see if it was as soft as he remembered. Most of all, he wanted to pull her from the water and find out if the passion and the heat emanating from her crystal clear gaze were real, and if they could vanquish all the horrible nightmares the war had created for him. How could any man leave this woman on a mountain to die? How could any man grow tired of her?

"You'll feel better in a few minutes," he told her.

"That's easy for you to say."

Her cryptic reply made him chuckle softly. "Indeed." Yet when he tried to walk away, he found he could not. "It's true. Your body's just now beginning to unthaw. The warm water should help."

With every intention of ignoring her until she was dressed and ready to talk, he turned his back. It worked for a moment, one brief second, yet he stopped, casually turned and leaned against the wall. With a perfect view of her silhouette through the privacy screen, he fought an overwhelming urge to stare. Focusing his gaze on every other conceivable object in the room, he felt as if he floundered in water so deep he'd never find dry land. At least five very long minutes passed before she finally spoke.

"You can leave now. I'm fine. Nothing is broken, nothing hurts. You can take my word for it." Her voice carried through the privacy screen to his bedroom...to him.

Once more his attention was riveted on her. Almost as if she'd read his mind, she sunk deeper into the water, crossing her arms in front of herself.

Again it was all he could do to keep his thoughts from the exotic slant of her blue eyes, from the fragility of her slender form, and her subtle sweet innocence. She needed someone...him. Not just anyone. She needed him. His gaze traveled back to the girl, studying everything, every movement, every delicate gesture, so evident even in the inviting shadows behind the screen.

"No. I won't take your word for it. I'd feel responsible if I let you walk out of here and you were still hurt. You need proper care and time to heal. You could have died out there." His voice was low and raspy. "As soon as you're through with the bath, I'm going to check your condition."

She whispered but her words stopped him, "I'm fine, really." The subtle tremor in her plea made him realize how vulnerable she was.

He continued after a lengthy pause. "Has the pain stopped?"

"Better..." she returned.

"Are you sure?" He felt like a fool standing outside the screen, interrogating her, but he had the crazy idea she'd bolt if he approached her now. Perhaps she was telling the truth. After all, she had no reason to lie yet. Perhaps she had every reason.

He had a mind to leave and let her have the privacy she craved, but that wouldn't help his peace of mind or her if there was anything else wrong. He had a thought to walk downstairs and down a couple of brandies. Charles was waiting for him. Instead, he looked one more time at the screen before he turned away. Before he gave into temptation and changed his mind, he walked to the fireplace and shifted a log or two with the poker. The sound of the fire crackled and hissed. When an ember popped and flew out to land on the tile, he pushed it back with his booted foot.

"Would you like help with your clothes?" he queried softly then wondered what he'd do if she accepted his offer. For a moment, he thought it over but...

"In your dreams." Her defiant whisper made him grin.

Distinctly and very clearly, he'd heard the scathing message and couldn't help but laugh at himself. Yes, she was right, in his dreams. Oh, and they were beautiful dreams too. He turned, looking through the screen and at the silhouette of her. Stood transfixed as he watched the graceful flow of her movements. He should leave now.

His conscience insisted that he stay.

Yet he argued that point too. No, it wasn't just the professional reason to see her well that kept him here, although that was most of it. A combination of curiosity and potent desire made him break all his rules. And so he was here, gazing at her through the screens, unable to tear himself away.

"You should be 'most normal now. Your toes, your fingers, do they still tingle?" he cleared his throat.

"It is none of your business," she told him politely yet firmly. Her calm indifference was nearly his undoing. "Really, I'm fine. You can go now. I appreciate your..."

"The devil. I don't mean you harm."

"...your help?"

He hesitated then, reflecting on a day long ago, a day that changed his life forever. On that day he'd made two promises. After setting the cross on his sister's grave, he vowed he'd never let anyone close again. It hurt too much to lose a loved one, but then he'd heard the soft sob, the sound smothered beneath the woodpile. He'd found Jessie that day and without a second thought, taken her into his heart. He'd loved her, cherished her. Vulnerable and alone in a strange world, she'd needed him, and he felt such a strong parallel between Jessie and this woman. He needed to understand why this woman bewildered him so and turned his well-ordered world upside down.

"Come downstairs when you're dressed." It was a command he didn't think she'd refuse. Then, with considerable determination, he left the room.

~ * ~

Charles sat in James' favorite chair, feet negligently propped on a stool, casually sipping his best French brandy.

"What took you so long, old man?" Charles' drawl was casual but it subtly implied a wealth of things.

James felt an embarrassing heat touch his cheeks. "Not what you're thinking."

Charles brow rose fractionally. "Now, what was I thinking?"

James ignored the question, stepping over to the sideboard to pour himself a drink. He sipped the brandy, relishing the burning heat of it as the liquid slid down his throat. Even as the silence lengthened between the two men, James knew Charles would wait for an answer. If anything, Charles was a patient man when he wanted to be.

"If she's not the guilty party, who is she?" James swung around, confronting Charles. "You're the sheriff. You're supposed to know these things."

"I've never seen her before, but she is pretty." Charles smiled. "She's gotten to you. After all this time, didn't you think to ask her?"

James grimaced. "I thought she was the lady you were after. Until a few minutes ago, there was never a question in mind who she was."

"You can't keep her here," Charles said.

"Why the hell not?"

Charles laughed again and downed what was left of his brandy. "I suppose you can, but will the lady be agreeable? Living in a man's home has certain implications she might not like. And of course there's Jessie to think of."

"What do you propose? A room in the jail or perhaps one over the saloon," James asked smoothly. "Perhaps she could approach the Madam who owns the brothel. Would that be more acceptable?"

"What makes you think she has no other options?" Charles slapped the question in his face. "She might have money of her own somewhere."

"I'm no fool and neither are you. You saw her when I carried her in. All she has is the ragged men's clothes she was wearing. No money. No kin. No means of support."

"You're assuming a great deal."

"And maybe she's a whore down on her luck."

"A very lovely whore, if you ask me."

"No one's asking."

Charles laughed again. This time he rose, stretching his long lose frame. "Then you'll make her your mistress? There's a small house on California Street just perfect for what you seem to have in mind."

James hesitated a moment too long and Charles cast him a quelling glance he promptly ignored. His mistress. Not a new idea by any means.

Indeed, it was very good idea. If anything, that thought made him even more responsible for her well-being, her protection. He wanted her. He wanted her safe. And he didn't want anyone else to have her.

Under his protection.

"Charles, what kind of lady would you find out in the woods alone? Abandoned?"

Charles rubbed his jaw thoughtfully for a moment. "Someone who'd lost her man. A woman down on her luck. Probably a lady of easy virtue who found herself in some kind of scrape she couldn't get out of."

"Exactly."

"You can't assume anything."

"Of course I can. Especially if the lady in question has no answers forthcoming. I have only her best interest at heart. I didn't rescue her to leave her to her own devices now that we're off the mountain."

"You don't know if she's in need of protection."

"But I will soon." James grinned. "Yes, I'll know soon, very soon." She was exactly what he wanted. Someone who would come to him, only him, willingly and passionately. "She needs me, Charles. She needs a safe haven, a place where she can rest and heal. I mean to give her that."

"What if she doesn't agree?"

"She will. And I'll find out the truth. Whoever left her up there to die will pay."

~ * ~

"I'm going to find out what that little tramp is doing in James' house," Belinda was archly saying to Attaway Morehouse over muffins and coffee in the breakfast nook of her home. "If you must know."

"How did you find out about her?"

"Charles came by an hour ago, talking up a storm."

"Charles?"

"My brother, the sheriff. Anyway, Charles says James has gone loco over this girl. He had the nerve to tell me there'd be wedding bells pretty soon if he didn't miss his guess. I'm not going to allow that."

Attaway looked appalled then she choked on the blackberry currant jam. "How? You can't mean..." she stuttered then blushed hotly.

Belinda nodded confirmation. "I'll do anything to get my way. You know that."

"Are you going this afternoon?" Attaway asked, wide-eyed and clearly fascinated.

"I won't let one minute pass." Belinda adjusted the lace at her collar then reached for her coffee. "He'll be very glad to see me." She smiled, showing her fine white teeth briefly. "After putting up with the little whore for the night. In fact," she paused dramatically for a second, "despite what Charles said, James has hinted he intends to propose to me."

"Really?" Attaway's gasp was so strident, Belinda almost shivered. "I don't believe you."

Belinda shrugged a delicate, ladylike lift of her shoulder. "You should, you know. James Lawrence will not be a bachelor for long."

~ * ~

A few minutes after James left the room, Alexandra leaned back in her bath and let her eyes close. She was warm, finally and sleepy. The water had a calming effect. She wasn't sure exactly when she accepted the fact her trip through the vortex had defied all scientific laws. For a while, she'd refused to believe what was right in front of her nose.

Faced now with overwhelming evidence she'd traveled backward in time, she was also beset with a devastating fear she'd never be able to return. She wanted to go home.

But how?

Minutes ticked by while she turned over every scrap of information she could think of. It was the vortex. Had to be. Her soft sigh floated up with the steam before she reached for a towel, still thinking furiously. Quickly, she dried herself and wrapped the towel around her before she walked to the bed. Surely she could allow herself a moment of rest before confronting Captain James Lawrence. Just one moment, she thought before slipping beneath the soft warm quilt on the bed. Her eyes fluttered shut. The trembling within her stopped.

She slept, to dream of James' arms around her and the heat radiating from him, the security she'd felt when he held her and the protective feel of his touch when he warmed her.

He was undeniably handsome.

Deep in her fantasy, she reached out to touch his jaw line, wishing all-the-while he'd kiss her.

Then a different man stepped out of the shadows of her reverie, interrupting the fragile peace. His perfect face was scarred and his grin terrified her. It promised retaliation.

"Be careful, pretty lady, because I'm going to find you."

Chapter Three

Soft sounds of winter, of snowflakes and ice, whispered against the window. Alex snuggled deeper into the quilted bed coverings, pulling the covers close then drifting asleep once more. The nightmares did not return, but she did dream of a handsome cavalier man. A man with jet-black hair and laughing blue eyes. The man who'd brought her down from the frozen mountain when she'd lost all hope.

His image and his husky voice haunted her imagination. Yet she knew none of this was possible, understood this strange fantasy was a dream she was sure to wake from. Her logical, scientific mind told her it could not have happened. Time travel went beyond the realm of all imagination. It was sci-fi at its best, a Jules Verne novel.

A soft musical voice penetrated the sleepy recesses of her mind. In the background she heard clattering dishes, smelled the delicious aroma of fresh baked bread. She shook off the last vestiges of slumber, and pushing herself away from the mattress, looked around the room.

The little Chinese lady stood at a table humming to herself, busy with a tray of dishes. Kim's back was turned away from her. She wore a black tunic made of padded cotton and baggy black trousers. Embroidered peonies decorated the fabric, and Alex thought she had never seen anything so perfectly done. Kim's long black hair, sprinkled with gray, and braided neatly, fell to a point just above her waist.

Alex smoothed the long white folds of the nightgown she wore then pushed her hair away from her eyes. She looked up to see Kim smiling at her.

A blue calico dress was draped across the foot of the bed. From the table, Kim picked up an assortment of underwear, which she held in her arms. A pair of matching blue slippers rested on the braided rug in front of her. Alex sat for a moment thinking and absorbing her surroundings as the seconds ticked by in her mind. A second later, and with tears in her eyes, she held the dress in her lap while she recalled days long past in her great grandmother's attic. Amidst cobwebs and dust, Alexandra had searched out dresses such as this and giggled with her friends when they admired themselves in the mirror. This was no longer a fantasy, nor did the dress hold whimsical notions of romance in some bygone day.

Alexandra was well aware she wasn't free to dream, understood this wasn't an illusion that would vanish when she closed the lid of an old trunk. She was really and truly in another time.

Her stomach grumbled miserably, reminding her she hadn't eaten in hours. She heard soft laughter float across the room along with the enticing scent of tea and bread.

"Hungry?" Like a soft summer breeze, Kim's question floated across the room.

"Yes." Alexandra swung her legs from beneath the warm quilt, her feet resting now on the cold floor. "Kim, how," Alexandra looked at the soft white cotton, fingering the buttons at the neck then back to Kim.

"I helped you. Mr. James came by to talk to you, but you were sound asleep. You're to come down to his private sitting room first thing."

Alexandra's eyes widened and she blushed, felt the heat slowly covering her cheeks. "I see." But she didn't really. "Where, where did he sleep?"

"In the adjoining room."

"I'm sorry. I didn't mean to put him out of his room."

"I'm sure he didn't mind. The clothes are for you. James sent me to the neighbors this morning."

"Thank you," Alexandra fingered the clothes. "This morning? I didn't mean to sleep all day. And all night. I..."

"You were tired."

"Kim, what year is it?" She was desperate, her heart beating like a drum. Her entire life hinged on Kim's answer.

"The year?" Kim looked puzzled. She hesitated, "Eighteen sixty-eight, why?"

Alex's breath stopped for a second as she accepted what she'd already guessed. "I, well, I wasn't sure." She wondered what to tell Kim next or how she was going to explain to James she had nowhere to go. No home. No family. No way to support herself in this strange world. James would want to know everything. Oh, and she didn't think he was going to believe what she had to say.

Escape sounded infinitely preferable to confrontation.

"He expects you downstairs in the next ten minutes."

Alex held the dress tightly in one hand next to her chest and watched Kim pad quietly out of the room closing the door behind her. A few minutes later, she was dressed and peeking out the door. The stairway was long and frightening. Jessie's little voice floated upward, giving her a moment of hope.

"Well, Alex," she murmured. "You've got to beard the lion in his den if you ever want to go home." And if all this is true, if she had traveled back in time, she was going to need all the help she could get.

Alex considered herself a woman with a purpose, with goals. Passionately involved with her studies and learning, she'd had a purpose. The ultimate woman of the new century; a vulnerable woman, despite her driving ambition. That was the way of her time, or so it seemed. A woman could never easily have it all, a career and a family, she had to be willing to sacrifice, but Alex hadn't been willing to do that. Perhaps this was her penance, exile into a land where a woman had no rights, none except what the man in her life would allow. And because she was desperate, she was willing to do just about anything, except perhaps windows, if it was the only way she could obtain his help.

~ * ~

The object of her thoughts found himself disconcerted at that moment when he walked into his private sitting room and found Belinda waiting for him.

"How did you get inside?" James asked in a quiet voice, making a mental note to have a word with Kim.

"The front door was unlocked." Belinda's smile was polite, her pose demure, as if she lounged everyday in his private rooms. Which she didn't. The problem was, in truth, she did feel at home with him. There were many times only a year ago, in the Jacksonville Hotel, he had seen all her secret treasures.

James, however, had not seen her for at least six months, nor did he have any intention of renewing a relationship that had played its course. "So what brings you here today? You must have a good reason," he asked her smoothly, his mood somber. The minor irritation of delaying his conversation with the young lady upstairs, of whom he still didn't know her name, vanished with this unexpected disturbance.

"The rumors floating around town." Her statement was rude and pointed. For one strained moment, James debated returning tit-for-tat.

"The rumors, if there are any, don't concern you, nor do they warrant an explanation. Now, may I see you to the door? Ah, no, I believe you know your way around."

"I'm only looking out for your best interest."

"I see. Well, I suppose a thank you is in order. Thank you."

Her mouth formed a pert little moue then she smiled. "When will I see you?"

At the moment 'never' didn't seem like an appropriate answer, but for the life of him, he couldn't think of anything else to say. "I'll swing by your house tomorrow, for afternoon tea."

Her eyes sparkled, and his smile was one of relief. He loathed scenes of any kind.

He scooted her out the door, his thoughts back on the lady upstairs. "Go on home. I'll see you later. By the way, make sure Charles is there too. I need to speak with your brother. And don't bother yourself about any of the rumors. I'll take care of them."

Standing on tiptoe, she kissed him. "You're an angel," she giggled merrily.

"Of course," he said.

~ * ~

Alexandra had heard and seen enough in the few short minutes she'd stood by James' partially open door with her hand in the air prepared to knock. All thoughts of working for him in exchange for his help swept through her in the most embarrassing way. Not only did he have a lady friend, but she'd made him the recipient of rumors.

She reflected on her future and her destiny as she walked upstairs and to the window. She stared out at the rolling hills, studying the effects of the wind as it swept through the old oak tree by the house. Everything looked the same. The same mountains loomed larger than life in the distance; the same view she would have expected to see stole her imagination.

The snow had stopped falling. It melted now, seeping into the earth. In the sky, the clouds parted and the sun was bright, warming the ground once again, encouraging the flowers to peek out.

Alexandra knew she had to leave and she had to leave soon.

Wistfully, she traced a pattern on the glass. All she needed was her cellphone and a ride home. She laughed and it sounded bitter and hollow. She wondered where her cell was, somewhere in the woods. Of course it wouldn't work. There were no towers.

She felt horrible fear, and the certainty there would never be a place for her to phone home again. For a slender fragile moment, she felt terribly alone as trepidation mounted and despair threatened her usual dauntless self.

Who would ever believe she'd traveled through time?

How would she ever convince James to take her back into the hills? Take her to a strange vortex where all realms of imagination were defied? Where she would vanish once more. She breathed deeply but her racing heart didn't slow nor did the fear go away. Instead, it built and built until Alexandra wanted to scream out loud with the frustration and the hopelessness of her situation.

She suddenly knew what she had to do.

Without hesitating, she strode across the floor in search of her boots, ignoring the baby blue slippers perfectly matched to her dress. James' wardrobe furnished a jacket. She put the boots on and wiggled her toes in comfort. Next she slipped the jacket over her shoulders and started toward the door, intent on one thing, finding a way home. It wasn't sensible but it felt right.

~ * ~

James stood in the large living room, staring at his elaborate hand-carved mantel of golden oak and wondered how Belinda had managed to finagle a visit out of him and why his houseguest was taking so much time to make an appearance.

He rubbed the hard surface of what appeared to be a card with the lady's picture on it. He raised an eyebrow, thoughtfully, then turned to look at the stairs and decided, ready or not, it was time.

Oh, yes, the picture was hers, in color too. The photograph captured every lovely detail with startling clarity, even the smile, ah, Alexandra's smile. It was a smile he could not easily forget.

But the color picture was impossible, so he stared at it for a moment as if that would clear away the musty cobwebs. Nothing Kim had taken out of Alexandra's pockets made sense. He read the words on one of the cards.

Driver license. Driver license? Crissakes, Why did a person need a license to drive? And the dates on the license, he frowned thoughtfully. Perhaps the numbers weren't dates, perhaps they were merely insignificant numbers placed at random.

None of the other cards made sense or the numbers printed on them. And neither did the keys or key ring with the picture of the capital painted on its hard surface. And the little rectangle that lit up and told the time when he presses a button.

At least now he knew her name, clearly printed on a half-dozen hard surfaces, Alexandra McMurdie. The name fit. Her fiery red hair was pulled tightly from her face. And up close, the first thing he'd noticed was the dazzling smile then her eyes. Oh, those were eyes a man could lose himself in. He sensed the vulnerability and the passion too. Her eyes were cobalt blue and they reflected honesty, intelligence, compassion. They gazed back at him so compellingly that several seconds passed before he realized she appeared completely and utterly innocent. *Angel girl. My angel girl.* He'd have to keep his hands in his pockets until he could understand why her smile affected him the way it did and why the color of her eyes reminded him of a warm summer day.

His fist slammed against the mantle. By thunder, she'd taken long enough. "To hell with waiting."

He'd drag the truth from her. She'd tell him what she was doing on the mountain and who she was with. Henceforth, he'd have nothing but honesty from Miss Alexandra McMurdie.

Precisely one minute later, after stalking ruthlessly up the steps to the second floor, heated emotions simmering inside of him changed to cold, hard resolve. An innocent looking seductress had deceived him. Seductress? She was worse than that, he thought bitterly as he threw open the door and stepped inside his bedroom. She used him. Lies, lies and more lies. Nothing about her rang true.

James stood inside the door, searching the room for her. He saw the blue slippers in the middle of the room and a nightgown tossed haphazardly across his bed. As James absorbed every detail in the room, his jaw clenched into a tight line of anger. She wasn't there. In a few long steps, he entered the adjoining room. His gaze rested on every shadowed corner, stopped at his desk as if his hesitancy would cause her to materialize. She didn't.

Alexandra had fled.

He stood, unable to breathe, unable to comprehend her motive. He felt as if someone had slammed a fist into his heart. He stepped to the window and watched her stride away from his home toward town. She was almost a half-mile away, fading slowly in the distance, and he still couldn't move. The sunlight filtered through a few holes in the clouds and as the beams of light reached her, they cast her hair in flames. She disappeared around a bend in the road before he finally caught his breath.

"The devil," he murmured as he turned and raced down the back stairs. "If the woman wanted to go to town, why didn't she just say so?" He ran into Kim and toppled her in his haste. He wasn't ready to let Alexandra McMurdie go, not now, not for a very long time, perhaps not ever. He didn't intend to analyze his motives either.

"Oh, Mr. James," Kim asked as he helped her to her feet, "are you all right?"

"She pulled foot," he retorted sourly. "And she promised to talk. Said she'd tell me what happened. You all right?" he finished awkwardly.

"What can you expect?" Kim asked suddenly, dusting her hands on her apron as she righted herself.

"She is uncontrollable," he said, astonished that Alexandra McMurdie had the nerve to walk out on him. "And she needs...she needs...needs a..."

"Yes?" Kim raised an eyebrow.

"Protection." he said quickly and perhaps a little too eagerly. His protection. This wouldn't be the first time he kept a mistress, but he was positive it would be the last. And he decided, then and there, he wasn't about to give her a choice.

"You owe her an apology."

"The hell, I do." His mind catapulted back to the present. "And she owes me a lot more respect than I'm getting at the moment," he said very slowly.

"She's frightened. You've had such a dark look on your face, you terrified me. I doubt if you'd understand." Kim smiled and lowered her head.

"I saved her life," he returned softly. "And she's not leaving," he added in a deceptively quiet tone.

Kim looked up once more, her smile gone. "And you think she owes you."

"Of course not, but if I hadn't found her, she'd have frozen on that mountain." *And, I would have never seen her smile.*

"What about her feelings, Mr. James? You know she asked me what the year was?"

He studied Kim seriously, his tone confident. "It's a ploy, Kim. Can't you tell? She's the best little actress this side of Texas. Besides, the games she plays are irrelevant. I'm only trying to help. And no, I will not apologize to her. I've done nothing wrong."

"Then go after her," Kim said gently, "and bring her home."

"That is the point. I don't think she has anywhere to go. After I looked through those things you took from her pockets, I'm more convinced than ever."

Kim watched him then finally turned away.

A tiny bundle of energy whipped around the corner. "Papa, where is she going? I thought she'd be my new mother." Jessie hurled herself into his arms. "Don't let her go!"

James smiled and kissed her forehead, tightening his hold. "Now, Sugar Plum, I never promised she would be your mother, but I'll go after her because she needs us. She doesn't even have a warm coat," he finished softly and was startled by the tenderness he heard in his voice.

"Bring her home. Please."

"I'll try, but first you have to let go of me so I can hitch up the wagon. She's afraid of horses, you know," he smiled reassuringly at Jessie. He couldn't deny her a thing, and he knew where all this led. If he didn't change his tactics soon, she'd be one spoiled little hellion by the time she grew up. Still, he couldn't say no to her. After everything Jessie had been through, it was beyond his ability. James kissed her cheek and set her away.

The entire time he spent readying the wagon and catching up to Alexandra, he thought of the things Kim had found in her pockets and tried to sort it out. He couldn't and that bothered him. His anger had cooled though, and he felt ready to tackle this objectively.

He set the horse in motion, intent on catching her before she reached Jacksonville. For a moment, he had the oddest sensation she wouldn't like what she found there. He shook it off and urged the horse to a faster trot. Even as the horse came steadily closer, Miss Alexandra never turned around. She just picked up her pace, her strides lengthening when he closed the distance.

"Whoa," he said and grinned at the girl, hoping to see her smile in return. Her back stiffened with what looked like determination, and she made quite a picture. Stubborn woman. Damn stubborn woman. The little beauty was full of surprises.

"You didn't have to follow me." She kept on going, one foot after another, refusing to look at him.

"Nice day." His voice was regulated with a lazy insouciance. James leaned forward. One hand rested on his thigh and his other hand rose to leisurely tip his hat back.

"Go away."

It was like walking barefoot through the nettles, James thought, so when he spoke again he tempered his voice to sooth and coax.

"Go away? Seems I've heard that line before." Never taking his gaze from her, he watched the gentle sway of her skirts then the slim calf exposed between the rise of her dress and the top of her boot. "I don't think I can do that, darlin'," he said with feigned indifference.

"I'm not your darlin'."

James' dark brows shot up, his curiosity sparked. He didn't offer an explanation, just watched her and kept the wagon even, tightening his hold on the reins.

He swore softly, realizing the precarious position she had put him in. Capriciously and unwittingly, she challenged him, and with that challenge, she threatened him.

"How far to town?" she asked.

"It'll take you an hour or more, on foot. I'd be happy to give you a ride." He laughed teasingly, still smiling. He hoped to reach an understanding with her. If he could, he'd have her home soon.

James stopped the wagon and held his hand out to her, offering a ride. She ignored him, and kept going.

"I don't want your help," she told him firmly. Her dark lashes fell across her cheeks.

"I know."

Alex stopped to confront him. She brushed the hair out of her eyes.

"I mean it," she said and looked toward the town.

"Why?" his question was straight and to the point. She didn't make sense, of course little about her made sense, but he meant to find out why. He never did cotton to secrets and it seemed she harbored a very large one.

"Because."

He watched her nervously smooth the folds of her skirts. "I already owe you for the dress, and the..."

James didn't laugh this time, decided instead she'd carried this too far. She had become his obligation. Crissakes, but there was a new word to ponder, obligation. "Out here, Miss Alexandra, we help our neighbor. You don't owe me anything." He jumped from the wagon, landing in front of her. She stopped and cast him a glowering look then wiped the moisture from her forehead.

"All right, I give up," she sighed wearily.

"Good, I thought you'd be in a pucker all the way to town." He lifted her easily into the wagon then settled himself next to her.

"Pucker?"

"Yes," he said and the wagon began to move. "It seems to me you've got a bee in your bonnet, Miss Alexandra, and all I've tried to do is help." He'd intended to take her to town as soon as she was rested, but when she'd left without a good-bye, he decided he'd, well, he wasn't sure what but he knew he couldn't let her walk out of his life.

"Among other things," she snorted, and he wanted to laugh.

~ * ~

They came over the hill, down the road along Main Street, and turned on Oregon Street. The residents of the tiny community waved at James and openly gaped at her.

Rumors. Were they all talking about her?

They rode past the post office, the Table Rock Saloon, the General Store, and the blacksmith shop. She snapped her mouth shut. Turning slowly, she looked at him with huge cobalt blue eyes, unshed tears threatening to slide down her cheek.

"It all looks—almost the same—except the street isn't paved, and the buildings don't have the same name. What happened to the Jacksonville Inn? I thought…" her voice quavered and she brushed away the lone tear that slid suddenly down her cheek. "I wish this weren't true."

"Miss Alexandra."

"Stop," she said weakly.

He pulled in the reins then turned to her. "Welcome to Jacksonville," he said with quiet calm. "What do you intend now?"

"I'm going to find a job." Her voice was gently assertive, her sparkling eyes challenging his authority as if she knew he'd object. She jumped down from the wagon. Before leaving, she stood for a moment, inhaling several times. Then she purposely held on to the side of the wagon as if to steady herself. "I have to support myself, you know," she said quietly then started toward the General Store.

He waited expectantly, his gaze following her as she walked across the street. Even as the urge to run after her and stop her simmered deep inside him, he watched and admired her spunk and her dauntless courage. He wondered how long it would take for her to realize there were no jobs. And he pondered also just exactly what kind of job she was looking for. It didn't appear as though the lady would give up easily. Yet he could afford to be patient.

James hopped off the wagon and settled himself comfortably into a chair in front of the saloon. Casually, he watched as she went from store to store, watched as women went out of their way to avoid her and men leered openly. For a brief second, he felt guilt followed by anger. Knowing why the townspeople acted with such hostility, he accepted the responsibility. It was up to him to change it. The posse had ridden in this morning. The gossip must have spread faster than a wildfire on the windswept prairie.

"Nothing," she told him a couple of hours later, sitting down on the boards. Her hair was flying in the breeze. He watched her hesitate before she turned to look inside the Eldorado Saloon then back to him. "I suppose I could try in there."

"No, not by a jug full," he said quietly and, he hoped, with undisputable conviction. "I won't let you."

"It's not up to you." Purposely, she stood and dusted off the back of her skirt. With pursed lips and a distasteful frown, she peered inside again. "I have to, don't have a choice now. No one wants—"

"An adventuress..." He let the words trail off silently, begging for her to deny the accusation. His words tested and she didn't seem to understand.

"I suppose so," she said, still brushing the dust off her skirts. "I suppose you could call me that."

His gut tightened at her admission, and his voice grew low and husky. "You don't have to do that anymore." His words cajoling, almost begging surprised him. "I'll take care of you. There's a small house down the—"

"You don't listen very well," she said, looking exasperated with him. "I could wash dishes or sweep." Alex pushed the hair away from her eyes. "I make a great martini." She stepped around him, stopping suddenly. A small man with gold-rimmed spectacles stood in the doorway of the saloon.

"You lookin' for a job, Miss?" he asked.

Unsure at that moment what to do, James hesitated, hoping McAllister had a full stable of girls and this inquiry was due to curiosity.

"Yes," Alex told the proprietor then cast a smug grin James' way.

"I have one room," McAllister began. "I get fifty percent right off the top. Don't tolerate skimmin' and the rules are posted in every room. You can start right now. There's a man by the name of Sean Cassidy that just asked for you. He's new in town. Came here about three months ago. Been workin' for Beekman and the Wells Fargo Line. Takin' the mail out tomorrow." McAllister stuck his fingers in his suspenders and rocked back on his heels as if thinking. He didn't hear her sudden gasp of air. "Yup, when the posse rode in with your story, well, we've all been waitin' for you. What's it gonna be, little lady?"

"Don't be absurd! I don't..." she whispered savagely, her voice strangled. "Sean, my, God. It couldn't be. He's been here three months? How on earth?"

James heard every sweet beautiful word and practically caught her as she dashed from the sidewalk into the street.

"Whoa there," he cut in quickly. "The job not to your liking?" He followed her to the wagon. "My offer's still open. I'll take care of you, angel girl, see to your needs. I know you don't have money, but it'll be my pleasure."

Alex bristled. "Only if you'll let me work," she finished with a quietly commanding tone. "Perhaps we can reach an understanding."

"You don't have to cook or clean. Kim takes care of everything. You only have to..." Her chin tilted and her lips thinned in what he was beginning to recognize as one of the first signs her temper was about to heat up. "All right," he backed off but he liked her sudden flashes of temper and her occasional sarcasm. Yes, he had to admit he enjoyed her immensely. "I'll find something else for you to do." Yet he knew what he wanted from her.

Judging her expression, he wondered if it was possible.

His hand lifted her chin and his finger brushed across her lips, hoping to soften them. The gesture was, of course, futile. "Wait here. I have to send a telegram. I'll be back in a minute."

~ * ~

He left her standing alone. Her hands were clasped tightly around the back of an old chair, and she watched his disappearing back. This was harder than she thought it would be. How do you tell a man you're so desperate to get home you'll do just about anything, in exchange for his help, of course.

His long loose-limbed stride pounded on the wooden sidewalk. She traced his form from his broad shoulders down to his narrow hips and long legs, her lips suddenly dry and in need of water. She felt a shivering of pure sensual appeal sneak down her spine. He was sexy, she thought suddenly. Undeniably sexy.

She started forward but someone blocked her path. The man looked hideous. A scar slanted across one cheek. His hair was cut short, his face strangely familiar. After a moment of fierce scrutiny, "Sean..." she breathed, petrified.

Then she found herself slammed against a wall and held within the shadows of an alley. Her breath rushed from her lungs and her head throbbed painfully where it hit the building.

"Let me go!"

Sean raised a brow and smiled. "Ah, pretty lady, you disappoint me. Have you forgotten so soon? I haven't. I've been here for months, waiting, waiting for you. I wasn't sure you'd make it, though. But now that you're here..."

The words were spoken with a sneer. She detested him, abhorred everything he represented. Panic consumed her, but she forced herself to think, to control her fear. She balled her fists to defend herself.

She didn't know if she had the strength to fight him. "I detest you," she told him, "Let me go!" she cried out and hoped James would hear.

Sean clutched her arms, dragging her against him when she struggled to loosen his hold on her. His strength overwhelmed her, as did his audacity.

"Ah, but you owe me. We have some unfinished business together. You're under my thumb, Alexandra, oh yes," he whispered furiously. "Don't you remember what we started together?" He had wrenched her head back and had the terrible brashness to try to kiss her.

Where had James gone? He had deserted her when she needed him. No, she could do this by herself. After all, she was a woman of the twenty-first century, and she could take care of herself.

Just think, think, Alex.

She didn't have a mercurial temper or fiery red hair for nothing, she thought, as she swiftly drew back her knee and brought it up without compassion, hard against the man's groin. Once. Twice.

"No."

Sean swore violently and shoved her ruthlessly against the wall. His hands dropped to his sides and he doubled over in pain, his shoulder still pinning her against the bricks.

The sound escaping him was filled with agony, yet he spoke to her through clenched teeth, his lips stretched thin and pale.

"That's the second time Alexandra..." he began in raw fury. His face was livid and the thin white line of his scar stood out in stark relief. "I will never forgive you, and I will have vengeance."

Alex stared at him, terrified, frantic over his words. With all the strength left her, she pushed away from him. She started after James, running wildly, recklessly, panic stricken, shouting at him. All she knew at the moment was that she didn't want to be left alone.

She reached the telegraph office door panting and terrified, a cold sweat consuming her. It didn't matter though as she pushed on through, finally standing beside James, still quaking with fear and wondering at Sean's words. She clung to James, leaning her head against his arm. Soaking up the strength his presence offered, she tried to calm herself.

She was breathless, and her heart pounded alarmingly.

His hand hovered in the air above the paper and he waited, watched as if he expected an explanation. And all she wanted from him at the moment was his protection. She gulped air frantically. Her mouth so dry she couldn't speak.

At her silence he pulled her close and finished his business.

"Can we go? Please."

"All right, where?" he asked cautiously.

She did need him, despite what she thought or wanted. Sean Cassidy was out there and she had to tell James.

"I don't care," she told him weakly. "Anywhere."

James held her arm and turned her toward the door. She faltered. Before they left the office, James swept her off her feet and carried her all the way to the wagon. He placed her gently onto the seat and leapt up behind her. Seconds later James urged the horses forward. It was then she realized they headed out of town. The ride lasted an eternity. Finally, she felt the wagon slow and stop.

"We're going to have that little talk."

Her gaze traveled a full circle, taking in everything, the lazy creek, the trees, the mountains in the distance. She didn't know what to expect. Silence and brittle tension surrounded them.

His concern for her was obvious. Yet now that the immediate danger was gone, she was afraid to pose the question. When she looked in his eyes, they were cold and unreadable. The expression on his face was hard. Alexandra suddenly broke into tears. She sat in the wagon and sobbed. All the confusion and fear she held inside the last twenty-four hours suddenly found its way out, letting lose in a sudden barrage of sobs. He wrapped his arms around her, pulling her close; his hand wandered across her back. She allowed his soothing caress to heal her pain.

Alex molded herself to the hard angles and planes of his body, forgetting her resolves, forgetting everything except the warmth and the comfort he offered. With her head pressed against his chest, she heard his heartbeat and the soft whisper of air as he breathed.

Alexandra wiped the tears from her eyes then moved away from him, only to find herself caught in his gaze, transfixed, enchanted, and at his mercy.

She knew James' piercing blue eyes were studying her as he held her in his arms. She understood he questioned everything about her. Now, despite all he'd told her and the things she'd seen, she still harbored a tiny thread of hope. A hope that blossomed with his touch, perhaps he would help her find her way home, to the mountain, to the vortex.

"You promised to tell me what happened." His words were demanding and tough. At the moment, James Lawrence held the means to her survival in the palm of his hand. She owed him her life and her livelihood.

She riveted her eyes on James only to see him scowling at her. He looked confused and frustrated enough that he was for a moment at a slight loss for words. She couldn't help but feel a bit of empathy for him. He looked exactly the way she felt.

"I was attacked," she told him.

"When?" The ferocity of his question startled her.

"Just after you left to send the telegram."

"Are you hurt? Why didn't you tell me?" His tone was rough and hard-edged.

"I, I just did." Her voice was trembling.

"If you had mentioned this sooner, I might have been able to find him," he said, almost as if he regretted his harshness.

When she looked at him, she saw gentleness, a tender concern for her. She breathed deeply and gauged her response trying to justify her actions.

"Did he hurt you?" he asked again and once more his tone grew harsh. "Why?"

"No, I hurt him." She didn't understand why her voice trembled or why she wanted so desperately to trust him.

James's frown grew deeper and broader as his eyes focused on hers. "Tell me what happened. Tell me everything."

Alexandra swallowed the fear building inside. Out of the tangled mess of the last few days, there was little she could say.

"Alexandra?"

If she could have controlled her voice, she might have replied. But she couldn't. That was the point. She gasped for air and choked on her words. Calming herself, she breathed deeply and said a silent prayer, asking for strength and wisdom and the right words. This was so very important.

Finally, "He said he'd never forgive me. Said, too, he'd have revenge," she was shivering uncontrollably. She found herself in his protective embrace again. She didn't move, didn't want to. Instead she huddled within the security of his arms, waiting, using the time to think.

He had the nerve to smile at her. The all knowing masculine one, the one that confused her, leaving her speechless and out of breath. "You're not going to let him frighten you," he spoke softly, challenging her. "I won't let him hurt you."

"No? But he's not going to give up, you know."

She jerked her gaze away from him.

She had no proof of anything except her name, which he seemed to know all to well. She didn't understand until she remembered her pockets and the I.D. she'd put there.

"Why not?" he asked swiftly.

"Because he wants something that I have."

"And what is that?"

"He thinks I have his money."

"Do you?"

"No."

James didn't answer for a long time and she wondered if he believed her. His next response didn't help solve the problem. Instead, his reply left her more confused.

"Are you always so impetuous and foolhardy, rushing off into the unknown without a second thought? You should have stayed with the wagon. Waited for me. I mean to protect you, even from yourself."

"I've never been impetuous." The words murmured, soft and tremulous, made her question every facet of her life. "And I don't need your protection, only your help."

"Now, why don't I believe you?" An undercurrent of laughter softened his words.

She was surprised and puzzled by his accusations. "I don't know. I've never thought of myself in that way."

His brow rose slightly as if ready to argue. "You should. You know, everything you've done today has been foolhardy."

And he was right. So here she was, in another world, another time, hoping this man would help her find her way back through time. And he didn't even have a time machine. Her fingers curled into fists to still the horrible fear. *Please, God, let him want to help me.*

Chapter Four

For a short time, Sean had watched from the alley as James and Alexandra rode down California St. After they disappeared from view, he turned his attention to other pleasures.

He'd always had everything his way. He was big-man-on-campus, good-looking, with deep brown eyes, thick wavy chestnut hair, and a lean, well-muscled body. Every woman Sean knew thought he was a gorgeous hunk of a man, perfect in his dress, and manner, their dream date, from the incoming freshman to the graduate student. They'd voiced their opinions often enough. He found it hard to believe Alexandra thought his smile was arrogant and condescending.

His antithesis in every way, she avoided him. Alexandra McMurdie, heir to a veritable fortune, and "Alex" to her friends and relations, was the smartest woman he knew. Like her mother, Dr. McMurdie, she was completely unreachable, an iceberg to be exact. Too skinny for his standards with features too fragile for his taste, but Alexandra had an unyielding presence about her that instantly intrigued and compelled him to find out if he could tame her to his hand. Her piercing blue eyes flashed daggers when brought to anger and he hoped, perhaps, passion. Unbound, and in usual disarray, her hair formed a fiery halo of curls around her face. Even with the obvious strikes against her, he wanted her. She possessed his fortune and he'd have it back, one way or the other.

Yes, he would have had Alexandra, but she had surprised him. So he had followed her, raced after her at midnight, and found himself caught in a terrifying nightmare. His world had turned upside down. When he landed, after spinning through hell, he'd ripped his cheek open on the jagged edge of a rock. He had nothing now. His elegant good looks vanished, the scar giving him a demonic appearance.

It seemed as if he'd been here forever. After three months of waiting, his patience had finally paid off. When Charles Majors returned with the posse he'd been in the saloon, listening; heard the description of the girl they'd found on the mountain. He'd known instantly who it was. The ride through time had just taken Alexandra McMurdie a little longer. But she was here now and he'd find a way to have her.

He'd been raised to take what he wanted, the world and everything in it was his. He wanted Alexandra McMurdie.

Yet somehow, he thought, staring at the naked woman beside him, he'd lost it all. He'd never been able to tolerate rejection. Alexandra had posed a problem from the first day they met. He'd kept at her though, until she finally agreed to date him. He wasn't quite sure why she had relented, but he didn't complain.

Then, he thought with a sigh, he'd come so close to having her, and discovered she had become an obsession within himself. Now because she had followed him through time, he would find another opportunity to possess her.

"She won't escape me next time. I will have her," he told Belinda as she stretched out on his bed. He stared off in the distance all the while stroking her soft white flesh. "Under my thumb," and he hummed the Rolling Stone tune thinking of Mick Jagger and his bad boy image. His infatuation with the Stones was a legacy passed down by his father.

Alexandra's father and his had had opposing views about Iraq. Alex's father had enlisted in the Air Force, and without flinching, he'd packed his bag. His father on the other hand, left for the London School of Economics. At some point, before the war ended, Alexandra's father and his became partners, co-conspirators in something that might have been illegal. No one knew for sure, but some believed one friend had betrayed the other.

"When is next time?" Belinda inquired sweetly, interrupting Sean's reminiscing. "You know you'll have a devil of a time, since Lawrence is protecting her."

He flinched, playing with the girl's breast, noting the voluptuous roundness. She was pleasant to look at, but she wasn't Alexandra. He pinched her and she cried out. Then he rose on an elbow, one leg bent, tracing the contours of her with his finger, his mind blank as he stared at a picture on the wall.

"Alexandra has always been a challenge to me," he said, and his words were true. Something about her refusal to notice him ignited a fire within his blood. She was like a conquest he could not achieve. She would surrender to him. Even if the entire town knew Lawrence sheltered her, slept with her, he would have her. It would make the victory sweeter. Damn Lawrence. Damn his stubborn protectiveness. Any other man would have used her then put her out. Of course that was still a possibility.

He despised her and he wanted restitution. No one rejected him, especially not Alexandra McMurdie, the ice maiden. More than anything, even returning to his time, he wanted her to feel the pain. If there had ever been anything denied to him, anything refused him, he couldn't remember. Alexandra would surrender.

Alexandra possessed something no other woman he knew had. Her fiery red hair, aloofness born of arrogance, or perhaps the fire went deeper. Perhaps the fire burned in her soul.

Yet he was no closer to possessing her.

"Lawrence took her into town today," Sean rose from the bed and strode naked to the window. He looked out at the dusty street, leisurely watching the horses plod along. "I had her for a moment, actually thought I had won."

"She got away. And now you're angry."

He hesitated. "Yeah—she surprised me—never again though."

"You have a plan?"

He nodded. He would do anything to pay her back. She had scorned him twice. Oh, yes, Alexandra would pay.

~ * ~

A few minutes after they arrived home, James ushered Alex into his private sitting room. Looking at her for a brief second, he turned to the window. As if the rolling hills and the familiar setting could answer all his questions, he stared out the window for a long time before turning to confront her. James watched Alexandra furtively while Kim and Jessie bustled about with a silver tea tray and tiny little sandwiches.

Before he'd looked away, he'd watched Alexandra gaze at the newspaper on the table. He'd seen her eyes widen. She was holding the newspaper in one trembling hand, her eyes blank with what? Disbelief?

Her talent was, he decided, beyond compare, when she lifted a tear stained face to him. This had to be an act. Only a moment ago she was fine. He'd spent too much time trying to figure out what type of woman she was, spent too much time worrying about her, beginning to care about her.

She was sitting stiff-backed in the chair, so pale she looked most angelic. Angel girl. James stared at her, cursing his stupidity and the soft spot forming around his heart for her.

Surely Alexandra McMurdie should fit into one of the tight little categories he'd used to place every woman he'd ever known, but she didn't. None of the facts he had assembled so far categorized her. She was twenty-three, if the dates on license were correct. Unmarried, he'd thought, and that in itself put her in a very vulnerable position. All the unmarried women over twenty he knew were either old maid school teachers, whores, widows, or well-kept mistresses. A few hours ago she had bluntly admitted she was a prostitute, yet she'd turned down the only job offered in town, the one in the Eldorado that came with its own room and customers.

What baffled him even more was the relief he'd felt when she turned it down, then she'd accepted the position at his home, but he had the strangest feeling she didn't understand what he'd wanted.

His tiny housekeeper turned to him, saying nothing yet at the same time looking as if she was on the verge of giving him a well thought out tongue lashing. Perhaps he deserved one. After all, Kim had scolded him many times while he was growing up. She seemed to think it came with the job and perhaps it was why his mother insisted she follow him west.

"I'll be in my study when you feel more like talking. I want to know what you read in that paper." The door slammed behind him and the walls shook. A figurine of a dog rocked once, twice then careened to the floor. It's tail shattered into a hundred slivers.

He pushed the door open to see to the damage and cringed. Then his gaze traveled to the lady.

Damned if she didn't look at him again with those innocent blue eyes. Stubborn eyes. She was suddenly vividly feminine in her prim blue calico dress; or maybe in contrast to the dark masculine setting, her pale alabaster skin and fiery hair and the soft lush contours covered completely were more beguilingly female. Her long slender fingers, clutching the chair arms, were small and delicate. She seemed, in the short moments since reading that paper, to have changed in some indescribable way. He strode to her quickly, realizing he'd have to speak with her if she caught him staring at her.

By the time he reached her, she was nearly recovered. Frustrated, angry with her and with himself, he mindlessly ran his fingers through his hair; at that moment he reached for the bottle of brandy and poured himself a liberal drink. After swirling the amber liquid in the glass for several long seconds, he downed the contents in one gulp.

"What did you read?" He held the paper in one hand and studied every word written and even the ones between the lines; nothing noteworthy, nothing out of the ordinary, and absolutely nothing worth crying about. The news, inconsequential at best, boring in its entirety, rested benignly on newsprint.

He studied the paper a second time and the only item questionable was the date. Absurd, but true. Once a month the typesetter went on a binge and once a month he set the date wrong. This time only the year was printed incorrectly. Oh, yes, the man had been known to miss the year by hundreds. The town seldom knew how the copy would look, so they ignored it.

Kim carried on as if life was normal, pouring tea and setting out sandwiches. James glowered at her, wondering what she had laced the tea with. Foxglove perhaps, because the look she'd just graced him with was pure poison.

Behind them Jessie skipped down the steps, her braids flying. She passed the room full of adults and raced out the kitchen door. Her presence served as a brief glimpse of sunshine in an otherwise confused world.

The breath he held rushed out.

Silence once again invaded the crevices of the house, sneaking around corners, permeating the very air, and he grimaced at the strange ominous thoughts filling his mind.

"Alexandra," he began and the silence was broken. "Tell me what you saw," he said as his boots hammered on the wood floor.

She whipped around to confront him only to spill the tea she balanced in one hand. It sloshed out of the cup and pooled on the thick Persian carpet covering the floor.

"No." Her mouth snapped shut, her eyes squinting in protest at the sound of his voice.

She looked at him as if she regretted saying no. Then without further hesitation, she sat up straighter and stuck her little chin in the air another two inches.

Crissakes, what did he say this time?

Nervously, her hand shaking, she dabbed at the tea stains. By the time she'd finished, she wore a different expression. One he was beginning to learn and understand all too well. Her lips thinned perceptibly and her eyes darkened, taking on the hue of a winter storm.

"Don't say..." He tried to ward off her frontal attack, but it seemed she was primed and ready.

"The date, 2016," she told him and a winter chill invaded the room. "Tell me it's a joke, or not a joke."

"Joke?" He cocked his head and a smile crept across his mouth. It widened with appreciation as he watched her. Enjoying her show of temper, he thought of ways to change the anger to passion.

Hastily, he forced those thoughts to the back of his mind, filing them away for future reference. His smile deepened even more. "No joke," he began, "I'm beginning to see—"

She lifted her chin. "I don't think you do," she cut in melodramatically.

James wasn't expecting her to interrupt his speech, or to see her sit back and cross her arms over her chest then stubbornly stare at him as if this date had importance. Her actions took some of the momentum out of his plan of attack, and he sauntered across the room to gaze at the hills outside, to think, perhaps to gain the upper hand. Methodically, he clenched his hands behind his back and slowly rocked on the balls of his feet.

He continued for some time in this manner, but after awhile he changed tactics. "Then you must leave confusion and chaos wherever you go," he said with quiet disdain, noticing the sudden rise of color to her cheeks.

"I don't see how that has anything to do with this" she whispered heatedly, all pretense of a calm facade vanishing instantly.

"Ah, but you do. I can tell by looking at you that you leave a man disoriented and unable to think. Much too beautiful by any standards and surely you understand what you can do to a man. I have a mind to show you what I mean, but then..." he hesitated a moment too long.

"I'm not beautiful," she said quite distinctly, in a tone leaving no room for disagreement. "And as for the other..."

She handed him the paper, pointing to the date.

Except he smiled and laughed when she handed it to him, presuming for a brief moment she understood.

Alex sat up, instantly contrite. Anticipating her move, he bent over, only the smallest of spaces separating them. So close he forced her to move back against the chair. Deliberately and with calculated purpose, he snared her attention with his dark blue eyes.

James rested his hands on the back of her chair. "The typesetter," he said quietly, "does it once a month, sometimes more." His breath feathered against her cheek, the faint smell of lavender so very close.

"Does what?" her voice quavered.

"Gets corned," he replied smoothly. "Sometimes he misses the date by hundreds of years." He toyed with a wispy lock of fiery-red hair. Ran a long slender finger down the column of her neck, enjoying her shiver beneath his touch. Knew it was desire. She realized it too. Euphorically, he watched color slowly creep up her neck to her cheeks. And he ignored his upbringing, the code he'd lived by for so long, ignored everything but the soft warm feel of her skin against his.

Her eyes registered surprise, passion, before turning to panic. The devastating alarm, he saw, jolted him back to the moment, forcing him to automatically drop his hand. She pushed away then slipped from her vulnerable position only to dash across the room. He followed more slowly, handing her the paper. His brows narrowed suddenly. He had an aversion to dishonesty and lies. In this case it was her reluctance to confide in him that bothered him so deeply.

"By corned, do you mean drunk?"

"Of course." The becoming blush suddenly vanished and her skin paled. His dark brows shot up and he moved toward her, hesitating this time, wondering at the sudden change. "Now don't go into a conniption fit. I believe your imagination has gotten the better of you."

She looked as if she wanted to ignore him, but he wasn't going to allow it. It wasn't easy though. The mere appearance of that date had caused her pupils to dilate and her skin to become clammy. The mere sight of him had the same effect. She didn't look at him. Instead, she focused on the mantle.

"You've a lot of nerve. I understand now why I'm here, and what you expect from me," she said in that cold polite tone of hers, determination apparent in the subtle lift of her chin.

"I suppose I do, but then you need a place to stay," James replied with a calculated and hard edge to his voice. "I'm right, aren't I? You have no place to go." He went on, ignoring her look of righteous indignation. "I am at your disposal, Miss Alexandra, and if I've wronged you, well, then I apologize. If I've offended you, then I apologize again. I have simply offered you my protection, nothing more nothing less." The statement was casual and in no way did he expect a reply.

Alexandra's lower lip trembled, and she looked away but not before he saw the wetness in her eyes. "I don't need your protection." She waved her hands in the air. "I don't care if you ignore me. And you haven't really offended me. I just want you to leave me alone," she finished with a very ragged tone.

"Crissakes, I've said it all wrong. I'm sorry," James said, apologizing. Reaching out, he brushed a lone tear from her cheek. Taking her hand in his, he smoothed her slender fingers with his thumb. "I can't leave you alone. It's only, oh, hell, you need me."

"I don't want anything to do with Sean Cassidy," she told him. Her shoulders drooped and her words lost conviction.

"Who the hell is Sean Cassidy?"

"A friend of the family." She turned away from him then, staring at the fire that blazed merrily in the fireplace.

He longed for things a gentleman shouldn't; wanted to walk to her, pull her into his arms until all her pain and fear were resolved. Yet all the while he couldn't ignore the heat that spiraled inside him when she looked at him. All it took was one gentle look, a suggestion of a smile for him to lose perspective. Frustration, anxiety, the need to protect her, certainly but something else lay between them. No matter how she exasperated him, she caused him to look within himself and ask questions he'd never before thought of.

"How much do people know about this?" she asked with a wary emphasis.

He didn't answer promptly, weighing the subtlety and content of his reply. "You're not from these parts, are you?"

She let her eyelashes flutter shut, opening them slowly.

"I didn't think so. You have a face I'd never forget," James said softly, more to himself than to her. "Portland, perhaps?"

Her blue eyes were dazed.

"Where do you want me to start?" she asked bluntly.

James raked his fingers through his hair, a nervous gesture. "To begin with, I have a hankerin' to know just how you ended up on that old mountain trail. The only thing that's up there is a lost mine, and I'll be damned if you think that I'm fool enough to believe you were looking for it."

She tossed her hair back and paused a moment as if concentrating, her glance challenging. "The Blue Bucket?"

He met it firmly. "Don't whitewash it," he said with a small smile. "You must realize your presence here has raised a lot of questions."

"The Blue Bucket? The lost mine that no one's ever found? No, I wasn't looking for it. It doesn't exist. After all these years, I'm not foolish enough to believe I could find it."

He arched a brow high, amazed at her quick answer. He didn't tell her she was the absolute center of attention in this small town, discounting his role in bringing about the gossip surrounding her. He didn't say he had no intention of letting her leave. Instead, he spoke with a casual blandness. "Exactly, then what were you doing?"

She appeared perplexed. "I didn't want to be there, but I didn't have a choice. Sean brought me there and he wanted, to..." She shuddered as if recalling some terrifying horror. "I hit him and ran. When I got to the Oregon Vortex I went through the fence. After I found the crooked house, I went inside. I only wanted to get out of the rain, but the moment I sat down, I felt strange and my head started spinning." She was babbling now, going on and on and she couldn't seem to stop.

"Oregon Vortex, what's that?"

"It's, well, it's a place where strange things happen."

"You mean the Forbidden Ground? The Native Americans called the land that because their horses wouldn't go there."

His brows rose a fraction. "You were running from Sean. This the man you saw in town?" His gut clenched and an incredible fury overwhelmed him. It brought back other memories, too, memories best left alone.

"Yes," she kept her gaze away from his. "I was so upset by what he tried to do to me that I couldn't go back."

"He's your husband."

"No." she gritted disgustedly, her hands tightening and untightening at her sides.

"Your protector then?" He continued to question, to pry, to delve into her past, praying that wasn't the case, but if it was...

Alex stiffened then confronted him. "My what?"

"You did say you were an adventuress," he spoke quietly as he closed the distance between them once more. Ah, but he hoped this time she'd deny his accusation, yet despite the ambivalent situation he couldn't help flashing her a wicked grin.

"Yes," she said softly. "But I think you have a different definition for adventuress," she retorted pertly, this time. "To you, what is an adventuress?"

"A prostitute."

"No. I thought you meant someone who liked to travel, have adventure, you know."

"A woman shouldn't travel alone," he told her.

"That's archaic."

"Well then, maybe your protector," he amended, willing to concede anything, anything at all. "A man who takes care of you in lieu of certain favors."

His definitions seemed to float past her. "No." Her voice bordered on coolness. "You don't understand. He was a friend. At least I thought he was, and I won't do what you seem to be implying. If you want, I'll go."

"And where will you go? Back to Sean?" He remarked lightly, disregarding the tension sweeping through him.

She looked up astonished. Her voice was barely audible when she spoke. "No."

He hesitated and for one surprisingly brief moment, he thought he saw a touch of guilt in her eyes, perhaps a need for honesty, then it vanished. She was holding back something.

"Ah," he said grinning at the paper, searching for a new line of questions, "two thousand sixteen. The date is only a little off. But if you are from around here, you should be used to these mistakes," he strode to a chair, sitting back in a lazy crossed-arm pose, and continued, "Now you've peaked my curiosity. Tell me about this man, your protector."

Surprisingly, he saw tears well in her eyes. "He's nothing to me." She brushed away the moisture from her cheeks then closed her eyes. "Don't you listen to anything? He's not my protector."

He inclined his head, his brow raising. "Well, you're not going back, at least not to him."

She looked up startled. "This is not your concern," she told him. Her voice held a polite conviction. But a dark shadow seemed to slip over her eyes before disappearing without a trace.

"Oh come on, Miss Alexandra, you can't want to hook up with that critter again." He was suddenly afraid she meant to do that very thing.

His tenacity made her eyes widen, "It's not your concern and I never said—"

He laughed ruefully at her outburst.

"You're wrong. As your doctor and your new friend, I want to help."
He closed the distance between them once again. He had moved swiftly
beside her, silent and without warning. She looked so innocent, so sweet.

Ah, but is she an angel or a devil in disguise?

James realized instantly he'd gone too far in his assumptions and too
quickly. "I didn't mean to ruffle your feathers. I apologize. Think of this as
your home. Please." He didn't care about the small-minded people of
Jacksonville, but he knew she would. For some unknown reason, he only
wanted her to stay. His fists clenched and unclenched at his sides, and he
had hoped for more control.

As he approached she stiffened, tilting her chin in one swift motion.
"Fine, but I'd like to know exactly what I've said. Bear in mind I'm willing
to leave. All I need is a job and a place to stay and I'll be out of your life."

"No."

She laughed at that. "No?"

"Oh? But Miss Alexandra, you have neither a place to stay or a job,"
he said softly. "Hang up the fiddle, Miss Alex. You are staying here. I will
do all that I can to ward off the rumors."

"Why? Why would you want me to stay here?"

"I saved your life. That makes you my responsibility," he admitted
albeit cautiously, "but it's the truth isn't it?" She shouldn't deny his
hospitality and in the same breath continue with the charade she could find
a job other than in a room over the Eldorado.

"Yes, but—"

"You have nowhere to go," he interrupted.

"You've been more than kind," she bit out sarcastically, "and now
you can consider the debt fulfilled."

"No, dash it all," James cut in swiftly. "I would more than willingly
find a home and a job for you, but as you must have noticed, no one is
hiring. Now, if you'd graciously accept what I'm offering."

Alex slumped into the chair, the stiffness surprisingly gone and told
him quietly, "I don't think I understand your offer."

He rubbed his hand across his jaw, caught up in thought. When he
looked at her confusion was clearly written on her face. "I'm not sure I
understand either." It wasn't that he didn't understand. It was just that he

was suddenly embarrassed to tell her. And he didn't want her to leave, not yet anyway.

"When you figure out what you want, tell me." She stared at him for a long heart-stopping second as if she waited for him. Finally she let out a breathy whisper, saying skeptically, "I suppose you're right. I do need a place to stay."

"Of course I am." He walked back to his chair, turning his back on her and the conversation as well.

"I'll stay on my own terms."

"Miss Alexandra." Clearly intrigued, James sat up straight in his chair. His grin stretched broadly across his face. He was suddenly relieved her disposition had improved, and satisfied she had acknowledged the dire straits that had befallen her. He leaned forward. "And your terms?"

"I'll write them down and you can sign them," she volunteered swiftly.

"All right, and I'll do the same."

She didn't look pleased with the idea and he couldn't understand why. At times, the way she acted supported all the circumstantial evidence surrounding her, all his preconceived ideas, but at other times she looked as pure as freshly fallen snow. He didn't want her to leave and he didn't want her pushed from his home by misunderstandings.

"What did you have in mind?" he asked.

"Well," she began, "I'm willing to work. I'll do anything."

Her prosaic honesty startled him for a moment.

One dark eyebrow rose a fraction and a grin inched across his face again. "Anything, Miss Alexandra? You'd best be careful what you promise."

She let out a stunned cry of amazement. Oh, and he knew he'd gone too far, perhaps played his hand too soon.

"I promised nothing."

"Ah, but that's not the way I heard it."

"You have no right insinuating something like that," she whispered adamantly.

"Really, but I could have sworn," he said and grinned knowingly.

"Are you cuttin' up a shine?" he asked.

She flushed deeper then braced herself against the power of his hold. "I didn't lie, I just didn't imagine that you'd... well I didn't think..."

"But you just lost your protector. It has been my understanding that young ladies in this situation need to look for another man. I won't let you go back to Sean Cassidy." And that was the truth. If she tried to go back he'd fight her every step of the way.

"Sean was not my protector. I will be no man's mistress. I'd rather starve," she promised him her eyes wide and beguilingly innocent.

"If you don't change your mind that is a likely scenario, starvation," he said, enjoying the game and her denials. "Or you might find yourself on your back in the Eldorado. As you well know there are very few ways for a woman to earn a living. Although I distinctly heard you turn that offer down." As long as she stayed in his home she could do anything she wanted.

"I have an education. I can teach. I'll find a way."

"We have a competent teacher. And you sure don't look much like a school-marm," he argued. With each passing second his voice grew increasingly husky.

Her mouth snapped shut then she sputtered, "Of course you do, but I could help."

"Not with your credentials."

She stared at James and her tone faltered, but she brazened it out, "Can we start over? You know, pretend we just met."

He gave her a lazy humorous look. "Perhaps..."

She sucked in her breath, "You don't believe a person can change then?"

"No, not that much." He stared at her hard for the next couple of minutes. Instead, "How old are you?"

"What does that have to do with anything?"

The day had been more taxing than he would ever cared to admit. At this moment, he wasn't sure if her age mattered, but he still intended to find out how old she was. His thoughts and preconceived ideas had been shattered into a million tiny pieces by Miss Alexandra. Just when he thought he had her figured out, she would do something or say something that would make him waver. He was confused one moment, furious the next, then condescending as well. She was a puzzle he couldn't solve. The pieces just didn't fit together.

"A hell of a lot," he countered obstinately. "You're no misty eyed virgin. In fact, you're a bit over the hill and I'm sure, fair game. So, how old are you? Be honest—"

"Fair game?"

Crissakes, he hadn't meant to say that.

"How old, Miss Alex."

"Alexandra."

"Miss Alexandra," he grinned.

"Twenty-two. And if you want everything pin pointed, I'll be twenty-three on February eighteenth.

"Good," he stroked his chin and perused her from head to toe. "You don't look that old," he paused, "I'll let you know exactly what I expect."

"Really."

"I'll be here for you. Anything you wish for you have only to ask, and if it's in my power, you'll have it," he continued in his stiff manner.

He was suddenly very pleased with Alexandra.

And with himself...

Alexandra looked reticent.

And her sweet innocence mystified him.

She was an exquisite piece of baggage.

And still...

Just the thought of her made him smile.

Chapter Five

Belinda's mother, Nora, pursed her lips as she studied the intricate needlework pattern in front of her. For a few more seconds, she continued her ardent perusal then she cleared her throat and began speaking to her daughter. "You really must apply yourself more diligently to catching James Lawrence. I've had the wedding dress on hold at Worth's for almost a year. Truly, Belinda, I thought you all but had a proposal months ago," she paused, spreading the material in front of her. Nora looked up at her beautiful daughter with deliberation, her cool, disdainful eyes taking in Belinda's dishabille and derisively went on. "I suggest you do whatever it takes to secure a place at the head of his household."

"But mother, I've already tried that. Our relationship simply didn't last," Belinda replied without a bit of embarrassment at her disclosure. She negligently lifted her lashes to look unabashedly at her mother.

"If your brother found you in a compromising situation, I'm sure James could be forced to do the right thing by you," she said, exasperated, and took several tiny controlled stitches.

"Actually that thought did cross my mind, but James doesn't even want to be in the same room with me since the little tart took up residence in his house." Belinda scrutinized her teacup. When her mother gave that level of attention to her stitchery, she was irritated. Belinda smiled and soothingly coaxed, "Tell me, what has Charles done this time?"

"He's too honest," her mother grumbled. "He turned down a chance to run for office because all politicians are liars. Says he likes it here. Says, too, that the town and the job suit him just fine."

"Mother, it's all right. You know you can't make Charles do anything he doesn't want to do."

Nora Perkins wanted the best for her daughter, and in truth, considering the small town she was forced to live in, had done admirably. But when she first saw James Lawrence ride into town and realized his wealth and statues far out-distanced anyone in the state, she'd known he was meant to be husband to Belinda. Over time though, the problem had been convincing James Lawrence.

"As for Lawrence and his little strumpet, I've already figured out a way to get rid of her."

Her mother stopped her grumbling and glanced up in surprise. Setting aside her stitchery, she curiously asked. "Anything you can tell me?" she probed, well aware of her daughter's agile mind and liaisons with unscrupulous men.

"It's best you don't know," Belinda replied sweetly. "But it does have something to do with Sean Cassidy, the new Wells Fargo driver." She flaunted a small smile.

"Be careful," Nora told her daughter bluntly. "Cassidy is dangerous, in case you haven't noticed."

"Oh, I've noticed."

"I don't know what they both see in Alexandra, but Sean Cassidy wants her. It shouldn't be too hard to lure her away from the house. When that happens, all I need to do is let nature take its course. And you, mother, will see that Charles comes along just in the nick-of-time."

~ * ~

That morning Alexandra overslept, waking finally to the happy chattering of conversation coming from down the hall. She was sleeping in the adjoining room to the master chamber. With a sinking feeling, she realized this wasn't a dream, and she was really and truly waking up in the wrong century.

Wistfully Alex opened the bedroom window inhaling the cold winter air. Endless rolling hills changed to foothills, then merged with the rugged Cascade Range. Gold Hill, Sardine Creek, and the Oregon Vortex lay out there somewhere to the north.

Her ticket home.

For one brief moment Alex let her body slump against the top pane of glass, her forehead pressed against its coldness. She hadn't asked him for help yet. Maybe later today, she cowardly decided, and pushed away from the window. The chill air seeping through the thin glass sent shivers running across her shoulders and down her back. Surely James would help her go back to her own time. Surely he wouldn't insist she stay.

She turned, leaning against the window frame. Her back to the chilled air, Alexandra inspected the plain room in front of her. Despite the suggestive nature of it, Captain Lawrence had put her in the room joining the master suite. It was so very different from his. The room looked as if no one had entered it for a long time. Kim had cleaned the room thoroughly; no dust, no cobwebs, no clutter to make her think that way, but it felt lonely, empty somehow.

As Alex walked to the large roll top desk, she was determined to make the list she'd proposed earlier. A small figurine of a horse sat on top of the desk. Alex picked the object up then turned it over in her hand.

"You must have been made with the most tender care," she said to the fragile clay figure. "How many years have you sat here?"

She gingerly set the small sculpture back, pausing a moment to look at it once more then pulled out the chair and sat down. When she looked in the little cubbyholes in front of her, she noticed several reams of paper. There was ink and the old fashioned kind of pens she loved as a little girl. She studied them, openly curious at first, wistfully but not stopping, then as a historian intrigued by their fundamental simplicity. She smiled whimsically, a small laugh slipping through her loneliness.

Alex heard James' quiet tread as he walked into the room.

In a matter of a few seconds, all humor vanished. "What are you doing? Writing your list?" He lazily asked, watching her. "We'll compare lists tomorrow. I'll let you decide what it is you want to do." His husky voice pounded inside her head and sent a flutter down her spine. "I'll be in the library if you need me." With that said he left.

Yet, if she were honest with herself, she'd have to admit he was the first man who had ever completely dazzled her. The thought struck her like a forceful blow when she recalled all that had gone on between them and all he seemed to expect from her. And she was not adverse to any of it.

It took a full five minutes for cooler reason to prevail over the swift cryptic response. "Naturally." She had been beside herself with confused and incoherent feelings, yet her sarcasm didn't seem to surprise him.

She respected the captain. He made her feel protected and fragile, made her feel that perhaps she did need him. Which, of course, was his intent. James took her breath away and made her, for a brief moment, entertain thoughts of staying in this century.

Alex lit the lamp.

As she wrote, she stopped now and then to gaze out the window, more committed and determined than ever to return to the vortex, even if she had to walk there by herself. It seemed a bit ludicrous to list household chores she somehow knew she'd never perform.

Somewhere between the first and second item on the paper she became sidetracked and began writing other things. She documented her fall through time, the cold paralyzing terror she experienced on the mountain, and the blessed relief she felt when James Lawrence rode into her life. Then she wrote more, scripted unbelievable things, described miracles and mysteries. With a perverse sense of humor and with bold handwriting, on the front page no less, she dedicated the knowledge within to James Lawrence, hoping he would someday find it. While she wrote an idea made its way into her head. A miraculous revelation, she'd earn her keep, pay her room and board by writing essays. The suffragist movement had taken root, and while she wouldn't change history, she could add moral support. Determined and eager, Alex set to work on her first series of exposes, "Education and the American Woman," equality in all things.

Hours later, physically and mentally drained, she leaned back in the chair. After setting the pen in its holder, she gave herself a well-deserved pat on the shoulder. Cat-like, she stretched her aching muscles.

A childish giggle erupted in the hallway snaring her attention. Kim called out to Miss Jessie and they both laughed. From the corner of her eye,

Alexandra glimpsed bare feet, long legs then an impish face. Jessie stood for a brief moment in the doorway and after a curious peek inside, she vanished.

Miss Jessica, she was a charmer, that one. Alex laughed. Her mommy? Surely Jessica Lawrence didn't think she was a candidate for that pedestal-like position. Her father thought she was a prostitute. Alex started to laugh hysterically, shaking her head, wiping away the tears that suddenly welled in her eyes. The longing for home unbearable.

Impossible, absolutely, utterly impossible. Seductress, prostitute, adventuress. Mother? In a different century she was known as an ice maiden.

"Miss Alex?" Alexandra felt the little girl's hand on her shoulder before she heard her.

"What? Miss Jessica, you shouldn't be here. Your father wouldn't like it."

"You're crying, Miss Alex. I don't want you to cry."

"Oh, darling," Alexandra turned and hugged Jessie then quickly let her hands drop to her side. "I was laughing, but Jessie you have to go. Where's Kim?"

"Didn't look like it," Jessie interrupted.

"I know. Maybe it was a little of both." She was torn between a blossoming concern for Jessie and the horrible loss she knew she'd feel if she returned to her own time. A small sob tore from her, and she felt a heart rending stab of pain, recalling once again her resolve to stay detached from the little girl.

"Papa says it helps sometimes to talk."

"And I'm sure he's right most of the time."

"He's always right."

Alex ruffled Jessie's hair then picked up her hand. She decided for the sake of everyone concerned she'd better make this short, even though Jessica deserved her time and compassion. "Come on," she led her to the bed and they both sat down. "Jessie...can you keep a secret?"

Jessica's eyes lit up and her little face seemed to glow. "Oh, yes,"

"Good, then I'll tell you something I've never told anyone else, but when I'm finished you have to promise to go. Okay? I don't want you getting into trouble." Alex paused for a heart beat then squeezed Jessie's hand, "I'm afraid, Jessie. I'm a very long ways from home, and I don't think I can a find a way back."

"Oh," Jessie's smile vanished. "If you really want to go home, my daddy will take you." Tears suddenly appeared in Jessie's eyes.

Alex frowned. She hadn't thought. "It's too far even for your daddy. But perhaps he can help."

"Oh," Jessica crossed her legs and a little furrow creased her brow, her tears dried up as quickly as they had appeared. It seemed to Alex she was trying to understand.

"Miss Jessica," Alex's voice wavered, "why do you think I'm going to be your mother?"

Jessica beamed again. "That's easy. You're the only lady Papa's ever brought home. And you're so pretty."

"I am?"

"Uh huh."

"But ,Sweetheart, Captain Lawrence and I don't even know each other. And I know he doesn't love me."

"He must. He brought you home. Besides, if he doesn't, he'll learn to love you," Jessie's wide-eyed innocence touched Alex's heart. "I love you," Jessie finished.

What indeed, she thought. *Out of the mouth's of babes.* "Jessica..." Alexandra's voice was stern and full of reproach yet she hadn't intended it to sound that way.

"You don't understand. I want you there next time I wake up crying. I don't know why, but you're going to be my mother," she finished stubbornly.

Neither Jessica nor Alexandra were aware they had a visitor, a very amused visitor. James was leaning negligently against the door jam, listening. At the sound of a smothered cough both girls jumped. The implication hit them before the sound of his words.

"Miss Jessica," James' voice held warm concern and a touch of embarrassment, "go to your room, sugar plum. I'll speak with you later," his voice was tender as he looked at Jessie.

Jessica didn't even blink before she raced from the room. Alex closed her eyes, hoping he'd go away, but she heard only the little girl's running footsteps until Jessica's door closed hard.

When she opened her eyes and looked up, James was thumbing through her journal. Alexandra suddenly felt James's gaze rest upon her, considering her, testing her. It felt as if he analyzed every breath. The man was standing with one shoulder leisurely propped against the doorframe, staring at every sentence, every unbelievable word she'd written.

"Jessie's mother?" he inquired. Boldly looking at her, he allowed his gaze to roam over every curve of her body, hesitating momentarily on her stocking clad toes peeping out from beneath her skirts. After a slight pause, he moved upward in a brief inspection of her feminine assets that left Alexandra feeling as if he wanted nothing more than to devour her.

He's protecting Jessica, she reminded herself.

"It was her idea," she replied hesitantly then shot him a curious look.

"So you say." His eyebrows narrowed as he seemingly thought about what he'd overheard.

"Yes, I do," she sighed but was tempted to laugh. His audacity never ceased to amaze.

"Perhaps we should continue where we left off," he said with a languid smile. "I'm really quite interested in your list."

"I haven't made one."

"Then we'll have to make do with mine. Come here," James said.

"I'm afraid that wouldn't be a good idea. I'm not going to be here much longer."

"What makes you say that?" he asked into the chilling silence that seemed to follow.

"I'd like you to take me back to the hills where you found me. You can't keep me here against my will," she hesitated.

"Feel free to leave. You're not my prisoner."

"I know." If she told him the truth, he would never believe her.

"There's nothing there for you," James said looking out the window toward those very hills.

"I know, but..." Alexandra started then quit. If he could only understood the upheaval in her life. The past few days had become a nightmare she didn't care to think about let alone remember. Yet she had to remember because a way home existed. She intended to find it and she needed James' help.

"I'm only asking for one day. Is that too much?"

"No, of course not." His smile was lush and inviting when he turned back toward her. "And since we're on the subject, perhaps we could discuss exactly how you wound up there in the first place."

It was time to tell him as much as he would believe. "Sean Cassidy brought me up there, expecting certain favors. I refused him. Then I ran. After that I stumbled around in the dark for several hours."

"I found you."

"Tackled me."

"I thought you were a murderess."

Alexandra had seen the hesitancy before he answered, the instant transformation of his features. His poise was as impeccable as his charm, but she wasn't sure he meant what he said. It seemed to her he was merely placating her until he could think of a suitable argument to forestall her plans. And what if she didn't find the vortex. She'd have to make another trip, or possibly more.

"What is it—exactly—that you're looking for?" he asked her softly.

"A vortex," Alexandra replied swiftly, hoping he wouldn't question her further.

"If we don't find this place the first time, what then?"

"I'll stay," she told him with a cool detachment she didn't feel.

"Then we've reached an agreement," he said so low, the words were a throaty resonance as he stepped closer. He was much too close, she thought with alarm before she scooted back to the farthest reaches of the bed.

The scent of him filled her as he sat down on the bed so very close to her. Suddenly, she wasn't sure they'd just agreed to the same thing at all. Their gazes met and he held her immobile for a fleeting second before she broke away, sliding the length of the bed to eventually end up standing at the open doorway.

"You'll come to like it here," he smiled easily, almost affectionately.

Just the thought made her cheeks glow with unfulfilled yearnings.

She shifted uneasily. Enchanted by his subtle promise, her gaze flew swiftly back to meet his. Instantly, she found her soul captured and held prisoner. Her body as well as her resistance melted under his ardent gaze; her knees shook and she felt a strong hot shiver run the length of her spine.

Perhaps she wasn't made of ice.

But after the horrible night with Sean, she'd sworn...

Heat rushed through her body, coiling deep inside. She denied it, all of it. For her peace of mind, for her conscience, she refused to admit James left her mind in turmoil and her physical well being in jeopardy. "You're very sure of yourself."

"Of course," he told her, with a soft chuckle

"When can we go?" Alexandra asked, her feeling an ambiguous confusion of fear and the need to reach out to find her identity, to find home.

He smiled, and grinning like a Cheshire cat, sauntered to a chair by the window and sat down, looking extremely pleased with himself.

His long legs, encased in buckskin, stretched out in front of him drew her attention. His moccasins were knee high, fringed, and beaded. A knife handle protruded from the top, peering over the fringe, mocking, threatening, and announcing to the world this man protected his own. It was a curious feeling to know a man that self-assured and possessive.

"Give me a few days to check things out." His voice, soft, resonant, and warm sent chills colliding inside her.

Stormy blue eyes so heated at times, now remained steadfastly on her lips and she couldn't help but feel nervous.

"Do you have any idea what you do to men? Ah, darlin', perhaps you do," James said, his smile as warm as a summer day.

"I don't. What do I do?" she queried, surprised by his insinuations and her inability to understand the situation. She was mature and intelligent, strong and principled, she reminded herself, yet suddenly she had no control of her life and she didn't like the feeling.

"You, my sweet lady, are absolutely exquisite, perfect in every way. The very brilliance of your smile, when you choose to bestow it, could lead an innocent man astray."

"What?" She was momentarily shocked then she almost forgot

herself and smiled. He sounded as if he recited a poem, a very bad poem. Yet her mind was confused and frayed beyond repair, her nerves unraveled. She battled to control herself and her precariously teetering emotions, since she could hardly fight the man who had saved her life. She wanted off the wire it seemed she walked. Politeness was highly overrated in this situation.

"You are the most beautiful woman I've ever seen."

"You've gone blind," she returned immediately. "And if you are not, then you are the first man to think it."

A lazy smile curved into his lip, and his brow arched high once again. "Blind? You have not looked into a mirror lately."

~ * ~

James suddenly found himself studying Alexandra down to every fine curve of her exquisite body. His eyes kept returning to her lips, almost too lush and full for her face; the provocative little pout she managed more often than not, and the enticing pink tongue that darted out to trace their line. It enhanced her huge cobalt blue eyes that slanted just a minute. The high fragile cheekbones and the fine almost too white skin framed them to perfection. He found he couldn't keep his eyes from her. A long tendril that had come lose from the spinsterish bun she wore whispered soft against her neck, floating on her collarbone. It was the sweetest sight he'd ever seen, and he wanted it to last forever. Yet those beautiful eyes smoldered when they met his.

Angel mine, how long will it take before you're in my bed?

"When I return, I'll take you to the hills to search for this vortex. If that's what you want. Once, if we don't find what you're looking for, we won't return," he said.

When she lifted her chin, she made him think of a queen looking with disdain on her loyal subjects. "I'll be waiting."

Admiration seized him, but when he saw her grip her fingers around the chair, he wondered if any of his presumptions about her were right. James suddenly understood he'd taken her by surprise this evening.

She smiled slightly when he approached, his nearness seemed to make her nervous and he didn't like that. James rested his hand on her shoulder. "Do not believe in miracles," he insisted. His gaze, melding with hers, drew slowly to her lips, downward, falling upon her breasts, hesitating, then followed the path back to her eyes.

"Oh, I do, Mr. Lawrence. I have for a couple of days now."

That caught his attention and made him smile. When he'd told her he'd make a list too, she'd become a different person. Not so self-assured, in fact, that little spark she'd first let ignite between them no longer existed and he wanted it back.

The gentlemen in his family had all but died. The greater part of his family had lost most everything in the war. As the youngest son of a wealthy family, he'd spent the first part of the war fighting for the North. Then two years in a southern prison camp had left him less than a man, worn, defeated, and struggling to understand.

When he'd come across the remains of his sister and her house, he buried her, picked up Jessie, and left. He'd headed west with the baby girl in front of him and nothing behind him. Not once did he look back or regret leaving. So, searching for his future, he'd found Jacksonville one hot, August day and decided to stay.

He didn't like the feelings Alexandra McMurdie stirred in him, but the fact remained she rekindled memories in him he'd all but chosen to forget. And it didn't help with little Jessie pleading for a mommy. Not that Miss McMurdie was looking either, she wasn't he could tell from the way she held him at arm's length. That was another piece of the puzzle that didn't fit.

Instinctively, his eyes rested on her profile. Her lashes fluttered once, twice, and fanned out on her cheekbones. The steel rod bent; she sank against the headboard as if exhausted.

His thumb rubbed against the shiny smoothness of one of her cards. Intrigued by its hardness, everything about them absorbed his thoughts. The numbers, all of them including the color portrait of herself, and what seemed to be a date. A date that hadn't occurred so he'd dismissed it from his mind. Dismissed it until she'd acted strange and her words had spoken of things that didn't exist. At least they didn't in this world.

The world he knew was nothing like the one she'd described in her diary. The devil but she made him think about the impossible, another time, and a person transposed. She had him weaving fantasies in his mind. No, her peculiarity was explainable. He'd had second thoughts about intruding in her private world, her personal beliefs, but when he'd seen the dedication on the front cover of her journal, he couldn't resist reading.

The evening he found her would forever be clear in his mind. She'd almost died that night, and if he hadn't been in the posse, she'd have met a far different fate than the one she faced now.

Her beautiful skin still bore scratches from the bushes she'd rummaged through and her clothes had shown marked signs of wear. When he'd first set eyes on her, she'd seemed the most beautiful creature on earth.

Yet Alexandra had closed herself to him and the world. He'd find a way to open Pandora's box...Alex's heart.

If she'd admit the truth, he was her only friend, and the only person she knew in these parts. She had no one else to turn to.

They were both individuals, unique somehow from the norm.

They were kindred spirits, both running from the past, looking for freedom. It gave him another reason to look at Alexandra in a different light.

"Tell me something," he said after what seemed hours of silence.

"Yes?" Her huge blue eyes had shadows beneath them.

"Anything. Anything you like." His smile spread slowly across his face.

"There's nothing to tell." Wariness and exhaustion clearly apparent in her tone, her lashes fluttered softly across her high cheekbones.

"You're wrong. I don't know anything about you, and if you give me reason to trust, I will." His voice had dropped an octave. The long length of his thigh brushed against hers and he felt the sudden heat of her body join with his. Every muscle tensed.

Her gaze flew again to meet his. Silence pounded into the quiet room but still they said nothing. Nothing seemed to matter. She rested her hand on his.

"All right, what do you want to know?" she said and he felt her body trembling against his hand.

"First, you have to promise—"

"Promise what," she interrupted him.

He was fascinated. At one and the same time, she managed an intriguing deception. He imagined she knew what she was about though, playing the bewitching innocent one moment and the next a provocative seductress.

"The truth, angel, only the truth."

She nodded and he sat patiently and watched. In the guise of blatant boredom and total disregard, Alexandra raised her eyes to gaze into his and with a radiant smile and a sarcastic hint to her tone, "The truth? I have no idea what that is anymore."

James chuckled. The cards appeared immediately and she blinked in recognition and reached for them.

"Not so fast." He held them away from her. James felt an unexplainable surge of anger he immediately tapped down.

"They're mine."

"Of course they are, but they hold a wealth of information about you. Don't they?" He was tempted to kiss the confusion from her. He held off though.

"You can have them. They're of absolutely no use here."

"What are they made of?" He held one up to the light, raising it in his hand. He looked back at her, a questioning brow arched high.

"Made of? I don't understand," but her eyes gave her away. Her lips creased together in a slender white line and she looked back to him.

"Do tell. One question, darlin', only one question and you've lied. After your promise." His eyebrow had risen in mocking disdain. With the silence frozen between them, the tension seemed to go on forever.

"If I told you the truth, you wouldn't believe me."

"Try me." His voice was intentionally hard and unrelenting.

"I can't," she said, softly, and her hands trembled.

He tapped the card on his chin, studied her face. As if to test her word he said, "You can't or won't?"

He hesitated beneath her scrutiny. Watched her carefully.

Her smile looked funny and her brow creased when she nodded. "Both."

"I don't know what to think," he said. "I'll be the first to admit I don't know everything. The card exists, is made out of material I've never seen before," he thought a moment more in concentration. "Can you explain the color portrait?"

He paused then, frustration rising within him. He waited for a denial, an answer, nothing. "If you leave me no alternatives," he said confronting her openly, "I can't help but write my own story about you."

Her lips quivered, even as she held the bottom one between her teeth to stop it. "Color pictures do exist, but I can't tell you the mechanics of it." Ironically she was babbling again and he almost regretted his questions. "My area of expertise is the environment. I'll receive my doctorate in environmental engineering this spring," she paused to take a breath and push back a tear. "Well I don't suppose that's true any longer."

He didn't miss the tear or the defeat in her voice and for a moment it made him regret his callousness. She sounded so sincere and so knowledgeable. Trained actress, consummate liar, or what, he wondered, the words, the smooth talking, all part of her training. And nothing she had said made sense. What the devil was an environmental engineer?

James stood. "You're full of surprises but it doesn't matter. Not to me anyway. Eventually you'll trust me enough to tell me what I need to know." He rubbed his jaw never taking his eyes from hers. "When I get back, darlin'." Her eyes widened instantly surprised. "When I get back we'll discuss these things in detail."

Chapter Six

How do you respond to a man who wasn't even alive when you were born, whose values and moral codes were products of a different century? How do you say, "I have a mind of my own, and if someone would give me a chance I'm perfectly capable of taking care of myself? And how do you tell someone as sure of himself as James, "You're wrong about me. I'm not what I seem to be."

With a heart-felt sigh, she rose from the chair. Her gait was slow and thoughtful as she stepped to the window. Looking down at the yard, she watched as he walked toward the barn. When he looked back to the window, she smiled hesitantly, "Bon Voyage," she said softly, "have a safe journey."

When James left for the week, it had given her a moment's reprieve, a time to consider and perhaps determine a course for her life. Then one week turned into three and she began to use every moment to her advantage.

With diligence and tenacity, Alexandra wrote to magazines in the East and sent her articles to newspapers all over the country. Ideas flowed non-stop. Writing was a remedy for the loneliness she couldn't dissolve. The days slipped by. Sunshine and fresh spring breezes warmed the earth; flowers nudged their way into the gardens and the fields. Kim went into town to purchase supplies and send the articles for her.

What would James think when he read the essays? Alex sat back and gazed pensively at the title of her newest manuscript. "Women, Economics, and Survival." She delved into the options men gave women, the restrictions they'd placed on behavior, and even the moral code, which they developed in order to prioritize or rank women. Females didn't have many options. The restrictions were mountainous and the categories were despicable.

James was a man who categorized women and placed restrictions, but it was all done under the name of protection. His code of ethics were decidedly Victorian, but then, she admitted, he didn't know any other way. Perhaps she could teach him.

And she was a fool.

He'd find out soon enough she wasn't fair game, and to her utmost delight, he'd find out she could take care of herself. She meant to push James Lawrence from her thoughts until he could accept her as an equal. And how long would that take? It was only 1868. The challenge that thought presented loomed large and clear. Suddenly, the door slammed against the wall.

James Lawrence filled the doorway. He was back. Why was it that until this moment Alexandra hadn't realized how much she had missed him? Unconsciously, Alexandra rose to greet him.

He stepped inside, his moccasin-shod feet silent on the wooden floor, and pushed the door shut with a negligent sweep of his arm. "Your week's up."

Alexandra's heart was beating wildly. From the low, husky, deliberately provocative sentence.

"Days ago."

His stormy blue eyes flashed as he stepped closer. Yet somehow she managed to stand her ground and return his gaze.

"When did you come home?" she whispered breathlessly.

"Been home a few hours. What the devil is this? Angel girl. I assume you meant for me to find this since it is dedicated to me. It is, shall we say, for the lack of an appropriate adjective, interesting reading. The first few pages I saw the other day didn't begin to pique my interest. But this. Space shuttles, and moonwalks, probes on mars, perhaps you'll give Jules Verne some competition. I hear science fiction is quite the thing now and you have an astonishing imagination." He raised his eyebrows in mild inquiry.

Once again Alexandra wondered how she could possibly tell James that it wasn't her imagination. How could she tell him that someone had truly walked on the moon?

"I don't know what to say." Alexandra murmured in a breathless rush.

"What did you mean by this? The truth, Miss Alexandra." He held papers and her journal. Before she came downstairs, she'd stacked them all together in a nice neat pile. He must have thought...

The slow easy drawl vanished, and she suddenly wished for the light teasing air it gave his voice.

Because he enunciated each word so clearly and in such a provoking tone, she knew he'd read everything, even the essay. Thank the Lord it was only the first one, and she lifted her eyes to heaven. He couldn't possibly know she'd sold them.

"I didn't mean..." She reached for the journal. He seemed to hesitate, almost as if he considered giving the manuscript to her. Then he clearly changed his mind and held it away. She started to speak then quit with a soft little whisper, her hands falling to her side.

"It doesn't matter. I thought it was your list, Miss McMurdie. The one we spoke of."

"It does matter," she gasped out for a moment furious with his out-right audacity. "You had no right."

"Really? But darlin' you dedicated it to me. Right here on the front page, it says... "His smile unexpected, his brilliant eyes aglow with amusement."

"Yes," she interrupted. "But I never intended for you to..." Lips thinned, she glared at the sanguine man.

"I see."

"No...I don't think so."

"Then help me understand."

The sunlight slanting through the window defined the classic structure of his features, the perfect, aristocratic nose and the strong cheek bones depicted the teasing light in his eyes. He held the truth, her story, in his hands. And she had no conceivable way to explain time travel.

Even as she hesitated though, Alex saw his fist clench and his knuckles turn white. She saw the shadow of doubt in his eye. His jaw remained tense, and the pulse still throbbed at his neck, but she knew he controlled himself and his apparent curiosity. Forced to look at him, she waited while a brittle tension developed around them. She knew the truth needed unearthing, needed telling, but only when he'd believe her.

"I'm waiting." His eyebrow rose as if questioning her, but his expression held an underlying trust and a not so subtle hidden meaning. He was smiling in that slow, gentle way she had come to associate with him. "It's only a matter of time and I'll learn all your secrets," that smile was saying as vividly as though he spoke the words aloud.

Before she could answer him, his unspoken words caused a pink blush to creep up her cheeks, her burgeoning awareness of him evoking a myriad of sensations in her traitorous body. "I know what you must think. It's beyond understandable. I just faced the truth and realized nothing is as it seems. Riddles, mysteries, the unexplainable, the universe, all are one gigantic puzzle. Somehow I stumbled into one, a puzzle I mean, and I can't find the way out." She held out her hands in supplication.

"That's very good, Miss Alexandra, very good.

"You don't believe me."

"Be realistic," he cut her off and waved a dismissive hand. "Riddles? Mysteries? Puzzles?" he queried. "What's to believe?" His impatience and confusion were clearly obvious. "Is this a ploy...a game of some sort?"

"No game." She struggled for an explanation, staring at the paper. Nothing else clarified who she was or what she knew. He couldn't understand how she appeared on that road and neither could she, but it had happened.

"I am realistic," she said in her own defense. "Perhaps too realistic."

"That's a matter of opinion," he countered, his voice softening. "I need to understand all you've been through and what I can do to help."

Alex stared hard at the rigid tension of his muscles, at the brilliant lights in his eyes. Horrified, she remembered every word she'd jotted down. Recalled her vivid descriptions of the vortex and the beckoning light that seemed to call to her. Recounting her rapid journey through time, she'd foolishly added detailed accounts of machines and events that wouldn't exist for years; the Internet, computers, Facebook, Instagram and so many more. She'd spoken of cars and planes and even walking on the moon. Her ideas, her comments on women's rights and sexuality were scandalous. She'd come across one of his old medical book and almost choked when she read the section on abortion and contraception.

While her head pounded and her stomach churned with foreboding, she looked for a way to convince him. Even her calm inner voice couldn't subdue her anxiety. "It's all true..." she hesitated. "If you read that, you know I don't belong here."

"A fairytale I'm sure. You have one hell of an imagination. Do you really believe this?"

"Of course I do. It's all true." Her gaze swept upward and locked on his again. The contact shattered every coherent thought.

"Don't get huffy." He paused and rubbed his chin then smiled as if he enjoyed the discussion. "I suppose there should be a better way, but..."

"It's all true," she reiterated. Alexandra backed up and let out a long quiet breath.

She fell silent and wondered what had just gone on in this room. She wasn't precisely sure, but no smart woman would want to go through it again.

James steepled his fingers in thought and peered over them to place an accusatory look. Still leaning against the doorframe, he had the appearance of a predatory male animal.

"Convince me," he stared at her in veiled amusement. "I'm a good listener, but whatever you do don't take back your words or play me false."

"I've nothing else to say. It's all there," she nodded to the journal.

"I should have been more direct. Perhaps we should talk about...sex," his mouth quirked in a half smile.

Alexandra saw and swallowed a chuckle of her own. Without prudence, Alex knew she tended toward the impetuous...she messed things up terribly...words came out in a jumble. This time she bit her lip to control her words and hold back a grin. "Sex?"

"Contraception, if you like," he replied knowingly. The soft look in his eye told her he might understand, but then again he might think...she groaned, and heat rose once more to her cheeks. She knew she blushed. For once in her life she had no idea where to begin. And James stepped closer.

"What do you know about contraception?"

Alexandra grinned...but only a little then she moved back in an unconscious gesture to hit the wall.

"Can I throw something at you?"

"If you're willing to answer the question with a demonstration," he said, his arms open wide.

For a long time she eyed him warily, completely unsure of him and his intentions. "That it's every woman's right," she finally told him, coolly regaining her poise and the polite tone she always used. "Pregnancy is great deal more harmful than contraception. James..."

Her cool arrogance in the face of such a scandalous topic only seemed to push him nearer the brink of outright laughter. "I'm listening."

"When are you going to take me back—to Sardine Creek—to the vortex?"

If anything she'd said had taken him by surprise, this apparently did. His eyes turned a smoldering deep blue and he stared at her for a very long time. He didn't bother to hide his emotions. "I haven't decided."

"You promised," she reminded him, all humor vanishing, her tone of voice taking on a decidedly chilly air. He had to take her back, at least try. The change of topics had shaken them both. It was so quiet she thought she could hear the future turn into the present. After his answer and her reply, nothing more was said between them. She stood proud and stubborn, refusing to budge an inch. He'd followed her when she backed against the wall; his forearms on either side of her head keeping her from moving, and she didn't dare breathe. He didn't touch her—just looked. Finally, he turned from her and walked to the window. "It could dangerous, if what you've said is true."

"You believe me? I have to take that chance; it's my ticket home," she said softly.

There was no longer any reason to hide the truth from him or erect any more barricades. Her presence here was a mistake, one he had to come to grips with. It was up to her to convince him, but she was suddenly not so sure she wanted to. Her feelings for James were becoming disastrously tangled with her yearning to go home. She must set her priorities straight.

There was really no question when she paused to consider all the details. Traveling back to her century was the only feasible alternative.

He was whispering even though there was no one around to hear. "Ask for something else. I don't want to take you back. Forget about Sean. You never have to see him again. I promise he won't hurt you."

"All right," she was prepared to bargain. After all, she didn't want to see Sean anyway. She'd find a way back by herself if she had to. "In that case, I'd like your word." She hoped he would grant that one wish. "Your word you won't tell anyone what you just read."

He laughed outright, "I'll think about it."

"James," Alex said, furiously, "you can't tell anyone."

He arched a brow even as he slowly walked back to her. "You don't know much about me. I won't bargain. Besides, everything you've written here has merit, well almost everything."

"You agree with me?" she asked incredulously, her heart thumping wildly with relief. "Do you believe the other part?"

Alex drew a deep breath and forged ahead.

He nodded but said nothing. Waited. "You're expecting more than I can give at the moment."

She was right in the first place. "I wouldn't believe me either."

"You shouldn't have such a vivid imagination," he said softly, staring at her, reaching out to gently trace the line of her jaw.

She was speechless. "James, I..."

He raised an eyebrow again, a smile curling his lips. "So be it. Let's change the subject."

James didn't wait for her to respond. Bending his head low, his lips touched hers softly, brushing twice across them like heated velvet before he lightly traced over her mouth with his tongue and sent liquid fire sweeping inside.

She drew back in a shy response, but it seemed he felt the fire too, and from the startled look in his eyes, she knew there would be no turning back. His hands held her in place, his fingers weaving into her hair, and the other hand dropped to her shoulder. His thumb caressed her neck, smooth against rough, eternity passed and she denied herself nothing. It was far from innocent. The kiss, just a breath, a touch, a moment only, but the impact hurtled through her only to end in a soft warmth stirring within herself. Nothing in her experience came close to the spiraling sensations she felt, not even her journey through the vortex.

Then his mouth opened hungrily over hers. His hands moved down her back, pressing her closer and closer to the hard length of his body. He kissed her thoroughly, compellingly, passionately, and when her trembling lips parted for his probing tongue, he crushed her into himself.

Alex came alive in his arms, molding herself into his embrace, winding her hands around his neck. She gave herself completely to the unrelenting demands of his hands and mouth, and as she did, she forgot everything else.

A giggle, a swish of skirts, and a pattering of little feet scurried across the floor. The laughter light and airy warned her and she felt the moment rush back to reality.

Alex pushed frantically against him. James heard the same noise and he paused, slowly ending the kiss. He looked at her, his gentle unguarded expression surprised her and promised more. His arm tightened around her shoulder, keeping her near.

They both looked into twinkling blue Lawrence eyes and an amused mischievous grin.

"Jessica," Alex whispered.

"Mommy?" she asked, looking pleased.

Instantly James' sense of humor abandoned him. "No, sugar plum," he said, his tone instantly curt.

The smile on Jessie's face sputtered then vanished in a cloud of confusion. "I know what I saw. Amanda said her mother and father kissed all the time. Amanda told me only married folks kissed. So you must have married Alex. That was a kiss."

"True, about the kiss, wrong about the marriage, and she's not your mother."

His words and tone left Alex with the terrible truth. She meant nothing to James. After what she'd thought...what she'd felt... She wanted to run from him; felt as if she'd died inside.

She moved to leave, but his hand around her waist tightened, pulling her possessively close. Alexandra could not utter a single word in her defense. It was at once cold and hateful, and for a brief detached moment all her confusion vanished. But then, under the ever watchful and curious eyes of his daughter, her transient musings was abruptly jerked to a capricious halt.

"But, Papa," she protested.

"Run along, sugar plum," he cut in. She did but stopped at the door to look back and smile. A smile that would melt the hardest heart, even his.

Alexandra spoke but her words were a hoarse whisper. "Rest assured this won't happen again."

"It will," he said, "but not where Jessie can see or interrupt. You can depend on complete discretion from this instant forward."

"I don't think this is a good idea." Alexandra said determinedly.

He pulled her back into his arms and she felt his strength encircle her. His hand braced at the small of her back brought her tight against him, "Have you told Miss Jessica that you'll be her mother?"

"I haven't—I mean—when Jessica makes up her mind to do something, she's hard to avoid. You know that."

"Then why does she think..."

"I've never." Alexandra struggled not to lose her temper completely.

"No?" he cut in. "I don't intend to marry anyone," he released her and this time his grin unnerved her.

"Neither do I," Alexandra shot back. She pushed away from him and started from the room.

His face was set, his breathing ragged even while he lounged negligently on the couch. He stopped her exit. "Giving me the mitten, Alex?"

She whirled around, ready to deny him. With her anger threatening to boil over, she didn't know what she'd do, but his expression surprised her. He was so sure of himself, too sure. She was trembling. Frightened? The horrifying ride through time was nothing compared to what she felt when he kissed her, when he looked at her in that dangerous way of his, she'd almost lost all sense of herself.

"I haven't read all of it yet, but I will." He tapped the journal against the palm of his hand.

"Just because I believe in a woman's right to make her own decisions and live by her own values and rules, doesn't mean...doesn't..."

"You want me, Alexandra. You returned the kiss." He smiled contentedly but didn't say anything more for a moment. "If all you're worried about is a baby...well, I'll take care of that also."

Too stunned to move, Alexandra watched James disappear up the steps. She heard a door open then a soft cadence of words as he talked to Jessie. Closing her eyes, she ran an unsteady hand through her hair.

This was all her fault. She had written of TVs and radios, computers and telephones. The list was endless. They could find no common ground, no unity. Two people from opposing worlds could never know or understand each other. Her fanciful mind twisted and turned this relationship into something special because she had found herself inescapably drawn to him.

~ * ~

It had been so easy to find her. And he had watched them argue. It amused him. He stared at the house now, and in the darkness and the quiet with only the night breeze to hinder his thoughts, Sean Cassidy was satisfied.

Humor touched his lips once more. If she resisted, then to hell with gallantry. He was not a man to take no for an answer, and he decided she would not elude him for long. He wouldn't allow it.

He leaned back, cocking his head to one side before looking toward the house, confident, sure of his prey, for he did have her cornered. Alexandra could do nothing without him knowing about it.

Sean rubbed his chin and thought some more. An ice maiden, yes, but beneath the cold exterior he sensed heat and passion. He loved women and what they could do for him and to him. In fact he changed partners regularly with amazing ease rarely thinking of any one's needs but his own. He oozed charm when he wanted to impress a woman but his relationship with Alexandra had passed that stage.

Ah, but would she go with him willingly. Perhaps not, but either way, he decided, he'd have satisfaction.

Sean smiled with pleasure once again, thinking of returning to his century and the little cabin he had tucked away in the hills. He thought of hot running water and the conveniences he'd always enjoyed. Very soon now, Alexandra, very soon.

I'll wait until he leaves you alone, my sweet. Perhaps tomorrow or even the next day.

The moon slid behind a black cloud, darkness surrounded him.

It was midnight.

~ * ~

"I'm not going to just fall into his bed," Alex murmured. The vow, she knew, was an utterly useless waste of time. After the kiss they'd shared the day before, all he'd have to do is crook his little finger and she'd come running.

She was dusting his library, carefully examining the rows of books, pausing over his selection. An original of *The Voyage of HMS Beagle*, her finger traced the lettering, slightly in awe of the masterpiece. Alex jumped when his voice sounded soft and husky next to her ear.

"I think I'd like that."

"James. You've been listening." Her outrage died a sudden death when she noticed the soft smile curling slowly around his mouth.

"I'd like to see you tumble into my bed." He pulled out the book and handed it to her, an unspoken question glittering in his eye. "If you like, I'll get you a copy of Jules Verne's *From the Earth to the Moon*. I can order— other things, too. If that would change your mind," he told her softly, almost encouragingly.

She accepted the book, bending to the task she'd given herself in what seemed to be an attempt to ignore her blossoming pink cheeks.

"I'm not going to hurt you," he said very softly. "You're perfectly safe."

"Safe from who—and what?" she replied calmly while she turned her haphazard dusting to the table by the bookshelves.

Crossing the distance separating them in three swift strides, James pulled the feather duster away and said in a level voice, completely self-assured. "Sometimes I'm a patient man. You've got more time though," he said again, amused by her question. "I've planned a trip. I'm going hunting."

Her eyes opened wide at his cryptic words then she blinked, a frown suddenly creasing her forehead. "I've seen him, Sean Cassidy. He was staring at the house."

"You've what?"

"He's out there."

"Why didn't you tell me?" he asked, his voice fierce as if he had every intention of protecting a cherished possession.

"Until you told me you were leaving, I forgot. James, take me with you. Please."

"You're not going anywhere," he told her gently. "Stay in the house. I'll have one of my men sleep downstairs."

"But Sean..." she nervously clenched her fists.

"Forget, Cassidy."

"I can't stay here...without you." Her words brought to mind a terrible truth. A truth she was loathe to admit. Just the thought of Sean Cassidy made her skin crawl, made her long for the protection James offered.

"I'll be back," he told her. "Count on it. And you'll have to make the best of it. You'll be safe here."

The steel rod found its place again. "I can't stay." She swung towards him, her face suddenly pale. "I'm afraid of him. With or without you, I'm going to find the vortex and go home."

"I don't have a choice," he said frustrated with her stubborn streak. "If I take you with me, you'll only get in the way."

"Please."

"No."

She paused then quietly folded her hands in her lap and answered with a very meek, uncharacteristic, submissive, "Very well."

She peeked up at him from beneath her fringed lashes, but her eyes didn't give anything away.

He clenched his fingers into fists at his back as he strode swiftly to the window. The rolling hills of the Rogue Valley were green now from the long winter. Everything was fresh and clean. He turned swiftly back to Alex, started to speak, but she cut him off.

"What are you hunting?"

"It's none of your concern." James met her gaze for fraction of a second.

Her eyes widened in anger and disbelief. "Maybe it is. I—"

"A woman should know her abilities, her place in life," he interrupted her. "So should a man." His eyes twinkled in merriment but Alexandra was too furious to notice.

~ * ~

She continued in her own impetuous way, "I've been hunting before."

"Oh?"

"With my grandfather," she shot back stubbornly.

"Now the question is whether to believe you," he teased and he meant it good-naturedly. "But then I have no qualms about letting you have your little fantasy. Actually, your imagination is refreshing, reminds me of a cool spring breeze. It makes you all the more attractive."

"Don't patronize me."

He smiled and his voice was light, "I'm not. You think I should believe this balderdash. I can't, won't, and have no intention of allowing you to come. It's too dangerous."

"Only men allowed...chauvinist," she whispered.

"As you wish," he said smoothly fighting the fear he felt and hoping what she had said about Sean Cassidy was not true.

Angel mine, I don't trust you in those hills.

No longer completely indifferent to her stories of the future, James was bent on tearing them apart. Alexandra was different...too different, to be a product of this century. She knew too much, her thoughts too progressive and unique. No one could imagine all she'd written yet something inside caused him to argue, to find flaws. He desperately wanted to find a viable, logical reason for everything Alexandra had penned.

"I'm going."

"Think so?" he asked a touch of sardonic amusement tinged his voice, even while he contemplated ways to keep her here.

"You can't stop me."

"Oh?"

"You're right of course," she conceded, and it seemed she easily rephrased his words to her advantage. "It might prove dangerous for a man also."

"Do tell, but I'll only be gone a short time. You've been through enough. You won't enjoy sleeping on the ground and eating food cooked over a campfire, besides it's cold," he said softly and with the best intentions. He expected her to accept.

"I like roughing it and the weather's been unseasonably warm."

He turned on his heel, wondering what he could do or say that would convince her he was right. Several long seconds passed before he cleared his throat. Yet he stood so very still, his arms crossed against his chest, leisurely watching her, his face and expression intentionally guarded. And he continued in this manner for several more seconds before he spoke. "So you miss me already. I like that in my woman."

"I'm my own woman, James," she corrected him. But there was more than a hint of stubbornness in her tone and in her tilted mouth and arched brow. "You have no say in this. I'm going."

That didn't work, he thought with a grimace. One way or another Alexandra would stay. He wouldn't argue over the inevitable. She was his woman, even though he hadn't meant to say it so blatantly, and he intended to keep her safe, even from himself. The future was all that mattered now, but he was a man of his word and he intended to honor it. The only way he could was to separate himself from the woman who haunted his dreams and teased his waking hours. She couldn't go. He wouldn't be responsible for his actions if she did.

"As long as you live with me," he paused for a few tense moments, remembering a time long past, years when he'd had no control, days when the danger threatened and he'd lost, "you will do as I say."

"I'll move," was her terse reply.

"Whatever pleases you, but the only place you can afford is above the Eldorado," he said softly, the threat clear. "Is that what you want?"

"You know it isn't. We've been over this before. I prefer this house to other accommodations but what I don't understand is—"

"The way I think?" he asked, narrowing his eyes, concentrating on her answer, moving closer. "That makes two of us then. I don't understand you either."

"You could explain," she countered.

"You don't want to know." He turned then, prowled the room and didn't look at her, but his tone was solemn. Almost as if he couldn't help himself, he began, "Five years ago I was a surgeon for the union army. Fought for the north because my home was there. Night after bloody night, I watched men live and die at my hands.

"One night I went with the ambulance to collect the injured. When the men were separated, I discovered my brother-in-law, Jessie's father. I could only hold his hand and watch him die. That night I promised to look after his girls. We both knew he was never going to see them again.

"By the time I'd finished patching everyone else, he was buried in a mass grave. I wrote the letter home, but it was the hardest thing I'd ever done. His death wasn't my fault. I knew that, but before I could get leave to visit, my unit was trapped and I was captured."

Alex choked. "So, you went to prison."

"Two years. I escaped, though."

"You were lucky," she said so quietly he could barely hear. "I've read about the prisons."

"It wasn't all luck. I made it to my uncle's home in Virginia. I knew that land like the back of my hand. Played there every summer with my cousins and brothers and sisters. I hid in a cave behind a beautiful waterfall. I cried when in the morning light the pool beneath shimmered blood red. And later I discovered the horrible devastation the Union Army had left. They burned the house, left the foundation and scorched timbers, nothing else.

"A tragedy," she murmured softly. "My father died in a senseless war too." The silence seemed to go on forever as they watched each other. "I still don't understand what this has to do with protecting me," she whispered.

"Didn't think you'd see my logic. To make this as simple as possible, I protect the women in my life, those I care about."

She cast him a strange look. "You can't protect everyone. You should have learned it's impossible."

"Maybe I should have learned, but it's my duty and I'm honor bound."

"You don't have to think of me as your duty."

"Sarcasm doesn't become you."

"You convinced me. I've abandoned all plans of stealing a horse and riding beside you as an equal."

"You don't fool me. I read your journal...remember." She blanched but he didn't look at her or wait for a denial. "The trip is too dangerous and that's final."

Her mouth snapped shut then she smoothed the folds of her skirt. Her smile appeared innocently deceptive. "You're right of course. It was foolish of me."

He ignored the meek tone in her voice and continued on in the same even conciliatory way. "And don't expect me to believe you'd ride a horse. You're scared of them. You wouldn't make it to the gate before Matilda bucked you off, and she's the most docile mare in the stables." He walked to the window then turned around slowly. The steel rod was back and it made him smile. For some unexplainable reason, he liked this side of her, the stubborn passionate side.

"I know." She turned from him. "You should understand. I'd be so much safer with you."

He turned then inhaled deeply. It didn't sit right with him, this deception of his. Hunting...lord yes, he was going hunting. Hunting Cassidy. "That's not true, now if you'd give me your word. I don't like the idea of looking over my shoulder days on end. And I will. You know that don't' you?"

"I can't, you know...give my word." Her eyes closed and dark lashes fanned gently across her cheeks.

Crissakes, she looked innocent. "That's what I was afraid of. In that case, I'll secure your presence here in another way."

"It's not possible."

She faced him and waited as he came to stand beside her. The red of her hair shimmered in the early morning light. Spirited and proud, she sparked the protective nature inherent in his upbringing, inbred through generations. And she reminded him of the one moment in his life he'd rather forget. He hadn't fulfilled that promise, but he intended to make good on this one. He would keep her here in the protection of his home. He would keep her safe.

The issue of the moment seemed minor. He'd already guessed she had come to the mountain not by the usual means. His time away would give her precious moments of privacy. She needed that privacy, needed the time to come to grips with the facts she so vehemently denied. He couldn't understand why she refused to accept these facts even with the overwhelming evidence. All he wanted was the truth, not some fantasy she had imagined. He wanted to know who or what she was.

"You're right," she said with a glint of humor in her eye. "If you don't want to wake up tonight and find me beside your campfire, you will have to think of something."

"I already have. You surprise me though. Didn't expect you to admit it."

"It's not duplicity. Truth, only the truth and you have my solemn promise of that." She was smiling at him. Traces of humor laced her tone and sparkled in her eyes.

"After that speech, you know I'll have to take every precaution."

She ignored him again, turning her attention to the window and the hills that lay to the north. Gold Hill and the Oregon vortex. Her fists clenched suddenly and she whirled around to confront him. "You're going to Sardine Creek."

James blanched. Never, never in all his planning had he expected her to guess what he was about. Before he could move to the door and escape further questions, she intercepted him. "Tell me."

"Hang up the fiddle. You're not going."

"Wanna bet? You can't stop me. You don't have time." She tossed the words in his face.

"Ah, angel eyes, you're so very wrong."

"I'll do anything I have to."

He raised an eyebrow, watching the expression on her face turn from confidence to panic, and drawled in that slow sexy way of his, "Is that a fact?"

Her eyes went from clear cobalt blue to a dusky faded indigo and she backed away. "You wouldn't?" she gasped.

A slow even grin caressed his lips. She backed up one more step, watching, waiting. "I reckon I'd do most anything to keep you in one piece. Now, what did you have in mind?"

"Oh no you don't. You won't get any ideas from me."

"Then I'll have to use my own methods. Can't have you following me. I..."

He didn't finish. Alex swirled then bolted. Instantly, he captured her around the waist. In a few swift moves, he had her in his room, brandishing the key in one hand. "I'll leave a note where Kim can find it. You'll only have to be here an hour...or two...three at the most," he said just before he quietly closed the door and locked it.

~ * ~

The loud staccato of hoof beats reached the room and she laughed. Before he could disappear, she ran to the window. It stuck and she had to wrestle with it for the longest time. With muscles she didn't know she had and one last grunt thrown in for extra power, the window finally opened.

Alexandra leaned out. "Detestable man. Wretched, wretched man!" She shouted at the top of her voice, hoping he'd hear. "I'll have my revenge, James Lawrence. Have it when you least expect it. Perhaps tonight. If I have to, I'll shimmy down the trellis."

"Good luck, darlin', but there is no trellis." For a fragile half second James regretted his actions but the hell of it was, he couldn't think of anything else. She'd had the audacity to admit she'd follow, taunted him with the threat. He had no doubt she'd carry through with her promise, and he didn't want her anywhere near Sardine Creek.

Knew also that Jessie would help. Despite his orders, he knew Jessie would come to Alexandra's aide.

But he'd look forward to it, and thought of it as just another challenge. He could accept anything as long as his girls were safe.

But what if she'd been right about Sean Cassidy.

Damn, but he hoped she stayed put.

Chapter Seven

"Miss Alex?"

Alexandra whirled around, vacating her post at the window. "Jessie!" Her hand flew to her chest. "Oh, my," The last words said with one soft breath.

"Why did papa lock you in?" Jessie moved inside the bedroom, swinging the key from a long chain. "I heard you yelling out the window. When I came up through the kitchen, I found the key on the table."

"I don't know what to say. He thinks he's protecting me."

"Papa is like that."

Alexandra looked slightly askance at the little girl, "Can't fight city hall."

"What?"

"Never mind, sweetheart. But why?" She looked at Jessie, stunned yet extremely thankful for the needed help.

"I like you," Jessie told her without mincing words. The grin Jessie flashed Alex was missing an upper front tooth but endearing nonetheless. "I want you for my new mother." Alexandra hugged her close then kissed her forehead. "And you're pretty."

"Jessie, I like you, too, but I will never become your mother," Alex said. Tender concerns for Jessie warred with sheer logic and the irrefutable fact James would never marry her.

"Of course you will," Jessie said adamantly.

Miss Jessica's huge blue-violet eyes gazed into her own. "If your father finds out about this, I don't want to think of the consequences. He's going to be furious."

"Papa's funny."

"What in the world am I going to do with you?" she murmured affectionately and ruffled Jessie's long black hair. "Will you help me? I need supplies, just a few things really. Ask Kim. Meet me in the kitchen in five minutes. Now scoot."

Jessie's eyes twinkled and she rushed pell-mell out the door and down the steps. Alexandra watched dumbfounded for a few brief seconds before realizing the devil's little helper had just come to her aid.

After that it was no surprise to discover Jessie took care of everything. Clothes, a pair of denim pants and a shirt, lay neatly on the bed. Matilda stood saddled and ready in the barn. With Kim's help, Jessie assembled a sack lunch for her to eat on the way

"Will James punish you?"

"No," Jessie grinned impishly at Alex, "he'll get angry. He might make me stay in my room. He'll tell me again that I mustn't disobey." Jessie giggled. "He always forgives me."

Alex looked to the heavens and closed her eyes a moment. "Jessie, honey, I'm not going to be your mommy. James and I...well, it would never work. I don't belong here, and I do want to go home terribly," she said, but Jessie wouldn't give up. Nothing Alex could say would change her mind.

"You can do it, Miss Alex," Jessie said when they walked into the barn together. "Papa told me you were afraid of horses, but Matilda's easy to ride."

Alex looked at the old horse with a little trepidation. "I certainly hope so." She offered Matilda a sugar treat then petted the horse's nose, prolonging the inevitable. Hoping to stop her trembling hands she desperately gripped the bridle all-the-while telling herself she could do it. She could put aside twenty-three years of apprehension and ride Matilda.

She landed on her backside twice before she finally mounted, the old horse snorting her displeasure. Exactly ten minutes later, Alex smiled grimly at Jessie as she rode the old mare north, towards Sardine Creek and the vortex.

"Papa was wrong."

Alexandra distinctly heard the words. She laughed and it almost sounded hysterical. Matilda whinnied in response and began to canter. Even as she clung to the reins, the landscape raced past, bushes and spring flowers blurring into one color. Slowly, the road changed to grassy fields when she turned toward Gold Hill.

A few moments later, Alexandra shielded her eyes against the glare of the warm March sun. The weather had unexpectedly turned balmy three weeks ago. The rain had stopped and the earth gradually blossomed with the first signs of spring. Daffodils dotted the fields and wild irises poked out from the ground.

Her gaze stretched as far as the horizon, and she liked everything she saw, all the beauty surrounding her, the fresh clean air. A slight breeze ruffled her hair and golden beams of sunlight kissed her skin. In only a matter of days now, a light dusting of freckles would pop out across her nose and cheeks.

If her luck held, she'd find herself face to face with Captain James Lawrence before the end of this day. May the best person win. She smiled delightfully. At the moment she had the decided lead. Putting her index finger to her lips then swiping an imaginary one in the air, she whispered, "Chalk one up for old angel eyes, James."

Alexandra smiled with elation and the feelings that surged deep inside would have warmed the devil himself. Then with renewed determination and a stubbornness born from years of practice, Alex headed toward the foothills of the rugged Cascade Range. Oh how she wished she could see General Lee and James. With nothing in front of her and nothing behind her except blue sky and low rolling hills, only the wind whispered in the tall field grass. A jackrabbit suddenly darted across her path, and Matilda faltered a moment before picking up the pace once again. The unease and curious foreboding that seemed to surround and hover nearby frightened her. A sixth sense, an uncanny intuition, but surely no one was following her.

Everything looked normal, yet...

Alex urged the horse faster, recalling Sean Cassidy vividly and his vile touch.

Despite her fear of the horse and Sean Cassidy, she clung tenaciously to the reins and her stubbornness came in handy more than once as her backside threatened to slip from the saddle. Gritting her teeth, she held persistently to her pride and the horse. Hours later, with tired muscles plaguing her, she began to find a rhythm and felt a renewed burst of energy.

Yet she knew someone followed her.

A shadow, slight sounds that didn't belong...

"No," she murmured. "Dear God, don't let it be him."

She didn't fear the wilderness or camping, only the illogical and, she told herself, irrational feeling Sean Cassidy was close. She felt a moment's trepidation when faced with the coming darkness, then a sinking feeling she'd seen that craggy boulder at least one other time. When the sun began its descent behind the coast range, even when it almost disappeared and the rosy glow of a perfect sunset appeared, she kept on, determined to find James. She was even more determined to keep the man that followed from catching her. Surely, she moved faster than a lumbering packhorse. She should have met James by now. That couldn't be the same piece of granite she'd passed an hour ago!

But it was. Thoughts of James intruded, were pushed aside, suppressed, then ruthlessly stole back into her consciousness more vividly than before. With a long heart-felt sigh she realized she'd begun to care for him and she wished desperately he was here—with her.

And she had no idea...no clue...

A long, shrill, piercing scream shattered the night. Matilda reared and Alex clung desperately to Matilda's neck. Then she slipped from the saddle. In a jumble of waving arm and legs she landed, sprawled and bruised on the ground. Matilda whinnied and bolted past her.

Fighting her fear and the pain in her shoulder, she inhaled deeply, forcing herself to think logically. Her soft moan surprised her. Cautiously and very gingerly, she tested each muscle, each bone then looked skyward directly into the eyes of the cat.

~ * ~

James heard the scream and watched Matilda dash across his line of vision. His loud piercing whistle stopped the horse instantly.

The scream came from a cougar. He knew the sound all too well and was sure Alexandra needed rescuing again. As he circled around the boulder, a cat stared at him from a tree. Large yellow eyes threatened and waited for its prey to make a fatal mistake. Alex lay in front of him staring wide-eyed at the animal. Then to his amazement and relief, he watched Alexandra slowly sit up and push an errant lock of hair from her eyes. Now she sat on the ground, her hair swirling in disarray around her shoulders. A streak of dirt smudged her cheek, and she looked slightly embarrassed and very disheveled, but otherwise fine.

"Son of a bitch!" Fear for her then a blinding fury that she'd so easily disobeyed him, crept along his spine. His reaction was instant. "Headstrong little fool." He should have never left her on her own. Stubborn woman, she'd told him she'd follow and against all odds...here she was. He'd underestimated her. But it wasn't the first time and he suddenly felt sure it wouldn't be the last.

James nudged General Lee forward. The woods were canopied in a lush dark green, and here the dusky evening was darkened and cool, the temperature dropping swiftly as soon as the sun began its final descent.

James watched her and once more he felt an irreversible crawl of fear grip his heart and slowly radiate outward. It was something he'd never felt before. He understood fear because he had lived with it so long, but this was different. This had him circling around the rocks, watchful and so very careful, intent on one thing.

A twig snapped. The cougar watched threateningly from its vantage point in the trees. James trained his rifle on the cat and was ready to use it if the need arose.

He swore softly.

There was a cataclysmic silence.

He saw the cat tense his muscles, preparing to spring, its eyes riveted on Alexandra. The cat screamed again and crouched lower as it eyed its prey. James fired high. The shot, smashing through dense foliage above the animal, frightened it enough to stop the attack. Once again James aimed carefully, firing one more time, the bullet missing the animal by inches. The cougar vanished into the forest.

James inhaled deeply, his eyes brilliant with fear, gentle forgiveness demolished by intense anger sweeping through him. Three quick strides brought him to her side. His heart lodged in his throat at the sight of her, and he didn't breathe for several tense seconds. Anger still warred with terror, emotions he thought he'd long ago vanquished.

He had never expected to find her quite like this or feel the underlying sensations welling inside. He'd felt an ungodly terror that for a brief second had paralyzed him. His inadequacies paramount in his mind threatened to override his common sense.

Until he pulled her to her feet...until he felt the warmth of her body next to his.

Easily maneuvering her, he lifted her into his trembling arms as he would carry a child. Caught in mercurial emotions, he didn't hear her gasp of pain nor did he see the one brief moment of agony that swept across her features. With a stubborn and resolute determination to see her safe, he helped her on his horse and mounted behind her. They rode then, her horse following placidly behind them.

The camp lay straight ahead. Firelight flickered and danced through the spaces between the trees. Alexandra relaxed against him and her breathing slowed to normal. He thought she'd never felt so vulnerable or so very fragile.

James didn't stop until he came to a small clearing near the creek. The smell of simmering beans and hot coffee tantalized his senses, and the aroma lingered deliciously in the cool night. His stomach rumbled its appreciation, but after dismounting, he ignored it. James gingerly lifted Alexandra into his arms and carried her to a fallen log. He set her down gently then stepped back, distancing himself from her and battling the overwhelming fear and anger warring inside.

Unable to resist the silent yet beguiling call, her innocent, wide-eyed stare issued, he stepped forward again. His fingers rested on her waist and his face was so close he felt her breath. His voice was light, but challenging. "Stay put," he whispered then left to take care of the horses. In the oppressive silence that followed, Alexandra didn't budge or speak.

Beneath the layer of sweat and grime covering her, she looked madder than a hornet and paler and more vulnerable than she'd ever been before. When he approached, she might have trembled slightly, but she didn't back away. James hid the smile twitching at the corners of his mouth.

She looked as if she wanted to mount his horse and run. When his voice came sharp and demanding behind her, her breath escaped in a soft rush.

"Are you hurt anywhere?" Nothing but concern and a little fear registered in his voice.

"If I was, it would be too late now. Don't you know you're not supposed to move..." she got out before the pain in her shoulder stopped her. "My shoulder's bruised, but I don't think anything is broken," she finished weakly.

"Little fool," he muttered then straddled the log, resting a forearm on his thigh. Several long seconds past before he was ready to deal with Alexandra, his fears, his fury and the danger she'd placed herself in. She'd had no business riding into the rugged mountains alone, and she'd had no tangible reason to defy his orders.

"It doesn't hurt," she said quickly then fell silent. Beside her he clenched his jaw, squeezed his fists until the tension in his muscles forced him to stop.

"I didn't realize," he began in a soft deceptive voice. "Didn't think you'd really come after me."

"James?" Alexandra's eyes widened perceptibly then darkened with what he hoped was desire.

"Ah, darling," he whispered, pleased he'd managed to spark an emotion in Alex even if he didn't intend to capitalize on the passion he saw.

She didn't move but her eyes remained focused on his. "I was afraid to stay in the house without you," she said. Her beautiful blue eyes clashed with his volatile gaze.

He forced himself not to stare at her, forced his gaze away from the smooth ivory skin of her neck the fragile fullness of her lips. The urge to touch, to taste welled up inside of him, swept through him.

James grunted then stood abruptly. Two quick strides brought him to the fire and the coffee; at the same time distanced him from the subtle sweet innocence that was Alex and the compelling need he felt to have her in his arms—to possess her. He poured two cups of coffee then set them on a stump nearby. "You should have been more afraid of what could have happened to you out here."

"I only wanted to go home," Alex said, looking up at him her eyes wide, lashes spiked with unshed tears.

James stretched his legs out in front of him and wondered why he couldn't understand her. The minutes ticked by, and James had almost regained control of himself when Alexandra decided to speak again.

"The vortex is around here somewhere. It's my ticket home."

"You've placed yourself in a great deal of danger." His gut ached and a shiver swept through him. He was beginning to understand how deeply she believed in her story of travelling through time.

"It was necessary. I have to return to my life." She looked at her feet as if to hide her thoughts.

He wasn't about to let her hide anything from him—not now—not when he was beginning to care about her. He lifted her chin and their gazes met. The slope of her lips slightly downward, the longing in her eyes she tried to hide by lowering her lashes all evoked a wealth of dominate male emotions.

"Home?" he asked. He turned his head away for a moment, fighting the surge of frustration—and fear—that had possessed him. Perhaps she'd had a good reason, but she'd put her life in more danger by disobeying him. When he thought of what she encountered in the forest, what almost happened—he felt physically and emotionally sick. It was a double miracle that neither horse nor rider had fallen prey to the cougar.

"I can take care of myself."

"I should have chained you to the wall and kept the key with me."

"I'll have my freedom, you know," Alex continued as if no one had interrupted. "You can't..."

"That was a cougar out there, Miss McMurdie. You didn't have the ability to fight it," he cut in dryly. All feelings of amusement or relief vanished and his fingers twitched with a repressed urge to love her so hard and so thoroughly she wouldn't have the energy to do anything so stupid again.

She lifted a hand in the air. "I had my rifle."

"Went with your horse, which I might add has more sense than you."

Her chin rose and he was sure he heard a little snort of disagreement before she looked away.

"Alexandra."

"I thought I'd catch up with you before dark," she told him as if she finally realized what almost happened. Her beautiful eyes grew wide and wary.

"You did pass me, and you managed to make two complete circles of the same territory before the cat stopped you."

"You frightened me. You had no right," she gasped, astonished at his confession. "It was you all along."

"Since you came into the forest," he told her. "I should have taken you back then."

Her eyes grew even wider and more frightened, "The forest. But then..."

"What?"

"I thought...I felt," she threw a rock into the fire then another, threw a pinecone and watched it sizzle. She turned to face him, and her hands were clenched tightly in front of her. "I thought that someone followed me from the house." Her voice trembled.

"There was no one else," he told her then caught her hands and held them a moment. His thumbs grazed her wrists and he felt the terrified beat of her pulse. "Who did you think? Cassidy?"

Alexandra watched the fire, the brilliant orange and yellow flames, shivering convulsively, unable to stop. It crackled and hissed, but the night devoured the heat and the little clearing was cold as ice. "I wasn't lost," she said quietly, staring blankly into the blackness, into the forest. "I kept the sun behind me."

"That is likely why you ran into trouble," he said with disgust, his anger rising again. "So how did you determine where it was when you entered the forest?"

"I guessed," she said lamely. "How long?"

"Hours. I was with you for a while, hoping like hell you'd get your wits about you and go home." But that thought sent his nerves spiraling. She'd thought someone had been following her since she left the house.

He watched as the tension in her muscles increased and each little panting breath rasped slowly in-and-out.

"I don't believe it." Instantly her soft blue eyes smoldered and she snatched her hands away from his. Her small fragile fingers molded into fists. Slowly, her nails dug into flesh, and her shoulders trembled uncontrollably. "You had no right to scare me."

"How did you get out of the room?" He continued, reminding himself not to be taken in by the intense emotions she made him feel. "And I had every right. I wanted you to learn a much needed lesson. Now, Miss McMurdie, how?" He saw her hesitation then the sudden frown. Instantly, her lashes lowered as if she meant to hide something from him once again.

"Didn't..." Her voice so quiet he had to strain to hear.

James guessed the truth immediately. "Jessie," he whispered softly. "She won't come out of her room for a week."

"She was only trying to help." For a half-second she lowered her lashes but then she straightened. Her gaze focused on him. "She appeared in the room seconds after you left, brandishing the key and grinning mischievously. It was all her idea. And did you expect me to turn her away when she meant to free me?" A rosy blush slid up her neck to settle on her cheeks. "I'm not a fool, whatever else you may think of me."

"Jessie must have had her ear plastered to the door or she wouldn't have thought of it," James pointed out.

"She thinks of things all on her own. That child doesn't need help dreaming up trouble. She had all my supplies and clothes ready, just as though she'd planned this for a week, but we know that was impossible, don't we? Once she makes up her mind, no one can stop her."

James mulled that over while he watched her turn slightly away from him. He watched her loosen the top two buttons on her shirt, couldn't take his eyes from her as she slowly exposed soft white skin and the suggestive swell of her breast. Damn provocative gesture. The innocence on her face stopped him short, and he had the craziest notion she didn't think anything of the expanse of skin showing above the last button. Didn't she know it tore him up inside and was all he could do to keep his hands from exploring what she revealed? Crissakes, she tempted him. An angel who could beguile the devil himself. He braced himself against the driving urge firing his blood and the tempest that seemed to rage within. With every breath in his body and every beat of his heart, he wanted to touch her, needed to, and he was sure she felt it too.

He finally tore his gaze away and tended the food he'd reheated. Alexandra flinched as she reached for the cup James had offered earlier. Her fingers trembled and she lost control of the handle. Coffee spilled to the ground, mixing with the leaves and pine needles that carpeted the floor.

"I thought you weren't hurt." His voice was husky as he picked up the cup then dusted the needles from it. Without asking, he poured her more coffee.

"Neither did I, but the muscle's cold and it's starting to tighten."

It surprised him she'd admit such a thing. She acted so matter-of-fact and sounded so knowledgeable. He poured another cup of coffee and handed it to her. Because his silence seemed to overwhelm her, he let it continue, enjoying the upper hand he held momentarily. He watched her as she sipped her coffee, and he hoped he'd brought some stability to the volatile situation. When he finished thinking, he picked up his drink and sat down a few feet away. He was confused and even a bit amused at her reticence. James thought about the journal and the words she'd penned, recalling the flowing description of inventions he'd never heard of and the philosophies and attitudes so beyond this time.

"When are you going to throttle me?" she interrupted his thoughts, a saucy smile curving her lips enchantingly. "I'd rather you did it now and get it over with."

The wind chose that moment to howl through the trees overhead and a drop of moisture hit a rock near the fire. It sizzled and hissed on the hot spot, mimicking his frayed emotions. Their gazes met across the dancing flames, and he saw the concentration etched on her forehead, noticed the concern in her eyes, and he suddenly wanted to test her.

James hesitated then smiled wryly.

"After I have very thoroughly bedded you." He spoke slowly, the teasing note clear in his tone enjoying the curious look she graced him with. Yet he meant every word.

If she'd only let me, I'd bury myself within her, deep inside.

"In your dreams," she teased then suddenly stopped.

"I've been thinking about your journal. Been thinking about you." He strode the distance between them and sat down next to her, thigh against thigh. After a brief hesitation, he touched her chin and turned her face so he could look into her eyes. They were so close her breath whispered soft and gentle across his lips and she didn't try to pull away. When the pressure of his fingers vanished, she opened her eyes.

James rose, slowly walking to the fire. After he watched the flames for several seconds, he turned back to Alexandra.

She rubbed the goose bumps on her arms, but when her fingers touched her shoulder, she cried out. He heard and was instantly beside her. "I'll take a look," he said genuinely concerned.

She flushed slightly when she realized what he intended.

"No," her voice quavered. Her body swayed until she braced herself with one arm. "Don't, please."

"You don't hear very well." James bent to one knee in front of her. With practiced skill, he undid her shirt. Before she had time to raise her hand in protest, he'd eased the shoulder and one sleeve down her arm to reveal an ugly swelling bruise. An unrestrained ferocity swept through him at the sight, his body tightening into knots.

"I suppose I don't."

She shook from the cold or perhaps his fingers against her skin. Whatever it was, she didn't stop shaking and her teeth began a painful staccato as well.

James stood, his face a stoic mask. He untied the bandanna around his neck and moved swiftly to the cold mountain stream that meandered through the clearing. With calculated determination, he tried to ward off the painful visions suffocating his thoughts and the horrible bloody scenes that instantly flashed into his memory when he'd looked at the ugly bruise. He broke out in a cold sweat. For a second, he wasn't sure he could help her.

The frigid water he splashed on his face doused the tremors surging through him but not the anguish or the debilitating memories. By the time he returned, he'd soaked the bandana and his shirt, "This will feel like ice," he warned her as he placed the bandanna on the bruise and secured it with bandages from his saddlebags. "First thing tomorrow morning you're going home."

"Impossible," she shook her head emphatically. "I could get lost again. You wouldn't know. Just think how that would make you feel," she said, using his fears against him.

He stared at her for a long time, mulling everything over in his mind, debating every possible scenario. Finally, exasperated past his own endurance, he spoke softly. "To hell with returning then. Have it your way. We'll find the damn vortex and you'll be home faster than greased lightning." His voice was ragged with desire and uncontrollable fear spinning heatedly within.

"I wouldn't have it any other way," Alex whispered, but he didn't miss the slight tremor in her voice or the moisture in her eyes.

James swore softly. "What the devil does the twenty first century have that we don't?"

She kept her mouth closed and shot him a politely condescending look. His fists clenched.

"Tell me. I have to know why."

"A million things. A thousand comforts," and she breathed deeply. "Air conditioning in the summer and central heating in the winter. Fast cars and and even faster women," she grinned, quickly brushing the tear from her cheek then winked at him. "But don't think for one moment I'll share your bed. I'm not one of the fast ones."

He snorted then mumbled something under his breath. "Fine, but do you really believe this vortex can take you back? If you recall...you don't know where it is."

"I have an educated guess."

James ran his fingers through his hair, looking at Alexandra thoughtfully. What the devil happens now? Then without a moment's hesitation he was laying out the blankets and settling in for the night. He pulled out a huge fur and draped it over the blankets.

"What are you doing?"

"Exactly what it looks like. Join me?" he drawled. A slow lazy smiled curved his lips, a seductive smile, he hoped. His eyebrows rose suggestively.

There was a strange cast to her blue eyes and he watched them slowly darken. She didn't move or say anything for a very long time. Alex rose from the log where she was sitting and walked toward the fire. About halfway there she turned. Her hands were clasped in front of her, and she smiled tentatively. At that moment, he thought he'd never seen anything quite so beautiful. Firelight cast a reddish orange glow behind her, highlighting her hair and the soft curves of her figure. Somewhere in the forest a bird called to its mate, breaking the silence.

"In a while," she murmured then lowered her lashes.

"Uh, uh," James shook his head. "Come here. Now."

Alexandra had been looking at her hands, but now she looked at James. "Couldn't we meet halfway?"

"I don't see why. The ground's cold...the blankets are warm...can't we sit and talk awhile?"

"Is that what you want to do, talk?"

"No and yes. Come here. I promise I won't do anything you don't want me to do." James smoothed the fur then pulled it back. His gaze shifted to meet hers again and the expression on her face surprised him.

"That's what I'm afraid of," she said softly, so softly he had to lean forward to make out the words.

"What are you afraid of?"

"I...myself..."

He hoped he understood. Lord, but if she meant what he was thinking.

"I won't touch you if you don't want me to. Besides, I'm a curious man and right now I want to talk. After all, a man wants to know everything he can about his woman."

"What if...what if I want..."

"Come on," he said softly. "Sit down and tell me about the fast cars and even faster women." He paused. "What the hell is a car? Tell me that where you come from children no longer die from small pox. Tell me that men no longer die from the infection caused by surgery."

"All that? I don't think we have enough time."

He thought he heard her laugh nervously but wasn't all that sure. Then the fire shot a piece of burning charcoal in the air. The brand glowed for a brief moment in the increasing darkness before it fell silently to the ground.

Alexandra watched the sparks then as if she'd just made up her mind, she came to him. He made room for her and resting his arm on the old log, he created a snug little space for her.

"Are you humoring me, or do you believe?"

"Both," he said honestly. "I'm not sure of anything anymore. Convince me."

"Okay, I'll tell you about the fast cars but not the faster women." She stepped forward then kneeled on the fur. "But wouldn't you rather hear about EKG's and CAT scans, or perhaps...no, I don't suppose you'd want to hear about laser surgery. Actually, I don't know very much about those things either except they exist and save lives." Alexandra sat back on her legs. With the dark backdrop and the firelight playing on her face, she made a charming picture. James moved to make more room for her. "And...children don't die of small pox. It no longer exists. Because of a wonderful vaccine and incredible determination on the part of the medical community, the disease was wiped out years ago." She hesitated, her eyes suddenly looked sad and wistful.

"It's cold." James patted the empty spot beside him. Alexandra looked up. His gaze followed hers. The stars were so bright out here it felt as if he could reach out and touch them. When their eyes met again, she nodded and sat by James.

With a characteristic possessiveness and concern, he cradled her injured shoulder. For several minutes, he savored the knowledge that she'd come to him, savored the feel of her body next to his. Incredible, everything was simply incredible. When he started out this morning, he had no idea anything like this would happen. "Start with this miracle vaccine. I want to know everything."

Several hours later James felt as if he had been the one to step into a new world. No wonder she wanted to go back. How on earth could anyone choose to live with the hardships of this time? He pulled her closer. Crissakes, he must believe her.

"Umm..." Alexandra snuggled into him. Her head rested on his shoulder, and he held her hand in his. Umm, he thought, my sentiments exactly.

"Alex...Alexandra..." James lifted her chin slightly so he could see her face. Her eyes were closed. She was sound asleep.

In a very cherishing gesture, James brushed her hair aside and kissed her softly on the forehead. Without waking her, he pulled the covers over them and lay down to sleep.

Sometime in the middle of the night he woke to the steady drip of rain and he curled his arm around her waist protectively. The pleasure of the moment and the heat of her body next to his lent a feeling of permanence and belonging he'd never known before.

Security he'd always disdained and pretended he didn't want.

He held that thought for a fleeting moment.

This strange beguiling woman from another time gave him warmth and created new and tender feeling deep inside, but she threatened everything he'd planned.

She held him in the palm of her hand.

He was hers for the asking.

But she didn't belong here, and she vowed she would never belong to him.

So he would have to convince her.

What then?

He felt as if she'd turned his well-ordered world upside down.

Chapter Eight

It was the crow screeching next to his ear that woke him. No, perhaps it was the cold fingertips just beneath the waistband of his pants that woke him. But the reason no longer mattered because those same small fingers had slowly moved an inch lower. He groaned and sucked in his stomach muscles. The move was a reflexive action, but he almost regretted it. Her fingers slipped lower. If she didn't wake up soon and realize what she was doing, he wouldn't be responsible.

Crissakes, on the other hand, he didn't want her to stop. Yes, he did. When he made love to Alexandra, it was going to be on his bed with soft pillows and quilts surrounding them. And she was going to know exactly what she was doing.

"Umm..." Alexandra snuggled closer. Her hand moved so close, very close. Instantly, he was rigid all over. Every part of him tensed in desire with an inexplicable need. He was proud of himself because he was doing everything possible to hold himself in check, and it wasn't a simple task.

It seemed a blissful eternity, but there was no question in his mind when Alex woke. A small gasp penetrated the cold morning air. Her body went dead still—then—she yanked her hand away. He felt an aching regret, but he didn't say anything. Before too many seconds passed, she pushed away from his chest.

"Good morning. Did you sleep well?" James smiled at her.

Alexandra looked down at him with sleep-clouded eyes, bedroom eyes, he thought. Her mouth was slightly open, seductive and pouting. Her cheeks were a soft pink, flushed almost the color of a sunrise. After blinking a few times, she brushed her long hair from her eyes. He watched, completely enthralled by the vision she made.

"James?"

"Yes." He knew his grin was smug but he couldn't help himself. Despite the discomfort he felt right now, he'd loved the feel of her fingertips so close to him.

"What happened last night? I..."

"Don't you remember?" He kept grinning and suddenly felt like a little boy, teasing his favorite girl. "I ravished you and you loved every minute." His eyebrows rose suggestively.

She pushed farther away, and the cold air swirled in the empty space between them. His smile must have been infectious because she suddenly grinned too. "For some odd reason, I think I'd remember if you—ravished me. The last I recall about last night is having your arms wrapped around me and watching the stars."

"I'm disappointed." James stopped grinning and tried to look remorseful.

"You scoundrel. You know very well nothing happened."

"I do?"

"James!"

Before she could say one more word, he swept her beneath him. The feel of her soft curves and warm body beneath his was heaven.

"James, stop it. You can't possibly think to..." Her voice slowly faded to a whisper. When their gazes met, it seemed to James as if the world stood still. All humor vanished, replaced with potent desire and a burning need he understood all to well.

"The devil, Alexandra...what you do to me." His control was thinly balanced, and he could feel her body softening against his. Her scent confirmed the rising sun and whispered of dawn. Unexpectedly, she slid her hands up his chest, and he heard his ragged gasp of desire. Her eyes were clouded, yet they had a curious power over him. James was entranced by them, paralyzed for a second in time.

Just as all rational thought dissipated, the sound of the old crow that woke him had him swearing and moving away from Alexandra. Now he lay on his back. His arm rested across his eyes. Despite his chagrin, he was accountable for what happened. He rose quickly. She was sitting cross-legged on the furs, her hands resting in her lap.

Alexandra looked stunned, almost embarrassed by what happened. Yet she was smiling. As he watched, she reached out her hand. It wavered a second before she quickly brought it back to her lap.

"James, I..."

"I'm sorry. I know I promised. This won't happen again." His words were curt and he groaned inwardly when he saw the pain in her eyes.

"You're right, I suppose." She turned away from him, straightening her shirt and tucking the ends into her pants as if nothing had happened.

He felt he'd invaded a private sanctuary. For a second, all movement stopped. The calls of the animals receded into an eerie stillness, and even the shrill cry of the jay ceased.

~ * ~

"Here we are." James shifted in his saddle so he could see Alex. The warm sun beat down on a rutted out trail.

Alexandra squinched her eyebrows together, searching. "Here?" she asked. "I don't understand."

James pointed to the ground. "That's where I found you. Do you remember anything?"

"No."

"You told me you could find the vortex."

Alex pursed her lips, looking thoughtful. "You should have asked sooner. The vortex is by Sardine Creek. All we had to do was follow the water. Sooner or later we would have stumbled on it. Although I'm not sure what will be there."

"We've traveled at least three miles from where we camped."

"I followed that path," she said softly.

James looked into the forest for several minutes before he finished. "The horses need to rest, and I'm hungry."

"Are you angry?"

"What makes you ask that?"

She shielded her eyes from the sun and looked north then turned back to James. "I think it's the scowl on your face. Or maybe it's because you haven't said a word to me since this morning. You don't want to take me to the vortex, do you?"

"No." James dismounted and led General Lee to a grassy spot. A tiny creek pooled nearby. He picked up a rock and threw it in then watched the ripples spread wider and wider until they finally blended with the rest of the still water. "If anything you said is true—and not a product of your imagination—the vortex is too dangerous."

A bold squirrel scurried across an old log, scolding the intruders. Alex smiled at the animal's antics before it, too, dashed off to find safety amidst the fir trees.

"Shouldn't you be gathering nuts, little fellow," she said as she watched him go. When he reached a limb high above the ground, he turned and gave a last parting word.

Alex returned her gaze to the little pool and James. She stood in the same spot for a long time, staring at the water.

"If you weren't looking for the vortex, what were you looking for?" Alexandra had dismounted and now she stood an arm's length away from him. Both of them watching the currents swirl around a large boulder. Both of them letting the silence continue unchecked.

"Sean Cassidy." He threw another rock and it skipped across the smooth surface. "I want to find him before he hurts you."

"Sean?"

Crissakes, he hated the way her voice sounded, hated the tremulous fear and he was struck with the need to banish that fear. Suddenly, he couldn't stay away from her, he stepped forward and his arms encircled her. She leaned against him. His body supported hers. He tempered his voice and he spoke quietly.

"You made finding Sean impossible, angel eyes. With you along I won't risk it. All things considered, I'd rather take you to Sardine Creek and the Forbidden Ground, and I think you know how I feel about that." James rested his chin on top her head and breathed in the delicate lavender scent.

He felt the fine silken texture of her hair. Her softness lay against his chest, and he pulled her closer as if the strength of his embrace could protect her from the demons surrounding her.

He didn't miss the sudden relaxing of her muscles either.

He teased her now, charmed her. Seduction wasn't paramount on his mind, only her happiness, and when the time to make love was right, they'd both know. He prided himself on his patience, so now he'd test it.

"I'm not sure I do know how you feel. I..."

"I think your search is dangerous," he interrupted. "I think it's foolish to risk your life on something unexplainable," he reminded her. And," he continued as he turned her around, "you insisted on this trip."

When they stared at each other for so long, he felt as if he became a part of her. She pulled him into her soul, inviting him to understand her thoughts and feelings.

And he wanted to understand everything about her.

He rested his hands on her shoulders, slowly allowing his fingers to stray down her arm then back up, trying not to startle her.

Her eyes were huge and the stubborn pride shining within them left him with little doubt he would have to take her back to the creek. He would have to convince her he'd tried to locate this strange place. A difficult task—a very difficult task because he didn't want to find the vortex.

"Is it so hard to understand?" she asked with the slightest quiver to her voice. He let his fingers tighten around her shoulders then a moment later relaxed them.

"No, that's where you're wrong. I do understand," he said softly, trying to soothe her. "The longer you wait..." his words softened as he felt the slight tremor beneath his fingers. Lord, he thought, the longer she waited the harder it was going to be for him. As it was now he didn't think he could let her go.

Longing filled his soul even as he looked at her. Reverently, he stroked her cheek. Then he played with the tight bun she had secured at the base of her neck, hoping he could loosen a few strands. She tried to move away from him. Instantly, he dropped his arms.

"I...I...James...you can't want me. I'm not afraid, but you think I'm..."

"An adventuress?" he added softly, his voice husky.

He reached out and caressed the soft strands of hair that had slipped loose, twining them around a finger then letting them fall. They curled against her coat. He thought of the past and the future, thinking of Alexandra, her strength and her beauty.

She surprised him at every turn.

And at that moment James rather believed she could have taken care of herself. Despite everything he knew her to be, despite Sean Cassidy, despite the fears he had for her safety, when he looked at her he saw spirit and bravery. She possessed a quiet undaunted courage.

She nodded. "Yes, but I'm not...you know. At least not the way you think of it."

His laughter was swift and light, as if all the days of anger, fear, and frustration no longer mattered. His face came closer to hers, and he held her chin gently within his grasp.

"I would never hurt you," he said, softly repeating a vow he'd made to her earlier, a vow he was determined to keep. "You're safe with me."

She walked away from him, and he wondered what she was thinking. Despite the coldness of the little mountain pond, Alexandra undid her shoes, dipping her feet into water. Mischievously, a smile slowly spread across her face and her eyes twinkled.

What the devil, James thought just before a cold spray of icy water hit him in the face. He blinked the moisture from his eyes. Another cold blast hit him, and he heard her laughing.

"Alexandra?"

"The water is wonderful." She skipped up the creek, deftly landing on rocks.

She reminded him of a water nymph or perhaps a wood sprite. Before he had time to respond, Alex had almost slipped from view, her laughter floating through the forest.

"Son of a bitch!" he whispered fiercely. "What's she up to?" Before he had time to think and despite his confusion, he started after her. She surprised him, darting out from behind a tree. In a second, she'd stuffed a handful of grass down his back and fled once more. And once again her laughter spilled through the spring air.

James couldn't resist the siren's lure. He ran after her, slipping around the trees, always keeping her in sight. After several minutes of diligent hunting, he caught up to her. They circled a large tree, neither gaining an advantage. Finally, James feinted to the left then turned right. Alex must have fallen for the ploy because she ended up in his arms, laughing.

"You caught me." Her laugh sounded almost breathless. "It took you long enough."

"You're beautiful, Alexandra. You know that?"

Her large blue eyes gazed into his and his breath caught in his throat. He couldn't take his eyes from hers. She moistened her lips. Her hands rose and she flattened her palms against his chest. He felt his heart thunder against her fingertips.

"I want you," he said. "I've wanted you since the first moment I saw you. Tell me you want me."

"Yes." The word came out breathlessly, like the whisper of the wind.

"Do you know how much more I want you now than I did this morning? But not here. I want it to be special...perfect." His mouth brushed lightly across hers before she could answer.

"James," A single tear slipped down her cheek and more moisture formed in her soft indigo eyes. "Would you believe me if I told you I've never—"

"No," he cut her off gently before she could finish. "Don't lie," his frustration mounting at her obstinacy and the confusion she had created in his mind. "Don't try to pretend. You're not innocent. Your speech, the clothes you had on when I found you, everything about you denies that fact. But it doesn't matter—not to me—not anymore."

The warm moisture from her breath was clearly visible in the cold air. It hovered an instant then disappeared. "You're right. I'm not really innocent. I know too much, more than I should, I suppose. But that doesn't mean..."

"Alex," he said softly, his voice husky with desire. "I don't care about the past."

When she looked at him, her eyes held moisture and unshed tears. "That's not the point either." She wiped at the tear slipping along her chin.

"Then what is the point?" He wanted to understand, truly he did. Yet everything she told him went beyond his experience.

"You don't trust me," she whispered, struggling within his embrace.

"Ah...trust. It's not a matter of trust. The stories you've told me go beyond the believable. They defy all the scientific laws discovered by man." He freed one hand, resting it at the small of her back and slowly pulled her closer. His fingers continued lower, exploring, tempting. She moaned softly but did not protest. He smiled contentedly before dropping his arms, remembering his vows.

He released her but the promise still lingered.

Only a breath separated them.

Her body trembled with desire, and he understood.

"After you read the manuscript, I thought..."

"What is it you want me to believe? I have so many questions."

Surely she could tell him about Sean and the part he played in her life. James shut the images of Cassidy from his mind then laughed softly at her reply. "Little minx, you know I can't believe everything." He looked at her with a mixture of doubt and amusement.

She assumed the angelic look he cherished. With strands of hair finding their way from the confining bun now curling wildly around her face, she appeared to him as an avenging angel. A red headed avenging angel. He chuckled at the imagery.

"I want to go home."

"You are home," James was confident. Sure that eventually she'd understand how life-threatening travelling through some vortex to another time could be.

His hands rose to her face. He brushed her lips with his thumb; he closed his eyes thoughtfully before he looked at her again.

"Perhaps we should start over," James said.

Helpless to let her go, James caught her shoulders and pulled her against his chest. "Alexandra," he whispered against her hair. "I'm going to kiss you."

She seemed to agree as his mouth traveled within inches of her. His hands roamed her back and gently brought her closer. He could feel the rapid beat of her heart against his chest even through all the layers of clothing they wore. Then he heard her gentle sigh as he pulled her closer still, and it pleased him more than he'd ever imagined.

She drew a shuddering breath then softened in his embrace.

He brushed her lips with his, then the tip of her nose. Before he had time to restrain himself he had closed each of her eyes with a soft caress. His mouth lingered close to her ear. But she pushed away as if unsure of herself.

"No, don't shy away," he whispered. "Hold still."

She looked down, concealing her face and emotions from his gaze. Her fists came up to his chest and rested there.

"You're beautiful, Alex. I'll not let you go. Ever. So forget Sean. Forget Sardine Creek and the vortex. They don't exist for you any longer. And at the moment, I don't care why you're here, just that you are."

He paused, for breath or to think, he wasn't all that sure.

He watched as Alex slowly began to respond. "Perhaps you were sent to me, perhaps you were meant to be my guardian angel," he whispered. Anticipating her reaction, he knew she wanted him when her tongue came out to moisten her lips.

She looked up and their eyes met.

He leaned forward and kissed her mouth, very softly. He continued kissing her until he felt a response, felt her heart beat out of control. Then he lifted his mouth from hers.

"You realize how much I will treasure this moment. Your taste, your scent, it's nothing I've ever known before," he murmured.

"I don't think..." she started, sounding as if she was about to deny him again. Yet, even as his lips closed over hers, her body molded with his. She was soft and pliant. And she was his.

James resumed control and checked his pounding heart. He felt desire and need beat in his veins. He told himself this was all he ever wanted, convinced himself to let her go, and he tried, but her hands were sliding into his hair, her mouth was yielding, softening to his intimate kiss.

And even now he felt her gentle surrender.

He cursed the situation.

His breath drawing raggedly, James gazed into those passionate eyes while his hand plunged into her hair, holding her head captive as he abruptly lowered his head again. His mouth opened over hers with uncontrollable demand, slanting hungrily. He felt Alexandra's body respond to the undeniable sensuality of it; her arms stole around his neck, and she pressed closer, kissing him back. With unrelenting pressure, he parted her lips, his tongue probing—exploring. Alexandra returned everything; she drew his tongue into her mouth, her fingers sliding across his shoulders and down his back in an innocent caress. Desire surged through James unchecked, and he pressed his hand against her back, forcing her into blatant contact with his hard arousal. His hands slid carelessly over her then tightened when she melded her body tighter to his, seemingly unaware of the audacious evidence of his lust thrusting aggressively against her.

Instinctively, his hands moved toward her breasts then he remembered, and he tore his mouth from hers, staring blindly over her head as he debated with himself.

"James..." she whispered. And she sounded puzzled and slightly breathless. Swollen lips, huge dilated sapphire eyes, flashed at him. She raised her trembling hand to her mouth.

"Let's walk," he said huskily.

The air was warm and the trail was narrow and winding. James talked to her as they walked slowly along the creek bank. Told her tales of his boyish pranks and hours spent in the wild forests where he grew up. They laughed together as if they were bent on ignoring the desire simmering between them. Several hours later, they stopped in a secluded outcropping of rocks. Large fir trees towered behind and over the boulders. James shoved his hands into his pockets. Uncertain of his mood, he leaned against the rocks and watched Alexandra.

Then without speaking a single word, he placed his hands on her shoulders and pulled her against his chest.

He looked down at Alexandra and saw her laughing at him, her twinkling blue eyes soft and surprisingly innocent.

"Don't worry," he said succinctly, taking her arm and starting to walk back to the horses. "I'd never let anything bad happen to you. Not like someone else we both know. Tell me everything about that night I found you half frozen in the mud, your clothes in tatters then I'll help you deal with it...with Sean."

She said nothing, merely closed her eyes, but when she opened them again, he enfolded her in his arms.

"Was our meeting the coincidence you pretend?" he asked suddenly. Did you plan it?" He waited, but she didn't reply. "I don't believe you traveled through time to end up here," he added.

She laughed, a hard brittle laugh. "You don't understand a thing. I didn't plan to travel through time."

"Can you explain why Cassidy was here three months before I found you?" The tone was full of concern, even his eyes showed interest.

A cold breeze swirled around him, and the sun disappeared behind a great black cloud. It was an omen perhaps but he tried to ignore it.

"Alex, talk to me. I need to know."

She crossed her arms over her chest and turned her head away. "I don't know why. I don't know anything."

"That's what's so frustrating for me."

"Ditto."

"What?" He ignored her remark. "Tell me everything that happened that night."

"I did once already," she told him honestly.

"Try again, maybe you'll remember some detail. Try closing your eyes and thinking back to the day in questions. Tell me about Sean Cassidy. Everything." She stared at him then nodded in understanding.

"If it means that much." She moved away and looked for a place where they could both sit.

James didn't wait for her to find a place on her own. He pulled her along until he found a cozy little nook sheltered from the elements.

He watched her, a tepid smile crossed his lips, and he knew he wouldn't like what she was about to tell him, but there was nothing left for him to do except listen patiently.

"I've known Sean ever since I can remember," she continued speaking without pause, seeming to gain strength with each word. "We grew up together. We were neighbors. By the time we reached high school though, we were very different. He was an athlete, every girl's dream date, and I was a bookworm," she finished, her voice slightly defiant.

James didn't move, other than to let his hands drop away. "But you were with him that night. Why?"

"Because he badgered me for a date. It went on for weeks, and finally my mother begged me to go with him. I figured one date couldn't hurt. I was wrong, of course." She paused, her face growing paler the longer she spoke.'" By the time she finished, it was a deathly shade of white. "Mother will think I'm dead."

"You don't have to finish."

"You're wrong. I do have to finish. You deserve to know. Besides people are supposed to talk about things that bother them."

"What makes you say that?"

"Freud, I suppose...or maybe it was someone else."

"Freud?"

"Yeah, anyway...we went out for pizza. Not much of a date but there you have it. It was more than I wanted to do, so I didn't care."

"Pizza?"

"You're full of one liners aren't you?"

He looked at her but he didn't say anything.

"Pizza—I'll make you one sometime—don't suppose you have any pepperoni? No, well..."

"Thought you couldn't cook?"

"Oh, I can't, but I'm sure I can explain the process to Kim."

"I'm sure you can, but you've gotten off the subject."

"I have, haven't I? When we finished eating, I expected him to take me home. He didn't. Instead he headed north out of Medford. I protested, but there wasn't much I could do when we were going sixty-five miles an hour on the freeway."

"You can explain later," he told her dryly.

Alexandra grinned. "My pleasure. Before I knew it, he'd turned off at Gold Hill and was heading into the hills. When he stopped the car, I expected him to turn around, but he didn't. It was then he explained his plans. The fool had the audacity to tell me he was going to make it so we had to get married. Of all the archaic attitudes."

With those words, a frigid wave of cold enveloped him. He didn't believe what she'd just implied. Archaic attitude? Of course it wasn't, but then, maybe it was.

And he let those thoughts linger in his mind.

"Sean thought it would be easy to get me pregnant. He figured I'd throw myself at him just like every other girl on campus. When I refused him, he hit me. Not very hard, but I realized then that I had to get away." Alex kept on talking, baring her soul to James. By the time she'd finished, the sun was past its zenith.

"He hit you? I'll kill the bastard."

She grimaced. "I got my revenge."

He wasn't going to ask how. He had a good idea. They had to go home tomorrow because he hadn't planned on two people when he'd packed. In another day, his supplies would dwindle.

He had accomplished nothing on this trip. Sean was still out there waiting for her. Until he could find him, Alexandra's life was in danger.

Chapter Nine

How many angels are there? One...who transforms our life...is plenty.

Traditional Saying

The quest along Sardine Creek to find the vortex and Sean Cassidy failed. Alexandra sat upstairs in her bedroom, absently turning one of Jessie's old dolls over in her hands, trying to accept the fact she might have to stay in this century forever. One button eye hung precariously from its face. The lopsided grin on the doll did nothing to ease her fears or her loneliness. She let it slide to the floor.

"Come on, Alex, old girl. Quit feeling maudlin. It's time to put the blues away. Just because you made a fool of yourself the other day doesn't mean you have to hide away." She berated herself. "I acted like a child, splashing water and throwing grass. What must he think?" She touched her fiery cheeks with her icy fingertips.

"Snap out of this girl and soon. It won't do to dwell on all your misguided actions and crazy fantasies." She'd flirted for the first time in her life, and now she felt the repercussions. "Find something to take your mind off him. Soon." She drummed her fingers on her leg then rose from her sitting position. "Kim likes the veggie garden weedless. I could stand a little dirt under my finger nails." Laying everything else aside, Alex walked down the steps.

"Good morning, Kim," she called to the spry little housekeeper just before the door swung shut. The ground smelled of fresh spring rain and wind. Alex breathed deeply.

"Ah, now what should I tackle first?" Something hairy and rough rubbed against her leg. She looked down. "Oh, my. Shoo!" Kim's pig grunted at her feet then stared at her as if she was supposed to pet it. "Go away." She stepped back a little too quickly, stumbling on a rock in the process.

Piggy grunted several times before spying something more interesting on the other side of the yard and pranced away.

"Thank heavens. You're not human, you know that don't you?" Alex called to the pig. As if disputing her words, Piggy stopped instantly and grunted again. A noise that sounded disrespectful and patronizing.

Precisely two hours later, Alex rested back on her knees. Swiping a dirt-smudged hand across the bridge of her nose, she surveyed her work. Little beads of sweat dripped from her brow, sliding down her cheeks. The pig nudged her back. When Alex didn't respond, it nudged her again, this time decidedly harder.

Alexandra landed on all fours, suddenly nose to nose with the beast. "How did you get in front of me? Go away." She pushed and shoved but the pig didn't move.

"Stop grinning at me. Don't try to hide it. I know you're smiling—now just go away before I turn you into bacon."

The animal emitted that same annoying sound, "You wouldn't dare," and trotted off.

"Pullin' weeds?"

"What? Oh my, you scared me." Alexandra turned to find Jessie looking down at her. "I thought maybe the pig could talk after all."

"Nope. Don't think so," Jessie said matter-of-factly.

Alexandra stifled a giggle. "You didn't just hear it? Said plain as the nose on my face, 'You wouldn't dare.' Then curled its little tail tighter and trotted off."

Jessie cocked her head suspiciously. Her eyes narrowed. "You're pullin' my leg."

"You're too smart for me. Come on, I have to go wash up."

A little while later Alexandra leaned against the window, admiring the neat clean rows of vegetables. Lost in dreams and memories, she still felt a little lonely, and now, looking over the hills, she longed for home, for another world so very far away. The emptiness inside her, overpowering at times, settled in the pit of her stomach.

The sun had just set, and the colors hovered on the horizon. Blazing golds and burnished pinks blended with the faded denim of the sky. A planet stood out against the darkening sky, and Mt. McLaughlin stood in bold silhouette the other direction.

The world hadn't changed so very much and neither had she, at least not perceptibly, but she wasn't in the world as she knew it, and nothing was at all like it used to be. James had seen to her wardrobe; modest, and practical except for the slippers. She looked at them beneath the hem of her skirt then pursed her lips. For the sake of her aching toes, toes that didn't want to fit into the uncomfortable shoes James expected her to wear, she had taken to going barefoot whenever he was gone and the weather permitted.

A breeze swirled through the open window then onto the floor. It lifted the doll's hair before dying. The curtains at the window fluttered and after a second, lay still against the hard frame of the window.

Her breath shuddered and died within her. She knew the search parties had given up by now. No one would look for her much longer, except her Mom. Her mother would never stop praying or give up hope. And Sean...what of him? He had survived, but she hadn't actually seen him again since that terrifying day in town.

Suddenly, she felt ill. Her head whirled crazily and her heart pounded desperately.

"Dammit!" she swore and clutched blindly at the windowsill.

She'd hoped she'd never feel that terrible rolling sensation again. She wanted this to end. Now. Not tomorrow or next week.

Dressed for the time with her hair neatly tucked into a chignon and decorated with lace, she looked as if she belonged here. The dress made her feel fragile and vulnerable, but she knew beneath the dress she was the same.

Alex had always chosen to meet her problems head on, and this case was no different. This experience or this century had somehow strengthened her. The calm and collected demeanor she strove for still existed.

I want you, James Lawrence. The wonderful security you offer. I can't resist you. One look and my body trembles with desire. All you have to do is glance my way and my knees shake and my mouth goes dry. You have a gentle side to you, sensitive beyond words to the irrational terrors that cloud my days and nights.

And now...

James waited downstairs for her to put in an appearance, and she'd decided he could wait all night. Out of sheer perversity, she wanted him to wait for her. He had left a week ago, without a word, without a moment's consideration. If he wanted her, he could come here. He had gone hunting again. This time he'd managed to slip away without her.

"Miss Alexandra...are you there?" It was Jessie who knocked on the closed door.

Her little nose peeked around the edge of the opening door. By the time Alex saw her entire head, Jessie was grinning mischievously.

"Hi." Jessie skipped to the bed. She stood in front of her for several seconds before she plopped down beside her.

"Hi, to you too." Alex turned to Jessie and they both laughed. The little girl managed to raise her failing spirits in only a few short seconds, such a precious little...sugarplum. She used Captain Lawrence's pet name with a smile. When Jessica Lawrence set her mind to mischief, she was anything but a sugarplum.

"Was he mad at you?" Her tiny voice and insatiable curiosity breached the silence.

"Furious," Alex almost laughed, nodding her head to emphasize her statement. "Did he send you to bring me downstairs?"

Jessie nodded with the age-old wisdom of a child who knew her parent very well. "Not exactly," the little Miss countered. "He doesn't act like he cares. But he does. And I suppose he'll be mad at me if I don't bring you with me. One time I fell out of the old oak tree. I broke my arm. He was mad at me then. Not at first but later after the doctor set it. He told me I was never to do anything that stupid again." She giggled. "He was very angry, but he never did anything."

"I thought he'd make me stay in my room," Jessie continued. "I didn't like it when he yelled at me, but he said he wasn't yelling."

"I can well imagine," Alex agreed and ruffled Jessie's dark head. "Sometimes it's easier to be there."

"Of course he never does what he says, but then I'm never sure. Maybe that's part of the plan," she continued with more insight than a little person her age should have.

"Could be," Alex agreed and really thought about what she'd said. It did make sense, a great deal of sense.

"You have to go to dinner," Jessie told her, "I know you don't want to talk to him. But..." Jessie hesitated a moment then looked up with a sheepish grin. "But then sometimes Papa does things that I don't understand.

"Miss Alex...the other night when you came into my room...what did I say?"

"The nightmare? Do you remember anything?"

"A little. I remember the wood all stacked around me and the spiders." Jessie shuddered and her heart shaped little face turned bloodless. Alex held out her arms and the little girl snuggled into them. "I remember the bad men, too."

"Ah, Jessie, I'm sorry, but you know James will never let anything happen to you again."

Jessie sniffed once and wiped her nose on the sleeve of her dress. "Now, don't do that," Alex scolded, reaching into her pocket for a clean handkerchief.

"I remember the silence too. After they left it was so quiet. I wanted to call out for my mommy, but she'd made me promise to stay still. I don't know why I can't ever remember more of the dreams, only that they scared me."

"I have dreams, too, Jessie. And they're a lot like yours. The silence and the darkness..."

"Miss Alex?"

"Yes?"

"Are you going to come to dinner?" she asked again.

"No, I've got work to do." Alex looked at her writing desk. "I'm not really hungry either." Sometimes she didn't think she'd ever feel hungry again. And she wanted so desperately to find a way to comfort Jessie and herself.

"Work?" Jessie asked wide-eyed. "You're always writing. What's so much fun about that?" She looked curious for a moment then, "I'm always hungry, and Kim cooks the best dinners. My stomach is grumbling right now. Want me to bring you something later?"

"No."

"Are you unhappy?"

"Jessie," Alex started, "I don't think that's the right word." She rose and walked to the window. A shadow darted behind the woodshed, and she whipped back behind the curtain with a shocked little cry. Her back slammed against the wall, and her hand flew to her mouth. She fought to control her panic.

"Afraid then," Jessie cut in.

"Sometimes," she said, trying desperately to hide her fear and at the same time catch her breath.

"I know." Curiosity came to life in Jessie's eyes, and she seemed to mull the words over in her mind.

Alex gulped air then fought the dizziness and the terror. "Sometimes at night when the house creaks," Alex steadied her trembling legs. Despite her all-consuming fear, she walked to the little girl, ruffling the child's hair.

"Oh, Kim says the same thing." Jessie studied Alexandra with her huge eyes, and Alex felt sure Jessie knew what she'd seen.

Before her knees could buckle, Alex collapsed on the bed. She looked at the window, wondering if Sean was out there. Lord, why couldn't he leave her alone?

"What's wrong?" Jessie's question brought her back to reality.

"Nothing...nothing," Alex said softly, but it took all her strength to hide her fear.

"You sure?"

"Yes," Alex said with more determination than she felt. "Now scoot. If you don't show up for dinner either, then we'll see furious."

Jessie stared at Alex for a long time. "I think you're right," she said. "If you change your mind...about the food..."

"Go before your father comes up here and scolds both of us for missing dinner."

For the longest moment, Jessie looked at her quizzically. "Are you sure?"

"No. Tell James..." she moistened her lips and her gaze swung to the window. "Tell James I need to see him. As soon as he's finished eating—that is."

She watched Jessie scamper out of the room then she wilted onto the bed. Terrified of the strange apparition, she closed her eyes and told herself over and over that she was safe here in this room. With James here nothing could happen to her.

But if it was Sean out there, she knew she wouldn't be safe anywhere.

"James..." she said wistfully, remembering his strength and courage, the way he protected and sheltered the people he cared for. He would keep her safe. He promised.

Jessie poked her head in the door again and scurried across the floor. "Jessie...what?"

Jessie stopped at the end of the braided rug and ran her foot across one of the ribs. "If you bolt the door, the bad man can't get in," she told her just before disappearing out the door again.

"Jessie, wait." Alexandra lunged for the door, desperate to stop Jessie.

The little girl must have heard her frantic plea because she appeared at the door again. They almost collided. Jessie's eyes were wide and puzzled.

"What do you know about the bad man?" Alex rested her hands on Jessie's shoulders.

"Nothing. I knew you were afraid, and when I feel that way, I bolt my door so the bad men can't get in. Papa doesn't want me to do it though. He says if the door is bolted, then he can't get in either. He told me that when I have the bad dreams about the men that hurt my mommy, I'm suppose to come to him and he'll protect me. You can do that too."

Alexandra smiled and pulled Jessie close. Jessie came into her arms, and Alex cradled her next to her heart. "I'll lock the door, just until James can get here. Now go." Yet she could not dispel the vivid picture of herself running to James' bed in the middle of the night.

Jessie hugged her back. "I'm not going."

The curtains on the window fluttered once more in the evening breeze. Alex ran to the window and slid it down hard. Then she stepped to the side and pulled the curtain back so she could watch the yard. Nothing. Absolutely nothing stirred in the ominous black silence.

She closed her eyes, willing the fear to recede, pushing it from her mind. Until James caught Sean, she didn't have a life and she didn't like the feeling. Lord, she didn't want to live in fear any longer.

As if in a trance, Alex walked to the door. Within a few seconds, it was bolted tight. Would it keep Sean out? "I wouldn't count on it. It probably wouldn't keep anyone out." She knew if Sean wanted her tonight, he would come in, bolted door or not.

When Sean Cassidy decided he wanted her, nothing would stop him. Not even James.

She lay back on the bed thinking of a way to find Sean. They had already gone into the hills searching for him. James had spent hours scouring the countryside. Alexandra suddenly knew she was the only one who could make Sean Cassidy appear. "Impossible—maybe, maybe not." But did she really want to try? Did she want to be a decoy?

Jessie spoke, "I told papa everything. He wants me to stay here with you. I told him we'd lock the door just until he gets here."

~ * ~

The old grandfather clock chimed twice and the echo faded slowly before Alex heard someone outside her door. When she heard the steps hesitate then stop, she held her breath and tensed. She waited, hating the silence, then praying for some sound that might tell her it was James and not Sean at the door.

"Alex, are you awake?"

Her breath rushed from her lungs and her eyes closed, relief washing over her. She wanted to answer, but she couldn't get the words out, and as the time passed into an eternity, she began to tremble so hard she didn't think she could move. More than anything she wanted to open the door and her heart to James. Her hands gripped the bedspread, and she wadded it into bunches beneath her white knuckles. The bolt on the door drew her attention, and she focused on it.

"We're sleeping. James, we're fine. I...Jessie's asleep." Every part of her quivered despite all her efforts to the contrary. She could not swallow. She could not breathe let alone talk. She was sure her heart had stopped. "Just wait, I'll get the door. Don't go away." She pleaded so softly she thought he would never hear her words through the thick door.

"Alexandra." The sound of his husky voice pounded through the closed door. "I don't want the door bolted. It was a bad idea."

"I'm coming," she told him, and her voice quavered and dipped to almost nothing. "What about Sean?"

"He won't hurt...never mind. If I promise no one will hurt you tonight, will you open the door?" His tone softened, imploring her to do the one thing she wanted more than anything else.

"You don't know that," but she knew he did. She rose and on wobbly legs approached the door. Flustered and confused, she fumbled with the bolt.

"I promise, no one will hurt you."

"I'm not afraid," she cut in. *Liar*, she was afraid of herself not him, and she was definitely afraid of Sean Cassidy.

"If you're not afraid, then why don't you open the door?" he asked softly, and the tone of his voice sounded terribly strained.

"I am. It's just that, well, I can't breathe. It won't budge." Oh, she'd trust him with her life and her virtue, but that wasn't the issue here. She looked at the window then back to the door. If you're not afraid...oh, but she was.

The bolt finally sliding free, she opened the door slowly then waited until the surprise on his face vanished. Expeditiously, she moved a few steps back into the room. The door shut softly behind her and clicked. James entered and now leaned against the door, arms crossed against his chest. With his knee bent, one moccasined foot rested on the wall. "I was concerned."

"Sean's out there," she said, her voice a shaky whisper. She began to reach out to him then brought her hand back to her side. "At least he was earlier."

"Jessie told me. I've searched and he's gone. It's time I put Jessie to bed."

Jessie lay sprawled on the bed. Her body had turned sideways across it, and she had her doll tucked beneath her chin. James picked her up and carried her to her room. A few minutes later he returned.

"She told me what you did after you looked out the window. Jessie was worried about you."

"I don't want her to worry. Jessie shouldn't know about Sean. I've never said anything to her." Alexandra didn't like the thought Jessie might be caught in the middle of all this, and she couldn't help but feel her stomach churn.

"The devil."

"Sean wouldn't think anything of hurting her. You have to keep Jessie away from him. I'll leave." She blinked and her eyes focused on her feet as she debated with herself in the suffocating silence.

"You can't run from him, or us. Where's the courageous woman I've come to know so well?" he asked. "Sean's not out there right now. He's left."

Compelled to look up, she didn't even remember what she'd wanted. His dark blue eyes held her transfixed. She strove to breathe, and her heart pounded rapidly, thundering around her.

"There's no need for you to stay here then."

He started toward her but changed his mind. His voice was on the teasing side as he tossed back, "Ah...is that regret I hear?"

It was. Alex felt the heat of her blush as it spread slowly across her cheeks and wondered what mischievous spirit had possessed her. Instead, she continued to stare at him and watched him grinning at her.

"No, you misunderstood." She hoped for a last minute reprieve, and was unable to understand why she was denying him.

"I hope not," he said.

"Mr. Lawrence."

The sudden formal use of his name made him pause mid-stride then he began walking toward her again. This time he walked slowly, too slowly. He stopped in front of her and she could barely think. James held out his arms for her and his whispered, "May I?" was her undoing.

"Yes," she breathed.

With tender concern, he pulled her from the bed where she had retreated and into his arms. His fingers sweetly threading through her hair before he lowered his mouth to hers.

His kiss tasted of spring flowers and promised forever. The stubble of a day's growth teased her skin as his mouth sought hers with a gentle urgency that swept through her soul and left her hoping for eternity. His tongue teased her lips, tenderly moving them to part to his demands then it filled her, and the kiss deepened. She melted into him, moaning softly.

His hand found the swell of her breast and rested upon it. She didn't pull away or refuse him anything, having not the power to say no and it seemed he knew. She had known it would be this way. The languid warmth brought on by his kiss swept the length of her, and the sensual stroke of his tongue tore a sob from her throat.

It was that sound that stopped him, seemed to make him think. For several seconds, he held her against his chest as if he refused to let the moment end. Suddenly he let his hands fall away. Her head fell against his chest and his whispered, "Alexandra...I," startled her.

"I don't understand," she told him, and her hands fell to her side.

"I know. Neither do I. But I promised and I can't guarantee that you won't have a child from what we do."

"A child?" A child, yes.

"I told you I'd keep you safe and I meant it. I'm sorry."

He traced her kiss-swollen lips with his thumb. His eyes were smoldering, his features taut. He turned and began to wander the room, stretching the silence into what seemed like hours.

"I thought you might want to go with me tomorrow to the mine. I'm hauling equipment."

"To the mine," she repeated dazed and unsure of herself. "You don't, I mean, yes. I would like to ride with you," she told him without stopping to think.

"We'll leave first thing in the morning, and since you're already asleep, you'll have lots of rest," he teased, a half-smile on his lips.

Alex hesitated, remembering her words only moments before then her eyes grew wide with wonder at his sudden change. She laughed. "I will, won't I?"

He nodded his agreement. "Meet me in the kitchen at five, since you didn't eat dinner." He approached her and tenderly touched her cheek before pointing to the bed.

"I know," she interrupted the lecture that was sure to follow. "I'll be there with bells on." When she noticed the strange look on his face, she laughed.

He walked about the room, looking over the odd assortment of things that had collected here. "Bells on? Not to change the subject, but the town is planning a ball and minstrel show to raise money for a bell for the Bigham's Knoll school. You're invited, you know." He stopped, looking at her as if he expected an answer or at least eager enthusiasm.

"Why? Whatever for? They despise me...think of me as a fallen woman, and if you had your way, I would be," she reminded him.

His eyebrows rose a fraction. "Because you're my house guest."

"Since when?" She blushed but didn't change her argument.

"While we were gone, Kim explained to the people in town that you were a relative. A distant cousin it seems. Kim's quite creative with her stories, don't you think?"

"I suppose, living with you would make people believe we're sleeping together. Especially since you weren't the only one on the mountain that night. I'm sure everyone knows exactly what we're doing."

"Hardly, since we haven't done anything."

"I don't want to meet anyone," she said. "I won't be around here long enough to make friends."

"Do we have to have this argument? I won't take you near the vortex again, and you can't get there on your own, so forget any plans you might have."

"You really do believe I came from another time?"

"Believe?" for a moment he turned away from her. "Despite all my previous doubts, yes."

"Yes?"

"As hard as it is to imagine, I believe you came from another time.

"I want to go home where I can be myself, where I don't have to worry about what everyone or anyone thinks of me." For a man, he was certainly naive. If he expected her to associate with the town folk while she lived under his roof, he was crazy. "I swear, understanding you is impossible. I know what everyone is saying. I might as well take out an ad in the Post and confirm the rumors."

He gave her a long look. "If anyone says anything to you, they'll have to answer to me."

"I just want to go home before it's too late."

"You think the vortex might close?"

"I have no idea what it's capable of."

"Will it be so hard to live in this time?" He stopped her and reached for her hand.

Alex felt his warmth and his strength as he enclosed her hands in his. "There is nothing here for me. My friends and family haven't been born."

"Sometimes I feel the same hollow feelings in the pit of my stomach," he said and watched her.

Her eyes widened. "I feel as if I've lost everything."

A slight smile touched his feature. His fingers rode sensually over the soft contours of her cheek then to her lips. "You've gained my friendship. And now, well, I want everything between us to be perfect."

"Are you asking me to stay here, with you?" Her voice quivered. "But I don't belong in this time."

He fell silent, his eyes narrowing.

"Maybe, maybe not, but either way I have to know you'll stay."

"I can't make any promises."

He dropped her hands and moved back to the window. "I understand."

Determined to learn more about him, she changed the subject. "You've been mining the area. How much do you make?"

He turned to give her his complete regard. His eyes twinkled when he replied, "Oh, about a thousand a month."

146

The mining equipment she'd noticed out back would cost, but even so he must have a sizable bank account for a man in the 1800s.

"Then stop," she couldn't understand why he still worked and defaced the mountains when he must have more money than anyone could spend in a lifetime. She pressed her point, "It leaves scars that will last forever."

"I intend to quit. As soon as I can, I'll sell it all. Of course then someone else will do the same thing, and it will go on until there is no more gold."

"You're right, quitting won't solve the problem."

"What?"

"Don't sell the land or the equipment."

He snorted, just a little before he fell silent.

"The last female who tried to tell me how to run my life I threatened to throw over my knee and spank. I wanted her full cooperation. Of course, I can think of at least a thousand other things I'd rather do with you."

Instantly, her tightly held breath threatened to explode in a rush. But she finally saw the humor around the edges of his mouth and she relaxed, confident in her assumption, "Did it work?"

"No, Miss Jessica still has me wrapped around her finger. I can think of several other methods to change your mind. Speechless, angel eyes?"

She'd fallen for the trap, had even seen it coming.

Two could play at this game.

"I hear old J.C. Whipp makes a good headstone," she said smoothly, staring at him. "Wonder what the weather's like out there on the hill, cemetery hill, and if you don't stop calling me that..." She picked demurely at an imaginary piece of lint on her skirt then glanced back at him.

He blinked, studying her, his hand raking through his long black hair. He seemed clearly puzzled, and Alex wasn't quite sure what to say next.

"Never, it suits you, more than your name," he retorted and started to leave the room. He stopped just before leaving to add, "You do have angel eyes, and just one look into them is magical."

"Magical?"

"Mysterious," he countered.

"Hold it right there!"

Without a thought in her muddled brain of the consequences, Alex charged after him, swooping around him to block the door, bringing him up short. Unfortunately, she hadn't decided what she'd do when he stopped.

"Changed your mind?" he drawled and quickly back-stepped to the bed patting a space beside him after sitting down.

Alex smiled benignly. "No, but have you?"

"Well, I'll let you go to sleep." He looked slightly embarrassed. "Since we have to get an early start."

"I thought that was an invitation."

Her question seemed to fluster him. He never lost control quite so thoroughly. "No, I mean it was, but you're not ready," he murmured. "Didn't we just discuss this?"

"You discussed it. I listened. But you didn't think for a minute to ask me how I felt. You know though, I have to earn my keep," she teased.

He thought he saw her lips quirk in a smile as if she was enjoying herself at his expense, as if she hadn't expected this reaction from him.

Instantly, he understood the game and he liked it, but he wasn't going to let her win. It challenged him but he stifled an urge to laugh. He'd let her have her way for now.

"See you in the morning, angel girl."

Chapter Ten

James stood in the gazebo, staring toward the town of Jacksonville. A breeze, crisp and cool, whispered through the dry, old oak trees, rustling the leaves. The pink blush of dawn cast a rosy cheer on the horizon. It would be warm today, almost hot, perfect for an outing. Turning his thoughts to Alexandra, he ran his fingers through his hair, frustrated and confused. At times he felt so inadequate, so powerless. Alex feared Sean Cassidy, the man who attacked her in town, the man with a scar slashed across one cheek. He'd looked for him, oh yes, he'd searched everywhere, but Sean Cassidy seemed always to be one step ahead of him.

I'll keep you safe, angel girl.

His promise to keep her safe was an empty one, at least until he found this man who threatened her. He closed his eyes against his helplessness and vowed to keep her close to his side.

He would take her with him today, up into the hills. It was beautiful country. It was paradise on earth. Eden.

A curious chill seized him. There was danger in the hills, but if she'd told him the truth, there was danger here too. It was at these times, the uneasy times, he wondered what brought her here and why. Wondered if there was perhaps some unseen hand that guided her here, into a world where she didn't belong, hoping she'd find a way to become part of it.

Why did it all seem so complicated?

He shouldn't have asked her to go along, but he wouldn't rescind the offer now. He didn't want to. He cursed softly, entered the house, letting the door bang closed behind him.

She would be safe. He would keep her at his side, next to him every second. They would take the well-traveled roads, and he'd show her the mine then they'd return.

He strode up the stairs to Alex's room.

Alex woke with the first knock on her door.

"Rise and shine, angel mine."

~ * ~

She heard his singing, somewhat off-tune as he made his way down the steps. The sun peered in through the window in a blaze of glory, and she rubbed her eyes. Alexandra groaned and pulled the pillow over her head, burying herself in the warmth. Just as her eyes closed again, she remembered the wake-up call and what it meant. Scrambling as if the devil himself were after her, she threw off the covers and stumbled out of bed.

Alex ran to the window. Drawing the curtains aside, she peeked out on the day, delighted with the brilliant sunshine and the cloudless sky that greeted her. Opening the window, she breathed in the crisp clean air and the fragrant scent of spring. The promise of adventure hovered there, too, and her heart skipped a beat. Adventure, yes, she could hardly wait. Turning dreamily, she leaned against the wall. After a moment's hesitation, she pushed herself away and twirled in circles around the room until she was dizzy. Thoroughly exhausted, she let herself fall across the bed, giggling.

She stared at the ceiling and touched a finger to her lips. Last night had been a revelation of sorts. James had unequivocally admitted he believed her. He had also admitted he wanted her. Yet, she had slept alone. James Lawrence was a gentleman, and he'd never take advantage of her. What new revelations about James Lawrence would today bring?

Following a barely perceptible sigh, she rose and dressed for the day. Quickly winding her hair in a conservative bun, she glanced a second time at the mirror.

Not quite satisfied yet in a hurry to go, Alexandra dashed down the steps and whirled into the kitchen. With a rush of wind following her, she stumbled to a halt as she passed through the door. James had eaten and was leaning back in his chair, one foot propped on a stool. He was smoking a cheroot. She'd have to tell him to stop that but not now.

"Morning," he looked up. His bold admiring gaze swept over her then returned slowly to her face.

"Yes, it is, isn't it?" she said cautiously and ventured a brilliant smile. The wicked imp inside her wanted to ask him if he liked what he saw. But of course she didn't.

James didn't say anything else but watched her for the longest time. His stare made her fiddle with the buttons on her dress and smooth the folds of her skirt. Eventually, she sat down to eat. When she pushed her plate away, the look in his eye stopped her. It made her stomach roll. She looked for something bland. The buttered bread caught her attention. She ate it then washed the crumbs down with coffee.

He was dressed for work in blue jeans and a flannel shirt. His brogans replaced the moccasins he usually wore. In case of rain, he'd slung two ponchos over his shoulder. The shirt he wore was buttoned only part way and his sleeves were rolled up.

"Ready? I believe it's time to get started." He waited for her to rise.

"Yes," she nodded, but when she observed his face, she saw admiration. A soft wondrous smile touched her lips as she looked from James to the absolutely gorgeous morning waiting for them outside.

He picked up his hat with an easy grace and motioned to the door.

"C'mon then. We don't have all day to waste."

Alexandra pushed her apprehension to the back of her mind. Determined to change their relationship in some small way, she walked through the door, heading toward the wagon. Loaded with all types of mining equipment, the cart sagged. She squinted at the pieces, trying to recall each one and its use.

"Alexandra?"

"Oh my." His hands wound tightly around her waist, lingering there. "James." Before she could complain, he deposited her in the seat, and the sound of his laughter floated in the air.

"Ah, Miss Alex, you don't have to fend for yourself anymore. I intend to take very good care of you."

He was humming. It was a catchy tune, and her toe began to tap in rhythm with the music.

"You'll enjoy the ride," he winked.

"Oh, yes, I think I will. In what direction are we going?" she asked. The promise of adventure and the exciting sensations he elicited suddenly had her breathless.

"North." He handed her a bonnet and looked knowingly at her head.

"Really." She positioned the hat and tied the ribbons under her chin, grateful her nose wasn't about to become bright red. "That leaves it wide open."

He didn't miss her sarcasm and he laughed again. "Suppose it does." His grin widened and his lips twitched with suppressed amusement.

Horrid, wonderful man.

He leapt into the wagon and clicked at the horses. Weighted down by the heavy equipment, the wagon slowly began to roll. James looked relaxed and confident, leaning forward with his elbows on his thighs. The wagon moved along an old trail and steadily climbed higher into the hills, wheels creaking.

His thigh touched hers then their shoulders met. As the wagon rolled along and the sun warmed the air, she found herself relaxing into his body and her lashes fluttering and threatening to close.

A sudden dip in the road startled her, and Alex's eyes opened instantly. "James."

"Hang on, darlin'."

"To what?" she croaked.

"Why me, of course." The road stretched out in front of them and the landscape changed gradually. She heard water rushing nearby and chattering gray squirrels in the trees.

His hand rested on her leg, and she looked up at him.

"Enjoying yourself?"

His softly spoken question made her stomach flutter. "I, well, yes." When he squeezed her leg and removed his hand to point overhead at a large circling bird, she let out her breath. Before long, his hand returned. The warmth of his fingers penetrated the fabric of her skirt, and she knew an instant surge of desire. Lord, but she couldn't think. What on earth were they talking about?

"It's going to be a hot one."

"What?"

"A hot one."

She puckered her mouth in concentration, hoping to pull some thread of information from her mind. "Hot." And she looked at him rather hopeless and confused. "My mind wandered."

"Do tell," he teased. "Very hot," he winked and arched an eyebrow.

"I don't..."

"Of course you don't, but when you're ready, I'll collect." A single dark brow shot up, and he urged the horses on with a click and a swish of the reins. She knew she heard him laugh.

Oh, how he did tease, and the strangest thing was she liked his teasing and the light banter that went with it. It made her want to know so much more about this man.

"You were talking about the weather," she whispered.

"No, you should tell me about your mother," he said pleasantly.

"I should? Why?" She was still confused.

"She's a doctor. I find that incredible."

Alex held her breath, staring out over the forest. "Why? Because she's a woman."

"Absolutely."

"You're archaic." When he lowered the reins to stare, she continued, "I shouldn't expect you to think any differently than most, after all you're a man and a product of your time."

"I certainly hope so," he drawled.

Alex laughed softly. "When my father died, she put all her efforts into her work."

"Did she ever remarry?"

Alex shrugged. "No, Mom feels there was only one person she could ever love."

"How did he die?"

"Iraq, a war that was just as senseless as the War Between the States, but I guess you couldn't tell him that. The war was all but over, still the U.S. kept sending young men, and in the end, I never knew him."

"Iraq?" His question sounded poignant yet at the same time curious.

"He was among the first to be sent to Kuwait and among the Marines who infiltrated Bagdad after Operation Desert Storm. He stayed in Bagdad and was there when they caught Hussein. He didn't leave the area. It seemed as if he would stay there forever, trying to keep the fragile peace."

"That was it? You never heard from him again?"

"Never. Actually, in the interim, mom got to see him a couple of times. During his service in Iraq they met several times in Hawaii. His R&R. But that was before he went missing. He was officially listed as a POW then it changed to MIA."

"POW? MIA?"

"Prisoner of War." She paused, "missing in action."

James gripped the reins tighter and urged the horses on. His grim expression told her he didn't like what she'd just told him. "I hoped there wouldn't be any more wars. It must have been hard growing up without a father."

"It was but I had a good life. By the time I was in high school, most of my friends had only one parent. It seemed normal enough."

"One parent? Normal? You're not making sense. Why would most of your friends have only one parent?"

"Divorce mostly."

"You mean to say that people in your time don't take marriage seriously?"

"No, I, well. They do but it's different. I don't want to talk about this now."

"Suit yourself," he said after a long pause. And she knew he'd broach the subject again.

His hand moved on her leg and the pressure of his fingers, even through the fabric, sent warmth radiating through her. Her heart raced and the wind kept pace. It swirled, picking up pine needles and dirt that littered the ground, sending them on in a tiny funnel cloud of energy.

"I like it here," he said, changing the subject. "Reminds me a little of home. The forested valleys and the long winding rivers, it feels like God's country. He breathed deeply and looked around the forest.

"God's country," she placed her hand over his. She didn't understand the sensations his touch gave her. Didn't understand the tempest that invaded her when he left his fingers there.

He stared at her. All his attentions focused on her, and she felt as if he looked into her soul. "Would you like to stay here?" he asked. She looked away and tried to concentrate on something other than James Lawrence

"Stay?" she queried, her voice trembling.

His fingers traced lazy circles on her leg, kneading, encouraging the sensations to build. Seducing.

Lord, she couldn't think when he touched her.

"I want you to stay," he said.

She didn't know in what context he meant the words. But she wasn't ready to accept her fate. She wanted to go home, missed her friends and her mother.

"Why didn't you let Jessie remain back East?" She planned to keep him talking, hoped to keep his mind off her.

He watched her a moment then let his gaze drift back to the trail. "You don't want to know." A dark shadow dropped across his face. He took his hand away and she felt the emptiness, the loneliness. It seemed as if the sun had just slid behind a cloud. Suddenly, his mood had changed; the sorrow clearly written on his face, and she knew a moment of tenderness for James.

"She's a lovely child but..."

"Alex, leave it alone," he cut in, and his voice was almost menacing. She watched the muscles tense in his arms and thighs. Watched the set of his jaw tighten and the lines across his brow deepen.

"I suppose I'll have to. I like her, she's a breath of fresh air."

"Alex—"

"Oh all right but you shouldn't keep things bottled up inside you. It's not good for your, health. And the smoking will kill you too. You should really quit. If you cared about her, you would."

"Crissakes, Alexandra, stop."

It took her a moment to realize she'd said more in the last few seconds than she should have. He cared about the little girl, and she knew his feelings were sincere. "But the smoke will give you lung cancer. Who will she have to take care of her when you're gone? You have to admit she's a handful and not just anyone will do."

He stared at her hard and she could hear the grate of his jaw, hear the fury in his words. "I've taken care of her in my will. And Alex, I haven't changed my mind. I don't want to talk about this."

Alex kept on though. She continued perhaps because of the anguish she'd felt with his last words. "So, she'll have someone who loves her? How can you be sure?"

"Alexandra, it's not your funeral, besides, we're all going to die."

"That doesn't mean you have to rush things."

"You're crazy as a loon, you know." His tone of voice had changed to total frustration. She decided she liked him that way. It was a vulnerable side he seldom showed.

Alexandra laughed. "I know, but..." She kept at him, nudging him for answers. She wanted to know everything and she was willing to risk almost anything.

"I wanted to get her as far away from the war as I could," he told her.

She inclined her head and studied him, wondering what made the man so difficult. "Of course, so you overlooked every other possibility."

James was the one shocked at that point. "Excuse me?" he asked incredulous.

Alex blinked and looked at him puzzled. "What did happen?"

"Dammit, Alex. Her father died at Gettysburg, and I couldn't save him, no one could."

Chills suddenly tumbled in the pit of her stomach and she held on to James, turning so she could grip his arm. Her nails dug into him, and she felt him flinch but he didn't move, didn't deny her the opportunity to cling to him.

Her fingers tightened, leaving nail marks, and she couldn't erase the tragedy from her mind. But then Jessie was lucky to have James, even if he let her run wild. Her hand automatically covered his. When she realized what she'd done, it was too late to retrieve it. Before she could protest, he enfolded her hand in his and a callused thumb stroked the inside of her wrist.

Even after she'd had a minute to catch her breath and still her racing heart, she found herself speechless, almost breathless. She felt the warmth of his touch creep up her arm then sweep through her and the sensation offered comfort. Protection. In the subtle gesture, he offered a wealth of feelings she'd never before known. "Is that when you headed west?"

"After I tied up a few loose ends."

"Didn't anyone else want her?" Her voice cracked.

She's such a beautiful child. He cherishes her as if she were his own.

"I never asked. It just seemed the right thing to do. The rest of the family still fought. The war wasn't over. Mother would have taken her, but I didn't want to burden her. Besides I didn't know how far the fighting would reach and I didn't want her anywhere near the danger."

She had to agree he'd done the right thing for Jessie. "And you've never looked back?"

"Not once. I wanted a new life for both of us. And I thought if she was far enough away, she wouldn't remember what she'd seen that day." James shrugged as if none of this had affected him. She could feel the pain inside him when he talked about his past. A new life, yes, it's what she'd have too.

"If people still fought, did you desert? How could you just leave?"

"I received a special assignment in the West from General Grant. He was a friend of our family and he understood."

"Do you ever hear from your family?"

"Mother threatens to come see me as soon as the train reaches here. I'd like that, but that's a long ways away. Although I know she wants to see us."

"And you won't go back?"

"No, I won't go back, at least not right now. It's too soon. Maybe in a couple more years."

Alex wished she hadn't asked him about Jessie and the war, but she couldn't seem to stop. "Did you find them?"

"The deserters? The ones who killed Jessie's mother?"

Alex saw the pain in his expression. She berated herself, knowing suddenly she'd brought the memories back so callously, with no concern.

She felt his body stiffen then shudder as if defeated.

A baby had been deprived of her mother. She wished he'd caught them. "Did you kill them? Were those the loose ends?"

"Killed them? I would have tortured them."

"You did?"

"No," he cut her off, "I couldn't find them. Not because I didn't try but it was taking too long. Jessie needed me. So I gave up."

"And you left." But she didn't stop. Her lips flattened to a thin white line, determined to talk with him until he could accept what happened and perhaps ease his conscience.

"Soon as I gathered the supplies," James said harshly. "Jessie was two years old."

"And you've been here ever since."

"Four years now. Jessie doesn't remember her mother or her father. But I think she only saw him a couple of times, and a baby that young doesn't remember." James released her hand and stared down the trail.

"I've seen pictures of my father. He was handsome. Always in his uniform, so proud. Mom used to talk about him all the time. I have a picture of them both here in my locket."

James regarded her seriously, his gaze moved to the piece of jewelry at her neck. "At night, when she goes to bed, I tell her stories about her mother. I never knew her father very well. There won't be much for her to remember about him, not even a picture." He said it so casually, as if he didn't care, but Alex could see his eyes. The pain was tearing him apart.

"Have you tried to find out about her father? When she's older she going to want to know."

"No."

He looked at her again, and she knew she'd lost him, at least for now.

A tear slid down her cheek. She turned to look over the woods. The wagon slowed and turned off the trail onto another smaller one.

"I guess I've said too much." Alexandra made a feeble attempt to hide her feelings from him and perhaps apologize. "It's just that all this made me think of home and how nice it would be to—"

"Forget it, Alex. The road back is too dangerous."

"You don't know that." She wondered at his words and their implications. It sounded as if he understood the vortex, the mechanics of it all.

"I do." He turned his icy stare on her. "You're staying here."

She shook her head and her eyes narrowed. "You can't know. No one does."

James kept his silence a moment.

"It doesn't work like one of your TVs. You can't just set the channel and go where you want. You have no idea what happened, or how, or why. Use your head, Alex.

"I have another life. One I'd like to live again." She turned from him.

He was right. She didn't have any idea how the vortex worked, and instead of going forward, she could end up even farther back in a time more dangerous.

"Ah, Alexandra, I care what happens to you, more each day." He stared at her a moment longer. The silence deepened. "Ah, darlin', you don't understand."

"Then tell me. Explain it to me."

"You can't put your life in danger for a childish whim. You're here now and you have to accept it," he said patiently. "You don't know what could happen. Take a minute to think. If you got mixed up in it again..." His eyes fixed on her as if waiting for an answer.

"There's nothing to think about."

"You have to resign yourself to this. It's your fate."

"Perhaps, but—"

"Alexandra, I've told you things I've never told anyone else."

"Don't go there."

"Ah, Alex, I can't let you leave me, not yet, maybe not ever."

Her eyes were wide, questioning, "What if I decided to stay. What then? What would happen to me? You have to understand how alone I'll be."

"You'll have me."

"James."

"Yes," he smiled.

"Stop, I—"

"We're here," his tone of voice startled Alex. Her eyes suddenly rested on one of the most breathtaking views she'd ever seen.

A sheer wall of granite stretched to the sky. Douglas fir trees surrounded the boulder, their branches reaching out as if to caress the solid rock wall. A small creek wound its way around the base of the cliff, rushing helter-skelter over the rocks. Wild flowers and lush green ferns carpeted the forest floor.

The sun slid from behind a cloud, and a beam of light shone on the mountainside, illuminating the rough surface. Then a cloud enshrouded everything in shadows.

Alex wrapped her arms around herself and wide-eyed stared at the rock as if in a trance. She tried to deny the cold rush of fear suddenly sweeping through her. With all her willpower, she tried to block the terror that was suddenly overwhelming her.

Another breeze caught her hat, and she grabbed for it almost tumbling from the wagon. Alex sat down, her hat now tucked under one arm. She waited for her heart to slow.

The oppressive silence that followed brought to mind all kinds of memories she'd rather forget. But she shook off the feeling, thinking she was letting her imagination cloud her judgment.

The day waited for her, beckoning with all its splendor. She didn't intend to waste it by brooding over her disagreement with James. It was a futile argument anyway, because she was determined to try to go home.

Chapter Eleven

Alex wadded her skirt up in one hand and scampered to the top of an ageless boulder. After examining the view by making a slow three hundred sixty degree turn, she dusted the dirt and old pine needles from the top of her high rocky perch and sat down. With her knees drawn tightly to her chest and the tips of her shoes peeking out from beneath the hem of her skirt, she watched James work. His bare back and broad shoulders glistened with sweat. He was angry with her. She knew the reason why. But there was nothing she could do about it.

Bored and horribly out of sorts, she scratched a little stick figure on the solid granite rock she sat on, surreptitiously casting sidelong glances his way. He never looked up. After a deep sigh and little snort of derision, she rested her chin on her knees. Wistfully, she closed her eyes and let the sun dry the moisture around them. The warmth felt like a gentle caress. It possessed a healing touch, and as the hours passed, she tried to push the feelings of abandonment away.

Memories, she thought sadly, were not always kind. Some memories did best when left in the shadowed recesses of a person's mind. She wouldn't apologize for what she'd said to James. No, she didn't owe him an explanation. If anything, he owed her one for his rude behavior now.

He looked at her and the dark expression on his face sent a wave of guilt ricocheting down her back and made her heart race wildly. Alex tried to smile, but it fizzled and died before he could turn from her.

I'm in love with him.

Despite her unwanted and startling realization, she was not foolish enough to think she could have a lasting relationship with James, nor was she stupid enough to believe she could fit in this world. She was suddenly positive of only two things: She wanted to live the time she had left with him happily, and she wanted to return to the twenty-first century.

Yet she was afraid, terribly afraid of her future and her past, and uncertain of how she would continue in this century if she couldn't find a way to go home. The thought weighed heavily on her mind, and she wished she had the ability to reach Sardine Creek and the Oregon Vortex without his help. She shielded her eyes from the intense glare of the sun and looked north in that direction.

With a heavy thought filled sigh, Alex went back to her musings. Her knowledge of time travel was limited and not very enlightening. Perhaps James had been right in implying she should never travel near that curious and dangerous place again. Time travel had always held its place in the world of imagination and folklore, yet she'd never taken the concept seriously, and she had no idea what could befall her if she ventured into the unknown again.

Alex slipped from the rock. In one swift move, she gathered her shoes in one hand, and without thinking of the possible consequences, she walked down a tiny animal trail leading to the creek. So lost in thoughts about James and the beauty of the forest, she forgot Sean and the danger. Once in awhile, she'd stop to look at a wild flower or search for a hidden morel. A tiny Lady's Slipper poked its head out from behind a large fern and behind it a dozen Indian Paint Brush grew in a clump. The fiery orange red of its blossom called out to the honeybees, inviting them to sip.

She continued down the path, searching out guideposts and sticking determinedly to the trail, a trail that led north. And as she walked, the dark canopy of trees closed in around her.

She followed a parallel course to a little stream. Every now and then she'd bend over and pick up a rock that glittered or just looked pretty. He'd said they took out one thousand dollars a month, so one would surmise that if she looked, she ought to be able to find a nugget or two.

Curiosity pulled her closer to the stream until she was standing on the edge. The bank slowly crumbled where her feet touched. Soft dirt slid into the water, sending myriad of ripples to the other side. Alex couldn't resist. Before a few moments passed, she had her shoes and stockings off then tucked the hem of her skirt into her waistband. Sucking in her breath, she waded into the cold bubbling stream. The water so clear she could see the bottom and everything in between; a small fish stuck its head out from behind a ledge before it scurried back for cover. Cold and inviting, the water glistened and shimmered. Where there was no current, the water reflected the sun as it cast a colorful rainbow across its surface. Above, the thick green canopy blotted out much of the sun and the sky; shadows danced with the breeze stirring the leaves. Still, the beams managed to filter through and play on the earth then glide across the rippling water. When she looked towards the heavens, it was green, as far as the eye could see, green until the forest blended into the aquamarine above.

The rock she'd picked up wasn't gold. She smiled. It was fool's gold. She knew it well. It made her laugh though. Gold fever. She tossed the worthless pyrite into the air, catching it when it came down before throwing it again. Now her toes felt as if they were ready to crack and break. They were so teeth rattling cold. Ignoring the discomfort, she kicked the water and watched the drops fall back to earth, felt them touch her cheek then fall again, this time rippling the little pool of water she stood in. A crayfish startled by her presence dashed beneath the cover of a rock. She giggled and wished James was here with her.

She understood why he took life so seriously, knew he had a tender side, a vulnerability she couldn't disregard. More than once as she'd watched him at work, she'd wanted to reach out to comfort him.

Alexandra closed herself from the thoughts filling her mind. Torn between a man she just realized she loved and a home in the future, she felt a gut-wrenching stab of pain.

Her toes were numb and her legs were tired. But that part felt good. It was the indecision that bothered her and made her heart feel heavy. A small waterfall tumbled to the riverbed in front of her. Alex stopped a moment to watch. It was so peaceful. She hesitated, enjoying the serenity then, without another thought, she scrambled around the little waterfall. Her shoes lay on the bank downstream. Putting her cares and responsibilities behind, she skipped and hopped along the flat rocks.

Someone's hand suddenly pressed firmly over her mouth, an arm wound around her body, yanking her backwards. The man and his overpowering strength muffled her startled gasp. Alexandra froze for a moment, paralyzed with terror. Regaining her wits, she tried valiantly to free herself.

She knew the strength and the power of James. Knew his body well. She knew the feel of his chest and his arms wound around her waist, the callused pads on his hands formed from hard work.

This wasn't James.

No sandalwood and tobacco, just sweat and a sickly aroma, an odor that reminded her of another time and place. A shudder wracked her body. She groaned, desperate to see this man's face to confirm the truth. Struggling wildly in his arms, she almost succeeded in wrenching lose. His grip tightened painfully, biting into her skin and he allowed her no room to maneuver.

This man revolted her; she felt her skin crawl and she cried out, but the sound never came. It wasn't James. He was too tall and thin. She grew limp in his arms and faked her compliance, hoping for a chance to scream or run.

"That's it sweetheart, just relax and I'll be real good to you." The man's voice rumbled behind her.

"Sean."

"Now, if you'll come along willingly, I can free your hands." His voice was cold and hard. She cringed and prayed for rescue, prayed for James to find her.

Prayed also Sean would take his hand away. She wasn't greedy. All she wanted was one second, one second to scream, one second to let James know she needed him.

An old bandanna was suddenly stuffed into her mouth. Before she could spit it out, her hands were secured with a length of rope. The earth turned and when he threw her over a horse, she felt her stomach knot.

Alexandra moaned as he mounted behind her and the horse continued up stream. She fought her nausea and her pounding head. Then she hoped for a little, no, a great deal of ESP, and she focused all her thoughts on James.

They left the stream behind, heading higher into the hills, moving north. He talked and laughed unconcernedly while she hung precariously upside down from his horse. There was hatred for what she'd done to him in his voice. As if it were a lifeline giving her strength, Alexandra clung to that hatred as she bounced against the horse. His hands bit into her back, holding her possessively. With a silent moan of desperation and a last valiant bid for freedom, she bucked against his powerful hold and accomplished nothing. He laughed again and the sound sent countless tremors down her spine. The horse slowed. She heard the saddle creak as he dismounted, felt the horse move slightly, and as soon as he pulled her off, she bolted on wobbly legs.

He tackled her and the wind rushed from her lungs. Stunned for a moment, she lay motionless as he rolled her over and pinned her to the ground. He held her on the forest floor with the length of his body. She'd sworn she'd fight, but he held her unmovable beneath him, and even though he wasn't as large as James, he was stronger than she was.

When their eyes met for a second, she was catapulted into the future, reliving another time, another place, just like this. A place she'd tried to push to the back of her mind.

She struggled frantically. With a wild and reckless abandon, she fought against Sean Cassidy and the horror and pain he intended for her.

He'd followed her for revenge. And she'd fight him with the last breath in her body.

Tears welled in her eyes as his hand found her breast. "Not much, sweetheart, but enough," he said with a low laugh. "Can't get away from me, Alexandra baby, and what James Lawrence has sampled I will too. You denied me once but never again. You and me sweetheart—satisfaction through eternity." His laughter sounded demonic, and she fought the wild panic tearing at her.

She fought him with all her strength, clawing and kicking at him. It was the implication of his words that renewed her energy and determination.

"Well, you got fight in you. I like that too." His gravely voice sent tremors down her spine, and she brought her knee up hard, hitting his thigh.

When her knee hit him, it gave her an opportunity, and she yanked desperately at the bandanna he'd tied over her mouth. For a fraction in time, a scream filled the air and shattered the eerie calm that had descended over the little clearing. Startled birds flew into the air and began their own chatter as if in an attempt to help defend her. A cold wind swirled around them. The sky grew dark. The chill in the air grew frigid, and her terror echoed off the trees. His fist connected with her cheek. She gasped in disbelief as the pain rocked through her body and the nightmare began again.

"Your kind of satisfaction goes a long way, sweetheart."

Pain exploded in Alexandra's head, but it was a secondary concern. When his hand moved to her breast again, she fought harder, struggling against him.

Alexandra's head spun. Her stomach rolled.

He yelled at her and shook her against the ground. His curses flew. "Don't hit me," he growled, "if you know what's good for you."

She didn't. It didn't matter in any case. She knew what he had planned for her. She was crying, though; tears, hot and acidic, stung her eyes and hung in her throat. She watched him, waiting for him to move, and she was determined to find a way out of this. She saw the fury grow in his eyes, and she fought against the panic threatening to consume her.

"Bitch! You whoring, manipulating little bitch! I'll take care of you," he said his words slow and even. His voice harsh. Now fury seized him, and he turned into a crazed man. His hold upon her tightened, and his fingers bit into her skin, wringing a gasp of pain from her.

Alexandra had almost passed the slim line of sanity and was on verge of hysterical terror. The cold fear of death invaded her. Then an icy calm came with the acceptance of death freed her from the pain she knew would follow. And that gave her power.

He pulled her up, whirled her about by her arm and bent it until she thought it would break then shoved her against a tree. Trapped completely, as if she hadn't been before, she now feared for more than her virtue. She'd driven him to a point of madness. Before she could breathe, he was on her, hitting her over and over. He didn't leave one part of her untouched; her chest, her face, her stomach. Her body cried out in pain.

Slowly, she blacked out. She slid down the length of the tree to land in a rumpled heap on the grass. Still he continued, and through an ever-darkening haze, she knew the pain and wished only for an end.

~ * ~

When she painfully opened her swollen eyes, she was still lying on the grass where she'd fallen but something heavy covered her. The stars shone above her, and a black cloud floated across the moon. Alexandra was cold and the throbbing hurt drove all thoughts from her head. Her body cramped and ached, and she flinched when a hand rested on her forehead. She whimpered, unable to help herself or stop the sound that came unbidden from her mouth. At least he hadn't killed her. She vaguely remembered the sound of hooves as she slumped to the ground alone.

She stared at the sky, barely breathing because it hurt too much. She didn't know how to cope with the pain because she'd never experienced anything like this before. It went beyond all comprehension that a man had nearly beaten her to death.

Alex tried to sit up, but James stopped her, begging her to rest.

"Ahh, don't say anything now. God, Alex, I'm sorry. I couldn't protect you. You know I'm going to have to look at you."

She wanted to tell him it was all right. That he'd saved her, actually.

Sean would have killed her.

But she couldn't say the words, her mouth bruised and swollen, hurt.

She gripped the arm he offered and pulled herself up. A cloud of pain rolled through the length of her. Her head swam and her stomach felt nauseous. She worked to control it. The pain consumed her, and she let James ease her back. She just wanted to go home.

~ * ~

James stared at her, sucking in his breath in disbelief. When he noticed she'd wandered away, he was terrified, and he'd dashed after her in a blind panic. When he discovered her path led north toward Sardine Creek, his body reacted violently, instantly enraged. His anger became overpowering. He had been torn between going after her to throttle her himself or just letting her have her way. Then when he'd discovered the tracks of a man, a burning jealous rage consumed him. He'd known immediately the man was Sean.

When he first saw her, he'd felt such relief before it turned to horror. As he stared at her face, bruised and swollen, his fear for her overwhelmed.

He realized he hadn't drawn a breath, and his grip on her arm had tightened. She moaned and he wanted to absorb her pain and bear it for her. As gently as he could, James undressed her. She didn't move and it relieved some of his fears. When he got her blouse and skirt off, her chemise still covered her. The ribbons fell away under his nimble fingers, but the view greeting him sent chills down his spine. Rage spilled within and tortured his mind. He searched inside himself for a reason and came up with nothing. Her body was covered with bruises just beginning to swell and color. Sean Cassidy would pay.

All he could think about, all his mind would allow was that he failed to protect her. She had warned him Sean would not give up.

She didn't deserve this!

Jesus, why?

She hadn't done anything except be in the wrong place. He looked at her again. He had to get her home where she could rest. She needed laudanum, which he didn't have. The trip down the mountain would hurt like the very devil, unless she remained unconscious, and for that he prayed.

James tucked the ends of the poncho around her, and as carefully as he could manage, carried her down the mountain to the wagon. It wasn't easy, walking through the stream and across ground that had never seen a path, but he finally reached his mining site. He prayed the pain would keep her sleeping, but even then he heard sobs and saw tears flowing down her cheeks.

He felt his own agony for her. His deepest fears resurfaced with the knowledge he'd failed her.

She didn't wake up and still she felt pain. He would kill the man who did this to her. Unlike the time with Jessie's mother, he would find him and see that Sean Cassidy paid.

When they arrived home, the sun had long since dipped behind the mountains. The sky didn't twinkle with stars. Instead, covered with low-lying clouds, the blackness looked solemn and foreboding. He felt as if some unseen force watched and condemned him. The ride down had been slow and torturous. Kim stood on the porch with a worried frown, and Jessie all but tumbled down the steps when she torpedoed out of the house. Kim started down the stairs, eyes huge with fear. "What happened, Mr. James?"

"Don't have time for questions at the moment. Get laudanum and bandages, ice too. Someone beat the hell out of her, and I didn't even know it was happening."

"Good Lord," Kim said and all but ran back to the house.

Jessie stood wide eyed, watching James as he lifted Alex from the bed of the wagon. She stifled a sob. "I'll stay quiet, mama. I promise. I won't be afraid." She followed behind, tears sliding unchecked down her cheeks, "I won't leave you this time, mama," she murmured. "I won't hide. I'm a big girl now and I can help. Uncle James taught me everything he knows."

James carried Alexandra to his bedchamber. As with the first time, it simply didn't occur to him to take her to a different room. She belonged here with him.

Kim pulled back the quilts, and he laid Alexandra on the bed then covered her. Jessie pulled up a chair on the other side and sat down. She watched everything her uncle did. The oppressive silence tore at his soul and thundered mutinously in his head during the long hours of the night.

By the time he'd finished and had the last bandage tied, both Jessie and Alex were asleep. He studied them as he waited for Alex to regain consciousness. His girls, he thought, and gently covered Jessie with an extra quilt.

Except for the first night when he found her shivering with cold and fear, he hadn't been truly afraid for her. But now he remembered that night in vivid detail, and the icy fear that seemed to surround her.

How could he have let this happen, when all he had ever wanted to do was protect her? Instead, he had coldly turned his back on her over a childish disagreement and allowed her to wander into the woods. In so doing, he had sent her into the ruthless arms of a deranged man.

He recalled all the callous, vulgar things he'd insinuated over the past few months. Each degrading thing he had spoken to her marched in his thoughts, bringing a sharp biting pain, so he punished himself by reliving everything.

His fingertips glided unchallenged over her body one last time rechecking for broken bones or damages he'd missed before. The bastard hadn't broken a bone, but he'd inflicted such pain, she'd feel it for a long time.

He cursed himself and the man who did this to her.

~ * ~

Alex didn't want to open her eyes. If she did, she knew she wouldn't be able to ignore the pain. At least when she slept, the agony was secondary. Sean had done this to her, and now she'd have to tell James. He'd have to let her go, if only to protect Jessie.

Sean wouldn't quit until he got what he wanted. She shuddered, pain surging inside her.

Then she heard James' voice, reassuring her, telling her he'd protect her, that nothing like this would happen again. He wouldn't let it. That he'd keep her safe.

Her eyes fluttered open. She couldn't help herself. The voice was compelling, and she had to tell him he couldn't have done anything to help. It was her fault, all her fault. She knew better, shouldn't have wandered away. When the haze cleared, she stared into James' deep blue eyes. For that one instant, she believed if any man could keep her safe, he could.

"Safe?" she echoed, sobbing with the wave of agony rolling within. With each tiny movement, intense pain shot through her. And she couldn't deny the soul wrenching torment.

"Yes, Alex. But first you have to get well. Drink this." His hand trembled as he held it to her mouth. A few drops of water spilled out and pooled on the blanket. He brushed it off.

"What is it?" she asked.

"Laudanum."

"I can't. It's opium." Alex pushed the glass away and more of the detested mixture spilled.

"Dammit, Alex, do you have to question everything?"

"James, it's addictive. Don't you have a Tylenol or something else? No, I don't suppose you do."

"Alex," he began patiently. "This is all I have. I won't force you to take the medicine and I won't give you much, just enough to help you sleep. I know what I'm doing. I won't let anything happen to you. Never again," he added quietly, "never again."

She did want the pain to go away, and she needed to sleep.

"You have to take this, Alex, please." He carefully lifted her head and forced her to drink.

"It will be all right," he promised. "Just go to sleep and next time you wake up, it won't hurt as much. Then if you don't want any more, I won't give it to you."

"You shouldn't have done that, James."

"I know but forgive me this time."

~ * ~

For several days Alex drifted in and out of consciousness. She didn't feel like crying anymore, only floating in that surrealistic world she'd recently discovered. That's all she wanted to do, float and soar and drift through the sky with the birds and the wind.

"You're awake, Alex, I'm so glad. Papa told me to give you this when you woke up," Jessie said. "You've been asleep for so long."

"What is it?"

"Don't know. Papa said that you were to drink this if you wanted to, nothing more."

"Oh, Jessie, I don't want any more medicine."

"It's only water." Kim appeared in the doorway. "I have the laudanum if you want, but that glass holds only water."

Kim helped her sit up, and she sipped the water. The pain had receded, and she thought the swelling around her eyes had probably gone down. She could see better, and the room didn't appear blurry. She saw Jessie sitting by her bed looking worried. Kim didn't look much better.

"Thank you, I'm fine now. It doesn't hurt much. You'll see in a few days I'll be as good as new," she said.

"James drove into town to find out what happened," Kim said.

"I could have told him. He should have asked me."

"You know who did this to you?" Kim asked surprised. She took the glass of water from Alex and set in on the nightstand.

"Yes."

Jessie's eyes were wide.

"I know who. What I want to know is why?" James stepped inside the room. Once again he was demanding and self-assured. Ruthless. The gentle man who had soothed her pain had vanished. His eyes were hard and unwavering. Yet now she understood how the war and events that had transpired had molded him.

The pounding in Alexandra's head started again, and she whimpered. "Because he wanted what you have."

"What I have?" Suddenly, it seemed as if he understood. He swore softly then nodded for Kim to leave and take Jessie with her. James sat on the edge of the bed and lightly touched her cheek.

"I didn't want to tell you. I'm sorry," Alex searched for the right words. The words to tell him why Sean had attacked her and how he wouldn't stop, dear God, he wouldn't stop.

"It's my fault. I should have been there."

And she heard the catch in his voice, the self-recrimination. "No. You can't watch me every minute." A wave of pain hit her.

"He won't get near you again."

"You can't be sure of that."

"I can because I'm going after him, and I'll find him."

"You don't even know who he is?"

"I'm fairly sure. I saw him before he turned tail and ran like the coward he is. This time I won't let him get away."

Revenge was new to her, and she didn't like the fear it put in her heart. She couldn't allow him to fight her battles. She had to find the vortex and a way back to her time before something happened to James or Jessie.

Alexandra watched James turn to leave. She reached out a hand to stop him, forgetting her bruised ribs. But she overlooked the pain. She only wanted to stop him. His eyes went right to her bandaged ribs and to the exposed breasts above as the sheet slipped away. She gasped and yanked the cover back when she saw where his eyes had traveled.

"Did that hurt?" His voice seemed to waver.

"Only a little." She shivered, but not from the cold, only from the touch of his eyes upon her.

Alex heard him sigh as he turned back to her and sat down on the bed again. "You have to learn to lie still," James said softly, gently berating her.

"Please don't go. I can't relax..."

"Yes, you can," he said firmly. "I'll give you a little more medicine and you'll sleep like a babe."

"I don't want anymore."

Tears had started to flow as she spoke, and it wasn't all from the pain. The fear of him leaving, and possibly not returning terrified her.

"Alexandra, you have to stop worrying." He lifted her chin with a finger and looked at her. "I can take care of myself."

Alex didn't hear him. She needed him to enfold her in his arms and keep her warm. The safety she always felt nestled next to him was all she wanted at that moment. He dropped his hand and pulled her close. Some small treacherous voice in her mind urged her to let him hold her, reminded her that after she was healed she'd have to leave him forever, and that she was entitled to feel the warmth and security of his embrace.

He paused for a moment and he heard her sigh and felt her head move against his chest. Then she looked at him.

Their eyes locked and, "The devil," he said just before he moved closer, just before he stopped himself then brushed her cheek with his fingertips.

He began gently, as if he were touching a porcelain doll. He traced her lips with his thumb.

She felt herself weaken and surrender to his protectiveness. Unable to stop the inevitable even if she'd wanted to, she turned her cheek into his hand. His caress lured and promised what she could only imagine.

When his hand brushed the hair from her face and he held the strands between the tips of his fingers, she longed for the fulfillment of that promise. His eyes teased a path down the smooth column of her throat to the edge of the sheets.

"Dear God, angel mine, I've waited a lifetime for you," he whispered. "You have to accept your fate and stay with me. Didn't you know, I was meant to be your guardian angel?"

His hand drifted to the top of the sheet and he tucked the coverings around her.

"James," she said when he froze.

"I want you, sweetheart, and that's a promise. But not now, not when you're hurt." He looked at her, saw the bruises and the stark white bandages.

"I'm fine."

She didn't recognize the words, didn't really know she'd said them but knew she would say them again. Soon, before she left forever, she wanted him to make love to her.

James gazed at her, and the look on his face was filled with pain.

"You're not fine. And I'm a fool." He rose to leave.

Frustrated by feelings she didn't understand but wanted to, she watched him walk out the door, knowing he was the only man for her, the only man she could ever love.

She didn't belong here, not in this time.

She had to leave to insure his safety and Jessie's.

Her moisture filled eyes gazed out the window, toward the vortex, toward her future. North.

Alex cried in silent misery.

Chapter Twelve

Moonlight drifted through the open window, brightening the room, drying the pain-filled tears on her cheeks and her pillow. A moment of beauty and peace permeated the silence and her thoughts. She'd lost all track of time since that day in the woods. Her pain had betrayed her and she'd slept, waking only long enough to sip water and soup. James had insisted on the laudanum, and she'd given in to his demands.

She touched her lips and cheeks. Her fingertips traced a line to her ribs. Ribs that still ached. The pain had dulled now and only occasionally throbbed. She felt better and thought with the morning she might make it out of bed. She'd tried once before but had met resistance in the form of swirling walls and a floor rising to meet her much too fast.

James had been there for her. Dimly, she remembered him lifting her in his arms before placing her on the softness of the bed.

Jessie had helped her, too, pulling the covers snugly around her and whispering encouragement. The little girl had been at her side every day, patiently talking to her when she woke and bringing her things. Jessie had told her James had hired men to guard the house; that she couldn't leave without protection. Alexandra brushed an errant lock of hair from her eyes.

Now it was the middle of the night, and James was at the foot of the bed, standing over her. He didn't move, just waited and watched.

He held a glass of water in his hands. Someone should tell him to get some sleep, she thought wryly. He spent his days looking for Sean Cassidy; his evenings sitting at her bedside.

He leaned closer, his voice soft and warm against her cheek. "Do you need anything?"

She blinked and focused on him. Sometimes just opening her eyes made her head throb, but it didn't this time and she relaxed. "Water, please." she added, "You don't have to stay here all the time."

"It makes me feel better," his tone soft and weary with exhaustion.

"You don't look like it." Alexandra said with an attempt at a smile.

He handed her the glass and let her drink. "We'll have a long talk in the morning. For now, though, I want you to rest. Tomorrow you can tell me what happened."

"I don't know if I can tell you anything that would help."

He didn't say anything, just studied her. "Go to sleep, Alex. I'll be in the chair if you need me."

~ * ~

He walked from the room minutes after she closed her eyes and knew she slept. Last night he'd sat awake in the chair across the room from her, watching her and fighting the crazy urge to go to her and hold her, to tell her he'd give her anything she wanted. Yet the image of Alexandra hurtling through space, living out her life in a world he couldn't grasp in his thoughts, where he couldn't see her or talk to her, left him feeling empty inside. He vacillated between frustration and possessiveness, to misery and indecision, cursing his inability to keep her from danger and away from Sean Cassidy. He was afraid he'd let his fury get out of control.

He should have never allowed her into his heart. He turned back for one more look at her. She lay so still.

And Lord, she was beautiful.

In that lay his greatest frustration. This woman. This strange, beguiling, tempting woman from a different time had finally succumbed willingly to her passion and he'd turned her away. Had to, because she had become important to him in ways he wasn't ready to acknowledge. He'd seen the pain in her eyes when he turned from her, and now he didn't know if she'd give him a second chance. He wasn't sure if he deserved one. He had placed restrictions on their relationship, restrictions he'd known she wasn't ready to keep. Yet he presented them almost in the form of an ultimatum.

He didn't know when he'd started to believe her, truly believe her. But if she did come from another time, he had no right to keep her here.

James turned again and walked down the steps into the parlor. He poured himself a drink and downed it at once then poured another. Thoughtfully, he walked to a chair by the window, sipping the wine and gazing into the distance.

He liked everything about Alexandra. She was beautiful, inside and out, and wouldn't even admit it to herself. Feisty and intelligent, he knew she could teach him things he'd never dreamed of. Yet she had an irritating habit of dropping opinions when they weren't asked for. He didn't like it when she called him a male chauvinist. The name sounded somehow degrading when she said the words. Weren't men supposed to be chauvinists?

Kim approached him. She'd matched his steps down the hall and now she stood beside him. "I can take the tray to the kitchen," she said quietly as he turned. James ran his hands through his hair in a nervous gesture.

Authority and male dominance had been thoroughly ingrained in James, so his voice left little room for argument, "I'll take care of it."

Kim didn't answer for a moment.

"My room is next to the kitchen. It won't be a breath of trouble," she said finally.

James laughed. She had set him in his place. Made him realize how he'd acted since he'd brought Alex home more dead than alive. "You win," he said. "I haven't been easy to get along with, have I?"

"No, you haven't, and it's about time you learned who the real boss around here is, Mr. James," she teased.

James wrapped an arm around Kim's shoulder and pointed to the kitchen. "Let's both get a cup of coffee."

"She's going to be fine."

"Enough," he cut her off. It didn't take a mind reader to figure out what Kim was going to say, and he wouldn't allow her to continue the argument. She'd said her piece days ago. He hadn't listened then and he wasn't about to listen now. Miss Alexandra wasn't going anywhere. He had to find a way to make Alex believe that.

They moved through the parlor and into the big kitchen. The room was spotless because of her efforts, and she poured them both a steaming cup. Finally, after sitting down, she let the words slip, "You have to do this for Miss Jessica."

"Do what?" he asked, instantly surprised and concerned.

"She needs a mother," she told him seriously. "She needs the comfort and the nurturing only a mother can give."

"She has you," he said obstinately. Kim's words hit a tender nerve.

"That isn't enough and you know it. I'm more a grandmother than anything, and you know that also."

James didn't know anything of the sort, and he didn't have any idea how this conversation had skyrocketed out-of-hand.

"I'm not going to marry," he said through gritted teeth then sipped the hot coffee. "You're crazy as a loon, Kim, you have no idea."

"You're wrong, Mr. James," she said and lowered her head to study the rim of the coffee cup. Her bony finger traced the outline of the handle, and as she thought, he watched the lines in her aged face deepen. Her hand trembled a moment then faltered. Huge all knowing eyes suddenly stared back at him. "Every little girl needs—"

"Jessica doesn't need a mother. She has me," he cut in.

"She loves you but it's not enough." Her chin tilted and the gesture reminded him of Alex.

"It is."

Kim released a quiet sigh and rose from the table. "I hoped you would come to realize Miss Jessica loves Alexandra." With those words hovering in the silence, Kim left.

James stood abruptly and strode outside, slamming the door behind him. And he wondered at everything that had changed in his life when he found Alex.

The coffee cups sat alone on the table, half full.

~ * ~

Two weeks had passed and she finally felt whole again. Sometime soon she would have to talk to James. Until he understood she belonged only to herself, she could never allow him to make love to her. Until he trusted her, she could never allow him to touch her heart. Her fingers traced her lips, remembering with vivid detail their last kiss. She'd never forget the gentle brush of his mouth against hers. And she wanted to relive the moment. But she was afraid of it and the power of the man, afraid of losing herself to him, afraid she already had.

They weren't meant to be together. He didn't want to marry, only possess; she couldn't accept that. He'd said nothing of love or commitment.

Alexandra closed her eyes and lay back on the bed. Sunlight floated dreamily through the window, and she basked in the warm April heat. It was absurd to think of James as anyone she might have a future with. *We're as different as night and day. We'd never get along. Brought up in two different worlds, with very different philosophies; we'd never understand each other.*

"No." She turned herself face down on the bed.

I don't have a future here. And he'd absolutely refused to take her into the hills again. He'd said the very idea was too dangerous. If she stepped into the vortex and it took over, she could end up just about anywhere, but she could see no choice.

She rolled over and counted the tiny lines on the ceiling. Thirty, thirty-one...

An old bullfrog croaked beneath the window and she could hear the calling of the birds, "Chick a dee, dee, dee."

Alex rolled onto her back, pulled a pillow to her stomach and pounded it a couple of times in frustration. The motion set off a ripple of pain.

~ * ~

James showed up at the door shortly after Jessie went to bed. Two of the men he'd hired to keep an eye on the house followed him into the room with an old army cot. He had several pillows in one hand and two quilts slung over his shoulder. He pointed to a spot next to his bed. The men set the cot down then left.

She watched wide-eyed, felt a moment of panic, "James?"

"Don't say a thing," were his only words as he made the bed. "I'm not sleeping in the other room again, and neither are you."

Her eyes flew open. "But? I don't understand." She tried for the composure she knew wasn't there. She could see the tension in his movements, and when he looked at her, she could feel the fire in his eyes.

He kept making the bed, not once glancing her way; the sheets then a quilt and another one. The pillow followed and he didn't say a word, just kept moving. "I should have done this from the start."

"Are you going to tell me what you're talking about?"

He finished making the cot, not touching her but leaning close. "It's the only way to keep the demons at bay."

He still hadn't touched her. But he leaned closer still, suddenly his lips seared like a brand upon her cheek. After he pulled back, "Sean Cassidy has asked about you, and he has been informed that you are mine," he told her huskily. "I intend to make that statement true."

Alex blinked a few times before lowering her lashes. But James still stood in front of her when she opened them a few seconds later. He still looked down at her.

"Then you lied to me," she finally said after a long moment of silence. "You told me nothing would happen between us until I promised to stay. I haven't promised anything yet."

"I suppose you're right," he said and leaned casually against the bedpost. "I haven't changed my mind about the promise. Your safety is paramount. However, appearances mean everything, and I intend to sleep with you in this room," he said, and his tone didn't encourage argument. "Once upon a time I helped you look for the vortex. Of course we did not find it. And once I made a solemn vow to myself that I'd keep you safe. This is the only way I can think of to insure it. But if you want to go, if you have the will to leave, do it now."

"James," she whispered and struggled to sit up. Out of sheer perversity, she moved her legs to the side of the bed and stood. But she'd acted too quickly. Her head spun and her knees quivered. She sank to the floor. James was beside her instantly. His arms wound around her and he placed her on the bed.

"Now that we have that settled, this is where you belong, Alex, with me," he replied in a husky drawl. "I'm doing this to protect you, not humiliate you."

"But I..."

His lips twitched. "As long as we understand each other. Until you're healed, I want to be close to you, very close. And Alex, I'm tired of sleeping in the chair." He looked pointedly to the offending piece of furniture. "It's not like I'm crawling into the same bed with you."

She blushed. Since the beating, he'd spent every night with her. He moved the cot into the room for comfort. But, she amended, he only meant to have the cot for a short time. She turned a deeper shade of red. "There will be more talk, more rumors."

"Good. Sean's still out there. He knows I'm looking for him. If I catch him, his life isn't worth the bullet I'll put through his heart. The only person who can identify him lies in my bed. Now use your head Alex. Gossip doesn't mean a damn when a person's life is on the line. If you weren't still in pain, I'd be in that bed with you, so don't mention gossip again. I know you want me. Don't think to deny it."

Acceptance turned to anticipation as she watched him slip his boots off and settle himself on the cot as if testing it. "I haven't denied anything," she said softly. But her hands fisted in the bed covers as she fought her wavering emotions.

Without a single glance her way, he sat up and continued undressing. His hands worked the buttons on his shirt, and she watched, fascinated. Her gaze riveted on his fingers as they pulled the shirttails from his pants. She stared as he shrugged out of the shirt, folded it and neatly placed it at the foot of the bed. When his hands moved to the waistband of his pants, she turned away.

"You're taking this too hard," he said in an agreeable tone. "I don't hog the covers. My feet are never cold and I don't snore. You'll get used to me."

~ * ~

"Ready to go, angel girl?" James strode quickly through his bedchamber.

She stood on shaky legs. Before she could stop herself, she stifled a whimper and leaned against the bedpost just before James swept her into his arms. "Yes," she quivered. "But you don't have to carry me. As soon as my head adjusts to the movement, I'll be fine."

He opened his mouth as if he meant to say something but stopped. She felt so light, so fragile. "I like you in my arms."

"Where are we going?" she asked curiously then hastily looked toward the door.

"A favorite place of mine," he told her softly. "I've planned this outing for several days. The weather's perfect. The sun's out in all its glory, and I've already been to the spot and spread a blanket under a large oak tree. Jessie helped me and so did Kim. We put together a picnic lunch, embellished with hand picked wild flowers and a bottle of wine.

"And," he added, "I want you well rested. So I'm going to indulge both of us. I'm going to carry you all the way there."

"Oh," she murmured. Lowering her lashes, she watched his expression and his profile.

Alex had spent the last few weeks in excited anticipation, waiting for James to fulfill his promise. He would make love to her, or so he'd vowed. He had given her time to adjust to the idea, to heal from her wounds. She loved him, perhaps she'd loved him from the first moment she saw him.

James carried her down the steps and through the house. When the door fell shut behind them, the warm afternoon sunshine welcomed them. "Are you tired?"

"I'm fine," She rested her head against his shoulder. She laughed. "I should ask you that question. Really, you can put me down anytime."

"I intend to take absolute advantage of your weakness while I still can." Eventually he stopped, setting her beneath a tree, a smile on his lips.

He carried her as if she couldn't walk and handled her tenderly. His assumed role as protector of the innocent he took seriously. And the title she'd dubbed him with fit perfectly.

She watched him move about. He covered her with a light quilt, smoothing the fabric and tucking it around her. His tenderness and concern made her grin, made her forget the terror and fear that had consumed her for so many days. James presented her with the bouquet. "Hand picked," he said softly. "Miss Jessica scoured the countryside for the right colors. It's her contribution to the picnic."

She touched the flowers, "What's going to happen? I think Sean wants me dead and..." Her voice trailed off.

"I won't let him hurt you." James stared at her for a long time then finally sat down beside her. The silence grew around them, and she nervously looked for something to do with her hands.

His knuckles swept softly over her cheek and down her neck. With his touch, all thoughts of Sean Cassidy vanished from her mind. Alexandra knew she could deny James nothing.

With every passing moment, her need for him grew. The simple touches, the looks, and even the way his mouth curved made her long for him.

All she could think about, wonder about was James Lawrence, captain, doctor, miner and farmer. She wanted to know him better. A book, a romantic movie, none could hold a candle to the way he made her feel.

He frustrated her and confused her. Sometimes his passion and concern for her frightened her. She tensed with anticipation and longing when he entered a room. At times she wanted to pounce on him. Any of her friends would have told her to do it, encouraged her to take the initiative, but she'd never been like that. Her first attempt had failed miserably. Now she knew it wouldn't do to start something she didn't know how to finish.

Because of her new feelings, James made her uneasy when he stared and his gaze met hers. He had a way of seeing beyond as if he could read her mind.

"Sean's different somehow," she said.

"He meant to kill you," James spoke with a certain fierceness, but she thought she knew why.

"I know and if you hadn't been there, I'm sure he would have." Her tone of voice was wary, and she didn't want to pursue this any longer. She wet her lips and let her vision move back and forth across the hills.

"He won't quit, will he?"

"I, no, probably not," she said.

"He has to be found, you know." He looked to the hills. "Do you have any ideas?"

"Women; he has to have them, needs them, craves them." Alex spoke quickly and her voice faded to a breath. "He's always had more women than he could choose from. They followed him. They clung to him. That's why this is all so strange. We were friends once. At least I thought we were."

"The Eldorado. He must be at the saloon. Where else?" James fists clenched and he swore softly. "Someone there will know where to find him."

"Yes." She touched his arm. "When you go, promise you'll be careful."

"Of course."

"James, please, he's dangerous. If you won't think of yourself, you have to think of Jessie."

"I have to stop him."

"I know. It's just that..." she slowly exhaled and in time regained her composure. "He thinks I stole from him."

"Did you?"

"No, not intentionally, but there was a rumor." A lumped formed in her throat. "It all happened a long time ago. Well, not exactly a long time. James, this is impossible."

"Tell me what happened."

"Even though it occurred almost twenty years before, Mom didn't want the rumors to resurface. Sean's father wasn't anything like Sean. His father believed in truth and honesty, a model any son could be proud of. My mother couldn't see the truth behind Sean's debonair smile and handsome good looks. Sean believes the money I received just before both our fathers died is rightfully his." She fought to hold back the longing in her voice when she spoke of home, fought also to hold back the tears when she began again. "James, you know, I may not have a choice. I didn't decide to come here. It just happened. And I don't belong here. My future is over a hundred years away."

"No, it's not. Your future is here. I'm convinced you were sent here, perhaps by a higher power."

Her voice was paper-thin and it quavered as she spoke. "Have you listened to anything I've said? What is it you think I want out of life?"

"Everything." There was a strange catch to his voice. Alex watched him look toward the horizon, watched his expression harden then turn cold, and the deep breath he expelled tore at her soul.

James looked at her as if he was carefully considering her question, as if he realized how much depended on his answer. Now he touched her cheek, tracing the arc with his forefinger and tucking a strand of hair behind her ear. "I think you want to understand and categorize what has happened to you and deny how you feel about me. Yet, at the same time, you're feeling vulnerable and alone. The worst thing you can imagine is to lose the power to decide your fate or to have someone else tell you what to do. This entire scenario makes you feel as if you've fallen into a deep dark pit you can't find your way out of. But, Alex, is it really so dark or so deep? Can't you see the sunshine around you and the people who need you? Jessie needs you. I need you."

Alex didn't respond for a moment. She couldn't. A hard knot at the back of her throat prevented her from saying anything. It felt as if James had reached into her mind and pulled out the essence that formed her. But he spoke of need not love. It wasn't enough. If she were to stay here, she had to have more than empty promises.

"How can you be so sure? I..."

Her voice was both curious and intrigued. James hands rested on her shoulders and now he moved them down her arms.

"We're the antithesis of each other," he said. "I'm thinking we're very different."

She glanced up at him, her eyes filmed with unshed tears, "I suspect you're right," she continued. "I haven't looked at the whole picture. I kept dwelling on what you were taking away from me instead of concentrating on all you were doing for me. All my life I wanted to succeed and prided myself in the fact I could take care of myself. I didn't need a man, I told myself. Yet, when I discovered that I did in truth need you, I couldn't admit it."

Raising her hand, James kissed her lightly on the heart of her palm. "You're a very strong lady. I don't know anyone else who could have endured what you have. In spite of all the stubborn pride you have, I don't believe you'd have risked your life to prove anything."

It was true. "But what if you don't find Sean Cassidy?"

His hands instantly fell away. "No matter what happens, we have to take one day at a time. Tell me." His serious tone was at odds with the twinkle in his eye. "What do you think I want out of life?"

She was grinning mischievously as she threaded her fingers through his. "I think, sometimes you don't know how to let your hair down," her lips twitched and she laughed when she saw the curious expression on his face. "You're too serious. Most of the time you are opinionated and sexist, but then you say or do something that gives me reason to think you're really not that way. You live in a provincial little world and need to explore new ideas. Women can think for themselves. Everything isn't painted black and white. There always subtle shades of gray, you know."

"Are you through?" He appeared stunned but after a moment a smile began to spread across his face.

"It's interesting though, you don't seem to care what others think."

"I apologize, Alex, but it's the way of things. I did what I thought best."

"You don't have to apologize. I think it's admirable that you don't care."

"Then you don't mind if I make decisions for you?"

Alexandra searched his face, studying the lines of his slightly furrowed brow, the shape of his solemn mouth. His blue, bordering on mauve, eyes responded to her perusal by darkening, but this was one time she thought she understood what he was thinking. She squeezed his hand gently. "No, it doesn't have to be that way. I deserve at least a minuscule say in what's best for me."

"Do you now? But I'm just learning. Give me time to adjust to the modern woman. You can't expect to catapult all my emotions and thoughts through time instantly. I've had a lifetime to develop the way I think. I can't change it because you snap your fingers." He finished on a self-mocking note. Bending over, he kissed her on the nose then leaned back and grinned at her. "Though until a moment ago, I didn't realize I'd acted so high-handed."

Alexandra was undaunted. "You're not, at least not all the time. I think you can be protective to a fault and patient beyond endurance. When dealing with Jessie, you know all the right things to say. Yet, sometimes you don't listen very well at all. That's both aggravating and confusing." With uncomplicated forthrightness, Alexandra added, "It's also challenging." She watched as his eyes darkened once more. He was rubbing his thumb across her knuckles, the gesture more absentminded than planned. "With everything in my life so complicated, perhaps none of this matters at all. I feel like a helpless pawn, unable to change anything or act upon that which has already happened. Today, this moment, I can accept. And this helplessness is not your doing."

"The future?" The two words were almost said against his will.

"I don't know what that is anymore." Alexandra thought of her life more than one hundred years in the future. Ashland. Then Lithia Park with its endless green grass. The swans and the ducks she'd gone to see since she was a child. The Shakespearean Festival where she had enjoyed the plays. Medford with its Friday night football games and roaring fans.

The valley was her home, all of it, from Jacksonville to Ashland and the Applegate. She was still here, or there, but it had changed so very much.

Home was too far away to reach for; even the stars seemed closer, almost as if they were within her grasp.

His fingers had been stroking her arms. When she fell silent, he paused. "You have to figure that out or you'll never be happy. You have to decide exactly where your future lies."

"I know," she said softly. "But sometimes I feel as if I'm caught in a dream. Perhaps I'll wake up and discover none of this happened."

"Do you want me to be just a figment of your imagination?"

"It would make the rest so much easier." Alexandra didn't like the darkening expression on James' face when she said that. If she could call back the words, she would.

"Why do I have the feeling you're running away?"

Alex flushed and turned her head at his discerning question. He didn't sound at all pleased, "You can't be serious."

He merely grunted. "Why not?"

That was a good question. And she didn't have an answer. Perhaps she was running away.

James didn't fill the silence that followed immediately. "I don't want to think you're running from me."

"Neither do I."

James cocked an eyebrow. "I like that, angel eyes. What are you running from?"

"Myself?"

"Oh? I have a solution for that," he smiled wickedly.

She turned away from him, not daring to look closer. She didn't know what to do and practically fainted in relief when she heard the giggle from above and saw Jessica climb down the ladder of her tree house.

"She's not really running, Papa," Jessie said as Alex stopped suddenly to help Jessie down from the last rung. "She's in love."

"Why, Jessie Lawrence, I should wash your mouth with—"

"What?" James interrupted.

"Nothing," they chorused in unison.

He frowned before turning his attention on both girls. "I'll get to the bottom of this."

Chapter Thirteen

James moved up to the bar and ordered whiskey. A long mirror above the bottles and glasses gave him a clear view as he rested both elbows on the counter. The saloon reverberated with noise. Bawdy raucous laughter spilled out the swinging door into the street. With succinct and abbreviated movements, James turned toward Charles who leaned on one arm against the counter, lazily surveying the same scene as James. Both men remained silent.

"Alexandra?" A lecherous spark appeared in Charles' eye.

"Leave it, Charles. It's not your funeral nor am I a man to tell tales."

"Except Belinda is prone to telling tales, and I've heard more than I can ever recall."

Charles grinned then laughed outright. With a dramatic nonchalance, he poured himself another shot. As he watched the amber liquid fill his glass, he concentrated on James. After he turned to look over the smoky room once again, he raised his glass in a mocking salute. The whiskey gleamed brightly before Charles downed it in one swift gulp, his Adam's apple bobbing up and down.

For a Tuesday night more noise than usual echoed around the saloon, but it wasn't an average Tuesday night, and James had gone out of his way to seek a diversion from his thoughts. Smoke hung heavy in the room, and the barroom sounded loud and obnoxious. The tinny and slightly out of tune piano pounded on continuously. He'd rather have stayed at home and talked with Alexandra.

Impatient with himself, James drummed his fingers on the wooden bar as he felt an all too familiar tightening of his body. He straightened and rolling his shoulders, the tension slowly eased from his muscles. Then he resumed his position against the bar, his back to the mirror for a brief moment before he faced it again.

That was all it took, a gentle reminder, a vision in his mind and he'd lose control of his body. Alexandra had subtly eased herself into his life, threatening his plans for the future, toying with his emotions.

"The devil," he whispered fiercely then thrust her from his mind. Despite his preoccupation with Alexandra, he forced his attention back to the people in the crowded saloon. Where was Sean Cassidy? He wanted him, had waited for him patiently. Where the devil was he?

"Have you found Cassidy yet? Heard tell he's bragging about how he had your lady." Charles' prying question then his innocuous statement hit a tender nerve. James' fingers flexed around his glass.

James masked his fury well, his expression stoic, but he never removed his gaze from the opulent mirror hanging in front of him. "No, but then I've heard rumors that he visits one of the girls here at the Eldorado. I've also heard he left, has a shack somewhere in the foothills. And Charles, you shouldn't believe everything you hear."

"If he's smart, he'll—"

"If..." James let the word slowly trail off. "If he's smart, he'll skedaddle up the hills to Sardine Creek and disappear forever. I know for a fact that it's possible."

With an air of indifference, James perused each man in the saloon. His gaze hesitated fleetingly then moved on as he surveyed the room.

Noise from a high stakes poker game in the back snagged his attention for a brief moment. Several other tables had games in progress. A huge strike on the Applegate two days ago had renewed the gold fever in town. Any time a man brought in a large nugget there was cause to celebrate.

And celebrate they did, all night long.

James didn't feel like celebrating. He felt like making love to Alex. But he wasn't going to do that. At least not until he had a few things settled. One of those things was Sean Cassidy. "How is she?"

James looked up slowly, "She'll live. What's your interest in all this?" He turned his penetrating gaze on Charles. His eyes narrowed threateningly, his voice low and hard.

At the mention of Alexandra, James' muscles tensed once more and his heart thundered in his chest. A saloon girl bumped his arm as she passed by to pick up more drinks. Her long red hair caught his eye, and for a moment his breath caught in the back of his throat. But she didn't hold a candle to Alex, didn't even come close. He looked at the mirror again.

"Just curious," Charles shrugged his shoulders, proceeding to down his drink. If Charles noticed his nervousness, he gave no indication. Charles motioned to the bartender for another drink then exhaled softly. "Wouldn't like to see anything happen to her. She's a pretty little thing."

"Meddle in someone else's business for a change. I've had it with everyone's less than honest concern."

More whiskey burned a path down James' throat. He watched the customers behind him, hoping he could push thoughts of Alexandra from his mind and concentrate on finding Sean Cassidy. But it didn't work. No thoughts could entice his imagination the way Alex did, and no lady in this room had eyes the color of a summer sky. Quickly, he slammed his half-filled whiskey glass on the bar. The liquid sloshed over the sides and slowly spread across the counter.

"So, she's not in your bed yet?" Charles smug question threatened to send James' already frayed nerves out of control.

"Leave it alone, Charles. Alex is a lady." James' hand tightened around his glass.

"And you'd spread that gossip. Right. I'll tell you something, James. Ladies don't sleep around. If Alexandra is a lady, I'll eat my hat."

"Start eating."

Charles choked on his whiskey.

After spending weeks sleeping so close but not with Alexandra, James wouldn't mind taking all his latent frustrations out on Charles or anyone else who wandered into his path. No, he wouldn't mind at all, he'd revel in it.

"Alexandra's a lady from the top of her head to the tips of her toes," James said softly, almost reverently. He fell silent and leaned back against the bar. The whiskey had begun its work, pulling the agony and the fear, the pain and desire slowly from him. He shut his eyes but he could not shut his heart or his mind from the sweet reminders Miss Alexandra tempted him with, nor could he forget the subtle fragrance that was hers alone. He envisioned the velvet smoothness of her skin beneath his caress, beneath his lips, and he wanted her.

More than anything he wanted to go home and make love to her. His promises be damned. He didn't want to act the gentleman, nor did he want to wait until he had Sean Cassidy in jail and Alexandra's promise to stay with him. Both factors were too elusive.

But he had promised her; Sean Cassidy had left her terrified, and so he meant for her to learn she had nothing to fear. She wasn't fair game. He understood that. Until now he had managed to convince himself the path he followed had the markings of self-sacrifice and righteousness. But during the last few weeks, he had realized she had her own expectations and a moral code above reproach. It surpassed anything he had ever experienced or learned from his genteel southern ancestors. He stared back at the mirror, trying to forget his first erroneous misconceptions.

He could remember his words clearly. He'd understood perfectly, and he knew she deserved his trust and his undying respect. He could trust her now but there were other things to consider and hence the dilemma. Until he knew in his heart what he wanted, it didn't seem fair to push her into a relationship he didn't understand himself.

He could see her vividly.

Vulnerable and innocent, she called out each time she needed him, but he was always too late. Always too proud and stubborn, Alexandra did not know how to give up. No, she did not surrender, not even when the odds stacked up against her.

If he had an ounce of sense, he'd remain in town tonight. But he was compelled to go home. Bound by his need to protect Alexandra.

All she'd asked for was a way to return to her time. To her mother. Her friends. That wasn't much to request. She wanted her life back.

But he couldn't give that to her. He enjoyed watching her, talking with her, yet even though he denied it, she scared the hell out of him. She wanted more than he could give her. Perhaps she didn't belong in this century, but he intended to keep her here. He had to find a way to convince her to stay. So far he'd failed miserably. It was too dangerous to go through the vortex. That wasn't the reason he wanted her to stay though, and because of that, he didn't like himself very much.

He was a scoundrel. She was a lady.

He hadn't thought so at first because of the circumstance he had found her in, but now that he understood her, knew all about her and where she'd come from, he couldn't deny her background. If he intended to remedy the situation he'd callously created, he'd have to marry her.

It was all so simple. Marriage...

With caution and a great deal of wonder, with incredible calculation and determination, James began to plan, while all thoughts of his cold bachelor's existence drifted into oblivion.

Swiftly downing his drink, he mulled over the problems he would encounter. The decision felt good, but he couldn't guess how Alexandra would respond.

He wanted her, all of her. He wanted her heart and soul. He needed her more with each passing day, and he found it hard to continue the charade he had created for his own protection. With infinite patience and his best manners, perhaps he could tear down the walls that kept them apart.

Impenetrable walls.

Walls surrounded both of them. It wasn't surprising the lure of the future beckoned her. Warm running showers and electricity competed against drafty old houses. A quick car ride into town easily overshadowed a terrifying ride on the back of Matilda or a teeth-rattling ride in an old cart. He wanted to convince her she belonged here with him. He wanted to show her she had nothing to fear, that he trusted and believed in her. James moved from the bar, determined to go home and set things right.

"Fire!"

Instantly, men and women panicked, tables turned over, whiskey spilled and chaos erupted. People dashed between the tables, tripping over each other to race outside. Chips and cards scattered on the floor. Flames, blazing orange and blood red threatened the sky and spread like wildfire. Black, noxious smoke billowed between the buildings and engulfed the air. It crackled and thundered as the timbers of the Eldorado creaked once and fell. Fire raged skyward.

Outside, the heat of it all singed his skin. Then the hiss and fall of timbers shattered the night.

Smoke so dense only a small amount of light flitted through the haze. Vague silhouetted figures wove around each other. James coughed and brought his bandanna to his nose. The scalding air seared his lungs.

Men dashed back and forth in a feeble attempt to bring the inferno under control. Water sizzled as it hit the flames. Bucket after bucket unloaded its cargo. Old wood welcomed its fingers and ignited instantaneously.

~ * ~

With a fine sheen of tears clouding her eyes, Alex watched James ride General Lee down the road toward town. Over the past few weeks and despite her confusion and fears, she'd shared private intimate parts of her life, events she'd never shared with anyone else.

The knowledge he'd walked out the door with every intention of locating Sean and bringing him to justice left her terrified.

It was so dangerous for him to seek Sean out. Sean had changed. He had nothing to lose and oh, so much to gain. He was nothing like the football hero he used to be. But that time seemed an eternity ago.

She swirled the dishwater around the sink, pretending the work would relieve some of the horrible fears that came to mind when she thought of James pursuing Sean.

"Well then, Alexandra McMurdie, help him," she said pointedly as if it would give her the edge she needed. "If you're afraid for his safety, you should help."

Those few words gave her strength and courage. The fear and terror faded and was replaced with a growing sense of power and excitement. Just as James disappeared along the horizon, Alexandra decided to follow him, rushing down the kitchen steps and outside. Jessica and Kim would get along fine without her. He wasn't going to like this. She could almost hear his words, feel his anger. But it didn't matter. This was her fight too, and she didn't intend to have James sacrifice himself.

When Alex entered the barn, Matilda eyed her skeptically then looked heavenward as if searching for some tangible help. A sugar cube in Alex's pocket rolled through her fingers, leaving tiny grains behind. The treat was meant to placate the horse, and it always worked.

"Oh, where is Jessie?"

Upstairs in her room and undoubtedly asleep, she knew, and she didn't want Jessie's help, not really. She'd been so determined to do this on her own. It was a symbol, a symbol of her new perspective on life and her determination to live in this new century. Undaunted in the face of great anxiety, Alex proceeded on her own.

As she approached Jacksonville, an unnatural eerie glow tinged the horizon. The smell of burned wood permeated the night air. A few minutes later she watched flames shoot into the sky, heard the crash of timbers as a roof collapsed inward. With a horrible feeling of dread, she urged Matilda forward. Her heart caught in her throat when she saw an old lady leaning out the window of a burning building. Sounds of fear and death penetrated the night. A harsh wind, spurred by the heat of the fire rushed, through the town. It whistled around timber skeletons, fanning the flames ever higher.

The elderly lady screamed hysterically. Heat penetrated Alex's clothes, yet, she couldn't leave the lady to the mercy of the fire. Alexandra searched for help. No one, not one person caught her eye as the town's people raced frantically with buckets of water. Another glance at the burning building terrified her, yet she knew something had to be done now. Impulsively, she dismounted and dashed inside. Matilda was left to graze beneath an oak tree.

"*James! Dear Lord, I wish James could hear me. I need you,*" she cried out, but her words were in her mind. Through all the noise and confusion, her silent call for help was destined to vanish.

Just as she stumbled from the inferno with the old lady on her arm, tiny embers caught on the hem of her dress. Flames curled around her ankles, snaking their way slowly upward.

"James," she cried out again, searching for him and beating at the fire. A shadow of a man darted from the back of the saloon and disappeared into the blackness. "Sean," she breathed, then frantically turned her attention back to her smoldering skirt.

Alexandra heard him first then watched transfixed. A fraction in time, a second, that was all. Fanned by the winds of the fire, his words bolted through the night.

"Alexandra!"

Alexandra stood petrified with fear, watching the flames eat at the hem of her dress. James struggled through the wild chaos of people separating them. Only a heartbeat later, he tackled her and they rolled along the ground together. Smoldering material singed her flesh as he beat at the flames until the fire was extinguished.

She watched James. His fearless blue eyes looked hard and they held a hint of fear and perhaps fury. "You scared—you scared the hell out of me," he said suddenly, smoothing the tangled web of hair from her eyes.

"What happened to her?" someone asked.

She tried to speak then coughed. Her throat was raw and sore from the smoke. His weight covered her, pressing her into the wet mud beneath them. She smelled the damp earth and the cold seeped through the thin layer of clothes she wore. But she didn't care. James hands stroked soothingly along her arms then up and down her spine as he pulled her to a sitting position. Tears lined the back of her aching throat and she clung to him.

"It's all right, Alex. You're fine now. It's over. Don't worry and don't try to talk. The devil, but I'm never going to let you out of my sight again."

Now that the fire was under control, many of the town's people gathered around her curiously.

"Go on now," James told them. "She's fine."

Slowly, one by one, they left to attend to other business.

I don't want to talk. All I want is to close my eyes and forget the flames and the billowing noxious black smoke. His gentle kisses traced her forehead then she felt his lips brush hers and she heard his voice.

"What are you doing here?" James asked.

The sound of his voice made her tremble.

"When I saw you in flames, I was so afraid."

Drawing a shattered breath, she tried to tell him she came to help him find Sean. *I need his soothing touch and the comfort of his arms. I need him desperately.*

196

"No, don't answer that. I don't think I want to know."

His voice sounded different. There was an edge to it, a slight hardness that caught her attention. She couldn't imagine him frightened.

Her gaze met his once again, and she looked at him in wonder. His eyes were moist with unshed tears. Neither spoke.

With the silence came the realization he cared for her, truly cared for her. And she wanted to tell him she'd stay.

Despite her efforts, no sound came from her throat.

His fingers curled possessively around her shoulders and he pulled her up until she sat across his lap. The blaze in his eyes spoke of his fury and his fear. But that gave her comfort too and she leaned against him despite everything.

"Are you hurt anywhere?" His hands were touching her, everywhere, examining her methodically, expertly.

He shouldn't fear. She was safe. With gentle concern, his knuckles brushed her cheek, and with unwavering tenderness, he traced the line of soot running along the bridge of her nose down to her chin.

In response she could only nod, her throat so raw she wanted water. "Fine," she wheezed. "You came just in time. My super hero." The strange light radiating from his eyes was for her. Alex struggled uselessly to understand if it was caused by a tender concern for her or raw anger at what she'd so impulsively done. Then the expression was unmistakable. The fury emanating from his gaze was so strong she trembled beneath its intensity. His complete change made Alexandra's heart squeeze in a terrible painful way.

"You should be home now. Safe. In bed," he gently berated her. "Can't you learn to stay where I leave you? No, don't answer that either. I know it hurts. Hush. As soon as I can, I'm taking you home. The fire is mostly out. The saloon's demolished as well as some other buildings, but we managed to save many of the structures. And I don't want you talking for the next twenty-four hours." James lifted her from the ground in one swift motion. His purposeful strides carried them to a grassy spot where he finally set her down.

"Sean ran out the back. Escaped again. All the commotion..." Her hoarse whisper tore a ragged gap in the stillness around them.

"Sean?"

"Yes."

"He won't get away," he said. It sounded like such an empty promise to her. A assurance he had no means to keep. He had tried so hard to find him, and each time he'd failed.

She wanted to tell him it was all right.

"I mean it," he nodded, and she knew he would have gone after Sean if it hadn't been for her.

Terrified of the inevitable encounter between James and Sean, she wanted to keep James from going after Sean, but she knew how impossible that was. James wouldn't stop until he caught Sean Cassidy, until he knew Sean could no longer threaten her.

"The man's a damn ghost," he muttered.

It hurt to speak but she had to know. "Is the old lady? Is she..."

"Margaret? She's fine. She's better than you. Does that please you? If I hadn't heard you scream my name, why then the fire would probably have killed you."

"I didn't call for you. You must have imagined it," she whispered to him.

"I heard you distinctly." He punctuated his soft drawl by raising an eyebrow.

Unable to control her precarious emotions, "I didn't call you," she whispered.

"You scared me to death."

"I didn't mean to," she said softly. "But I couldn't leave her there," she rasped out. "I'm sorry."

He bent close to hear. "What would you have done if I hadn't come along?"

"I...I don't know."

"Ah, hell," He ran his long fingers though his hair. "It doesn't matter now. Just be quiet and I'll get you home."

"I can get myself home, thank you. You don't have to worry about me. You can go after Sean, you know." Smudged with black smoke from the fire and charred wood, the dress ruined beyond repair, she hadn't decided if she wanted to walk all the way home or ride the horse. She wanted a hot bath, a warm bed, and really didn't want to argue with him.

"Let me be the judge of that," he told her. "Cassidy can wait. You can't."

"I'll ride Matilda." Her voice was raspy and with each softly spoken word it seemed to hurt more.

"That's very interesting. Where is the old horse?"

"Right over..." She looked around, searching for Matilda. But she didn't see the horse. Matilda had disappeared, vanished in the hazy smoke filled night. The horse had deserted her for greener pastures. The fire must have frightened the poor old beast, and she hadn't even noticed.

"The horse is the smart one here. She's probably at home, safe in the barn, munching on her feed," he grinned.

Yes, she thought, the horse was more intelligent than the two of them put together.

"I'm going for my horse now, and I don't want you to say another word."

"All right," she said in a hoarse whisper, defying his order. After a slight hesitation, she rose on trembling legs and headed out of town.

"Stubborn woman," he grinned.

It didn't surprise her when she heard the pounding hooves. It didn't even surprise her when he swept her onto the horse without stopping.

"Where did you learn how to do that?"

He took a deep breath, his eyes brilliant with anger yet an underlying tenderness vanquished the other emotion. "A Sioux chieftain taught me."

Despite the questions, his answers brought to mind she said nothing more. She didn't want to chance breaking the fragile peace that existed at the moment.

It didn't take them long to ride home. Matilda stood at the stable door leaning placidly against it as if it was holding her up. General Lee nickered a welcome.

"Go on," James told her. "I'll join you as soon as I see to the horses."

Chapter Fourteen

By the time Alexandra finished her bath, she knew James had retired for the night. She'd heard him enter her old room, heard Kim's lilting Chinese while she readied James' bath. Even then she'd half-expected he might not come see her. Too much lay between them now. In her haste to help with Sean, she'd single handedly got in his way. It was long past time to apologize for her behavior. After all, she owed him so much, she'd never be able to repay him. But as things stood now, he fully intended to ignore her.

She wasn't about to let that happen.

Before she could change her mind, she rose from the bed, James' bed, and walked to the other room. She stood at the entrance for a minute, staring at the closed door, wondering what she was going to tell him. She took one last breath for courage before turning the knob and stepping through the now open door into the bedroom. Behind her, the door closed slowly, and the soft click that followed sounded ominous in the quiet stillness.

She raked her hair off her forehead then gave it an impatient shake. The darkness settled around her, encompassing her thoughts, tearing at her self-concept. She'd never done anything remotely this provocative before. Here she was trying to seduce this man who'd saved her life more than once. Her heart gave a little lurch and she almost fled. Yet, she didn't.

The old grandfather clock in the hallway chimed. Alex walked to the window, watching the fog gather on the glass where her breath touched it. As if it could warm her heart and chase the loneliness away, she picked up a blanket off the cedar chest and wrapped it around herself. Alexandra drew a shaky breath then turned to gaze at the man on the bed.

He tempted her so.

Her gaze traveled the length of him, lingering on the fine strong lines chiseled in his face, his broad shoulders. He was bare to the waist. Entranced and unable to tear herself away, she watched the heavy rise and fall of his chest, listening to the husky rasp of his breathing.

Alexandra swallowed hard and tried to ignore the little tug at her heart when she watched him. Feeling an impulsive surge of heat and mischief throb in her veins, she refused to listen to the little voice of reason in her head. Instead, she pushed away from the window and walked farther into the tiny room, the room she should have been sleeping in.

The blanket caught on a nail and she tugged. Looking at him as he sprawled, disheveled and completely unconcerned on the wide expanse of the double bed, her breath caught. Shadows danced around the room, flitting across his chest and shoulders.

Then she heard his low husky drawl and she gasped, startled that he was awake. "Alex, what are you doing here?" He rose expectantly on his elbows. His voice was almost inaudible, but his words were low and concise. "If you chase after a man, you can't expect him to act like a gentleman." An empty bottle of brandy sat on the bedside table.

She gripped the blanket tightly and hesitated a moment before she spoke. "I'm not chasing you, and you always act like a gentleman." Her words were completely true. Alexandra smiled again even as her heart began to flutter and the butterflies in her stomach did a dance all their own.

"Oh, but that's where you're wrong, my love," he said very softly. "If you give me a chance, I can be quite the rogue."

"Impossible." Alexandra had the wonderful feeling he'd find a way to prove it.

He sat up quickly. "Your honesty is a whisper of fresh air, darlin'. But I am a scoundrel. I've failed miserably where you're concerned."

In disbelief, she could only manage a languid stare. His eyes twinkled, reflecting the moonlight like the myriad stars she'd just watched in the midnight sky. She cocked her head, wondering what on earth he planned now and how she'd stay ahead of him in this game he seemed bent on playing.

"I don't know what you're talking about." She wrenched her gaze from him, suddenly bewildered and more than ready to allow him the win.

"Of course you do."

"No."

"I can act like a gentleman. Let me prove it." As he began to rise, the covers fell daringly low, and the mattress dipped beneath his weight. Alexandra had the alarming thought he intended to stand, and an even better premonition he had nothing on beneath the one insubstantial sheet covering him. But then common sense prevailed.

"No," she whispered hoarsely. "Stay! Stay right where you are." Completely aware of what she was encouraging, Alex began to have second thoughts. She stumbled over the blanket's edge, holding one hand rigidly in front of her as if she could stop his advance.

"Yes," he told her.

Suddenly, her hands dropped to her sides, and the blanket fell to the wooden floor. "James. I'm not looking for one, a gentleman." Rising to the challenge, Alexandra cautiously stepped forward, slowly, so very slowly.

"You should be. You deserve the best. You deserve a gentleman."

"I'm not looking for one. I want a man in my life, and I've decided on you. So if you don't think you're a gentleman, I want you."

"You've fought this for weeks. You can't make me believe you've changed your mind," he said. Then he smiled. "The devil, but if that's what you want, I'll be happy to oblige."

"I didn't, I mean it is but..." *What a mess*, she thought then ran her fingers nervously through her hair. *What a confusing mystifying mess I've made of all this. I can't even put together two coherent sentences.*

"Come here..." he said slowly. His voice sounded soft yet a bit wary. For a fraction of a second, Alex hesitated. Yet at the same time, the deep resonance of his voice beckoned to her, and she wanted so very much to obey.

"Why?" Her voice wavered and she grabbed the blanket off the floor as if it would offer protection.

"Crissakes, Alex...you can't keep changing your mind."

"It's a woman's prerogative," she said softly. Her voice sounded strong and convincing. Their eyes met and she suddenly felt sure he understood all the confusion and desire that raged within her, understood and perhaps accepted her reasoning.

"Run now while you still have a chance, angel mine," he said quietly. "Run and hide."

But she didn't run. Instead, she stood her ground. Advanced a foot. Then realized he'd fallen asleep. She looked closer, pausing in thought.

One night to let him know how it felt to be completely at someone's mercy, her wicked juices began to bubble deep inside. The lure, the temptation, all were so very irresistible.

One night tied to the bed would do him no harm. It might even give him cause to rethink some of his unforgivable male ideas. *Superior male mind, hogwash.* Without one more thought and disregarding common sense, Alexandra pulled his arms over his head and bound him to the bedposts with his very own black silk scarves.

"A fitting touch."

Just as she finished, James mumbled an incoherent word or two. And while he remained asleep, Alexandra sat on the bed next to him. Automatically, she lifted her hand to his jaw. When her fingertip touched him, she trembled. The stubble of a day's growth tantalized the soft pad of her finger.

His anger would wake the house in the morning. Perhaps he'd just bellow. *Oh, I could hope for that.*

"Is this the part where you ravish me and have your wicked way, angel eyes?"

Alexandra jumped then scrambled off the bed. She should have used that time to bolt from the room, but something stopped her. Her face flushed with embarrassment. He'd caught her touching him, and she could do nothing to change that. Oh, Lord, but she regretted her mischief. And how long had he been awake? His eyes were hazy and barely focused, but his grin told her everything.

Then he laughed and she thought she faced the devil himself.

"I'm ready and willing but I'm not sure about the able," James continued. He flexed his arms, testing the knots.

Alex thought she might have untied him a few minutes ago, before she'd looked into his eyes and heard him laugh.

"How ready?"

"Come over here and find out." His voice beckoned seductively. It compelled. It resonated soft and low but she didn't think it came from the heart. He sounded too calculated, too smooth, an expert at seduction.

Alexandra thought a moment. She almost came to him, but some indefinable irrational logic held her back. It was no longer a question of cowardice. Her life balanced precariously on a slender thread somewhere between the past and the future, the thread so thin she could no longer tell them apart and she didn't know how to weave the two together. One mistake and she'd find herself bound here forever. "I can't. My feet won't move."

"Too bad," he said softly.

"Then you won't mind if I slip out the door and return in the morning." Alexandra eased in that direction.

"I'd mind. I don't remember when I've ever been tied to my bed by a beautiful woman. If she were to leave without seeing to the promise and the pleasure, yes I'd mind."

He didn't sound angry or furious. His tone was one of amusement and that left her confused. "What do you want?" she asked, with all the courage she could dredge from deep inside her.

"Why darlin', I want you," he was smooth and her body hummed with what...longing or regret or something entirely different. It was something she had no experience with or control of, but it was very definitely something she wanted to learn.

"Why now and not before?" she asked.

"You surprised me."

"I did, didn't I? Surprised myself if I were to admit the truth, but if I did, then I'd find myself in more trouble."

"Yes, you would."

"I'm not sure I should trust you." Her eyes traveled over his body, the same body she'd just spent admiring and longing to touch, undressing him inch by gorgeous inch. Her gaze stopped at the edge of the sheet for a moment then almost guiltily she looked back.

"That's too bad," he said pleasantly as if he knew exactly what she'd intended and didn't like it. His expression changed markedly as each second ticked by. Carefully concealed, the humor still existed, hot, potent, and threatening to erupt. She could see it plainly in the lines around his mouth. And she didn't understand. No, it was a puzzle. If she were in his place, she'd be furious.

"If I get too close, I'll regret it. I know I will," she said and managed to slide one foot closer to the door.

"Even if I promise to be good?" he said, slowly captivating her with his words.

"I don't know." Desire rose up like flames simmering inside her, catching at her heart and her throat.

"Come here and lie down by me. I could use a soft warm body snuggled next to me, that's all."

"That's all?" she moistened her lips. "You're sure. Do I have to untie you?" Her voice quavered again and rose an octave.

"Of course you do. I can't hold you like this." His manner of speaking sounded smooth as the best Kentucky whiskey, heating her blood and pushing her to the ultimate folly.

She was tempted, but he'd had too much to drink. An empty bottle sat on the nightstand, and his breath smelled faintly of brandy.

She quickly regained her equilibrium and her sanity then hoped her rational mind worked. Before she made that unalterable move, she thought over all the possibilities.

Then decided to untie him. Changed her mind, but...

It sounded like a ploy, nothing more. No matter how tempted she might feel to sleep with him tonight, it wasn't meant to be.

They had too much to discuss.

When it was time, she'd know it. "No, James."

"No?" His brow raised a fraction, a mocking inch. It was so very suggestive, "But I don't want to spend the night like this." A long pause followed. The meaning implicit.

Oh, she understood all too well.

"Go to sleep then I'll untie the scarves."

"Alexandra, please."

She lifted the blanket off the floor, wrapping it around her once again. "I can't, not without your word." Her heart raced and she felt heat surge to her cheeks. Adrenalin shot into her system. The thought of making love to him never failed to bring new sensations to her body. With longing and desire, Alex remembered another time and James' gentle touch, remembered the tenderness and caring they'd shared for only a few short minutes. "I'd do anything..."

"You would?" She closed her eyes for moment, the world beginning to spin and tilt crazily.

"Anything, Alex. I'd promise you the moon and the stars."

"I don't want the moon and the stars, just you." Her voice faded away. She heard the old clock chime, tasted the sweet promise of his love, and assured herself this was what she wanted.

Oh, yes, she wanted James. As crazy as the idea seemed, she yearned for his comfort, but the need wasn't powerful enough to overcome her anxiety.

"I promise. Now untie the damn ropes!"

"They're not ropes, and if you're going to start swearing, I'll come back when you're asleep and I know it's safe. You know a little BDSM never hurt anyone." Indignation seized her and she turned to the door.

"What? Never mind. If you wait that long, the promise is off," his tone of voice was silky yet strangely compelling. It gave warning. "One week was up a long time ago, angel girl."

"I know." Alexandra slowly drew in a deep breath and made up her mind. James Lawrence had promised; he always kept his word, and that simple fact allowed her leaden feet to step gingerly toward the bed. But the look on his face caused her to vacillate and she almost reconsidered. "Promise?"

"Alex," he whispered urgently.

"I just don't know." She'd done it for a reason, and now if she let him go... "No, I'm not crazy," she shook her head and her fingers clamped together into tight little fists.

"Untie me, now."

Alexandra unconsciously moistened her lips and stepped forward. The board creaked under her weight and she jumped back. Her breath came in short little gasps. Before she lost her nerve or regained her sanity, she shot to the bed and fumbled with the scarves. Only a few seconds elapsed before he had her pinned beneath him. The blanket fell away. "I knew it," she pounded on his chest. "I knew—"

~ * ~

"Hush." James let out a long heavy sigh. Even after giving his promise, he couldn't let her go, at least not without teasing her first.

She wore one of his best shirts, as a nightgown of sorts. Made of silk, the material felt cool and very provocative as it lay against his chest. He felt like a wild man, and it was all he could do to control himself. Even though she had the shirt buttoned to the very top, fanciful images of what lay beneath stirred him in a way nothing else ever would. Everything about her tempted him.

One hell of a vision enticed him.

Now her hair tumbled across the pillows. Fiery tendrils winding around his arms, and the soft curves pressing against his chest made his heart miss a beat. One hand rested beside her head; the length of him covered her, pinning her beneath him, and his other hand rose of its own accord to bury itself in her hair. Until this evening, he didn't think she'd let him do this. But tonight, before he'd teased her, he'd thought she looked as if she wanted to devour him, and he liked that look. He memorized her expression so he could hang onto the vision when the night grew cold and his bed lay empty.

His head lifted just high enough to see her breasts beneath the fabric. Her long perfect legs peaked out beneath the shirt, legs that could tempt a saint. With her lips pursed tightly, she looked like an avenging angel. It was all he could do to hold back the laughter that threatened, but he did.

"I thought you were a man of your word." Her words cut. He was a man of his word, and he intended to let her go, soon. But he had to take a small sample, a token to keep him warm tonight.

"I am, but sometimes a woman tempts a man farther than she should, and when that happens..." he tightened his hold on her then rolled so she now lay on top of him. "When that happens, she has to pay a price."

"I did mean to tempt you."

"One kiss, angel mine," he said. "For all the trouble you put me through."

"What I put you through? I'll have you know you deserved this. I don't know why you'd want to kiss me."

"I don't," he lied blatantly. "It's just that you wanted to earlier, and I'd hate to disappoint you."

"I know," she said softly.

"Then you admit it," he chuckled. "Just one kiss and I'll let you go."

He knew he'd won when her eyes suddenly lit with passion then darkened, and she innocently moistened her lips. He'd known she wanted this for a long time, since the first kiss, to be perfectly frank. He saw the desire warm her eyes.

"How do I know?"

"Because you said earlier, I'm a man of my word."

She relaxed but only a little. "All right."

James knew he wouldn't make this easy for her. If she wanted a kiss, she'd have to work for it. So he waited and watched her as she tilted her head to one side. "If you want the kiss...darlin', I'm all yours."

"You're insufferable," she said.

"I'll let you go when you kiss me."

She blinked hesitantly. "But I thought."

"That's one of your troubles. You think too much." His heart wrenched at the way she looked at him.

"There is nothing wrong with that."

"You argue more than anyone I know, and you have too damn many opinions."

She hit him on the chest at that. "After what you just said, I'm not going to kiss you."

"I can live with that." He closed his eyes and began to snore softly.

"Oh..." she let her head fall to his chest. He opened one eye and smiled. Her hair tickled his nose, but he liked the feel and smell of it. So fresh and clean it reminded him of a spring day. "Alex. Alexandra, I know you're not asleep, answer me."

The silence lengthened, and she squirmed on top of him. He groaned. "One kiss," he insisted.

"Only one?" She lifted her head off his chest, catching her lower lip between her teeth as she rose above him.

"Yes," he said.

"All right. But..." Alexandra moistened her lips again. Her hair spilled all about her, moonlight caressing the strands. It glowed and a fiery halo surrounded her. He longed to thread his fingers through the soft curtain and weave its silken length around his hands.

"Hmm, I've heard that before," he said, distracted by his thoughts.

"Beast!" Alexandra laughed and her fists pounded his chest again.

"Just kiss me, Alex, before I'm an old man and can't enjoy it."

He watched her curiously. The length of him shifted then stiffened, coming alive at the very thought of her kiss. A subtle warning played in his mind, but he ignored the thought. Let her come to him now, or run, for he could not bear this a moment longer. He yearned to touch every part of her and bury himself deep inside her. "Kiss me Alexandra," he said again. "Please..."

So she did.

"There," she said smugly. Her words hung softly upon the stillness as he tried to tell her how unacceptable that kiss was.

"Is that it? That's not a kiss. It was a peck, something you'd give a small child or your Aunt Winnie." He smiled to himself, because this sweet impetuous woman, this creature of haunting mystery and wild tempest, came to him.

"I don't have an Aunt Winnie."

He caught his breath. "Oh hell," he groaned. "I'll show you." And he let his lips brush hers. Again they glided across hers. His tongue traced the seam of her lips, his mouth closed over hers and he deepened the kiss. His mouth played with and enticed hers. A penetrating warmth filled him. He tightened his hold then suddenly released her lips. When she opened her eyes he was grinning at her. Her lashes fluttered softly against her cheeks. He let his fingers wandered over her body, creating a magic all their own, "Your turn now, but open your mouth," he whispered.

"What?" her half closed eyes opened seductively. "That one doesn't count?"

"No. I kissed you. Have you forgotten already?"

"I haven't forgotten."

"Good, then be quiet and kiss me." She did; immediately his tongue moved to open her lips and delve into the warm languid recesses that tempted him so. He couldn't stop, couldn't put her away from him. No, he didn't think he ever wanted to stop. James felt her muscles ease into his and waves of pleasure radiated outward. Flames raged and licked within him; all along his spine.

He stopped but only to rearrange her more comfortably on the bed. This time he kissed her ear and down the long column of her neck.

"James," she gasped as his hands crept up her sides and his thumbs played with the soft underside of her breasts. "One kiss...that's all you said. I..."

"Hush."

"Please."

James groaned, "Don't ask me to stop now..."

"Papa? Papa..." A small hand tugged on the blankets. "What are you doing to Alex?"

Chapter Fifteen

Heat, vivid and very real, flushed her cheeks. What indeed had they been thinking? For that matter what had she been thinking? Scarves? Black silk scarves. What would he think of her? She had spent most of the night pondering the question and had come up with absolutely nothing.

Now, several hours past dawn, rain descended from the heavens in a constant deluge. Puddles filled the wagon ruts in the road leading to town.

May sunshine. Where was it?

As if in answer to her questions, the clouds suddenly parted, and a tiny thread of sunlight plummeted to the earth. It lasted half a minute, but it was enough time for Alexandra to throw caution out the window. Instantly, she decided she'd put off gathering the eggs long enough. She was more than ready for a battle with the hens.

With basket in hand, Alex pushed open the door and walked leisurely to the hen house. For a transient and very precarious moment she teetered on the brink of sanity, almost changing her mind. She slanted her face to another beam of light, letting the warmth wash over her skin. Two days ago the temperature had soared, scorching everything. Two days ago. She sighed deeply then looked at the clouds. She would have enjoyed a little more sunshine. Yet, clouds were covering that tiny fraction of light and preparing to send more liquid precipitation downward.

Piggy sat beneath an overhanging eave, looking strangely innocent. A rooster dashed across Alexandra's path, squawking furiously at her as if he knew her intentions. Alex watched in disbelief then proceeded onward. Whenever she entered the hen house, she always felt as if she were doing battle. And indeed she was. This was war. The hens never gave their eggs willingly to her, and she hadn't mastered the technique despite Jessie's enthusiastic instructions.

Reluctantly, Alex pushed the door open. The hinges creaked ominously, as if foretelling the upcoming disaster. The little house fell silent. She felt sure every chicken in that room rested their little beady eyes on her and condemned her without a trial. "Murderer...murderer...murderer," they screamed at her. The eerie quiet lasted a full thirty seconds then the squawking began. Flapping wings sent up a fine layer of dust and debris. Her nose tickled and she sneezed, once, twice, then a third time. Her eyes watered and itched; she sneezed again.

"Horrible, wretched chickens," she swore at them. Piggy peeked in the door, grunted once then left. "Coward," she mumbled. The door slowly drifted shut leaving, her at the mercy of the hysterical hens. With cautiousness born from earlier trials and tribulations, Alexandra moved slowly toward the first nest. As she reached forward, the little beast pecked at her. She gasped and flinched back.

"You chicken you. I want those eggs. If I come back empty handed, Kim will have to send Jessie, or worse she'll have to come herself. She already does too much. Hand over those eggs, you worthless birds."

She reached forward again, bracing herself against the pecking and squawking. Despite her apprehension, she closed her eyes. Just as she felt the warm smooth surface of an egg, just as she was beginning to pull it from beneath the furious chicken, she sneezed again. Her body jerked, the egg, wrenched loose from its protective home, flying through the air. Alex scrambled to catch it. The egg splattered on her shoe then slid to the dirt floor of the house. Yolk and egg white mixed together and rested benignly in the dirt. The mother hen flew from its perch, wings flapping angrily. The other hens joined in, and the little hen house became a cacophony of noise and chaos.

Alexandra was no fool. She fled, hands held over her head. The egg basket still slung around her wrist bounced repeatedly against her back. Two feet from the kitchen door, she paused.

"Damn. I let those little beasts get the best of me again. I'm going back in there and prove once and for all time who the boss around here is."

"What's the matter?" Jessie's innocent question stopped Alexandra before she could return to the hen house.

"The chickens," Alexandra slanted a cross eyed look back at the little shack that housed her enemies, "don't like me at all."

"Want me to get the eggs for you?"

"I suppose. But you'd better wait until they settle down. I got them a little riled up. No, on the other hand, I better get them myself. You can help though." Alexandra and Jessie both giggled. The noises coming from the hen house indicated more than "a little riled up." More like a lot.

"Sounds like someone let the fox in." Jessie looked at the hen house then back to Alex. "What happened to the chickens?"

"The usual." Alex dusted her hands on her skirt, looking a bit sheepish then suddenly contrite. The usual, yes indeed, what didn't she do to them? Alex straightened, shaking off her failure and striving to keep the atmosphere lighthearted. "Well, then. What should we do?" Alex twirled around in several quick circles. Her skirt rose and fell in an undulating pattern. Breathlessly she fell to the ground on a grassy spot. Before she had time to catch her breath, Jessie joined her.

"Let's dance," Jessie said. "Not the way Papa does it. The way I saw you doing it the other night."

"Okay," Alex held her bottom lip between her teeth, grinning at Jessie. "So you want to twist again, huh."

"Like we did last summer," Jessie finished for her, hopping on one foot and gyrating in time to her own slightly off key lyrics.

"How about this one," Alex laughed. She bounced from her resting spot and showed Jessie a new move. "This is called the Pony Step. One, two, three; one, two, three." Her head bounced in rhythm as she agilely hopped from one foot to the other. The song changed and so did the beat. Her arms moving out in front of her, imitating a crawl stroke. "This is the swim." Then Alexandra changed again. This time her arms pummeled wildly up and down opposite each other. "The Jerk," she said then laughed at Jessie's bewildered look. "The dance, Jessie, I mean the dance, that's what its called."

"Oh no. It's sprinkling," Jessie giggled breathlessly. She imitated every move Alexandra made.

"The rain's wonderful."

The two of them danced and laughed. Neither one noticed the slight drizzle had turned to a shower. Rainwater ran from their hair and dripped to the earth. But the dancing and singing continued as if the sun were shining on a brilliant day.

~ * ~

James, covered with his long black poncho, leaned negligently against a tree. He watched fascinated as his two girls frolicked in the rain. The picture enchanted him. Every nerve ending in his body came alive when he watched Alexandra dance. Dance? He didn't think so. At least he wouldn't call it that, but where Alexandra was concerned, it was entirely too seductive. Passionate urges leapt to life, and he recalled the night before, remembered the sudden and unexpected interruption. Perhaps it had been for the best. Even though he already decided he would marry Alex, he had not intended to make love to her before the wedding night. Despite his best intentions, if Jessie had not peeked her little head in the door, he would have made love to Alexandra.

This had to stop. If he kept watching Alex, he wouldn't be responsible for his good intentions or his wicked thoughts simmering beneath his gentlemanly facade. No, he'd take the easy way out this time. The rain had molded her shirt to every soft contour of her body, and the picture reminded him of the time he'd placed her in the bathtub in an attempt to keep her modesty intact. Just as the water had revealed every secret to him then it did once more. When she swayed and turned toward him, he saw the dark outline of her nipples, the perfect form of her breasts. In an attempt to slow the racing of his heart, he looked away. The gesture was futile. Only a second later when he looked back, Alexandra had begun a different dance, a dance more seductive than the first.

Clenching his fists, he stepped forward. Neither one noticed him as he moved toward them. So caught up in the joy of the moment, they were oblivious to him. He grinned then wondered how on earth he was going to interrupt their cavorting without scaring them half to death.

Alexandra solved the problem for him. She twirled and twirled then slowly came to a stop. She was breathing heavily and grinning. Crissakes, she enticed him like no other woman ever had. When recognition came to her, she stilled. For a brief fraction in time, the earth stopped moving. Rain dripped from her forehead, ran down her nose then dripped again, landing softly in the V of her shirt then slipping inside. James watched, fascinated, thinking of his fingers following the same line.

"Papa?"

Jolted suddenly back to reality and his manners, he wrenched his gaze and his thoughts from the tempting and as yet forbidden territory beneath Alexandra's blouse back to her eyes.

"Dancing?" he asked softly, his eyebrow rose marginally with skepticism.

"Yes." Alexandra's smile grew and she spun again. "Dancing in the rain. Isn't it simply grand?"

"Oh, Papa, it's so much fun. Try it." Jessie hopped on one foot then the other again, imitating the step Alex had just shown her. Then she ran to James. She tugged on his hand, pulling him onto the grassy knoll. "You can do it."

James watched tenderheartedly. He hated to disappoint her, but he didn't really think he could do that. He'd look like a fool, and even worse, he'd feel like one. And he thought suddenly what if someone saw him? Before he could refuse, Jessie was twisting and pulling at his hands in a useless attempt to get his hips to move. Alexandra was laughing harder by the minute.

"Like this!" Jessie cried out. "Like Alex. Watch her." Oh, he did watch her. He'd watched her too much already, but he shot her another glance. It was an imploring glance, and Alex looked as if she knew exactly what he wanted.

"Not this time," she grinned. "You're on your own." Despite his initial hesitancy, he winked at Alex and tried. In less than a second, Jessie and Alexandra were facing him and dancing. Alex and Jessie sung a tune about twisting then started in on something that sounded distinctly like seeing the sign then the song turned into something having to do with eight week days.

Breathless, he pulled her into his arms and whispered next to her ear. "It's my turn, darlin'. Let's waltz." He thought he heard a slight choke.

"I can't waltz," she said.

"It's easy. I'll show you." Positioning her hands and pulling her closer than he should, "Doesn't anyone dance this way in your time?" They were so close he could feel the gentle rise and fall of her breasts, smell the provocative scent of her damp hair, hear her breath whisper her sweetness.

"Well," she hesitated, "we do but we don't really dance. We just sort of, move."

"Ah, darlin', you're in for a treat. Think in fours." James began humming softly. She was an agile partner, graceful and easy to lead in dance. Together, as if they were made for each other, the bodies completely in tune, they moved around the yard. James had thrown his poncho around her, and she was settled against his body. Time passed magically for them, but he began to feel the chill sweep across her flesh, felt the goose bumps on her arms. He pulled her close. Over her head, he saw Jessie grinning at him and clapping her hands in delight. Then beyond that he watched as Kim opened the back door and called for Jessie.

"Jessie," he said, "it's time you went inside. Kim will get you a warm bath and something hot to drink."

"What about you?"

"Oh, I have something else in mind." James spun Alexandra around and watched as Jessie skipped up the steps and disappeared into the kitchen. *Something entirely different*, he added to himself.

"What's that? Something wicked?" Alex asked, a mischievous smile of her own creeping slowly across her face, her eyes twinkling like myriad stars.

"Definitely. Yes, definitely something wicked. But first I have to get you dry."

"Umm, sounds rather ambiguous, don't you think? What about you?" She plucked at his wet shirt. "You're wet too."

"Then I guess we'll have to help each other." He waltzed with her all the way to the stables. When they entered, the fresh smell of hay and horse greeted them. General Lee nickered a greeting. But James didn't stop until he'd reached the back of the stable and entered a small room. With a quick tug, the door closed behind them. It was perfect. Quiet, private, and for the next few hours he intended to take wicked advantage of this opportunity.

"What do you think?"

"I think, Mr. Lawrence, that you have maneuvered me into a very compromising situation. What will Kim think?"

"Does it matter?" he asked softly.

"Yes," she looked at him and the expression he saw in her eyes was so sweet and so damn innocent, he faltered, his plans suddenly shattered.

"Well, then we'd better leave. But I have to tell you now that I don't want to."

"Neither do I." Her voice was whisper soft, yet he heard no sound of hesitation. Yes, he felt sure she meant what she said.

"Ah, darlin'." One long stride brought James to the bed. Quickly, he claimed the blanket and wrapped it around Alexandra's shoulders. For a moment, his hands rested there and he felt her shiver beneath his fingertips. He hesitated, weighing his words. "You have to take those wet clothes off, you know."

Alexandra looked at him but didn't say a word. Her bottom lip was caught between her teeth, and even as he watched, she began to shiver violently. "All right, but turn your back."

"Alexandra, I've—"

"Turn around."

"How about if I just close my eyes," he teased. The devil but he hoped she'd say yes. "In my wildest dreams," he murmured.

"James."

He turned. The sounds of wet fabric slipping to the ground was almost his undoing. But when his imagination darted into his brain sending images dancing though his thick skull, he tensed uncontrollably, his body instantly coming to life. The subtle movement must have startled her.

"I'm not ready."

James gritted his teeth. "Darlin', best you hurry. I've only so much willpower and at the moment, it's dangerously low on fuel."

"Okay."

"Is that, okay, you can turn around now, or okay, I understand?"

She laughed softly and he could envision her smile, tempting and innocent, beguiling and seductive. It was a smile that could reduce a man to a puddle of jelly. He didn't wait for further invitation. When he faced her, their gazes collided and he felt the immediate surge of passion between them. Crissakes, he'd made a mistake bringing her here. Dangerous, it was far too dangerous for this vulnerable man. Alone and unchaperoned anything could happen, would happen unless he had more constraint than he attributed to himself at the moment.

In a useless attempt to take his mind off the naked woman wrapped in his blanket, he strung a line across the room and hung her clothes on it. She sat in the rocking chair by the lone window, her gaze following him around the room. His shirt joined her clothes on the line.

"Warm enough?" His voice sounded strange and his question held a brittle tension that emulated his feelings.

Alexandra nodded, a sheepish grin curving her lips. "Yes. And you? I'd offer to share the blanket, but..."

"Relax, angel eyes. I don't want to seduce you. I just wanted to find a place we could be together, uninterrupted." The devil, but he did want to seduce her. He wanted to talk, too, so at least that part wasn't a lie. And his advice to Alex would come in handy for him too. *Relax, relax.* In these circumstances it was easier to say than do.

Forcing an air of nonchalance in his movements, he tried to saunter casually to the bed. It didn't help when the blanket slipped off her shoulder. He flinched and sat abruptly on the bed. After regaining his lost equilibrium, he leisurely studied the white shoulder she revealed. Then, as if the sight had no affect on him, he leaned against the wall, comfortably.

They both started to talk at the same time.

"Go ahead," James said.

"No, you. I wasn't going to say anything important."

"All right." The distance between them was palpable, and he longed to change that. He searched his mind for some way to bring her close to the bed. He wanted to hold her, just hold her, nothing else. "When you lived in that other world, what did you do with your spare time? Times like this, when you had nothing else to do? Or did you ever have time on your hands?"

"More than we knew what to do with." She stood suddenly. The rocker moved rapidly back and forth, empty now. Alexandra wandered around the room, picking up odd items then setting them back in their place. "If I wasn't reading or studying, I'd go to a movie. Sometimes, when I was in Portland, I'd go to a Blazer game."

"Enlighten me. I have no idea what you're talking about."

She inhaled deeply, pushing on the arm of the rocker as she idly watched it move. Then she closed her eyes as if thinking. "Movie or Blazers?" she finally asked.

"Blazers. You talked about movies in your journal. Remember? The one you dedicated to me." Casually, he brought his foot on the bed and rested his arm on his knee.

Her fingers trembled as she pulled the blanket back so it covered her shoulder. He wished she hadn't done that. "Blazers, that's hard. It's a basketball team. Do you know anything about basketball?"

He shook his head, delighted by the vision in front of him. "Nope," he said succinctly. "Come here." He tempered his voice to sound compelling yet innocent. "You'll be more comfortable, warmer, and..."

"You're cold." Instantly, she was beside him. Her obvious concern left him amazed and strangely intoxicated. He moved into the corner and pulled her back against his chest. Relieved she'd come to him so easily, he breathed in the lavender scent surrounding her.

"You need to dry your hair too."

"Do you want to know about basketball or not?"

"I think I'd rather dry your hair, but I'm sure we can do both. Tell me about basketball." As she began to speak, James pulled the pillowcase off one of the pillows and gently began to dry her hair. The tension he felt beneath his fingers began to ease. The story she told him was interesting, but it did not take his mind from her or the desire that built constantly within him. This was a sweet torture, and he wouldn't change it for anything. Football then baseball captured his interest. It amazed him, astonished him really, people actually paid money to see these athletes play games. And baseball, it had changed, at least the way people watched it. The huge stadiums the athletes battled in actually fascinated him, made him think of the Roman gladiators fighting the lions.

"Curiosity satisfied?" she asked. Her cheek was pressed against his chest and in the time they'd been talking, she'd snuggled closer to him. She sounded a little sleepy, and her eyes were huge and round when he looked down and saw her smiling at him.

"No." His knuckles whispered softly against her cheek then slipped tenderly beneath her chin, lifting it, tilting her mouth upward. In an innocent gesture, she moistened her lips. Good God, but he wanted to kiss her. One kiss, just one. He groaned and touched his lips to hers. After tasting her sweetness, exploring the texture of her lips, he pulled back. *Crissakes, Lawrence, don't ruin it now.* It was one of the hardest things he'd ever done. Looking into her eyes, he saw her desire, the sudden explosion of passion he'd ignited with the schoolboy kiss he'd just given her. With a teasing gesture meant to reassure her, he touched his finger to her nose. "Tell me about those cards I found."

"Why did you stop?"

"Because I promised."

"Oh, then you did just want to talk." She sounded disappointed. He grinned and he was sure she guessed his thoughts because when she looked at him again, her eyes were burning with unleashed passion.

"That's not entirely correct, but a promise is a promise. Now tell me, what do you use those cards for?"

Hours passed and they talked. His smoldering curiosity about walks on the moon and missions to Mars, easy money and bankruptcy was anything but satisfied. They talked about rockets and modern warfare. In minute detail she told him what the town of Jacksonville would look like in the future and why the county seat would go to Medford. Eventually, the questions and the constant discourse stopped.

Sunshine filtered in through the dirty window.

Alexandra slept.

James pulled her close, letting his chin rest on the top of her head, enjoying the intimacy. This time she'd taken him through what sounded like another Jules Verne fantasy. She'd used the words "science fiction" to describe several movies she'd seen, and he thought it fit her past life. He chuckled, or was it her future life? He certainly hoped not. What was science fiction to him was pure reality to her.

Alexandra had described a plane ride to him, taking him through the take off and proceeding to the landing. It had literally taken his breath away and sent his heart into his throat. The world in her time had shrunk. What amounted to days and even weeks of travel could be accomplished in hours in the twenty-first century.

"Umm..." she moved against him.

"Alex? Are you asleep?"

"Almost." Her breath whispered beguilingly over his bare chest, and her hand rested on his abdomen. He covered her hand with his, wishing he dared move it lower.

"Alexandra? What are weddings like in the twenty-first century?"

"What?"

"Weddings. Do people still get married?"

"Yes, of course they do, silly." She sat up, pushing away from his chest. He brushed the hair out of her eyes.

"What are they like? Weddings?"

"That's hard to answer. There are all kinds. Some people get married in a church, some in a garden, some still elope."

"What kind of wedding do you want?"

She laughed softly. He pulled her back, settling her between his legs. She rested her head against his chest. "I've never really thought about it."

"Never? I thought all little girls planned their wedding."

"I did," she admitted a little reluctantly. "But that was a very long time ago."

"Not so long ago. Tell me."

"I dreamed about a beautiful white dress with a long veil and lots of people at the wedding. But mostly I dreamed about a handsome bridegroom sweeping me off my feet. I decided then, that when I fell in love, the groom would always tell me how he couldn't live without me."

He sucked in his breath, feeling instantly guilty. He fell far short of that girlish fantasy.

"Am I handsome?" He tried to change the direction of his thoughts, the direction of the subject she'd just dropped at his feet. *Fool*, he berated himself. *You've no need to pander to her childish and overly romantic whims.* Yet, he felt a fierce desire to please her and to make all her dreams come true, a desire he had forsworn when his life had been ripped apart because he never intended to fall in love. It was a desire born by the autumn hues woven within her hair, by the sapphire flame of her eyes; by the perfect fit of her when he held her close.

She turned and hit his chest playfully, the blanket slipping far off her shoulder. The view it presented stopped his heart, and his breath caught as he waited for her answer. She hesitated.

His willpower deserted him, and he traced the same line he'd watched the raindrop take, down, always down until the tip of his finger touched the top of the blanket. The temptation she presented was more than he wanted to endure. Succinctly, he turned inward.

"I'm sorry darlin'. You don't have to answer that. It's time we went inside. Kim will wonder what happened and come looking for us."

Before Alexandra moved from the bed, "You're the most handsome man I've ever seen," she said breathlessly then stood.

It didn't take long to dress. James kept his back turned, but he couldn't help himself, he watched her reflection in the windowpane. She was exquisite.

When they exited the stables, the sun rested on top of the coastal mountains. They had idled away the afternoon, but he'd not regret the time spent. At the bottom of the stairs, he kissed Alex then sent her up the steps.

He stood for the longest time. Finally, he strode to the stables. General Lee nodded his head in greeting and sampled the sugar cube James offered.

Five minutes later, the two of them were galloping across the rolling hills.

~ * ~

Belinda's reception was cool and calculated when Sean strolled into her front parlor early that evening, as if he were born to a life of ease. "You're taking a great risk waltzing in here," she told him in her low, sultry voice. "But then you know I like danger. Have you figured out how to get rid of her yet?"

Sean stood with his back against the door he'd firmly closed behind him. "I'm working on it, Belinda. You know I almost had her. She was careless once. It will happen again."

"Really, sweetheart. So you're telling me that I need more patience," she chided in the sweet Southern belle voice she affected when it suited her. "Come, relax. Tell me what you've planned. Perhaps we'll have a time for a short contretemps." Her green cat eyes slowly raked Sean's lithe form. His jeans hugged his thighs, accenting his muscular build. His blond hair curled slightly around his ears where it was growing longer, framing the gruesome scar that would brand him for the rest of his life.

At the moment, she didn't care if he succeeded in his plans to rid her of Alexandra McMurdie. She could think of better ways of spending the evening. Her mother had left for Portland hours ago, and Charles was spending the evening at the jail going over wanted posters.

"Come, relax," she told him and delicately patted the sofa she was seated on.

"No. There isn't time. I heard he was planning on marrying her." Sean pushed away from the door then walked to a chair opposite Belinda and sat.

"The bitch doesn't deserve him. Coffee?" she inquired again. "Tea? Or perhaps me?" she added in her perfect sugary voice.

He snorted at her casual use of a phrase he'd thought coined in his century, and he wondered what she had in mind for James Lawrence besides marriage. She'd hinted at a pregnancy, urging him to hurry, but she was slender still, his glance quickly ranging over the gown she wore and lush curves beneath he remembered vividly.

"I'll need for you to deliver a note in a couple of weeks. There are a few loose ends I have to take care of. I'll let you know."

"There are a few," she moistened her lips seductively her eyes focusing on his lower anatomy, "loose ends we could take care of right now." Her eyes came up and met his with a practiced charm that would do any brothel whore proud.

Sean held his hand out to her, and she slipped her fingers into his hand. She rose and with his help and smiled.

Sean's eyes were hot. "Am I as good as he is?"

She tilted her chin to the side, her mouth forming a pert little moue, "Of course, darling. But you've heard how good you are before, haven't you?"

Reveling in her compliment, he said huskily, "Where's your room, Belinda."

"Not there. Here. I want you here in the family parlor. I want to look at this rug when my oh-so-righteous brother is sitting in that very chair sipping his brandy."

"You're a conniving little bitch, Belinda. But then you suit me just fine."

"And you're a bastard."

He threw his head back and laughed then pulled her hard to his chest. With one determined yank, he ripped the bodice of her dress, buttons flying through the air, her breasts spilling from the gown, his hands winding through her hair, ruthlessly tearing the pins from her scalp. Then his mouth met hers hard, aggressively, demanding surrender.

And Belinda did surrender, even when he called her Alexandra.

Chapter Sixteen

From her window up stairs, Alexandra watched James leave. It was a splendid sight, horse and rider moving as one. The vision made her think of gallantry and knights in shining armor, romance in its golden age. She remained at the window until it was too dark to see, finally sitting down to a light meal. Sometime after the clock chimed ten times, she heard James stride inside and go to the spare room. She curled into a little ball, cradling her pillow like a small child, holding her locket in one tight fist, and went to sleep.

The next morning, Alexandra waited until James and Jessie left before she peeked from behind the bedroom door and motioned Kim inside. Her appointment this afternoon was critical, so she'd dressed in the next best thing to a business suit she could find. The Garibaldi blouse slipped over her head, and she tucked it into her long black skirt. A quick inspection, a tuck here and there, and a huge breath of air announced she could do nothing more to achieve a conservative disguise.

"Are you ready, Miss Alexandra? Jessie's at Amanda's house, and she'll be there all afternoon." Kim smiled and nodded her approval. "You look very pretty."

Alex looked back to the mirror, examining the image. For good measure or perhaps to bolster her confidence, she patted the chignon and stuck another hairpin into it. She paused, briefly lost in thought, but a small smile flitted across her lips. Before she left the room, she rested her hands on the back of the chair, once again frowning at the image she presented in the mirror. "Thanks, Kim, but my knees are wobbly, and I'm so nervous I think I'm going to be sick." Alexandra sucked in her breath and headed for the door, determined to make a good impression on the banker. "Other than that, it'll be a fine day. I hope."

Kim tsked, tsked, for a brief moment then brought the real issue to the forefront. "Have you told Mr. James? He deserves the truth, you know."

Alex looked back. Kim had paused in the doorway, waiting for the answer. Of course James deserved to know, and she'd tell him just as soon as she found the courage.

"No, but I will." Alexandra swirled once, enjoying the swing of her skirt then moved down the steps. She didn't stop until she reached the wagon.

She heard Kim and her Chinese proverbs littering the air in a cacophony of discontent. Alex smiled again.

Alexandra had no second thoughts. She had no idea whether or not James was ready to hear this news. Not even a clue. It was simply too soon, and she didn't intend to risk all she'd worked so hard for on a weak conscience. If she told him now, it would threaten, the independence she'd been working for. She couldn't risk it. Before she could give James anything of herself, she had to understand this new life and who she had become.

Thirty minutes later Alexandra and Kim turned down California Street and stopped in front of C.C. Beekman's banking house and express office. Charles walked by them. His grin widened appreciably then he nodded, lifting his hat in a slow courtly manner. Two women moved across the street, staring pointedly at her. Alex's hand shook and the reins slowly slipped from her wooden fingers.

Charred skeletal remains of two building loomed in front of her. The fire could have spread much farther and done a lot more damage. The people in town had, for a time, put aside their differences and had banded together to fight the flames. But that was a couple of nights ago.

The street was relatively quiet for Monday afternoon. Perhaps it was due to the heat wave, perhaps not. The smell of fresh baked bread mixed with the delicate fragrance of honeysuckle floated in the air.

The sound of a closing door snapped Alex's attention back to her surroundings, and she turned toward the noise. A packhorse neighed its discomfort as it waited for its owner in front of J.A. Brunner & Bro.'s. She turned back to Kim.

"You feeling up to this? Your face is as pale as new fallen snow, and it doesn't take a genius to see your lip trembling. You don't have to do this," Kim finished.

In a state of anxiety, Alexandra placed one hand on her chest as if she could slow her pounding heart.

Kim didn't say anything more, but she did nod toward the bank. The silence was profound and stuffy. Sweltering in the heat, Alex knew a moment's doubt, an uncertainty she didn't like. *All right, Alex darlin', you are one valuable and special woman, don't let anyone intimidate you.*

A soft cool breeze fanned her hot cheeks, and she instantly felt an uplifting. It felt as if a quiet confidence passed through her. She could do this.

Impossible task that it was.

"Oh, Kim," Alex inhaled a deep breath then eyed the bank coolly. "I have such high hopes. You think they'll take me seriously?"

"You shouldn't have started this if you didn't mean to finish."

"You're right of course." Alex kissed the elderly lady on the cheek then jumped from the wagon. "Wish me luck."

Alexandra lifted the hem of her skirt from the dusty road and moved to the door. She stood in front of it for a brief moment, collecting her thoughts. Then with more courage than she thought she had, Alex stepped inside. She paused a moment to let her eyes adjust to the dim interior then boldly made her way to the office marked C.C. Beekman.

About to knock, her hand poised in the air inches from the door, it swung open. She instantly stepped back, giving way to the man who rudely sauntered through the door. She regretted her retreat the moment she moved back. After all, she had meant to stand her ground. A very tall, very thin, almost gaunt man strode from the room. It wasn't Mr. Beekman. Alex swallowed back her hesitancy and her nervousness. "Sir."

"Ma'am." He walked by her as if she was nothing more than an ornamental piece of furniture.

Ma'am, ma'am? Her eyebrows rose a fraction. She looked on either side then behind her. "Mam..." she murmured. "I'm not a mam..."

"Miss?"

"Oh, Mr. Beekman?" Her hand wobbled but she was determined to shake hands with the banker who now stood in the doorway. She stepped forward, her hand extended, intentions clear.

"Miss McMurdie."

"Yes."

"This is highly irregular," he hesitated a moment, looking at Alex as if he was taking her full measure. Before he continued speaking, he looked over the bank and its customers. "But I've arranged for the owner of the business to meet us." Beekman pulled out his pocket watch then cleared his throat. "He's late."

"Mr. Beekman, this may be unusual, but it is time I took matters into my own hands. I would like to buy the town's newspaper. I have sufficient funds to meet a year's payments. There should be no problems."

"Well, there are a few problems."

"Oh?" Alex's tone was cool and controlled. "I can assume there's more than one?"

"Yes, Miss McMurdie. But only one that matters. The owner refuses to sell to you."

"Why?"

The silence almost suffocated her. Politeness, inbred and at this moment very difficult to maintain, almost turned to fury before she stamped it down.

"Why?" he parroted then cleared his throat again obviously at a loss for words. "Well, a..."

"Surely, I have the right to know why the man won't sell to me."

Beekman pulled at the collar of his shirt in a feeble attempt to loosen it. Clearly discomfited by Alex's question, he nodded. "Suppose you do."

"Nora Perkins refuses because she doesn't want another...a...a parlor house in the area."

"That's ridiculous. It's a newspaper, Mr. Beekman. I don't intend—"

"It doesn't matter what you say. Mrs. Perkins is convinced of your—

a—promiscuous nature, and she won't sell," Beekman cut in, waving a hand as if to silence her. "And she does own the business. Perhaps we should go into my office where there's a little more privacy," he finished, lamely shrugging his shoulders to emphasize his lack of power in this situation.

Alex's temper was no longer controlled under the guise of polite conversation. Anger simmered beneath the surface of what appeared to be a calm and placid demeanor. If Beekman had known her better, he might not have cushioned his reply with hope. "That's her final—"

"Well, there's the little whore."

The people in the bank gasped simultaneously, turning in unison to stare at them.

Alex turned livid and Beekman looked as if he wanted to hit Belinda Perkins who had just sauntered her way through the bank.

"Miss, this is a respectable establishment," Beekman stated firmly. "Miss McMurdie is a valued customer."

"Ah, deposits a family's hard earned money here, does she?"

"Miss Perkins I earn my money honestly." Alexandra walked toward the young lady, her spine straight, her lips pursed, the light of battle in her wide all-knowing eyes.

"Whoring ain't honest," a man chimed in before Alex could defend herself. "Even if James is the only one. He's tired of ya huh? So now you're goin' ta solicit your wares here in town. Well, sweetheart, I ain't helpin'. I heard all I need to know about ya from that Cassidy fella'."

"I think it would be best if you left, Miss McMurdie." Beekman nodded to the vault and two guards stepped forward.

"James hasn't paid me a cent and I haven't slept..." Both Alexandra and Belinda ignored the banker and his subtle threat. Caught in a wave of bigotry and sexism, Alexandra drew on all her resources and retaliated.

"No wonder you're wantin' to branch out. But not with the town paper. No siree."

"I'm not branching out. I made my money through essays and stories."

"Yeah...heard about those essays too. Started a riot in a Portland saloon, they did. My wife read one, and now she refuses to have another baby. Insists I get some confaddled rubber or something like that. Well, let me tell you...only whores know about things like that. Those things ain't Christian. If God meant for us to abstain—or use such contrary devices—he would have—"

"Mr. Owens," Alexandra addressed the man before sucking in a deep calming breath then gritted her teeth against the anger she felt for him. "Women die every year in child birth. Sometimes the reason is very simple. She's had too many children. God never intended that kind of abuse."

"The devil will take your soul. You've no right to set crazy ideas into the mind of my woman. I own her. I think for her. And I decide if we're going to have children."

"I thought God did." Alex's tone was cool and mocking, her smile insolent. "Mr. Owens, you can't own a person. Slavery was abolished, thirteenth amendment, I believe."

Men and women curiously gathered around the three people. By the time Alex finished with her last statement, the battle lines were clearly drawn with the people lined up behind them. Murmurs of discontent changed to instant anger. Men and women openly debated the pros and cons of Alexandra's essays. Neither Alexandra nor Owens noticed but Beekman did, and he was adeptly maneuvering the crowd of rebellious onlookers to the door. Like wildfire, word of the confrontation spread through town, and the once peaceful California Street erupted with angry swearing men, men whose wives had read Alexandra's essays and begun to question everything.

Alex had never meant to cause problems within the family framework. Her concern was for the health and well being of women everywhere. There was nothing she wrote about that hadn't been published before in some form or other. She didn't understand the cause of all this fury over something so simple as birth control and women's rights. In fact, she'd thought she'd tempered her articles with a very conservative slant.

Alexandra scrambled her way to the wagon and Kim. She climbed into the bed and began speaking, hoping a calm reasonable approach would soothe the fiery temper of the crowd. Men and women tossed angry insults back and forth. A rock flew by her head, nicking her ear. Two gunshots resounded.

The crowd gasped and fell away.

James rode General Lee down the street. His rifle rested across his thigh and his gun was pointed at the crowd.

"Alexandra. Go home...now."

Alex rallied, about to tell James she had no intention of following his orders, but Kim tugged on her skirt and whispered, "Please." Gingerly, she moved into the front of the wagon and sat down. Before she left, she turned a rebellious look to James. One minute later they were out of town and on the road home, James, riding General Lee, followed about a quarter mile behind.

~ * ~

When they reached the house, Alex fled upstairs. Every word Mr. Owens said to her echoed repeatedly in her mind. Even though she knew James would insist she explain how she caused a riot, at this moment, she had to be alone. She recalled the look on Owens' face when he sneered down at her. The single word "whore" still tore at her. Whore...whore...whore...

A man could do whatever he wanted, whenever he wanted. If she had to stay in this world, she'd have to learn that fact and how to deal with it.

Damn Mr. Owens and any man like him. Damn this provincial little world. A man's world, but one day...

Blasphemous thoughts smoldered in her brain ready to spill out on paper, ready to shock the placid chauvinistic people inhabiting her new life. But she couldn't intrude on the present, couldn't change history, and if she foretold too much, who could guess what might happen? Even though she knew none of this was James' fault, she wanted to blame him.

What did she want? A scapegoat maybe? No, she wanted him to understand how she felt, to understand what motives drove her. Equality. He'd mentioned it the other night. Perhaps he had listened. Perhaps he understood more than she was giving him credit for. But she knew the only equality she'd find in this world would be with James and only if he were willing.

She found her way to the old tree house built several years ago on the solid limbs of a sturdy old oak tree.

"Jessie? You up there?" she called into the tree, suddenly feeling so very alone and empty. All her rebellious thoughts had suddenly dissipated along with her anger. She felt drained and strangely complacent.

Silence followed, a breeze whispered through the tree.

"Jessie, honey?"

Alex shielded her eyes, leaning back to see if Jessie had made her way to the little perch.

"Can I invade your space?" she asked then scrambled up the ladder without waiting for a reply. The wooden steps moaned at her weight but held fast. The rough bark on the palm of her hands scratched, but it felt right.

This wasn't the first time she found herself in a tree, but it was the first time for this special one. A board creaked and slipped from the sudden intrusion as she adjusted herself. Mistletoe grew unchecked from the old oak's limbs, and she tugged on a piece of it. Dirt, bark, moss, and a collection of tiny bits tumbled down; she blinked and shook the dirt from her hair. She smelled pitch on her fingers, and when she closed her hands, they stuck together.

One could see a very long way from here, and one could lose herself in their sadness too. Table Rock sat off in the distance, and she gazed across the horizon. The snow on top of Mt. McLaughlin had begun to melt, forming angel wings, a sure sign the salmon were running. The Rogue River wound its way through the valley, and Alex marveled at its beauty. She could recall how Bear Creek looked when it merged into the larger river, and she knew how changed this valley would appear in another hundred fifty years.

"I don't belong here," she said, a resigned catch to her voice, now more convinced than ever that was the truth. "I have to go back."

The air was hot and stale. The wind blew hard, swirling and dipping around the oak leaves. A few high clouds overhead charged the air and banded together with the thunderheads forming over the Cascades. Dark ribboned clouds hovered in the west and approached at an astonishing pace. A long hot summer in the Rogue Valley was in front of her, a season where a person would seek out the little swimming holes and shade. Hot and dry—one hundred degrees, and she had always loved the feel of the sun on her skin and the golden tan she had to work like the very devil to get.

She twirled the mistletoe in her fingers, frowned then remembered her first kiss beneath a sprig at Christmas time. She hadn't liked that kiss. She had detested the boy just as much as the kiss. He'd taken advantage of her, had the audacity to brag. Furiously, she pitched the fungus into the air. "Damn, damn, and double damn!"

If Jessie, and her ungodly penchant for acquiring a mother, wasn't enough to worry about, she had the confrontation in town to mull over. She wouldn't risk that again. And James, what would he think? He was bound to say something.

"What next," she murmured again.

She smiled at the new direction her thoughts rambled. Angel eyes, she thought a moment. James had said they'd take a man straight to heaven.

"Impossible." She let her head fall to her knees.

None of the men she'd ever dated thought she'd take them to heaven. But she'd never known a man quite like James Lawrence, and she'd never known a kiss quite like the ones James gave her. They were hot and wet and so very possessive.

With James, all the feelings he'd brought to life from the beginning made her wish she might have had a place here with him, a place in his heart and his future.

He'd frustrated her more than any man. And the desire he elicited within her left her breathless.

James was the man for her. Her heart beat faster and her palms got clammy when he was around, and she longed for him to enfold her within his arms. His kiss made her think of long, lazy days beside a stream and a picnic basket filled with fried chicken, potato salad, and a little hot salsa.

And Miss Jessica still believed she'd become her mommy.

Oh, but the seduction was sweet. She regretted Jessie stumbling in on them and the position that very childish act had placed her in.

If they hadn't been discovered...

Her head pounded and she didn't want to think about it any more. She just wanted to forget about the kiss and the desire she felt for James, but she couldn't help remembering. What she needed was someone to talk to. Jessie was too young, and she didn't know anyone else.

"James," she thought momentarily but shrugged it off.

Black dangerous clouds towered into the sky. They came closer and more threatening with each second. Alex laughed softly. At home she would have gone to her best friend to pour her heart out.

She leaned back, resting her head against the wood planks. The mere thought she had no one to talk to caused her to sink into a depression she hadn't felt since the first few weeks she was here.

Her mother, she missed her.

A drop of rain splashed on the wood and soaked its way through the grain. Another drop fell and she moved to the inside of the tree house, hoping James had made it rain proof. Alexandra stuck her hand out from beneath the cover and let the cool water splash against her hot skin.

Would she have a funeral? Flowers? No, her mother would undoubtedly bring balloons and rainbows and she would cry but only in private. If only she could find a way to tell her she lived and was happy.

Alexandra felt a desperate horrible weight on her shoulders, and she didn't want to come down, not ever. If she did, she'd have to face her problems, and it wasn't like her to run away and hide.

It poured now, yet off in the hills the sun shone brightly and a beautiful rainbow formed. Rainbows, and balloons, and flowers. Would she ever feel whole again?

To heap one surprise upon another Jessie crawled into the tree house, eyes beaming. "Hi!"

Alexandra's breath caught in her throat. She grinned. "Hi, to you, too."

"What are you doing?" Jessie asked softly, surprised by the adult in her tree house. Her voice held as much shock as curiosity.

Simple question, but Alex didn't know what to say. Her tongue tripped on the words, "Hiding from myself." She gave Jessie a weak smile and a shrug. After a few strained seconds, she pretended to watch the raindrops. Her sigh haunted the stillness and drowned the soft cadence of the drops that littered the earth. "You won't buy that, will you? No, I didn't think so." She answered herself before Jessie could form new questions. "It doesn't really matter anyway."

Jessie sucked on a peppermint stick, her little face tightening in a frown. She nodded her head as if thinking about what Alex had said. "Is he mad? I come here when I do something wrong. I like to hide up here too."

"Probably," Alex bit her lip to keep from laughing at Jessie. Miss Jessica was sitting there so smug and looking as if she had the answers to all the world's questions instead of just her own. "I did something very foolish today." After what he'd witnessed in town, he had every right to be furious.

"What did you do?" Jessie's innocent voice still held the curiosity of childhood, and she even looked as if she would help. Yes, Jessie looked ready to play her knight in shinning armor, and Lord knew she needed one at the moment. If any damsel in distress ever needed rescuing, she did.

Alex looked wistful. If Jessie could only help. "I, well, this is a little hard to explain." She watched Jessie's cute little face, her expression unreadable. "I guess you could say I caused a riot."

"Riot?" she questioned then after a lengthy pause. "Was Papa there?" Jessie wrinkled her little nose as if the very thought were distasteful, and Alex had to agree with the idea.

"I suppose you could call it that, Jessie. But actually it's all really very childish," she wiped the mud off Jessie's nose. "And the disturbance wasn't really my fault. It's just that James had to rescue me again."

Jessie giggled. "He likes to do that. He yells and stomps his feet. He can act real mad. You do like him, don't you, Miss Alexandra?" Huge hope-filled eyes gazed upward, and Alex almost gave into the pressure. She almost told Jessie how much she loved James, but she stopped herself.

Alex found an old quilt to share with Jessie and wrapped it around them. The rain kept up a steady beat on the ceiling, and neither one of them wanted to dash for the house. When the wind howled and the old tree swayed, she shivered and they snuggled closer together. The warmth of their bodies felt right, and they heated the air inside the blanket. She should have known Jessie would find a way straight to her heart and heaven help her, she had.

"You're precious," Alex said and hugged Jessie again.

"I still want you to be my mother," Jessie whispered softly, her head resting against Alexandra's breast.

"I know, sweetheart, but I can't."

Tears slipped down Jessie's cheeks, and Alexandra's silent recriminations echoed within her. Jessie sat up suddenly, wiped her eyes and stared hard at Alex. "Yes, you are. You are going to be my mother!"

Alex didn't know what to say. Perhaps Jessie had a point. She waved a dismissive hand and fell silent, not wanting to argue with the little girl.

Jessie was smarter than she gave her credit for, "You don't want to marry daddy, do you?"

"It's not that," she started and knew defeat at the hands of a six year old. No, it wasn't that at all. It was the fact he didn't love her. If he only loved her, she'd do anything, even give up the future.

"Then why not?" Jessie cut in. Her dark blue-violet eyes accused then flashed defiantly.

But Alex didn't have a clue how to answer her and looked away for a moment. "I don't know the answer, don't have any answers. It's quite impossible, this situation I've found myself in, and I don't know what to do." Alex rested her head against the wall. She smelled the rain, listened to the wind, and knew it sounded and smelled the same everywhere.

"I love you," Jessie said, her tone so sincere and wise that Alex hugged her. No wonder she was so dear to his heart. This little girl could worm her way into the coldest one. Alex combed Jessie's hair with her fingers, ruffled the silken curls then let her hand fall to her side.

"I know, sweetheart. And I'd love to be your mother. But don't get your hopes up. What you saw the other night wasn't what it looked like."

Jessie raised an eyebrow. "Oh," she said slowly, "it wasn't? I know why you don't want to live with us. It's because people are saying mean things about you."

Was this truly a six year old? "It wasn't what it looked like. The people in town have nothing to do with this. Do you understand? Say you understand. Please."

"I understand," Jessie's lip began to quiver, and Alex had the unholy urge to slither away. She'd hurt Jessie and that in itself was unforgivable. Despair tugged viciously at her heartstrings.

The rain dripped from the heavens at a steady rate, and the pair in the tree watched with nothing more to say. Minute after minute ticked by.

"Alex...Jessie..."

Alex started at that deep voice. She let out a nervous little groan before peeking over the edge of the floor. The ground zoomed toward her, and a wave of deja vu jolted her system. Dizzy and slightly off balance, she pulled back but not before she'd located James striding toward them. His hat was on and tipped low to avoid the drenching rain. He wore a long black poncho and his usual buckskins. From the look of things, he'd been searching for them, and if he'd been in the vicinity he could have heard every word. So much for being alone, she thought wryly.

"Papa...Papa," Jessie waved frantically, hollering at the top of her lungs and the belated "hush" that Alex threw at her lost itself in the noise.

"Is my other girl up there too? My Angel girl," James called sweetly.

"Oh, yes...Alex was here first," Jessie yelled. "C'mon."

"No!"

"Oh? Why not?" James asked.

James was smooth, real smooth but she caught the dangerous undertone. "Because there's no room." she cried out almost hysterically.

"Of course there's room," Jessie said, indignantly. Hands on her hips, Jessie looked from her father to Alex then back again.

James climbed the wooden steps to join them. He pulled his body over the ledge and scurried beneath the roof just as a gust of wind shook the tree, pummeling his back with huge pellets of water. The poncho dripped and he shook the water off. A few seconds later, he settled between the two girls and underneath the quilt with a grin that looked as if it could melt butter.

No escape, no way to flee, she blinked and found his arm around her waist, his fingers teasing her ribs and sliding provocatively upward. She sighed at his caress then blushed demurely.

"No? You don't want my company?" he asked Alex pointedly and brushed the underside of her breast with his thumb, sending shivers down her spine. She shuddered from the heat spiraling through her, and she heard the teasing quality of his voice even as he tried to hide it from her. "Do children have tree houses, you know, where you come from?"

"I didn't say that and yes, just like this one." She gasped for air, even as her cheeks felt the slight rosy stain his intimacy induced. "It's just that I wanted to be alone and this is more like Grand Central Station."

His eyebrows narrowed pensively. "Grand Central Station?"

Alexandra shrugged helplessly then explained.

"So, you don't want me here. You implied as much." He brushed his lips across her forehead.

Her breath caught and she swallowed hard. "It's not that," she began, "It's just that..."

"Why were you in town today?"

"Umm, well, I'll tell you later."

"All right, when?"

"Tonight?" She felt apprehension settle in her stomach, and she told herself he'd understand. But the other possibility always existed.

"Jessie and I were having a girl-to-girl talk and I...well, it was private," she said quickly in a fervent attempt to change the subject he'd just introduced.

"That's good you were talking because I think the three of us need to sit down and plan the wedding. What do you prefer? A garden or a church? Of course we could always elope."

"What?" Both Alex and Jessie gasped in surprise, but they had far from identical expressions on their faces. If the situation hadn't felt so serious, Alex would have dissolved in hysteria.

"I want to marry you. And we can either talk about the wedding or you can explain what happened in town today. Although I've a pretty clear picture in my mind."

Jessie clapped her hands in childish abandon, grinning from ear to ear. She kissed her daddy soundly on the cheek and rushed to do the same with Alex.

Alexandra stared at him, her gaze riveted on James, her insides rolling with confused emotions. She couldn't answer, couldn't think, couldn't even see straight. Indeed, she felt overwhelmed and moved to exit, but a huge hand still insinuated its presence around her rib cage kept her immobile. Her mouth felt dry and she coughed, sucking in air that didn't seem to be there for her, desperate for a reason behind his sudden and unexplainable change of heart.

The look he shot back was mischievous but held a subtle warning. "Don't say anything you'll regret, Alex."

"When, Papa?"

"Soon. I contacted the preacher a few hours ago. Before I ran into an angry mob," he added pointedly before continuing. "The arrangements are being made. If Alex agrees, we'll set a date. Sometime after the ball, maybe a week or two, I think would be appropriate. We can announce our engagement there."

Chapter Seventeen

Swirls of petticoats, lace, and silk, perfumed water and more pampering than Alex had ever received, greeted her the day of the ball. With the end of June, the weather turned heavenly. Languid warmth filled the air, along with the enticing scent of summer roses. The sky, a soft blue, stretched endlessly from one horizon to the other.

Every item including Alexandra's sapphire studded hairpins James had hand picked with the greatest care. New York supplied the dress, as if he'd known months before she would accept his proposal of marriage.

"I have a mind of my own. I could have picked out my own dress. Hoodwinked, bamboozled, and conned by the best," she murmured laughingly, but she wasn't sure who to hold responsible, Jessie or James. Perhaps they both had a definitive role in this issue. But then the dress was beautiful and it conjured romantic images, images she longed to hold next to her heart. If she could put her fears aside and forget her other life so far away, so unreachable, she could be happy.

The dress shimmered when the light danced on it. The blue satin looked too fragile to wear. A row of a dozen matching buttons running along its back fastened it. A low cut bodice fit corset-like from the tiny waist to the tops of her breasts. White silk stockings and matching slippers waited for her as well as sinfully delicate underclothes. She did want to wear everything but not to the ball, and not after her last encounter with the good people of Jacksonville.

When she'd slipped the dress over her head, she had done it with the greatest excitement only to discover the dress wouldn't button. Kim informed her she needed the corset.

The corset with its stays and uncomfortable boning bit into her skin, and she couldn't breathe, could barely move. A refusal to go almost slipped off her tongue, but she was determined to do this for James. She sucked in her stomach and had Kim try to fasten it one more time. The gesture was futile.

Without the corset, the dress didn't fit and without the dress...

"Hogwash!"

I'm not going to cry. I'm going to wear the dress even if I have to put that thing on.

Jessie watched the entire transformation, a smile delightfully lighting up her face. "You look so beautiful, just like a real fairy princess." Jessie danced up and down with excitement, while Alexandra, looking over her shoulder, silently stared at the back of her dress.

~ * ~

With a single-minded determination, James had painstakingly planned everything down to the smallest detail. She comprehended why she had to go to this ball, understood why it was so important to him. But the people of Jacksonville had made their feelings about her clear.

Whore. Take a family's hard earned money. Don't want a parlor house in town.

The announcement of their betrothal was tonight. *Lord, I'm nervous. A betrothal? Nothing is settled. What on earth is James thinking?*

Despite all her misgivings, she had given James her word. When she looked at Jessie, she saw the sparkle in her eyes. And because of that she knew what they planned was right.

"James, how could you do this to me?" she sighed softly as if having second thoughts again.

"Do what, angel eyes?" he drawled from his post at the doorway, his lip curling into a gentleman's smile. James leaned against the frame arms crossed, and he took her breath away.

His evening wear fit him perfectly; she wrestled with her frustration, her confusion, and her sudden urge to tell him how much she loved him, how much she wanted to stay here, in this time, with him.

"Talk me into going to this ball and confronting all those people. It's playing dirty and you know it."

He moved swiftly to her side. "Ah, darlin', you have to confront them sometime. They will be your neighbors. People you might have to rely on."

"I know that but do we have to involve them so soon?" Alexandra stood her ground, acknowledging the truth of his words even though she wanted to deny them. Her gaze met his, and she shot him an exasperated look.

"Eventually, you'll thank me," he told her succinctly and winked at her. "They're going to like you."

Volatile emotions sunk to the pit of her stomach. She felt torn between the past and the future, confusion simmering inside. *He needs me. Jessie needs me. This commitment will bind me to him for all time.*

"I love you," she whispered.

"What?"

"Nothing?" she managed to squeak. It was too soon to tell him.

"Despite what you think, I didn't buy the dress a size too small so you'd have to wear the corset," he grinned. "I estimated wrong. I thought you were smaller," he winked.

"Oh." She tossed him a dirty look. "Horrible, wretched man."

"I'd really prefer you didn't have to wear that thing. It's not at all good for the lungs. But that isn't the issue here, is it? Do women wear corsets, in your time? You can answer that later. I wanted everything to be perfect tonight. I hoped you'd enjoy yourself."

"You mean—I don't have to wear the corset?"

"Of course not," James began and his smile looked almost wicked. "Personally, I don't care one way or the other if you wear it, but if you want to wear the dress..." He raised an eyebrow mockingly.

"Oh, you'd like that wouldn't you. A modern day Lady Godiva," *Wouldn't it shock him if I did just that, attend the ball in my underwear. I've certainly worn less in public.* She stifled a little giggle. It would shock the good people of Jacksonville.

"The idea does have merit, but you'll have to decide that all on your own. Isn't that what you wanted? A chance to make decisions. I think you called the notion equality."

"Only a man would think that choosing between wearing a corset versus no dress at all was equality."

James roared with laughter. "Back to the ball, darlin', can it be that bad? I'll be at your side every minute. Promise." James straightened from his position and approached Alexandra. He stopped inches from her. Their gazes clashed. His hands rested on her shoulders, and he gently turned her so her back lay against his chest. The mirror reflected their images, and Alexandra stared at the woman in the glass as if she'd never seen her before.

"I like your hair down," he murmured and found each pin in her carefully arranged chignon and removed them, slowly, one by one. She listened to their sound as they hit the floor.

She moved away from him and steadied herself against the chair. "You think this will change how they feel about me?" Alex turned away from the mirror, her image, his image.

"Yes," he said, "give them time and show them who you really are."

"I'm not sure that's such a good idea. I think I've already shown them too much through the essays. I don't want to start another riot." Her voice whispered soft in the room, yet a trace of longing touched it as her heart reached out to him.

His fingers caressed her hair. The length cascaded down her back, and she watched as he held the strands for a moment before letting go. "Didn't you tell me once that a person could always make a decision and they didn't have to do anything they didn't want to?"

She turned to him. Her expression was soft and pensive. "I did say that once. I'm not sure it's true. I don't want to go to this ball." Alexandra stepped back, smiling. "But I don't seem to have a choice."

His hands fell away and he walked to the door. The languid smile vanished when he turned and spoke again. "I know, and I wish you felt different. Jessie and I will meet you in the parlor. Five minutes, Alex, and wear the necklace. Please."

Alexandra nodded then hurried to fix the damage he'd done to her hair. She called Kim and groaned as Kim laced the corset. After slipping the dress over her head, she glanced once at the mirror. The necklace of sapphires he'd insisted she wore sat on her dresser. She ran her fingers over the stones. They were beautiful. Carefully, she placed it around her neck and secured the clasp.

"Thank you, James," she whispered.

~ * ~

The carriage waited at the bottom of the front steps. A gold stripe along the solid black body and the decorative scrollwork gave it a regal appearance. It was elaborate and absolutely made for a woman's dreams. James stood at the top of the porch, and when she appeared, he ushered her out the door and down the many steps. Jessie and Kim sat in back, and James helped Alex to a seat next to him. Heat simmered between them as he set the horses into movement and they headed toward town.

~ * ~

The gaiety reverberated down the streets and out McCully Hall. Music flowed as they celebrated for a worthy cause, a new bell for the school. Jessie was all one gigantic smile.

When they entered the ballroom, an exaggerated hush gripped the revelers and everyone stared.

"I can do this," she breathed, instantly desperate for air.

"Is there any doubt?"

Alexandra stiffened, her chin tilting determinedly. She flashed everyone what she hoped was a dazzling smile. For the briefest second, Alex felt completely shunned, but she forced herself to ignore the stares and the subtle whispering behind her back, forced her chin a little higher. Bolstered by James encouraging touch at her waist and the slight tightening of his fingers around her elbow, she walked proudly into the gathering.

"The queen is back. My queen, angel girl. You're beautiful."

"James," Alex whispered, "don't leave me. Whatever you do, don't leave me."

He winked at her. "Keep that pretty smile on your face, darlin'.

244

You're doing fine. Want something to drink?"

Alexandra nodded. "Yes." She wasn't going to let these people intimidate her.

Jessie wasn't intimidated at all. The little girl started with the food, and it appeared as if she intended to eat her way through everything.

"Smile, sweetheart. Here comes Charles."

Alexandra looked up hesitantly. Her hands trembled and the drink James had just handed her dripped down the glass. She felt as if she'd just run a marathon and lost. "I'm not sure I can manage a smile," she laughed nervously.

James chuckled. "Guess what. The reverend is right behind him. What do you suppose he wants?"

"He looks fit to be tied."

"In a fine pucker," James agreed handily. "We could escape both of them. Want to dance?" James lifted the glass from her shaking hands and set it on the table.

Before she could reply, James waltzed her onto the dance floor, holding her scandalously close, breathlessly intimate.

"I'm going to make a fool of myself. You know I can't waltz." Her voice sounded soft and disarming. For a brief moment, it whispered against his cheek, and she wanted it to sound determined and strong.

"Relax," he whispered close to her ear. "Just follow my lead and whatever you do, remember to think in fours."

He pulled her closer, and she was sure it was too close for propriety. Hang propriety, she had her nerves to control. Within his embrace, she felt protected and cherished, and at this moment, she didn't care what the town of Jacksonville thought. She couldn't see over his shoulder, but she knew people stared, could feel their censor knifing into her back. Lord, he wanted her to make friends with these people. He was insane. Certifiably insane.

Alexandra inhaled deeply, hoping the oxygen would make her feel better. She wanted the confidence and the determination she'd had earlier. She wanted to please James. These people were important to him, and there had to be someone in the crowd who didn't think poorly of her. There had to be someone who understood. "Shouldn't I meet the reverend?"

James' grin disarmed her, instantly sweeping all her sense into a maelstrom of giddy delight. She'd known her question had pleased him, had known also he'd never push her to meet this man or anyone else here. If she was going to change Jacksonville's opinion of her, she'd have to set the wheels in motion. She'd have to act as the catalyst.

"You never cease to amaze me." James brushed his knuckles across her cheek. His gentle approval meant the world to Alexandra and she smiled shyly.

Together, they met the Reverend Royal and his wife by the long table filled with food.

"Good evening, Reverend, Mary Ann," James said.

The reverend nodded. Mary Ann smiled. "I could marry the two of you tonight," the reverend said quietly. "It would stop the tongues from wagging, you know."

Alexandra turned to James, questioning, her hand resting at the base of her throat. "Tonight? Could we do that?"

James stopped, turning his attention to Alexandra. His eyes held a wistful far away look, and she wasn't sure what he wanted. This was not at all what she had in mind for a wedding but...

He wasn't going to swear undying love and carry her off to his castle, but he needed her.

"I have no objections. It's up to Alexandra. You won't have your white dress or a long veil."

"I..." She felt too stunned to reply. Her mouth had gone suddenly dry and her knees threatened to buckle beneath her weight.

He wants to marry me today. Now.

I'm going to stay and love this man.

"Was that a yes or a no, darlin'?"

She gazed around the room, still dazed. The Reverend and his wife stood strangely unmoving, watching her confusion as if in a trance. Mary Ann had an all-knowing grin on her face, and the reverend appeared eager, too eager.

Was that how I looked? Eager? Was she eager?

Even the desire of returning to her time couldn't keep Alexandra from seeing James with Jessica, smiling and gentle, and with Kim. The love she felt for him was strong enough to bind her here, to him. When she married him, she'd give up all intentions to find her way home.

Alexandra wanted to know that kind of love in return. She wanted to make with James the home she had never thought to have, a safe haven in a curious world that had the power to yank her from one dimension to another, and the babies for Jessie to play with.

The knowledge of how completely and in how many ways she needed James scared Alexandra. Capriciously and unwittingly, he ripped apart all her rational thought processes, replacing them with emotions she didn't understand. She had no idea what curious power would envelope her if she gave in to her love for James.

"You two have been living in that house without a chaperone for too long," the reverend's voice was soft but his words sounded harsh to her and they implied so much.

"Can we talk about this?" Alexandra asked suddenly.

"Five minutes. Now don't go away. We'll be back and let you know."

With this expeditious proposal looming over their heads, James had changed. There was a glow about him. One that charged his movements and made his eyes flash. His volatile gaze pierced through her defenses, crumbling them to the ground, just like the walls of Jericho, she thought wryly. His vivid stare brought back the heat he aroused in her so easily, brought back the memories of his embrace.

"I don't think I can make up my mind in five minutes," she gasped out, shivering suddenly despite the heat. All the fears and uncertainties of the last few months settled in the pit of her stomach.

"It's all right if you don't." James looked over the dancing crowd. "This plan is crazy, you know, even though it feels right. I want to marry you and every instinct I possess tells me there won't be a better time than tonight. But I'm leaving this up to you. It's your choice, darlin'."

"I don't belong here."

"Hush, little angel, but you do." His expression and voice held so much compassion and longing. She could hear the yearning in his voice, see the fierce desire in his eyes. His hands trembled slightly as he touched her chin, raising it so he could look into her eyes.

Good Lord, was he frightened too?

"You belong by my side, forever."

"James." She felt as if she'd found everything she'd ever wanted. "This is all so sudden." Butterflies began to dance in her stomach. She loved him but he didn't love her. Jessie needed a mother but James didn't need a wife. Alexandra's pulse fluttered frantically. For a brief moment, she thought it had stopped. Reason warred with desire as she tried to make up her mind.

"Darlin', what difference does it make if it's tonight or in one month?"

He smiled at the reverend and his wife then gently guiding her through the crowd, he moved toward the door. Finally, they stood on the steps and even before they stopped, the words tumbled from his lips. "Alexandra, my very own, you can't deny this."

His mouth descended, aggressive, almost desperate but after the first few moments, gentled. He demanded a response, hungrily parting her lips and gaining entrance. Alexandra knew he meant to convince her. It was a heady thought. This wonderful man wanted her, desired her above all others. She wanted his touch, craved the intimacy he offered and his response was dangerous as their tongues met intimately. He no longer demanded, only waited as they moved closer together. On fire with yearning, her body melted against his. The sweet surrender that always followed his caress left her defenseless, and even though she'd already made her decision, she wanted this kiss and perhaps another.

"James," she gasped softly.

As he pulled back, he looked hopeful and eager. "Yes?"

"What will people say?"

"No one can see us," he said quietly, still looking confused but now appearing frustrated too.

She brushed her hands against her lips then touched his with her fingertip. Letting her hands slide down his chest, she pushed against him. "I don't want to go back in there, to my wedding, looking as if you've already had your wicked way with me." Her voice cracked on the last little phrase, and she shot him a weak smile, wondering if he understood what she'd just admitted.

His eyebrows rose dangerously. "Does that mean? The devil, is that really a yes?" he questioned. "Ah, darlin', my wicked way. I can hardly wait." His voice had suddenly grown husky, and his smile stretching nearly from ear to ear looked devilish. She gasped, startled by the sudden barrage of emotions zooming within.

"It wouldn't do to look ravished before the ceremony."

His eyes twinkled with humor. "How about after?"

Alexandra shot him a half-smile then nodded. "Perhaps."

"Ah, don't think for a moment that you'll get away unravished. If I understand correctly, this is our wedding night."

"Let's find the reverend."

~ * ~

The preacher stood in a place of honor, a podium and small stage had been set up while they were gone. Kim stood to one side. Jessie next to the preacher. Her wide beguiling eyes were innocent and held such expectation.

Alexandra stared at James for the longest time before finally nodding, certain this was right. All she had ever really wanted awaited her here, tempted her. Such simple words. James' hand tightened around her, giving her confidence. His fingers pressed reassuringly against her waist. It seemed he passed his strength on to her.

"Good, now just say I do at the proper time," she heard him whisper in her ear, and the warmth sent chills of desire down her spine and an almost greedy anticipation of the night to come.

It was true. He meant to marry her tonight.

The ceremony seemed to end even before it started.

There he stood, grinning at her, turning her around so the town's people could congratulate them and share in their newfound bliss. Charles came to kiss the bride. And Margaret kissed James. He pulled Margaret into his embrace, whispered something in her ear that made her giggle then swung her around. When the old lady landed on earth, she grinned at him, all smiles.

James slipped his hand in hers, and they ran through a shower of hastily procured rice to their carriage. Jessie sat in the back curled into the blankets there, her head resting on Kim's lap. Her eyes weary and dropping to a close, she moaned that her stomach hurt.

Alexandra allowed James to help her into the carriage, looking straight ahead while James bid his friends good bye; listened to the lewd jokes and laughter that followed them down the road.

As they left the town behind, the last of the crowd disappeared and they rode in relative silence.

"Alexandra?"

Her lashes snapped open and her head swiveled at the sound of his voice coming so close to hers.

"What?"

"Darlin', if it's any consolation, I'm sorry you didn't get your long white dress."

She watched him with a curious apprehension."

"Alexandra, what's wrong?"

"I, James?" She watched him, anxious yet determined, hesitant yet filled with an urgent desire.

"I won't hurt you. I know you were afraid of Sean, but I promise you that I won't do anything you don't like."

"I want you to make love to me," she said softly. She touched his hand with her own.

"I know that, at least I'd guessed. But, Alex, I want you willing. Will you come to me? Come to me with no fears and no regrets?"

"Yes. I'm just a little nervous."

"I don't know how to change that. I wish I could."

"After tonight, I won't have anything to be nervous about, will I?" she said brightly.

A full moon bathed them in a soft golden light. The road went on forever even as the crickets filled the night with sound.

A cougar cried in the distance.

James understood and urged the horses on in anticipation.

Chapter Eighteen

"We're here." Alexandra snuggled closer to her husband, her head resting against his chest. When his knuckles softly caressed the column of her neck, she opened her eyes slightly. "Wake up, sleepy head. We're home." Alexandra's lashes fluttered softly against her cheeks.

"James?"

He smiled and touched the tip of her nose with his finger. "Yes?"

Alex pushed away from him and stretched. "Home..." It did feel like home, she thought contentedly.

"It's really your home, Alex. I mean it. I want you to think of it as yours." His expression made her heart skip a beat, and she knew then he did speak the truth and knew also he'd do everything in his power to make it so.

She grinned and the little imp inside her head took over. "Does that mean I can paint it any color I want? Neon pink would be nice or perhaps a nice shade of puce."

James hesitated as if thinking it over and his eyebrows narrowed. As he started to give her an answer, he absently ran his fingers through his hair. "What's neon pink?"

Wicked thoughts returned two-fold but she restrained herself. "Don't worry. I don't think paint comes in that color yet, but maybe in a few years we could patent the shade."

"Can we discuss this later?"

"If you insist."

"I can think of a dozen other things I'd rather talk about. Stay here. I'm going to put Jessie to bed then I'll come for you. Promise me you won't budge an inch."

"Why?"

In a single fluid move, James jumped from the wagon. Purposely, he picked up her hand and held it. His mouth widened in a boyish grin and he winked at her. "It's a surprise, darlin'. Don't ruin it." He turned her hand over and kissed the heart of her palm. When he looked at her, his eyes were shinning and his soft laughter was endearing. "Promise?"

"Yes. I'll stay, but I don't understand."

"There are some things you don't have to understand, Alexandra. Some things are just meant to be lived. Don't try to make this logical. I'll put Jessie to bed then I'll come back for you. Now don't move."

James set her hand on her lap. Without hesitating, he lifted Jessie from the carriage and strode up the walkway with Kim following. Before he opened the door, he looked back at the carriage. When their gazes met, he nodded. She lifted her hand to wave but he was gone. The door stood open, and only the soft sounds of a hot summer night echoed around her.

This was heaven, Alex thought; it was more than she'd ever dared to imagine. Paradise was so very close she could almost taste it, feel it; hope for the future surfaced. Yet the unbidden call to the vortex still haunted her dreams, beckoning her back, subtly imploring her to venture within its mysterious realm once more. In this world of enchantment and the unknown, she was disposable, a pawn of little significance. Once, not so long ago, James had told her that until she could commit to staying in this time, he wouldn't touch her. Yet here they were. It was her wedding night, and she still harbored one very important secret from him.

"Alexandra?"

"Oh, my! James."

"A penny for your thoughts?"

She felt heat rush to her cheeks. "I don't think they're worth that much."

"I bet they're worth more."

Her heart fluttered. "You'd be wrong."

James held her hand in his. Tenderly, he brought it to his lips, lightly touching each finger.

"For you. I should have had it with me. It was my grandmother's."

Alexandra heart stilled, the ring shimmered in the light. An exquisite mate to the necklace she wore. "James..."

Before she could finish, James's hands encircled her waist, and he lifted her from the carriage. She gasped, startled by the sudden swift movement and the close intimacy. He held her for several breath-stealing seconds. In search of balance, her hands rested lightly on his shoulders. When she looked into his eyes, she saw compassion and desire. James wanted her, and the smoldering gleam she saw made a flame of longing curl deep inside.

As if in anticipation of the night to come, he let her body slide against his, causing her to tremble. The tips of her toes met the earth, yet he continued to hold her close. His chin rested against the top of her head, and one hand rested against the small of her back. With her cheek so very close to his heart, she could feel the rhythm of his life, the beating of his heart. New hope captured her soul, and she longed to tell him how much she wanted to stay in this time and with him.

"Ah, darlin'." James swept her into his arms and carried her across the threshold of her new home and into the parlor. Only the moon glow touched their features. "You deserve the very best."

"So do you," she told him, "I'm so afraid. Not of you, but..."

"We'll go to our room later," he whispered next to her ear. Shivers of delight coursed down her spine. The door clicked shut, closing out the rest of the world. James settled into a large chair, keeping her in his arms. She nuzzled into him, enjoying the moment, savoring it. He acted as if he never wanted to let her go and stared at her as if memorizing all the contours of her face.

"Our room?" Alexandra responded automatically. Yet her feelings were suddenly a mystifying confusion of desiring and not desiring, of common sense warring with potent emotions. "Can we talk first?" she tempered her words, recalling her promise to him. Willing. In the current state of her mind, how could she possibly separate her needs from her haunting imagination and the horrible nightmares she'd endured? How could she willingly go to him knowing at any time she might find herself wrenched into a different dimension? How could she give him what was rightfully his? He deserved a love that would last through all time.

"James, I'm so very frightened. Not of you but of the unknown. What's going to happen?" She had no experience in matters such as these.

A virgin at twenty-three, he'd scoffed, impossible. The ruse wouldn't work, he'd told her, and he'd also explained she couldn't escape his bed with such a blatant lie. But he was different now. He listened with a tender concern to everything she told him.

"Yes," he smiled down at her. "Our room." His tone was commanding yet strangely compelling. He sounded as if he were talking to a child trying to coax her to follow him. He was, she had to admit, coaxing a reluctant virgin, and he didn't even know it.

"I'd rather sit here a while," Alex said quietly, "with you."

He arched a brow. It seemed he noticed the panic in her eyes.

"Whatever you want," he said. "I want to make this night perfect for you." His fingers threaded through her hair, undoing the carefully arranged chignon. Hairpins scattered on the floor, and once again Alexandra listened to each one as it landed.

Everything about their liaison, beginning with their initial encounter on that frozen night in February was mysterious and complicated.

This was her wedding night. She belonged to him, now and forever. She'd promised to love and honor, but she'd also promised to obey. The wedding happened so fast she didn't have time to protest that one word. Obey? Obey. It did have a unique ring to it. She could try. Perhaps he could obey her too.

His wife. Forever.

She'd never thought.

Never thought what? A moment later she smiled at her absurd opinions. As if she'd had a choice in any of this.

A bottle of wine and two crystal glasses decorated a silver tray. The languid warmth of the night, the gentle light shimmering through the window, all spoke of romance and James' tender concern for her.

"Would you like a drink?"

She looked up suddenly, startled by the sound of his voice. "Okay." She laughed slightly. Her fingers nervously folded and refolded the fabric of her gown.

He stood and settled her on the chair. Alone. Emptiness surrounded her, cold air took his place and she shivered, missing the warmth that had encompassed her moments before. With each passing second, a brittle tension simmering around them grew. Awkwardly, she groped for words, the right words, but could think of nothing.

"What's wrong?" Instantly he was beside the chair, kneeling, the lines of his faced etched with a tender concern.

"Nothing. I just, I was thinking. This doesn't feel right. I mean, well, I don't feel married. It's as if I don't even know you." Her voice trailed away in a quiver of defeat.

He arched a brow. "Perhaps we should go upstairs now." His voice sounded tender and promising. "It might be easier."

"No. This is fine," she said, "for now." He'd have to understand. She wanted to come to him of her own accord, but at the moment she couldn't will herself to do that.

"Whatever you want, little angel. Whatever you need."

Tiny nerve endings on her skin prickled and danced, magically enchanted by the silky cadence of his voice. Still, she watched, not daring to breathe. He stood in front of her now and his hands caressed her. Slowly, he raised them, bringing her to her feet. Stiff but unresisting, Alex followed his lead. One finger separated from his grip and gently touched the underside of her chin, raising it, tipping her head back, forcing her eyes to meet his. Crystal clear with wanting, he gazed at her. She closed her eyes, hiding, escaping from what she didn't know.

The long black lashes that lay against her cheek fluttered open at his words. "Jessie's tucked away, now it's only the two of us." His eyes shimmered with passion, yearning, and perhaps even love. She didn't know, couldn't read his mind as easily as he did hers. She couldn't force herself to look away. Truly and irrevocably, he captured her in his gaze and transferred his feelings to her. The pull, a cosmic force, just as unexplainable as her tumble through dimensions, stoked a flame inside her.

With single minded purpose and trembling resolve, she shook the thought from her mind, summoning all her will power, "Is she all right?"

Her feelings for James were disastrously caught up in a tailspin of confusion.

"Don't be shy, Alex. You have no reason to act that way. Your experience doesn't bother me. I want you just the way you are."

"I'm not. It's just that Jessie didn't look well," Alex continued. She felt heat slowly build, and she knew she blushed.

"She ate too much. She'll feel fine in the morning. Concentrate on us, angel eyes. This is our night," he said.

"You're sure," her voice trailed off even as his thumbs found her lips and brushed them. Back and forth, soft and gentle, they traced the lush full curve that beckoned him.

"Don't change the subject again. I'm going to give you a wedding night you'll never forget." Their eyes met and she searched for confirmation. She saw passion darken his eyes. She trembled with anticipation, unable to deny her rising needs.

"I know, but the drink."

James hesitated as if he heard the anxiety in her voice, as if he knew how she felt. "Yes, I forgot," he laughed softly, and pulled her close. "It's all right. If you need to relax, if you want to wait a few minutes, I'll do whatever you want."

Alexandra nodded. "No, yes, please, James. This is new to me. I've never..."

He arched a brow and leaned closer still. Closer. Whisper soft and warm his breath caressed her cheek. "I've planned a night of seduction and wild passion." James brought her against him, and she felt the hard contours of his body. "Alex, don't pretend. Now, if you want to spend some time here first and it gives you courage..." he smiled. "It is courage you're looking for, isn't it? I must say that I don't understand, but I'll accept the excuse." He let her go and turned away. "Brandy...or wine?"

That brief moment together had shaken them both. They were both flushed and warmed from the encounter.

"Either one. I don't care."

"Perhaps both," James chuckled then poured them each a glass of brandy. He swirled his own, smelled the aroma, and gazed at her over the rim of the glass.

Alex had only tasted brandy once before, and the liquid burned a fiery path down her throat, but once the alcohol reached her stomach, it warmed and renewed her confidence.

She remembered the kiss he gave her at the wedding, hungry and demanding, and she felt the butterflies deep in her belly.

Absently touching her throat then the necklace, she ran her fingers over the sapphires.

"More?" he asked, eyeing her empty glass coolly.

"Yes."

"False courage, Alex. That's all it is."

"That would be nice," she wheezed painfully. "Can you fill the glass? I could use a little courage, false or otherwise."

"Are you sure? Or perhaps you're hoping to pass out and you won't have to perform your wifely duties?"

Her lashes flew open at the insinuation that was not even close to the truth. So much had happened to her the last few months she had no defense against any of it. The mystery was so difficult to understand, and acceptance had not been easy. Adjusting was even harder, but somehow she'd managed.

"Wifely duties? I never thought of it that way."

"No?" Their gazes met briefly, held only a moment before she dropped hers.

"No."

"Good. I'm not sleeping on that cot the rest of my life," he told her, and by the sound of his voice, she knew there was no room for argument. He studied her and it seemed he reached into the depths of her soul. To her astonishment, his hands were suddenly on the sides of her cheeks, gently exploring, caressing, discovering. "God, angel girl, what you do to me."

"What I do to you?" She struggled to understand his words then she remembered the night with Sean in the car. "Ice maiden," the words haunted her still.

The nightmare all of it suddenly came back to her vividly and with unerring detail. Desperately, she tried to shake off the images.

His gaze locked with hers now. Alex froze. She'd never seen that expression before, didn't know what to make of it. The heat and the ice, his look contained both, and the image threatened to shatter her peace of mind into a thousand pieces, sending fiery shards everywhere.

"Tonight and every night after you'll sleep next to me," he said gently. "What you're feeling now is nervous tension. The butterflies flitting about in your stomach will vanish. After tonight, there will be nothing to feel nervous about." His words left no room for argument, and she dearly wanted to accept all he told her as fact.

She tried to overcome her anxiety, "I know. But I'm frightened," the words barely audible whispered from her lips.

"There is nothing for you to fear. I won't hurt you. I promise."

"What if something happens and I go back?"

He sighed deeply. "We couldn't even find the place. This is your home now."

"But you don't want me. You don't love—"

"Don't deceive yourself. I want you. I kissed you and found I couldn't resist. You possess an innocence I thought never to see again. For a brief moment, I thought you had sent me straight to heaven, but I found hell instead every time you refused me." He held his hands out, beckoning to her, and she saw they trembled, and she watched his composure slip.

"You won't compromise?" Alex whispered, her eyes taking in all of James.

"No."

"Please..." she begged one last time. Alexandra waited. She felt as if she'd waited a lifetime to know his touch. There was a vulnerability about him that weakened her resolve. She was trembling again. She could not refuse him. Physical desire, curtailed and restrained in the past months was rising, impulsive and spontaneously, unaware of the tight restriction she had exercised in order to prevent such an intimacy.

"No." He pulled her towards him. Still paralyzed with fear of the unknown and mesmerized by the magic of his eyes, she was too stunned to move. In that instant, he was upon her and gently scooping her into his arms before she had time to resist.

"No more excuses." He started for the stairs and their bedroom.

Petrified, she sought a way to stop this. "Jessie, I need to see her," she said in a belated attempt to put off the inevitable. She'd always tucked Jessie in at night. Before she'd leave the room, she'd always given her a good night kiss and whispered a note of love to the child.

"Not this time. I've waited months for this night, and you're not going to find a way to put it off again." James responded in a low throaty growl that was vehement, not with anger but with frustration and yearning.

"Just let me kiss Jessie good night. Please. I always do. This isn't an excuse and I'm not really stalling for time."

"God knows I want to relent. I want you to feel this way about Jessie. But if I let you go this time, you'll think of something else, and this would inevitably become the longest night of my life. I'll bend. You can check on her later—after I've made love to you."

He didn't give Alexandra another opportunity to protest or seek a new diversion. He kept her well and thoroughly occupied. James no sooner entered the bedroom than he laid her on the bed. When his body came down to cover her, she sighed softly, forgetting everything else. His kiss sparingly potent, achingly tender, captured her attention and her body. Held captive by emotions and sensations, she allowed him the ultimate surrender, relinquishing her body without another thought.

Enchantment came slowly. Magically aided by his caress and the feel of his hard lean muscles pressing her down, she quivered beneath his touch. Every inch of her body that met with his came together in waves of untold pleasure. He held a power over her she'd never felt before or given to anyone else. Alexandra drew a ragged breath and forced herself to relax, then moaned with pleasure. While the caresses continued and became more and more intimate, she let her hands pull him closer. When at last his fingers slid beneath her dress, she knew her fears had been groundless.

Marriage, the word had bewitched her. It gave her permission for untold sins, but of course they weren't sins any longer. The guilt had vanished also. The inhibitions and ice had existed wholly because she hadn't loved the men who had ventured unasked into her life before. Now that she loved the man the restraints no longer existed either.

He wanted her, love might not have entered his mind but she didn't care. Nothing mattered except she could love him enough for the two of them. If he would cherish her and treat her with respect, she'd give him everything she could in return.

The heat inside her grew and spread. There was no way to stop it. It consumed her and even the cool night air caressing her skin didn't still the raging heat.

His hands touched newly bared flesh. He covered her mouth with his. Sensual undertones soothed her mind and allowed the fragile peace she so needed. A beautiful joining, a coming together of two people as one, and she was part of it. She wanted to return his touch and longed to feel his skin with her fingertips. But he wouldn't allow it. His hands continued their gentle seduction, roving everywhere, clearing a pathway for his mouth. James unlaced the corset and chemise to finally take her nipple into his mouth. Warmth deepened to a heated arousal, and she responded in kind arching toward him, begging him to take more of her, giving herself to him as a gift of love. The only wedding gift she had to offer. Alexandra gave of herself, and she prayed it would not go unnoticed or unappreciated.

Incredible, perhaps impossible, but the heat continued to grow, her body racing mindlessly out of control. The cool air caressed her fevered flesh but did not reduce the heat. She moaned and arched off the bed again. Her breath came in gasps as she struggled to understand the potent forces at work. With nothing else in her mind, she wrapped her arms around his waist and encouraged her fingertips to glide beneath his shirt, wondering at the ripple of muscle playing against her hands. Alexandra hoped to remember every one of these sensations the rest of her life.

He shrugged from his shirt and threw it to the floor. His boots and pants followed.

He began to move again and she lost herself in new and more potent feelings. She thought there could be nothing more, nothing stronger.

"Please," she whispered fiercely against him. Some unnamed force continued to build deep within her body, something unknown. A force that began to control each of her movements but she wasn't satisfied.

His lips trailed fire down the length of her body and back again, settling on her mouth, dancing attendance there only to move on to new places. His hands cupped her breasts as his thumbs lovingly fondled each crest, and his tongue ravaged a path down her belly, settling there then moving back to kiss her again.

A low moan followed by a whispered, "James," floated in the lover's bedchamber, and she gazed at him and knew this was right. She burrowed her hands in his hair and pulled him closer.

His fingers whispered against her stomach and drew with determined purpose to the soft curls between her thighs.

She gasped, startled, but he brought her closer. He whispered against her lips as he explored her further. She moaned softly and shivered, so captivated she pushed her hips against his hand as his touch surged intimately inside her. His lips scorched her once more. He caressed her with potent liquid heat in intimate spots, bringing soft moans to her lips as he possessed her breasts with his touch then his mouth. The liquid fire consumed her. Each new touch was passionate and compelling beyond measure, and she was hardly able to realize the first before another began.

She had never believed he would cherish her so completely, so thoroughly. He had married her because he desired her, and tonight he initiated her into his bed with tender concern.

"Alexandra," he raised his head. The next moment his mouth covered hers again, his deep rhythmic stroking continued, and an explosion of fiery pulsating sensation rocked her body. "Don't deny this again," he said.

He held her in his arms. His powerful frame still hovered over her, but now she didn't fear it, felt only the wonderful comfort and completeness his weight offered. Even as his tongue invaded her mouth, she felt him move against her. He teased and seduced her no longer, but moved with purpose, parting her thighs to his desire, crooning words of love next to her ear.

James eased himself between her legs, his rigid shaft poised at her entrance. He lifted her slim hips to receive him. She'd forgotten this part so caught up in her pleasure. Alexandra tensed, expecting the pain, hoping beyond hope her maidenhead had already been breached somehow. *Please,* she thought, *let it be gone.* She prayed as he easily slipped inside her. She was hot, warm and wet, and his entry stopped as suddenly as it had begun.

"Why didn't you tell me?" He sounded angry and she didn't understand.

"That I'm a virgin?" Alexandra did not turn her face away from him or try to twist free of his imprisoning grasp, but her eyes shone with a film of moisture.

"Yes," he said pushing forward suddenly and absorbing her cry of pain into his mouth.

The pain was astonishing, pulling her from the sweet web of magic that had surrounded her. She cried out and bit into his shoulder, tears stinging her eyes. James moved deeper into her tight passage until he filled her completely, moving, delving against her. "Horrid, wretched man!" she cried out.

"Bastard," he retorted with a gentle understanding, "God, Alex, I didn't want to hurt you. Call me anything you want."

She nearly laughed, but the magic consumed her pain and she was astonished again.

He stopped as if waiting for her. "It's all right. It's over now."

He flashed even white teeth. Then he lowered his head to kiss her. Alexandra clung to him with all the strength she possessed. A strength that diminished with each deepening thrust, and she fought for herself but lost to his greater power. She had never known a hunger so intense. Her body shifted and writhed beneath him. She stroked his back and felt the tension and control of his muscle and the ever-growing force within her. Then the pulsing was back, exploding over her, engulfing them, making them as one as he moved deeper.

"Alexandra," she heard, a low growl of pure animal pleasure emanating from him. They were one and she knew it would last forever.

He tilted back then, leaning on his elbows. His fingers whispering against her face, touching her heart. When she opened her eyes, she found him gazing at her openly, and she knew if he could he would have kept her from the pain. His eyes intense and fathomless met hers.

"I tried to tell you," she said softly.

"I know you did. But I didn't listen, did I? Perhaps because I've wanted this from the first moment I saw you. On hands and knees you defied me, and your courage touched my soul. You can't imagine how difficult it has been for me to give you the time you needed."

From the first moment he saw her? No, she couldn't believe that because she didn't remember the meeting except in dark hazy outlines. She couldn't believe any man would want her that much and for so long. It went beyond her realm of experience. Her tongue twisted in her mouth, and she choked on words that wouldn't come. Her heart raced as she watched him gaze at her body. All of it, and she felt tempted to cover herself. He held his breath. Only his eyes moved as she watched in confusion.

"I never thought," she whispered.

"Oh, but I knew."

That night, with the soft summer breeze wafting through the open window, the sound of crickets humming outside, the moonlight delicately painting the wall, and the smell of a lazy hot summer filling the air, with trepidation followed with assurance, they gave to each other their heart and soul and the promise of a future.

Chapter Nineteen

"Umm..." Alexandra nestled her head against James' shoulder. Her fingertips trailed lightly across his chest, met the light dusting of hair. Her husband's chest. Married, thoroughly, completely, and irreversibly for all time, and the thought sent little tremors of happiness rippling within. Alexandra McMurdie, no, Lawrence, was a married woman now. A smile stretched slowly across her face.

Daylight did bring a renewal of hope, yet despite all her newfound happiness, she could not purge her mind of Sean Cassidy or the threat still hanging over her head.

She might, after all, elude Sean and the horrible time machine that waited in the hills for her. She didn't want to leave, hadn't for so long now. She loved James Lawrence, loved him from the depth of her heart. What if she conceived?

James was not a man to toy with. Dangerous, and always masterful. If she were to conceive a child, his child, he would follow her to the ends of the earth or the universe.

They had taken no precautions.

She cast an appreciative gaze back to James, her husband now. He lay sleeping peacefully beside her. The ripple of muscle played beneath her fingertips. She ignored the fact her cheek rested on his chest and she'd spent the night doing the most delicious and unspeakable things. Yet, no matter what happened to her, she'd never forget what he did to her, how he touched her heart, the tempest he created within her. Nor would she forget the languid warm peace that had claimed her in the aftermath.

Despite her original apprehension, she had to admit waking up with James in her bed, although a new experience, filled the empty spaces inside her.

Alexandra slowly traced the hard planes of his chest to the edge of the sheet. Self-consciously, she ran her tongue across her lips. Once again she traced the length of his chest, this time with a fingertip. Crisp white linen sheets settled neatly against his body, a sharp contrast to his dark tan. Her thoughts turned wicked. She concentrated on the scintillating observation that he was naked. Naked.

With great strength of will, she kept her self from removing the sheets. Oh, how she wanted to see the source of all that marvelous pleasure he'd gifted her with, but she resisted momentarily. Then her resolve faltered and her hand moved irrevocably, hovered a moment then stilled instantly as a very soft masculine chuckle reverberated in her ear. An ear that was still pressed close to his heart.

She stiffened, startled by the sound. Then she let her breath out slowly and watched his muscles tremble with the heated contact. Instantly hot, hotter than a blazing August day, she snatched her hand from his chest.

Snagged in a compromising position, she smiled. What could he expect? Embarrassed now, irrevocably and thoroughly, she decided to brazen this out. An air of nonchalance, she thought suddenly, was necessary, but he interrupted her plans and caught her unprepared.

James enclosed her hand in his, palm against palm. "I don't mind if you look."

His amused tone surprised her. Now she wasn't at all sure how to proceed. But she did want to look her fill, and she felt another surge of heat flood her cheeks at that realization.

But she still had one secret she'd kept from him. It was an unforgiving secret if he couldn't accept it. She could only hope James would understand. Pushing all thoughts of revealing her career choice aside, she thought of lying here with him in the sunlight, thought of all the years they had ahead of them. She didn't intend to waste one moment on useless worries.

Instead, Alexandra brazenly let her fingertips tickle his flesh at the edge of the sheet, enticing and teasing a response. He growled, primitive and all male. She ran her finger the width of his well-muscled stomach, heard the rumble of excitement, smiled innocently, and ran the same finger back tantalizing and encouraging him. Felt her body stir and respond to the sensations she elicited beneath her fingertips.

She saw the warmth and passion within his eyes. "I don't mind either." Her fingers maintained the advantage, moving strategically lower, mischievously lower, so very wicked. He allowed her exploration and she reveled in his easy and compliant surrender.

"Keep that up, angel mine, and you might regret it." His voice sounded strained as he spoke, and she glanced at him, smiling impishly. She liked the words he spoke to her and the power she had over him. Slowly his fingers began a tantalizing exploration of their own.

"Never," she purred and her hand drifted lower, met his hard arousal and stopped as suddenly. Her gaze flew to meet his, and she saw his devilish smile.

"You're playing with fire."

"I am." She was enchanted by the magic, the mystery that surrounded them, and by his words. The world indeed had turned upside down. She was no longer an ice maiden. No, she was changed by some sweet madness he kindled within her, and the knowledge filled her with comforting warmth.

"You're not going to be able to put this one out."

"I might not want to."

He wound the silken strands of her hair around his hand, pulling her closer.

"Don't tease."

Her eyes widened, "I'm not. At least I didn't mean too. Does it hurt?" She liked the sound of his words and wanted to play even more.

"Don't ever doubt it darlin'," he drawled.

She didn't, not for a second. "May I?"

"Are you sure?" His tone held a hint of warning. The question asked for her benefit didn't sound as if he meant to allow her the freedom of choice. She had carried this too far to stop. "Making love to you was good last night but now...now...ah, darlin'."

"I've never been more sure of anything." She hesitated a moment, another thought stirring her mind, and she tried to withdraw her hand, but his fingers clamped over her wrist, immobilizing her then sending it lower.

"Touch me..." His ragged breath and pounding heart surprised her. Her fingers wound around his hard smooth length, and she held him, tenderly, almost reverently, still in awe of the power within him.

"Like this?" she asked even as she began a gentle assault.

"Perfect," he added, reversing their position so once again he pinned her beneath him. Her hands traveled to his neck. His lips feathered across her forehead, touched her eyes, closing them with the contact. Then he kissed the tip of her nose, finally settling on her lips. She opened, willing and eager for his kiss, blossoming under his tutelage. Their tongues met in a duel, a mating dance demanding completion. His hands came to rest beneath her breasts, enticing, teasing, but not quite touching the sensitive crests that hardened with desire. She arched against his supple fingers, yearning for more. He buried his face in the valley between her breasts, tempting her but still not satisfying her. Kissed the length of her body...

A sob shattered their lovemaking and the morning. They froze, listening, but it was as if nothing had been said. A strange, timeless silence echoed all around them. The mysterious tranquility of the house frightened her.

She lay beneath him, trembling.

"Jessie!" Alex called. They tensed and waited for a welcoming call. A sound to prove everything was as it should be, but it never came.

Another sob broke the silence.

She pressed against him, longing to stop the shivering and ease the sweet agony, but again a sob shattered the serenity.

"Another nightmare." James rose from the bed. Forgotten was the pleasure and the anticipation of their lovemaking. All need vanished and was replaced with a far different desire. Alexandra scrambled from the bed and threw on James' shirt that lay discarded in a rumpled heap on the floor. James stepped into his trousers, buttoning them even as he rushed to Jessie's room.

Jessica lay on the bed, giving the impression of a fragile porcelain doll. Sometime during the night she'd thrown off the covers, her nightgown entwined around her legs. Ebony curls, damp with perspiration, spread around her face, a face that appeared flushed and felt so very hot to the touch.

Dear Lord, what was wrong with Jessie?

"She's burning with fever." James rested his trembling hand against her forehead then moved to her wrist. "Pulse is weak and her breathing is shallow." He checked her eyes.

Kim appeared at the door. "Mr. James? Miss Jessica?"

"Don't come any closer."

"You heard her too?" Kim hesitated at the door, one foot slightly inside, looking as if she were torn with indecision.

"What's wrong?"

Alexandra was trembling as she looked at Jessie who appeared so pale and still. Jessie's eyes were open but she looked through her.

"Papa?"

"Hush, Sugar Plum. It's all right. I'm here now. Tell me where it hurts."

Jessie sobbed, her lips forming barely audible words. The soft cadence terrified Alexandra.

Alexandra brushed Jessie's forehead with the back of her hand. She gasped, startled by the intense heat. Then she looked at James. For a passing moment, she saw the pain and the fear clearly then he shuttered his expression, dawning a stoic professional mask, closing her from his thoughts.

"Kim, bring some water, cold water. And some towels."

As if anticipating his orders, Kim was gone. A few moments later she returned.

The bucket of ice filled water she set part way into the room.

"Alexandra, I don't want you here." James' precise and unfeeling command left Alex at a loss for rebuttal. She ignored him. Feeling as if she moved in slow motion Alexandra carried the bucket to Jessie's bedside. James was peeling Jessie's nightgown from her.

"Alexandra."

"I'm not leaving her or you." Alex turned back to the door,

retrieving the towels Kim had brought. Kim stood immobile at the door, peering into the sick room, ringing her hands. Tears flowed from her eyes.

When Alexandra set the towels by James, he glanced at Alexandra then dipped one of the hand towels in the ice water.

"Do as I say. Don't make this harder than it is."

"Send someone for the doctor," Alex said as she watched him run the cold towel the length of Jessie's arm.

"I am a doctor," he shot back and she stared at him, surprised at her forgetfulness.

"Okay."

"I don't need another doctor or a second opinion. I know what's wrong. There will be more cases. A great deal more. People will die."

Alexandra stumbled back, concerned and baffled at James' proclamation. All the time James talked he continued to bathe Jessie with cold water.

The tiny child closed her eyes, and for a while, it seemed as if she slept. Two hours later Kim brought food and left it by the door. Alex alternately stood and sat by Jessie's bed, sometimes resting against the wall, always watching.

"She's no better. She can barely draw a breath." His voice stretched pencil thin, wavered. Sweat soaked the back of his shirt and beneath his arms.

"James, you have to do something."

"I'm doing all I can."

She watched James purse his lips, furrows creasing his brow. He propped Jessie head against his shoulder and helped her sip the cool liquid he offered. His brow was lined with worry and fatigue.

"What is wrong with her?" Alexandra asked after James settled Jessie back on the pillow.

"I'm afraid..." his voice trailed off, sending goose bumps down her arms. Not knowing was far worse than understanding and dealing with the bad news she felt certain he was about to apprise her with. Once again he turned back to Jessie and placed a cold damp towel on her forehead.

"What is it James?" she asked again. She had to know if only to think straight, to regain a fading hope.

Kim was back. "I'll take the dishes."

"No. Leave them here," Alex said quickly.

"But..." Kim stopped. "I'm going to have to take them sometime. We both know she's not going to get well soon."

Alexandra gasped, surprised at the knowledge written so clearly on Kim's face.

"What is it Kim? What does she have?"

Kim bit into her lower lip then looking at James. After a few brittle moments, Kim left the room. Alex could hear the soft shuffle of her slippered feet as she slowly moved down the hallway then the stairs.

After the sounds vanished, she swirled on James, furious with him.

"Never mind," he said before she could question him again. "Send for the doctor and don't come back to the room." His change of tactics alerted her instantly. "If it's what I think, I don't want you anywhere near this."

"James," her voice wavered slightly her speech tentative. Not knowing terrified her and the concern written on his face made her next words falter. "I deserve to know." Her knees threatened to buckle. "Please, I have to know."

"Don't argue...believe in me." He moved away from Jessie, striding purposefully toward Alex. Grasping her chin between his thumb and forefinger, he lifted her face up to his. "Please."

"I want to believe but—"

"Just do what I say Alex and leave," he cut in instantly. "I don't want you anywhere near this."

"What is it?"

"Alexandra! You don't need to know. Now do as I say!"

"No, not until you tell me." It occurred to Alexandra she'd approached this the wrong way. And as quickly as the thought entered her mind, she shoved it angrily away.

His eyes were rimmed with dark circles. Already fatigue and worry claimed his features. "I know I'm about to have one hell of a battle on my hands. Alexandra, I want your obedience. I want you out of the sick room, and I want to protect you."

It was his turn for surprise. "No."

"Son of a bitch!" he grabbed her arm and ushered her from the room. "If it's what I think it is, I won't put you at risk. I took an oath. You didn't."

His grip tightened on her arm and his jaw grew formidably taut. She bristled with furious outrage. "You'll put yourself at risk," she challenged him, courageously standing her ground, and it seemed she refused to back down even at his request.

"Yes, she's my responsibility."

"Mine too or have you forgotten so soon? I'm your wife now, and it was because of this little girl that we came together."

"I need you healthy. Don't you see?" His tactics changed suddenly. His voice turned soft.

"But I might be able to help," she looked desperate. "I won't abandon Jessie, not even for my safety."

~ * ~

Forcefully and with a quiet determination that had always seemed a part of him, he held on to her with both hands now. He hesitated a moment, trying to think of the words. "This isn't the time to act stubborn," he told her. He didn't want to be harsh with her, but he didn't have time to explain everything. Expecting his commands to be obeyed, he didn't know how to handle this situation or his new wife. He was so very frightened for Jessie, for Alexandra. He wouldn't lose them. He would never survive without them.

Would never survive if he failed to protect them.

"I'm not," she stammered, "it's just that, I don't know how to explain this but James, there are diseases I can't get. I'm immune. A miracle of the century I came from."

He laughed, his tone harsh yet it amazed him, "Because you're a witch—you travel through time—you can't get sick—really, Alex." Then he saw the flash of pain in her eyes and regretted his words.

"I didn't mean it like that."

He watched her and berated himself for his callousness even as her pain turned to anger. She trembled and he knew she drew strength from her stubborn pride. Alex had to understand the danger. Had to realize he would not allow her to put herself in jeopardy. The risk of loosing both of them was a gamble he wouldn't pursue.

"No you're not a witch, you've had these diseases already. I understand that, but..." he continued, cautioning himself to reason but still unable to assimilate everything she said.

"No. I haven't had the diseases. Shots. Shots, James, I've had every one imaginable. Damn you, James Lawrence, I wouldn't lie about this!" she cried out frantically.

"Please, Alex, don't try to humor me. Shots?" He left her and went back to Jessie, his ministrations succinct yet also tender. "This is serious. Her life is in danger, and you're allowing your imagination to run wild." He knew what he wanted from her, obedience, blatant obedience at least until the danger passed.

"It's not my imagination. I know this is serious, but if it's something I can't get and you can, don't you see? I should stay with her. Reconsider. Please."

"I won't, can't allow you to put yourself in danger. Besides, she needs medical help that only I can give."

"Hogwash. You could give me directions from outside her room," she whispered fiercely. "Besides, at the moment there is nothing to do but bring the fever down. Any fool can do that. After all we've been through, you still think of me as weak and I hate it, James Lawrence. Do you hear me? I despise the pedestal you've put me on; not only because I'm not used to it, but because I'm anything but weak and fragile."

"I know that."

"I'm independent and strong. I can think for myself."

His response was curt. "Don't. I can't fight this disease and you too. Don't make me force the issue."

"You don't have to," she shot back, her fury clearly evident. "Male pride. Stubborn pride. You'll let the disease kill you because you're a man. And you won't let me in even though I may be immune. I can't believe—"

"You win. I understand. It's the way I was raised, but I'll listen." Suddenly, James pulled her in his arms and buried his face in her fragrant hair, his hands pulling her to him as if he could erase all his fears. He wanted to kiss her mouth closed and stop the truth from tumbling out, because he'd already guessed she spoke the truth, even though it was damn hard to admit. He was stupid to let his stubborn pride block their efforts to help Jessie. Stupid to let the disease threaten his health, if what she said was true.

"What do you think it is?" she asked.

"I don't like this," he said. His hand softly brushed Jessie's, cheek. "I don't want to take the chance."

"You have to."

"Just tell me what it is you think she has," she said, praying he'd tell her. "You said you'd understood, but you don't. One word could end this argument. One little word, James that's all it would take."

The fear he heard in her voice was replaced by resigned determination.

"I insist. I won't budge," she said with heartrending finality.

"That is a threat you can't carry out, darlin'."

"I know but I have to try. I'd fight you every step you moved me away from her room."

"Diphtheria," he interrupted callously then watched to see her reaction. She didn't cringe or withdraw, actually smiled as if relieved then exhaled suddenly.

"Good, then you'll let me take care of her."

"You're not above lying to get your way in this." His expression was serious even as his hopes soared. "Promise you won't lie."

She bristled at that, "I've never lied to you and I'm not doing it now. I've had my shots, TDAP, diphtheria, pertussis, and tetanus, can't get any of them." She waved her hand defiantly. "The list is longer but I won't bore you. Now, I'll take care of the patient. And wash your hands," she added with a smile that might have been triumphant in any other circumstances. "We're dealing with a highly contagious disease."

He held up his hands in silent surrender and awe. He'd have to send a man into town and place a quarantine on the house. A second opinion wasn't necessary in this case. He'd seen too many cases during the war and before not to recognize the symptoms. Why he had never contracted the disease went beyond his understanding as did the words Alex had spoken, but he knew of the advances in medicine over the last fifteen years and could speculate that what they would consider a miracle now could seem common place in the twenty-first century.

"You win." James turned to leave.

"No one wins, but when you come back, you'll have to tell me what to do."

"For now just sit by her and try your best to keep the fever down. I'll leave ice outside the door then I'll explain everything to Kim. And, little angel of mercy, I'm not leaving. I'm only giving you permission to help."

Tender feelings stirred deep inside him for Alexandra, and he smiled at the look of fear he saw in her huge blue eyes. Now that she'd won the argument, she was afraid but he knew she wouldn't crumble under the pressure or back down. And he knew all too well the terror gripping her heart. It had him in a vise. She wasn't afraid for herself. No, the fear went deeper than that. Jessie's life rested with her ability now, and of course luck. Failure would be her constant companion, and she had to survive that fear, accept the possibility of failure and deal with it.

Failure meant Jessie's death.

Success meant her life.

Days could pass before they'd know the outcome, and he remembered the all-consuming fatigue that accompanied the waiting and the fear. As much as she liked to believe she could nurse Jessie by herself, she couldn't. It simply wasn't rational to think she could do everything alone.

When he left for a moment, Alexandra promptly locked the door, wouldn't even let him peek inside the door. Despite all his efforts to persuade her otherwise, she kept it bolted from the inside. She opened the door only when she heard his footsteps move away. He had at the very least expected to gain entrance to the room.

Two days. Two terrifying days.

Hell, how did she do it?

Still, the surprise he registered when the door swung open on its hinges without protest stopped him.

"Alex, what the...?" He saw her curled next to Jessie, one hand rested on the little girl's shoulder the other tucked under her own cheek. She had in truth given up, admitted her frailty and allowed him a small measure of responsibility. Even grudgingly, he'd decided he'd accept it anyway he could get it. She needed him.

"James?" he heard her plea, "be careful," and her eyes fluttered closed.

Chapter Twenty

Was there no star that could be sent...to heal that only child?

Emerson, "Threnody"

Alexandra leaned back in the soothing hot water and allowed her eyes to fall shut. Every muscle ached, every nerve stretched taut, and now with the languid heat against her skin, she relaxed.

"Alexandra. Alex...come here." The command shattered the peaceful serenity in the room. She jumped from the steaming heat of the tub, water sloshing over the edge, soaking into the carpet. With only a sheet wrapped around her, Alex raced to Jessie's room. The terror in James' voice alarmed her and her heart lodged in her throat. Fear. Desperation.

Oh, God.

"Jessie?" Breathless, her heart pounding, she ran into the room. Alexandra's wet hair dripped down her back, soaking the sheet. She'd wrapped the towel around her toga fashion and tied it over one shoulder. Goose bumps spiraled down her arms, and she shivered uncontrollably.

Alex saw the tears in James' eyes. Saw the pain etched in every line of his face, imploring her, as if she could wave a magic wand ending the terrible uncertainty. She wanted to do just that. She wanted Jessie's life back, needed to hear her laughter.

His body trembled, shaking violently as he held Jessie's fragile hand in his. At the sight, Alexandra's heart pounded fiercely, terror rolling in her stomach. They couldn't lose Jessie now, not now.

Dear, Lord. How could this happen? They'd taken every precaution, done everything humanly possible.

"She can't breathe," Alexandra whispered.

They had regulated her temperature, kept it down, but now Jessie couldn't breathe. Exhausted by his fears and guilt, James had withdrawn from her.

Alexandra stepped forward, examining the child. She placed her head on Jessie's chest to listen, the sound of her breathing faint and so very shallow. "Isn't there anything we can do?"

The most precious thing in his life, wasting away in front of his eyes, and Alex knew he couldn't think of anything. Waiting for her to die was impossible—preposterous. When Alexandra looked out the window, it was almost as if she could see Jessie playing and dancing across the fields of wildflowers, her long dark hair spilling across her shoulders. It seemed impossible this precious child was dying. Helpless to absolve James of his guilt, she reached for his hand. It trembled beneath her fingers.

He refused her comfort, withdrawing from her. "I told Jessie I'd take care of her. Wouldn't let anything bad happen to her," James fingers lightly brushed Jessie's dark hair from her face.

"Then don't." Alexandra's quiet determined reply startled him.

"I don't know what to do." His anguish was echoed in his tone and betrayed in his fathomless blue eyes. He covered his eyes with his hands, giving into helplessness. And she heard the shudder of fear and defeat that wracked his body, her heart going out to him. Only a miracle could save Jessie now.

Help Jessie breathe. She'll die.

"James?" Alex ran her fingers through her hair, her lips trembling. She was worried beyond endurance but still determined. Images of Jessie dodging Kim's pig and chasing the chickens around the yard filled her mind and she angrily pushed them aside. "We can't just let her die," she cried out to him. Of course she knew if there had been tricks to pull from a little black bag, he would have done it days ago. With no miracle in the making, they were left to their own devices, their own intelligence. And finally, the horrible realization they might not succeed.

His face was drawn and haggard, and his eyes were filled with unshed moisture. He'd aged ten years in the last few days.

"I don't, I don't know what to do." He looked at her for a brief moment, his eyes narrowed in anger with himself. James turned away abruptly, his hands clenching and unclenching spasmodically. Only tightly leashed restraint kept him sane, yet to Alex his voice was too quiet. "Son of a bitch, I should know what to do."

Alex waited. She could do nothing without him. Finally, their gazes met and she felt as if she begged, pleaded for advice or a miracle. A miracle from heaven. Too much, too much to ask for. She had no knowledge in this field. She had no training other than a little first aid, surely...

Surely he could do something. God or James.

Perhaps the devil would bargain.

Alexandra paced.

This laughing, beautiful child did not deserve this. Alex looked for answers, prayed, and found only silence. Jessie was dying, fading before their eyes, and dear God, she'd die if they didn't do something soon. Jessie fought each breath. Every painful wracking breath forced past her lungs foretold the end.

"Hang on, Jessie. We'll think of something." Determination pulsed in every nerve. She'd watch her play again, watch her grow up, watch her fall in love and have children of her own. "Jessie, you're going to make it through this. You are, even if I have to breathe for you."

Breathe for her. A miracle. But how?

A light, the barest glimmer of hope fluttered in Alexandra's mind, a thought, yes a miracle.

Take this into your own hands. Breathe for her. Give her life.

"Papa, am I going to die?" Jessie's words were thin and she struggled with each one.

"No, Sugar Plum," James whispered back.

"I've seen the angel, Papa. She's beautiful, just like Alex."

~ * ~

Lord, no! Tears slipped from his eyes and ran down his cheeks unchecked. He'd given up, defeated irrefutably by a capricious deadly disease, but watching Alex face this problem gave him new hope. "Think of something? Dear, God, I wish..." He let his head fall into his hands again and closed his eyes, thinking...crying...praying perhaps. *If I can only remember how.*

Jessie and her first attempts to swim...Jessie running wildly down the stairs, yelling Papa...then the first time she'd said "I love you." Precious, tender moments and now...now there would be only silence.

"What are we going to do?"

James looked at Alexandra, his lips drawn tight and shook his head. Long drawn out seconds passed while neither of them spoke.

"You have to think of something. You're a doctor." Her words reached into his soul and tore at his heart.

"You come from a world that performs miracles every day. I'm open to suggestions."

"I don't know. I just don't know. No one gets this disease in the twentieth century. There's no need of a cure." Alexandra held Jessie's hand in hers, thinking. Thinking so damn hard.

"Breathe life into her. Find a way."

Her singular statement gave him pause to think. "I'm not God," he said and the wariness in his eyes reached out to her for understanding and compassion.

"Hang on, Jessie. Fight this, please." Alex lightly kissed Jessie's cheek. She set her hand back on the bed then turned to James.

"There is nothing I can do...nothing you or any of us can do except wait."

"No." Unwilling to give up she looked back at Jessie. "Look, James, look at her. We're all she has. You can't wait for a miracle. The situation is not hopeless either. I won't accept that. Together we can think of something. There has to be a way."

"I'm sorry." Slowly he walked to the bedside and stared down at his child. His voice trailed off, and the tears that welled in his eyes threatened to overflow once more. He'd saved her that day so long ago only to bring her to this. He should have kept her safe, should have protected her from this fate, but he couldn't have. Short of keeping her locked in her room, he couldn't have kept her safe from life. And that's what happened; life stepped in and called to her. Now she'd have to go. She'd walk with the angels now.

Alexandra moved to his side, her tears glistening in her eyes, but it seemed to James she spurned the inevitable, refusing to acknowledge a power in and above itself that called to Jessie.

"Look at her..." Alex commanded, her voice shaking with tempered emotion. "Don't quit before she does. Don't give up on her. If you do, you'll never forgive yourself. Just keep fighting. Everything will be fine." Her voice had taken on a mystical quality. It seemed the words came from somewhere deep inside, somewhere unfathomable and far away.

"Breathe for her."

James did set his gaze on hers and he did watch. Jessie fought desperately, struggled, and with each breath, she achieved a victory of sorts, even though it might be her last. With each little gasp, she gave them an opportunity to save her and, yes, he'd given up because he'd felt so helpless and afraid of his terrifying inadequacies.

He stiffened then, tried to think of Alexandra and that damn steel rod she stuck up her spine, and he did the same. It almost felt good, but he still didn't know what to do for Jessie.

"I think, just maybe, James, I just thought of this. You're a surgeon, aren't you?"

James looked up, surprised by her question. "Yes," he said cautiously, not sure where this conversation was going, not sure he wanted to know. He wanted to shut out her thoughts, but instead he listened.

"Then you can perform a miracle here today." Her words were crisp and metaphorically concise, but gave nothing away.

Instantly alert, he stared at her hard, remembering times best left forgotten, recalling memories he had denied for so long. He hesitated a moment before he spoke. "A miracle," he said, his fingers suddenly trembling. "Hardly. More people died at my hand than I can banish from my memory." His attention riveted on Jessie, his lips thinned forming a harsh line.

"It wasn't your fault."

"Oh? The ones that didn't die from loss of blood died later from infection. There were so many."

"You couldn't do anything about the conditions."

"I accepted my responsibility. I've put it behind me."

Alexandra wet her lips then absentmindedly bit the lower one, looking to Jessie then back to James. She inhaled deeply before she proceeded. "Can you cut a tiny slit in her wind pipe? At the base of her throat?" She waited for an answer, but it didn't come. "Can you?"

The silence lasted an eternity and beyond.

He pondered the question for the longest of seconds.

"The trachea? Whatever for?" But even as he said the words he knew. *Breathe for her.* She could still die. If she truly meant for air to enter there, something would have to hold it apart and keep the tissue and blood from going through the incision.

"So she can breathe," she continued warily.

"Breathe?" His tone was hesitant.

"I'm worried, James, scared to death. I'll try it myself if you refuse, but surely you won't leave the cutting to me." Her hands shook and her voice sounded paper-thin when she spoke the words. "I don't know if I can hold still long enough to do it. I don't even know if I'll faint. The sight of blood makes me waver." She was babbling again as if she suddenly realized how nervous she was. She stifled another sentence.

Miss Jessie grew more beautiful and delightful every day. She was precious, fighting for her life with the only means available. No, she wouldn't let either of them give up.

"We'll need, let me think a moment, something with a hole in it small enough to put in the slit." Her eyes were filled with hope but also fear.

The full implications of what she said registered instantly, and it slammed into his chest with the impact of a charging bull. James stared down at his trembling hands, sickness coursing through his stomach. He pushed the fear aside, thinking, demanding the very best from himself.

"It might work," he said with more calm than he felt. "Yes, it might work at that," he said, buoyed now by a shred of hope filtering into his mind, a hope Jessie might survive this.

"Are there any reeds at the creek?" she asked.

"Reeds?"

"Yes, for the straw. Won't that work? If you insert it into the hole, she can breathe through the straw until—until—I don't know. Maybe this won't work after all."

"It might," he thought for a moment, studying the situation.

"I'll get some," she turned to go and he caught her arm.

"No," he said softly then smiled at her appearance. The picture of her mounting Matilda and riding hell bent to the creek dressed in her white sheet was amusing, but he'd have to save the image for another time. "I'll go. But not to the creek."

"Oh."

His gaze was filled with warmth when he looked at her and she blushed. With all that was going on, she could still blush he thought, amazed.

"My sentiments exactly." His voice flat and lacking any emotion. If this was successful, he'd have time enough later for other pleasures. "I've something that will work better. It's hollow."

She turned her head slightly. "Where?"

"In my surgeon's bag."

"I'll get dressed." Alexandra stood on tiptoes to kiss his cheek.

~ * ~

Water boiled on the kitchen stove. She set all the instruments in his doctor's bag in the water. Alexandra ironed the clean dishtowels. Without question, Kim worked diligently and uncomplaining beside her. When everything was sterilized, they brought it to the bedroom.

"This has to work." Alexandra's eyes filled with tears while she prepared for the operation. The pounding of booted feet echoed down the hall, and she stopped a moment as if to listen.

She held Jessie's hand and, watched her little chest rise and fall with each labored breath. Sunbeams hovered above the head of Jessie's bed.

"Alex?"

"In Jessie's room. Wash with the lye soap I set out," she hollered down the stairs.

"Already have." James stood beside her, hands in the air. She tied a sterilized cloth around his face and hers. James tore his gaze from the faith he saw in her eyes. "What's this for?"

"Germs."

"I won't argue...you think this is necessary?" The look he shot her held respect and admiration. Despite trembling hands, he strode to the bed, surveying the patient and the precautions Alexandra had taken.

"Yes."

"I'm ready. I do know something about bacteria and sterile conditions. This seems to be an extreme." But then what? She came from a time superior in many ways to his, knew things that seemed on the verge of sorcery if one believed in that. "The ether is working. She's asleep." He paused. "Are you ready?"

"Yes." Alex looked away as he gently made the first incision then forced herself to concentrate on the operation. The sterile cloths surrounding the wound brought home the danger that existed with startling clarity. When the first trickle of blood oozed out, she swayed on her feet. The blood drained from her face, and a soft sheen of perspiration covered her body.

"Wipe it away, the blood. I have to see."

Quickly, she reached out to do his bidding. She breathed a sigh before she focused on the task.

~ * ~

The silence in the room lingered, but James felt a presence. It warmed his soul, gave him confidence and knowledge all would succeed despite the barriers and stumbling blocks.

The first attempt failed. Sweat dripped from his forehead, but still he proceeded. Stuffy, confined and with the window closed, the heat seemed to magnify. James looked at Jessie and the halo of light surrounding her slowly began to fade as the sun drifted behind a cloud.

Jessie's dying, the rhythm of her life gently fading.

Tears stung the back of his throat, and the scalpel trembled in his hand. For a moment, his confidence seemed to shatter into a million tiny pieces. *Breathe for her.* James stiffened with new resolve and drew a shaking breath, praying he could do this. His shoulders ached and he reminded himself one more time Jessie's life lay in his hands.

The devil, but Jessie lay so still it scared the hell out of him. Once a mischief-maker from the word go, now she clung desperately on a very fragile thread to life. His gut clenched with fear and pain.

When he looked at Alexandra, her back was slouched, and there were large dark circles around her eyes. He wanted to tell her how dear she had become to him.

"It's working," Alexandra's whispered words jolted him back to the present and the danger that still existed.

He hesitated, stared at Jessie's chest then bent to listen to the sweet sound emanating from her. "She is breathing." His voice was filled with awe and relief.

Suddenly, James heart slammed against his chest and he looked heavenward with a silent prayer. A smile curved his lips.

"Yes." Alexandra suddenly straightened and blinked away the moisture in her eyes. She watched as Jessie inhaled another deep ragged breath. "Will she make it?"

"I don't know."

Alex clasped her hands together in prayer. "Please, God," she prayed, "let her be happy and healthy again."

"You're not going to like this, but I'm going to say it anyway. You're not going to lock me out of the room again. You have to let me help. I need to." His hands rested gently on her shoulders, their faces so close together. "Tell me you understand."

"Of course I do," Alexandra said with deliberate calm. His words made her flinch. She swallowed hard and looked chagrined as if she suddenly realized the impact of what they had just done.

"You can't nurse her alone. The risks to me make little difference at this point. It's Jessie's life that's important." He held her hands now in a silent plea for her to abandon her stubbornness. Maybe she'd lost her fight, or perhaps she understood that Jessie wasn't out of danger. "The risk of one of us falling asleep is too great if either one of us tries to do it alone."

Alexandra went pale. "Yes."

"Is that all you've got to say?"

"Yes."

"Well, then, I should take advantage of the opportunity but I won't. It sounds as if I could get you to agree to most anything. Are you up to the first watch?"

"Yes."

He arched a brow then smiled. "Darling, wake up. It's me you're talking to."

"I know but..." Alexandra nodded and tried to return the smile, but tears shimmered in her eyes.

"Dear, Lord," he murmured as moisture gathered in the back of his throat. The tears wouldn't go away, and he didn't want to cry, not now when they'd just saved Jessie's life.

"I think I understand."

"You do? I wish I did," she whispered.

"I'm glad you don't. It's rather nice having you so complaisant for a change. I intend to enjoy it while it lasts, because knowing you, this mood won't last long. Six hours, Alex. Don't let me sleep any longer than that, promise." James placed her hand in his and brought the palm to his lips.

She smiled, a tired smile, but it was good to see.

~ * ~

"James...it's me."

He groaned then stretched in an attempt to wake up. "So soon?"

"It's working. Jessie is sleeping and breathing peacefully. Her temperature is still rather high, but I just bathed her so all you have to do for the moment is sit with her."

"You're beautiful, Alex. Have I ever told you that?" he asked as the back of his hand caressed her cheek and followed the long white column of her neck to her collarbone.

"Yes," she looked away and felt the fluttering she was only beginning to recognize as desire.

"Give me a minute and I'll be there." His tone was gentle and understanding, and he hoped it would give her comfort and reassurance. He left to splash water on his face and shake the sleep from his mind.

"I'll wait in her room," Alex said.

He was beside her in a few moments. Water dripped from his hair, and he looked fresh and wide-awake. She'd let him sleep longer than the six hours they'd agreed upon.

Jessie lay on the bed, her face still flushed. Her temperature hovered at the same spot. It hadn't increased and there was no sign of infection around the wound, and she was breathing. It was the most beautiful sight he'd ever seen.

Alexandra sat in a chair by a small table Kim had brought to Jessie's room for them.

A makeshift supper of cheese and bread lay on a small table in Jessie's room, and hot coffee. Alexandra yawned sleepily and tried to stifle it with her hand. She crossed her arms and lowered her head to rest on them, closing her eyes.

"What's this? Dinner?" His voice came low and behind her.

"No, but it will help tide you over. The coffee is fresh."

"Why?" He didn't sound angry. His voice was gentle, and he seemed to know the answer even before she did.

"I didn't mean any harm," she admitted reluctantly then stifled a yawn. "You looked so tired I had to let you sleep, and I looked in on you several times and didn't have the heart to wake you."

"We had an agreement," James said with a solemn look.

"I know."

Reaching out, James chucked her under the chin before he pulled her from her chair and hugged her. "Don't do it again. I can accept and forgive it this time but not again, do you understand."

"I was too keyed up to sleep anyway."

"Eat with me?" he asked.

"Will she live?"

"I don't know. She needs time."

"How long?"

"Another day or two, maybe three."

Nothing stirred in the room, not even a slight breeze filtered in through the slightly open window. They both seemed lost in the quiet so unnatural for this small space. A space that usually overflowed with laughter and noise. So much time had passed in the desperate struggle for Jessie's life, how could it take longer? Surely God would know by now if he meant to take her. Perhaps they'd made him reconsider, though. Alex realized they'd done everything humanly possible to change the course of events.

Alexandra looked one more time at Jessie then turned to leave. "Good night." Alex kissed James on the cheek and moved through the door. "Six hours." She reminded him.

"We'll see," he drawled lazily.

"We had an agreement."

"You were the first to break it."

"Stubborn." she whirled and left the room in a rush of determination and frustration only to slow and smile. "I'll just have to wake up on my own."

Chapter Twenty-one

"Wake up, sleepy head." James bent over the bed and feathered kisses across her cheek, wanting her more now than he'd ever imagined he could. *Wake up, angel mine.* His finger traced the gentle slope of her nose then the lush fullness of her lips. He traced the line of her jaw, and his mouth hovered inches above her.

You can't leave me now. We're bound together through out time. Jessie has seen to that more thoroughly than I ever could.

"Umm," Alexandra lay in disarray in his bed, her head on his pillow, her eyes dreamy. Still half asleep, she seemed more than willing to respond to his wake up call. The covers were pulled snugly around her, a barrier easily thwarted. At this moment, though, he just wanted to sleep by her and hold her near to his heart.

"You awake?" James traced the length of her slender arm down to the gentle rise of her hip. He felt Alex snuggle against his hand, and he held her securely, wanting to join her in the warmth. Jessie's fever had broken several hours ago, and he'd left Kim sitting with her. Kim promised to call if she needed him for anything. Days had passed and they'd spent them in hope and prayer, sometimes desperation, watching Jessie fight the battle of her life.

Jessie's alive.

Breathe for her. Together we found a way.

Alex looked so young and innocent, her copper curls swirling about her in disarray, the contrast beautiful against the pristine white of the sheets. A wave of guilt passed through him, but the feeling lasted only a moment. He'd been hard on Alexandra. Demanding, conjoling, and teasing her, in an effort to persuade her to his bed. When she'd all but thrown herself at him, he'd backed off, afraid of the commitment, rejecting her blatantly. Ending in the proposal at the tree house with Jessie as witness.

He'd do the same thing again if it would bring this wonderfully courageous woman permanently into his life.

After the wedding and their brief night of lovemaking, he'd known what he'd done was right. He felt as if he'd known Alexandra for all eternity, perhaps even loved her in another time. For the moment, though, this one fragile moment before she woke completely, he wanted to hold her in his arms, possessively and protectively. Quietly, he slipped the covers away, nestled his naked body next to hers, pulling her close. He held her for a second before his hand ran the length of her leg and worked the long white nightgown up so his fingertips met smooth silken flesh. When he reached his goal, he traced the soft contours of her inner thigh.

James felt young again, quickening as he continued the slow rise of her gown. Dangerously out of control and with a sudden unrestrained need for her, he unbuttoned the gown and pulled the white muslin over her head. Like the tempting sweet siren she was, luring him to unknown pleasures, he wanted her naked beneath him.

"James?" She was too damn seductive with her voice whispering sweetly in his ear and languid slumberous eyes beguiling him. "Is that you?"

"It damn well better be," he snarled, his voice was husky with amusement. Euphoric to have her in his arms again, he pressed her close to his fiercely primed body, his only thought to possess that which he deemed his. The feeling was novel, illogical, completely beyond comprehension and so vehemently powerful he struggled to deny the emotion.

She laughed softly against the pillow. "James?"

"Yes, love, do you want to go back to sleep?" His breath stroked her flesh igniting hidden fires. His hands trembled then maintained mastery, the feel of her soft body beneath his roving hands a heaven on earth.

"How's Jessie?"

"She's fine. Her temperature is down, her breathing slow and regular. She's going to be all right, love." He kissed her eyelids. The slow rise and fall of her chest tantalized and enchanted his senses; the gentle rhythm of her breaths as she inhaled softly, encouraged his fingers to touch, exploring at his leisure. As he settled himself next to her again, he cupped one breast in his hand and held it with reverence, cherishing the silken texture. Shamelessly, her body responded like quicksilver.

He grinned lazily as he watched her. She looked exhausted, and he wondered if he looked the same. He didn't feel tired, not any longer, not since the fever had broken and Jessie's skin had lost its pasty white appearance.

Alexandra's coppery lashes fanned her cheeks. They'd had so few hours of sleep since this started he wanted to let her sleep now, but his body had other thoughts, thoughts of blissful surrender.

Curiously, he touched a strand of her hair, brought the fiery curl close so he could breathe in the light clean fragrance lingering from her bath. His hand roamed and explored her body, memorizing the dips and curves of her form so new to him but so cherished. His fingers followed the length of her leg down to her tiny ankles and back to a sensitive spot behind her knee.

Alexandra whimpered. A pulse beat later, he turned her and their eyes met silently, comprehending the sensual mood; his mouth lifted in a smile of tantalizing appeal, and he said in a husky voice that touched her, "Should I lock the door first?"

"Should you?"

His caress, whisper soft and cherishing, continued its exploration, brushing the soft feminine curls between her thighs. For a second, his fingers rested on her rounded abdomen then spanned the distance between her pelvic bones. Perhaps they had a child growing there already, one to play with Jessie.

He suddenly realized he wanted a lot of children. Would she? They had never discussed children, hadn't talked about a great deal of things. Fate had intervened and taken away so much of their time.

His mouth covered hers a moment later, his tongue deep inside her with an intimacy that stopped his breathing for a moment. When he eventually allowed her a second's reprieve, Alexandra frantically whispered, "Are you sure Jessie's okay?"

James nodded, an attempt to placate the panic he detected in her voice, yet he could have no more left her at that moment than he could have stopped his heart from beating.

"She was sleeping peacefully ten minutes ago."

Alexandra sighed deeply, so relieved Jessie was getting better.

"Hush, darlin'," James murmured. "Trust me."

"James, let me see her first," she started to roll over, but he kept her pinned tightly against him. Her well-rounded bottom pushing against his hard arousal, and her back rested against his chest. She was waking up, and he could feel her burgeoning response to his touch, her wild unleashed passion. No longer half asleep, her body moved in rhythm, a cadence he set.

"Whatever you want, darling."

"James," she moaned. He caressed her body, moving downward to find her most intimate feminine parts newly opened to his touch, blossoming for him. She melted against him, and he recognized the erratic breathy tempo of her increasing desire.

It was more than he wanted to endure in his current state of arousal, and he abruptly turned her toward him, pressed her beneath him in a blur of movement, covering her a split second later. Like quicksilver, he was inside her, deep inside. So small and tight she welcomed him and he wanted to stay there forever. Then, for a brief second, he didn't move. Cautious at first, building, harder and faster until she moved with him as one. He found her swollen throbbing bud, caressed and tantalized the little pearl. She purred and the soft sounds she made as the passion grew enticed him. Orgasmic sensation flowed between them. Her body met each of his thrusts with one of her own, arching up to meet him. She shuddered and he knew she felt him deep inside, heard soft contended sounds, and he held her close one last second then his body surged hard into hers, seeming to touch all of her at that moment. The world spun and his senses exploded around him in a pulsing climax. He poured into her, greedy for release, uncaring of any possible consequences.

"James," she cried out.

They both lay quietly together, James holding her close, still deep inside. *I'll tie her to me. Give her a child to call her own.*

Then he paused a second before withdrawing from her. He tucked her in next to him, her back against his chest. His fingers spanned her abdomen, once more touching each hipbone.

He opened his eyes and heard her soft breathing, looked down and saw her eyes, deep blue and fathomless, and he reveled in her softness.

"Hush," he whispered next to her ear. "Go back to sleep. I won't bother you again. At least not until the sun is well above the horizon."

"In a minute. I do trust you, James, but I have to see her myself. Tell me you understand."

James nodded.

~ * ~

Alex lay awake staring at the ceiling, a smug well-contented expression on her face. The sunlight darted in through the open curtain, and it seemed summer had almost passed without them realizing. Birds twittered and chirped outside, and Alex felt good to be alive. The sun bore down mercilessly from the sky, the fields drying from lack of rain. Yet the mornings had the distinct smell of autumn.

When she'd first opened her eyes, she'd truly believed the early morning had been a marvelous dream. It wasn't. James had come to her at dawn, and they'd made love and slept. For once her world seemed right. Peace had settled around her, and she wanted to stay here, forever.

Enticing and commanding, she felt James's hand upon her hip, the steady beat of his heart next to her, and the gentle caress of his fingers. The length of his body, fitted tightly against her own, left her breathless.

His body half covered hers, one leg draped over her thigh in pure, unadulterated, masculine possession, and he pulled himself to his elbows to look into her eyes. "Sleep well? I did."

"Did I," she smiled dreamily at him.

James' face was very close; bright sunlight danced across his dark brows, enhancing his features, setting an unquenchable fire deep within.

"Umm," he said and tenderly brushed a stray lock of hair away from her eyes. Then he kissed her nose and began another careful attack on her person.

"James, stop."

"Why?" His mouth found her ear, and he nibbled there. Only a few short seconds ago she'd decided this could wait. Now she had to disagree with herself as his lips traveled over her body.

"We have to see Jessie." She tried to push him away, but he resisted and continued the nips and kisses that made her melt in a spineless mass of nothingness.

"Just looked in on her." He paused between the words to kiss her nose and eyes.

"How," she struggled to sit up, but he held her back, found her mouth in a soft, gentle, and enticing kiss that effectively stopped her speech. She pushed on his chest, denying the kiss. With no response forthcoming, he sighed and settled back, fingers laced behind his head.

"All right, go see her."

Alex kissed him quickly. "I'll be right back. Now, don't go away."

"Don't worry."

She didn't take long. Only a few minutes later his bride slid into bed.

Her head tilted suggestively, "Kim's with her. I have a confession, and I don't want you to make this any harder than it already is."

He paused, watching her then turned his undivided attention on what she was going to say. "Make what harder," he demanded casually as if he didn't have a care in the world.

"You're not going to like this." Her tone sounded hesitant.

"Talk," he replied with a grin, gazing down at her from under his long dark lashes.

"Yes, well. I've kept some secrets." Alex's cobalt eyes held James'. She sat up pulling the sheets around her, hiding herself from him, her modesty confusing her momentarily.

"Why? Don't you know you can tell me anything? You can trust me." His lashes lowered slightly over his increasingly volatile gaze.

"Can I? When all this started, I hardly knew you. I was afraid of what you'd think."

"God, Alexandra," he moaned, staring at her. He touched her, traced the soft contour to her chin then down her neck to her collarbone. "Afraid of what I'd think? What do I have to do to convince you?"

294

"I, James, we don't know each other. There are times I can only guess at what lies in your heart." She inhaled quickly and closed her eyes.

His fingers fell away. "Alex," he was sitting up now, his broad shoulders suddenly naked and intimidating. "What could you possibly have to tell me that would cause you to fear me? This makes no sense. You make no sense."

"I haven't told you something very important."

He rubbed his neck and frowned. His explosive eyes flashed, threatening, warning her again. "Alex," his tone frightening.

"I didn't mean to keep it from you this long, but everything started happening. The marriage, the..." she gasped for air, "you know."

"We've been busy and if you forgot to tell me, I understand," he softly acknowledged.

"I've been writing," she blurted out in a alarming surge of courage. "And I..." She hesitated, unsure of herself and his confusing reaction.

Momentarily at a loss for words, James merely nodded, "I know."

"James, my heart is beating out of control, and I'm so relieved I feel dizzy. I can't believe you know and you're not angry?" Alexandra said.

"Why should I be angry?"

"When you first read my journal, well..."

He traced her cheek with his finger and his lips twitched with amusement. Alex turned to gaze out the window.

"The devil, Alex but that was a long time ago. And I didn't read all of the manuscript." James noted. "Why didn't you tell me?" Then his head dipped and he nibbled the soft down of her neck. "I think," he murmured, his voice like velvet, "We should end this conversation."

She turned from him, shaking her head. "No, I don't think you understand."

"Oh, I think I do," he returned, his lips warm against her skin. "I want you now."

"James," she whispered furiously.

"Not now."

Only a few minutes later they both reached a pinnacle of satisfaction then drifted into a long languorous sated sleep.

~ * ~

Straight to Heaven

Just about the time the sun reached its zenith, James woke Alexandra. He kissed her warmly, propped the pillows against the headboard then relaxed against them.

"We've other things to talk about, angel mine."

"Jessie?"

"Yes, among others," his eyes twinkled with mischief. "You do know the result of our loving," he continued and the twinkle hadn't diminished.

"The result?" She slanted him a curious sideways glance and put both hands on his chest. "Of course I know. You've already told me. I take you to heaven," Alexandra kissed his cheek, his nose then playfully traced his neck in kisses. "And you take me to heaven."

He said nothing, just stared at her for the longest time with the silliest grin on his face. Boyish and full of mischief, he continued gazing, saying nothing, expecting her to come up with more answers.

"Don't tease." He choked on the words; perhaps she didn't know. She was, after all, a virgin. Crissakes. Now what to say?

She stared at him wide eyed as if she didn't understand anything and smiled guilelessly. "Result of what? Wasn't I right? I don't take..." Alexandra lowered her lashes and turned from him.

He groaned, running his fingers through his hair. He did have a way of putting his foot in his mouth. In his most tactless manner he blurted out, "Do you want to be pregnant?"

"Pregnant?" She started to laugh. At least he thought she had laughed. But suddenly she looked confused, totally out of her experience, and he'd put her there by his stupid questions. He should have let nature take its course and wait until the blessed event surprised her.

"It's a reasonable question," he said, instantly losing control of his languid teasing demeanor.

"What is?"

"Do you want a baby?" he persisted.

She thought a moment, her grin widening then she sweetly cocked her head to one side. "Sometime." She batted her eyelashes at him and he groaned, despairing of ever telling her the truth.

296

"Sometime might be sooner," he said. Not knowing what else to do he continued. "You could be having one now." And he pointedly stared at her stomach.

"This instant?" Her voice held just the right amount of awe and reverence to thoroughly frustrate him.

"No. Not exactly having it this moment, but you could have conceived." This wasn't getting him anywhere, and he didn't know how to salvage the situation.

"Conceived?" she blinked a few times. "I don't--"

"Listen," he cut in, "making love, what we've been doing together, when I'm inside you..."

She nodded politely in understanding. "Oh, my."

"That's how you make a baby," he finished, relived that he'd done such a fine job. Even though the blank look remained on her face, he couldn't have said it any clearer. She kept looking at him, and it bothered him a moment more then he caught on. Saw the slight twitch of her lips that she couldn't control any longer. Heard the giggle. Realized instantly what she had done so well.

"Did you read any of the journal?" she grinned.

"A few pages," he admitted then sighed. A smile curved his lips. After a few seconds, he leaned forward to place a chaste kiss on her mouth.

"Really?" she asked just as he very gently throttled her and wrestled her to the bed. Sheets flew and she giggled as he tickled her and threatened every dire consequence he could think of. Then teased her with seductive words, words meant to be spoken between lovers. She laughed and pushed at him.

"You'll pay for this, you little vixen," he swore even as his desire for her grew and she pressed her palms to his back bringing him closer.

"Restitution? Is that what you want?" She giggled again and he flipped her over so she lay on top of him.

"The devil, but I want more than that." His hand wound in her hair, and he brought her lips to meet his. He'd never kissed her like that before. Forceful, demanding, but tender, he coaxed her to respond and there was nothing gentle about this.

Trust me.

Love me.

Hold me close to your heart.

"Answer me now," he said when their lips finally parted. "Do you want a baby?" Alex didn't answer right away. The silence lengthened and she smiled at him, all innocence, and cocked her head in thought.

"At least ten," she said happily, watching the expression creasing his face. "Can you handle that?"

"Ten," he croaked, slightly off balance. "Let's start with one." And their lips melded together, his hands roaming as the sheets fell away. But in truth her reply meant the world to him. They wouldn't have ten children, but in one word she'd told him what he wanted to hear. She was more than happy to become the mother of his children, as many as he wanted.

But he spoke nothing of love and neither did she.

~ * ~

Muffled footsteps and voices slowly penetrated through the solid walls of their room. Kim's loud screech filled the silence and more muffled voices followed. Sudden violent pounding on the bedroom door brought home their vulnerable position.

James bolted upright, his heart pounding wildly. "No."

"Not Jessie. It can't be. She was getting better." Alexandra's eyes were wild with fear.

Sean. James thought and dove for his gun. He couldn't reach the weapon. "Son of a bitch!" he swore violently, stumbling on the sheets then cursing himself for letting his guard down and failing to protect Alex.

Naked, he groped for the gun, sprawling on all fours by the nightstand where he kept it.

The pounding continued along with a cacophony of noises beyond the closed door.

"James...James...are you in there. It's your mother. James."

"And father." Another loud masculine voice boomed with a hint of amusement. "Get dressed and we'll meet you downstairs."

In one quick move, James whipped open the door. The sheet he'd wrapped around his waist slipped an inch, his broad shoulders blocking the doorway but not the view. The gun instantly clattered to the floor.

The greeting Danielle Lawrence was about to make fell on thin air. Her mouth gaped wide with disbelief and astonishment then her eyes opened in stunned shock.

"Mother." James broke off, staring at what he momentarily thought was a hallucination, a trick of his mind, before he realized the image was real. His mother and father were standing perfectly still, looking at him and at Alexandra. Instantly, he stepped into their line of vision, but it wasn't soon enough.

"James, who...?" Alexandra asked.

Trying to buy time, James grabbed at the sheet then bent over to retrieve the gun. Alexandra looked like an angel. His mother looked horrified. Finally, realizing the precarious situation and the horrible thoughts his parents must logically conclude, he stepped back with as much dignity as possible and closed the door slightly. But not before he saw his father leaning on the door across the hall, studying the scene, his all-knowing grin widening by the second.

A model of casual arrogance, he hadn't changed much over the years. His eyes, Lawrence eyes, twinkled merrily. James heard him chuckle and knew down to the letter what he thought.

James glared at his parents, shaking his head. He peeked through the slight opening. "Mother, go away. Go down to the parlor. We'll join you when we can get dressed. Mother, what are you doing here?"

"Is that any way to greet your parents? We did call up here. Made enough noise to wake the dead." Chase said, in his slow insouciant drawl, clearly amused by his son and his mad scramble to decency. "Your mother tapped on the door, once, maybe twice." He laughed then looked to Danielle.

"You could have waited in the parlor." James cringed when he looked back and saw the deep red color that covered Alexandra.

"Are you going to introduce us?" Chase asked cheerfully, the twinkle in his eyes dancing mischievously. "Or leave us guessing."

"Get out of here, both of you," his mother cut into their conversation. Without warning, she pushed on James' chest as if she thought he would give way and allow her into the room.

"I can explain," James said.

"I'm sure you can, but I don't intend to listen to some harebrained reasons why this beautiful woman is in your bed. I didn't bring you up to take advantage of a situation like this. Out." She threw her hands in the air, gesturing for them to leave. "Out. Both of you."

Clutching the quilt to her breasts, Alexandra stifled a giggle then rolled her eyes at James. Chase had removed his long body from the wall and was turning to leave. "Don't argue with your mother. You know you can't win," he told James, offering an immediate solution to the problem at hand.

"Speak for yourself," James countered, trying not to laugh as he looked back to the bed, hoping for a better view of Alexandra. He was sorely tempted to claim his restitution for her earlier prank, but he couldn't do it. He'd find another way and another time, when it was just the two of them. For now, he had to redeem himself.

"We're married," was his blunt reply to his mother.

"Don't lie to me, James Lawrence. I'm your mother."

Chapter Twenty-two

Love was born with them, in them, so intense,
It was their very spirit...not a sense.

George Gordon, Lord Byron
"Don Juan: Canto IV"

"Your mother?" Alex asked hesitantly. "She doesn't believe we're married."

"I never got a chance to write. Even if I had, the letter would have missed them."

"You've got to explain."

"That's going to be difficult. She's made up her mind, you see, and I, a mere mortal, don't stand a chance," he sighed dramatically.

Alex fell back on the pillow, laughing, sheets lying provocatively across her breasts. "Don't lie to me, James Lawrence," she echoed. "That was a real minister who married us, wasn't it?" Her eyes sparkled and he thought she looked incredibly beautiful. She didn't stop giggling. James cleared his throat and she laughed harder.

She giggled again and he contrasted that to the vivid scowl he remembered on his mother's face and the deep grin that had spread slowly across Chase's. When his father's brow rose slightly, he knew his parents didn't believe him, not for the one brief moment.

"They think I'm your..." she gasped for air.

"Whore?"

"I prefer adventuress or paramour." She rolled her eyes and held her hand to her mouth, stopping the laughter threatening to bubble out. The sheet slipped a fraction, and he delighted in the view. She clutched the fabric, pulling it into place.

"Obviously, I don't find this quite as amusing," he said softly, his tone threatening. "Do you know something I don't?"

James ran his hands through his hair then shot her a warning look. But his lips twitched, and it was all he could do to keep a very real grin from spreading unchecked across his face.

"Oh, yes. I still know quite a few things you don't."

"It could have been Sean," he said, but after thinking that scenario over, he knew it wasn't possible. He'd heard Kim laughing, if only for a short time, when all the commotion started.

For a long time he stared at Alexandra then he moved. James pursued her, intending a wicked restitution. In exactly three strides, he was across the room, pulling the sheets from Alexandra's hands, tossing them on the floor. The next second he froze as if paralyzed. Entranced by the sight of her, he forgot all thoughts of his parents.

"You know that's not true. Not even Sean would be that bold." Alexandra entwined her hands around James' neck and pulled him down.

"So, you think that was funny?" he drawled, taking on the accent that sometimes infuriated her, kissing her face and her lips, the words smothered against her sweet-smelling skin. He wanted to taste every inch of her.

"Umm..." she nodded, running her fingers through his thick dark hair. Hot kisses marked a searing path across her.

"Answer me."

Alex nodded again, "Very." Laughter erupted, spilling from her lips, and he seduced her, at his leisure. He intended to thoroughly enjoy each moment.

She ran her fingers through his hair then across his back, gasping when his mouth covered her breast and his tongue laved the swollen crest. James paid homage to her, suckling the tip, rolling the coral nub with his tongue then nibbling gently. Her nails dug into his shoulders and he stifled a growl of pure masculine pleasure.

"Restitution," he smiled at her and covered the other breast the same way. She responded so sweetly. He hadn't meant to do this, but the sight of her caused him to forget everything. It made him disregard the knowledge his mother and father were in his house. Memories of his adolescence rushed to his mind, and it was almost enough to end the seduction, almost.

"James, no. Your parents."

But Alexandra's voice wasn't commanding at all. "No?" He listened for a reply.

"James, please."

He smiled. His name on her lips sent tremors down his too heated body and invited further exploration. He wouldn't end this for anyone.

"No? James, please. Which is it, Alex?"

"Yes."

"Good, I'm not finished, not by a long shot." His voice, primal and masculine, warned of her surrender and promised a gentle seduction. He needed this, needed to listen to the sweet sounds she made when he entered her and stroked her depths, yearning to revel in the sweet, raging tempest he aroused in her.

"Your mother."

"Don't have one." His voice was hushed, his expression wild and untamed. *I will make you mine, angel girl. Mine forever through all time.*

"James..."

"Ah, Alexandra...my angel."

"They're in the house. They'll hear everything," she pleaded yet at the same time her hips rose to meet him.

"No, little angel? No? This doesn't feel like, no. They'll go away."

"But, what if, they'll think--"

"Good, I want them to believe we're married." He smiled into her laughing eyes, continuing the assault. "You say one thing but, Alexandra, your body speaks a different language."

"You can't mean that. Your mother. I can't help what my body says." Her words were feather soft, coming in little gasps against him. It seemed she tried so hard to put him off, yet at the same time she clung to him with a quiet desperation and a need that went beyond anything he'd ever known.

"What if they come back?"

"They won't." His sigh rippled through the sudden silence, the sound strangely translucent. "My father will stop her, and if she comes in, it will be her embarrassment, not ours."

"How in the world could he stop her?" Alexandra asked curiously. "She clearly has a mind of her own."

"Stop her? He has his ways. Just as I have mine." His whisper must have pushed all thoughts of arguing from her head because she fell silent. Instead she moved beneath him, tightening her hold.

"You can't mean," Alexandra looked instantly alert. The subtle meaning of his words made the color rise on her cheeks even more.

"Hush."

They heard the moan of pleasure clearly through the closed door, the sigh then the husky masculine voice. "Kid, let's find the guest room before I make love to you here in the hallway." Chase spoke softly to his wife.

"It's down the hall," the breathy whisper floated on the air.

Alex stared at him. "That was your mother?"

"She's putty in his hands." James raised an eyebrow as if to challenge. "Just as you are in mine," he finished on a seductive note.

"I am not," she punched his arm, but he caught her by the wrists and stretched her arms above her head leaving her defenseless.

"Surrender, wife." His eyes and his lips twitched with amusement. His words so soft and gentle they took her by surprise. He looked at the woman beneath him, and his breath caught in his throat. She was so beautiful and fragile lying on his bed, surrounded by the fiery halo of her hair. "Surrender."

Dear Lord, he had to protect this woman. His wife.

He closed his eyes praying against the vision he saw. Shut his mind against the threat of Sean Cassidy.

"Never," she whispered breathily.

He chuckled at that, nibbling her lips before covering her mouth with his own. "They'll be busy as long as we are." And he gave his full attention to his new bride.

~ * ~

James was wrong. His mother and father were busy a very long time. Lunch had been served and cleared before Chase and Danielle made an uneasy appearance. When Alexandra's eyes met Danielle's, they both blushed.

"About time you two showed up," James' languid gaze rested for a brief moment on Alex before returning to his father.

James and Chase grinned at each other as if they shared a secret. Chase pulled his wife into his arms then kissed her soundly, publicly, and most thoroughly. It wasn't a chaste kiss either, and James watched Alexandra's complexion deepen to match her hair, yet she didn't take her eyes away. James laughed and beckoned to Alexandra.

She looked away and found a seat across the room. He acknowledged her independence with a subtle nod.

James sat in his favorite chair, fingers steepled beneath his chin, watching the drama. This felt like an inquisition, and he wanted Alexandra close, needed her by his side.

"C'mere," James said softly, projecting all his latent emotions in that one word.

"No..." she murmured, forming her mouth into an innocent moue then folding her hands demurely in her lap. "I don't think so."

The silence continued for some time before James finally cleared his throat. His hands now rested on the chair, fingers drumming. "As you wish." James rose, his stride purposeful. In less than a second, he assumed a pose at Alexandra's side, identical to his father's.

Chase grinned and Danielle's brow creased in study or disapproval. Chase stood behind his wife, one hand lightly resting on her shoulder as if in a silent plea for Danielle to mind her own business.

His mother was still beautiful, James thought suddenly. His father still stood tall and straight, his hair had only a slight dusting of gray. His parents showed only a few subtle signs of age.

His mother's look was intense as if in ardent inspection of his wife. Chase, on the other hand, seemed genuinely pleased to meet Alexandra and not at all judgmental. His dark blue eyes twinkled approvingly.

"You have a great deal of explaining to do," his mother started. "I expect you have a plausible reason for your behavior."

"Oh?" A slow smile curved James lips. "Do I now?" James replied smoothly. "You barged into my home unannounced. Someone taught me that wasn't very mannerly. Now, who could that have been?" he teased, but the tone of his voice was hard and he wouldn't allow his mother to put him on the defensive. "I believe you and my father have some explaining to do. Why didn't you write? I had no idea you would show up today or anytime soon. It's not as if you live down the street and can stop by when you get the urge."

When James innocently squeezed Alexandra's shoulder, she straightened, and, he thought, she looked regal. An urgent need to claim her, to set all doubts aside suddenly possessed him. He squeezed again.

Relax, I won't let anyone hurt you.

Kim entered, stared at the scene for a long poignant moment then set the tray of sandwiches and hot steaming tea on a table. "Mister James?"

"That will be all."

Kim bowed and silently left the room, a smile on her face.

He felt Alexandra's muscles tense beneath his fingers, and he tried to reassure her, gently massaging her shoulder.

She wants equality. Yet I told her a woman should know her place. And what the devil does that mean.

James smiled. When Alexandra finally relaxed, he moved from her side, pouring everyone tea. Then he winked at his wife. The vapor rose from the delicate china cups, disappearing slowly into the silent room.

Danielle sipped then quietly replaced the cup in its saucer. Her words, directed pointedly at James, filled the parlor. "We didn't barge in. We knocked, called, and made an unholy racket. I'm surprised we didn't raise the dead. So we had to come see if everyone was all right. What would you have done?" Danielle added in what sounded like a motherly attempt to put her son back on the defensive.

"You could have waited downstairs until we were up," James said patiently then brought his cup to his lips. He grimaced, eyeing the brew hesitantly. Looking toward the kitchen, he set it down without tasting. "It would have been the polite thing to do. I'm sure Kim would have kept you company." After setting the cup of tea on the tray, James helped himself to the brandy.

"True. but..."

"Kim did try to tell you, didn't she? What did you expect to find in my room?" Caught off guard and angered by his mother's attitude but unwilling to act chastised, James bit back a more caustic reply.

"Not what I found." Danielle quickly replied then tried to stand, but Chase held her down, his grip on her shoulder firm.

"Danielle," Chase said.

"You can't condone..." Danielle glared at Chase then shifted her attention back to her son. "Really, James, we had a long train ride then the coach ride from Roseburg was unbearable. The roads are archaic, and I'm not at all sure my backside will ever recover. I wanted to see you, and you didn't answer our calls. It was well past ten o'clock."

"And that's your excuse? It's your only reason for barging into my bedchamber. You embarrassed Alexandra, my bride of only three weeks. I almost shot you, you know." James drawled, his relaxed pose unchanged, his expression refined. Only the tightening of his fingers on his glass gave indication he was angry.

"You insist on this travesty then?" Danielle asked. "You expect me to believe you're married. Why, you've denounced that sacred institution for years. No, James, your excuse just isn't good enough. My youngest son needs a lesson in manners, and I intended to give it. You shouldn't treat women with such callous disregard."

"Danielle," Chase said, the command evident in his tone, "Hold your tongue before it's too late."

"I'd like to see a marriage certificate," Danielle said. "I won't have my son--"

"This is my house." James asserted. "And, mother, you have no reason to doubt me. If I say I'm married, I am. You're testing my patience."

"And you're my son. I can't believe you would do this in your own home. Kim told us Jessie was sick. What's wrong with her? And what ever happened to the boy I raised?"

"Nothing. I'm still here and very much the gentleman. Jessica has been very sick, but she's getting better every day. She'll be up and running around in no time. By the way, Jessie hand picked Alexandra," he said smugly, reminding her once again Alexandra was his wife. The upper hand was his even though he saw the flash in his mother's eyes.

"Aren't you going to introduce us to her?" Chase asked, interrupting what threatened to become all out war, his expression unreadable. "I for one will take my son's word on the matter."

"James," Alexandra whispered, pulling away from the heat of James' fingers, trying to brush them off. "Why is everyone acting as if I'm not here?"

James ignored Alex. "I intend to introduce my wife, since you asked nicely, and what about you mother? Would you like an introduction?" James said smoothly, enjoying the position he put his mother in. Crissakes, she deserved it. "And, Alex, I apologize. I never meant to exclude you from the conversation."

"You have no reason for the sarcasm." His mother started in again. "It seems the Lawrence men are all the same. I'd hoped it was only one generation, but somehow Chase managed to pass it on. I'd tell you about your father's younger days, but I wouldn't want to put any ideas into your head."

"Have it your way, but be nice. Alexandra could be carrying a grandchild at this very moment." James chuckled softly when he glanced at his wife then his mother.

His mother paled but the slow rise of color to Alexandra's cheeks, warmed his blood, heated other things, too. The devil, but he burned everywhere.

At the moment, James was eagerly pondering an entertainment directly related to the subject of grandchildren. A subject he'd relish sharing with his wife. Even with his parents, no his mother, blandly disregarding his marriage as valid, Alexandra appeared anything but untouchable. He decided she looked like a wholesome western lady in her blue calico dress, her hair in disarray, and her skin rosy with the flush of embarrassment. The bright copper silk of her hair was an enticement to touch; the rise and fall of her breasts a subtlety of movement beneath the high collar of her bodice. But just as he was about to call this meeting adjourned and move on to more pleasant activities, his mother's frown stopped him.

Danielle hesitated only a moment. "I hadn't thought of doing anything else. It's not her fault I failed to bring you up right. If she is expecting a child, it won't be a bastard," she threatened. "And it's you I'd like to run over with a carriage, not your..." Danielle stared hard at her son as if she doubted his sanity.

"Wife," he reminded his mother pointedly. "Now be nice, or I won't tell you her name." His reply, quick and to the point made Alexandra's eyebrows twitch.

"Alexandra McMurdie," Alexandra cut in as she stood and extended her hand in welcome. James' mother hesitated a moment then welcomed Alex into the family. Danielle cocked her head to one side, a smile lit up her face, and instantly her eyes sparkled. Danielle looked to Chase as if seeking confirmation.

"Lawrence," James cut in abruptly. "Don't ever forget it, Alexandra. Your name is Lawrence now, and I won't hear anything different."

"I did forget," Alexandra apologized softly, but her eyes were dancing with mischief. "It's all so new."

"Then it's settled," James said cryptically and wondered if perhaps he'd acted too harshly. "Alexandra is my wife."

Chase laughed. "See what you've done now, kid. James' wife doesn't like us, and we've waited so long for him to settle down."

Chase watched his son with an amused grin then looked at his wife. He leaned down and whispered something in her ear. Something that deepened her frown and caused her to push his hand away. His fingers slipped from Danielle's shoulder.

"Hmph," was all he got in way of reply.

"Alexandra," James said softly, "they aren't always this implacable. Sometimes they don't even bite."

"Just like you? Well, at least I understand you better now."

"Alexandra," he said again, "You're not helping."

"Oh?" His mother said drolly. "Now that I recognize your name, dear, I understand why my son has fallen in love with you. After all, she's become so well known back east. She's beautiful and intelligent and she's not afraid to speak her mind. Why, one of her essays created quite a stir in

Chicago. I believe it was the one on 'Women's education and the economics of sexual freedom. You are *the* Alexandra McMurdie?"

"Her what?" James' expression changed drastically. "What essay? Sexual freedom?" His mind began to churn, honing in on certain words and their implied meanings. Once more his fingers tightened around the brandy glass he held. His mother was grinning as if she loved his bewilderment. Her writing, the reams of paper he'd noticed on his old desk, everything was beginning to make remarkable sense. The riot in town when she stood on the cart using it as a soapbox. "Son of a bitch."

She's gone to far, risking her life.

This isn't the twenty-first century.

Alexandra gasped, looking to Danielle then shook her head. Danielle instantly shuttered her expression and closed her mouth.

James understood the subtle glances between his mother and wife, realizing that in those few seconds a wealth of information had been passed between them.

"Alexandra. Alexandra McMurdie Lawrence." His thunder rose with the definitive pronunciation of each name.

Even with the noonday sun pouring through the window, Alexandra looked angelic, her beautiful features strangely tense as if she hid something very important, her eyes in sharp contrast looked clearly annoyed beneath her lowered lashes. The fragile porcelain of her skin flaunted her feminine vulnerability. She proudly lifted her lashes and her chin as though she had kept nothing from him all these months. Thoughts of throttling her foremost in his mind, he struggled with himself and his rapidly escalating anger.

No, it wasn't anger he felt. It was something he'd never experienced before, something completely indefinable.

"That's what I tried to tell you earlier." A soft murmur, nothing more, gave explanation. She spoke knowingly, her gaze on the trees outside.

"I don't understand how something you supposedly wrote could cause a riot. Does it have anything to do with the people of Jacksonville ganging up on you the other day?"

She relinquished her study of the landscape, and her gaze swung back to the room. She coughed delicately. "You didn't let me explain," she whispered, "how I found work. What I did with my spare time. I wanted to survive when you threw me out."

Throw her out? Would she ever realize how much she meant to him? Could she ever adjust to this time?

His lips twitched but no longer with humor. "Writing? You've had months to tell me. What have I ever done? Why would you think I'd throw you out?"

"I've been sending essays and articles to magazines and papers all over the United States. I even wrote a book. I have money in the bank, James."

Chase cleared his throat.

"Money? How much?" James' tone was demanding.

"Quite a lot, actually. Enough so that I tried to buy the newspaper, but--"

"James." Chase cut in but was soundly ignored. Danielle rested her hand on Chase's.

"The newspaper? Son of a bitch, that's what you were doing at the bank that day."

Alexandra flinched. "James, I can explain."

"I certainly hope so."

But she didn't say anything for a long while. The silence was deathly and foreboding. Alex cleared her throat and blinked a few times. Danielle coughed behind the border of a crocheted handkerchief. "Can we save the explanation for later, perhaps a time when there is a bit more privacy?"

"Is Jessie up to visitors?" Chase interrupted again.

James and Alex sobered instantly, their concern focused on a different issue and their gazes met. "Well, yes, as long as you don't spend too much time...," his words trailed off and he smoothed his hand across Alexandra's shoulder then picked up her hand. "This beautiful lady saved her life," he said. "I owe her."

"Don't lie, I did nothing out of the ordinary. Besides, I thought I owed you."

Breathe for her. She taught me to believe in miracles.

"Owed?" Chase and Danielle questioned in unison.

311

James explained all that had happened to Jessie and all they'd done for her.

"Can we see her?"

"Yes, but one at a time, and you'll have to put on a mask. Alex says we can't risk infection." He could joke about it now, now that the danger had passed, but in those first few days, nothing had been farther from the truth. James had put up with it simply because it would do no harm.

"Please, James," Alex pleaded.

James nodded, "If that's what you really want."

"It is," she said so quietly he could barely hear her.

James's gaze met Alexandra's briefly before he led the way upstairs and down the hall to Jessie's room. Jessie had just opened her eyes and was asking Kim for a drink of water. She shared a smile with her visitors at the door.

"Who?" The whisper floated to the people converged at the door.

"Hush, sweetheart," James said and he was at her side immediately. "I bet you want to know who's here?"

Jessie nodded and touched her throat.

"And," James continued, "you probably wonder what's on your neck."

She nodded again, and James told her all about it. "An invention, Alex thought it up just so you could breathe, and these strange people are your grandparents. You haven't seen them since you were two months old."

Chapter Twenty-three

Two weeks later, the women gathered in the kitchen. The pizza Alex had promised James was baking. Another one sat on the counter receiving various toppings.

"Doesn't look the same." Alex pushed a tendril of hair off her forehead. She felt inordinately pleased though. While the Canadian bacon and the sausage toppings weren't exactly as she remembered, she knew they'd do.

"Smells good," Jessie's voice was a whisper but getting stronger each day.

"Does, doesn't it?"

"How 'bout if we check this one out. Should be just about done." Alexandra opened the oven door. A blast of hot air hit her in the face.

"Oh my, that aroma is enticing," Kim breathed, "I'm not sure I want to try it though."

"Be brave, Kim. It'll grow on you," Alex laughed.

"Grow on you," Danielle echoed a puzzled frown etched on her forehead.

"Grow on you," Jessie echoed softly and clasped her hands.

"Yup," Alex grinned smugly, just as she pulled the bubbling pizza from its hot spot in the oven.

"Can I speak candidly?" James' mother asked. The sunny weather filtered in through the window and the lazy afternoon breeze cooled the hot air in the kitchen. Danielle Lawrence looked apologetic. "I had no idea James didn't know about your essays."

313

Alexandra's eyebrows rose at the mention of her writing and at James' mother's obvious approval for her controversial although unique career. She placed the pizza on the table. Taking her time, she found a huge butcher knife and cut it in half. She paused. "James has tunnel vision at times, and at other times he's horribly dense. Right now I have no idea what he thinks. He refuses to talk about it, yet he's bought everything I've written. Last night he spent the evening reading, and the only time he looked up, he had the most insipid scowl on his face."

"He may be dense, but he has always held women in the highest regard."

"I know but..." She made another deft slice across the pizza.

Fascinated, Danielle watched. "He is a bit autocratic. Gets it from his father, I suppose." She looked thoughtful for a moment then grinned. "He really does respect women."

"I never doubted that," Alex shot back quietly, the pizza divided into eighths now.

"Good," Danielle replied, "but I'm curious about you, and I don't know where to begin."

Alexandra pulled the pizza apart. "Ask then. But I can't promise you'll like what you hear."

"Tell me about yourself, anything." Danielle cautiously reached for a plate and the strange food.

"I don't know. There's not much," Alex shrugged and hoped Danielle would give her a focal point some place to start.

"Wherever you feel comfortable," Danielle urged, eyeing the pizza and the dripping cheese warily. She bit into it, "Hot,"

"Want another piece?"

"Where on earth? Pizza? You must come from another time," she laughed.

At that comment Alexandra froze. "I'm going for a walk."

~ * ~

"What did I say?" Danielle muttered ten minutes later. One hand rested on her hip, the other shaded her eyes from the sun as she watched Alexandra disappear over the horizon.

"Leave her alone," James whispered. "Let her go."

Danielle's breath caught. "You heard?"

"No. I could tell by the look on your face you said something," he told his mother as he nodded to one of his men to follow Alex. "Keep your eye on her."

"I made an innocent statement."

"Tell me," he said without hesitation.

"All right, I told her she must come from another time."

"She does," he paused. "She stumbled through a vortex and landed here over a hundred years before she was born. Maybe, if I had some proof," he sighed and watched Alex grow smaller in the distance.

"You're joking."

"No."

"When you get to know her better, you'll understand. She's an incredible woman."

He spent the next hour convincing his mother. "I'll show you something. Don't know if it will change your mind," His eyes narrowed thoughtfully. "You know Alex spins incredible tales. If she isn't from another time, she's got one hell of an imagination. She convinced me when she took care of Jessie," James hesitated.

"Does she want to go back?" his mother asked.

"She did," James answered a bit hesitant. "She hasn't mentioned the vortex for a while, but then we've been very busy with Jessie." He looked back to the hill where Alex had just been. "We haven't had time to ourselves. When Jessie's recovered, I'll have to take her on a honeymoon."

"Oh, and you would leave your beloved Oregon?" Her eyebrows rose knowingly

"No," he winked. "I'd take her to Portland. Do you believe me, mother, or are you just humoring me?"

"I wish I could tell you that I believed," she shot back defensively.

"You don't have to believe, just accept."

"Well, assuming what she's told you is the truth and I accept this curious story, how does it make you feel? The thought she might want to leave."

Danielle's pointed question surprised James. He remembered Alex's attempts to persuade him to take her back up the mountain, recalled her persistence. He'd denied her though, but now if that was what she really and truly wanted...

"I won't give her a choice," he said. "She'll never find the vortex without me."

"James, you can't decide feelings." His mother went on, "You have to look to your heart and hers."

"You ask the hardest questions. I love her. What am I supposed to say?"

Danielle stared out the kitchen door into the blue summer sky, yet the air smelled as if a storm brewed.

"Remember after the war your quest for freedom?" she asked.

"Yes, but what..."

"Freedom, such an elusive word, but James, without it we have nothing."

"Mother." But it did seem as though this was all about freedom, the right to choose and that illusive thread of hope, which bound so many generations together.

"I know. I don't have an easy answer. I don't know what to think," his mother said.

"Just don't forget what you looked so long for and refuse to give Alexandra the same privilege."

With his hands in his pockets, he stared into the distance, towards Sardine Creek. "If she wants to go, I'll have to let her." But he knew it was a lie. He would never willingly let her go.

"I thought so, you love her that much."

His mother was probing, trying to make him look inside himself. But he didn't want to, was afraid he'd see too much. *Bind her to me, but that would take away her freedom.*

"It's not a question of how much I care for her. I don't want her hurt."

"She's happy with you," her mother said. She brushed a wayward lock of hair from his eyes.

"If only I were enough," he slammed his fist on the counter and winced at the pain shooting through his arm. A pain that at the moment felt good, made him feel alive and whole. A pain, which told him he still had some control of his life.

"If she loves you..."

His laugh sounded harsh even to his ears. "I tricked her into marrying me. I didn't tell you that, did I?" His tone was full of reproach and self-incrimination. "She never wanted to, and you speak of love? She's never mentioned it. I tried to get her into my bed from the day I found her. Alexandra refused me at all turns, and the only way I could do it, was to slip the ring on her finger. I'm not proud of what I've done, but I wouldn't change it."

"She didn't look unhappy in your bed."

"No. she's a passionate woman, and I'm the only one she's known. It's all new to her. The novelty will wear off in time, and she'll want to go back."

"Don't sell yourself short, or her."

He turned and their eyes met. "Just telling it like it is mother," he said bitterly. "Isn't that what you've always taught me?"

She smiled, hesitant at first. "I don't think so."

"I'd go with her. But you know there's no way in heaven she has any control over what happens. Nothing she's told me indicates there was a master plan to her little adventure. She could end up in any time. It's too dangerous."

"Have you told her that?"

"Need you ask? But she's a stubborn one. I don't know if she listened."

"Did you ask her if she understood?" her mother said dryly. Her eyebrows rose a fraction of an inch. She laughed softly, and her gaze focused on her son.

"Don't get cute with me, mother."

"An expression you picked up from the twenty-first century I presume."

"Yes," he said a bit sheepishly, "but it certainly applies here."

"You can't go with her." Her tone had changed. "It's an absurd idea, and you can't even consider it."

"Can't I?" he challenged.

"Of course not. You'd have a devil of a time living in another century. From what I've heard so far, it's easier to go backwards in time than forward. How would you deal with all the new inventions? What about the women? If her essays are any indication, women have more privileges, more freedom, they speak with a mind of their own. Perhaps they're even thought of as equals."

"That would be a blow. It might be nice to have them equal instead of superior."

She laughed at that bit of nonsense. "You know what I mean."

"Yes, I do and it's not a laughing matter. Women don't like that pedestal." he said reflectively, unsure of his mother's response. Men liked to put women on a pedestal and worship them. Or did they just wish for something that didn't exist, an allusive butterfly. Or perhaps it made them feel superior. James grinned at that foolish notion.

"Not when it's demeaning and subjugates," his mother continued slowly.

James thought a moment. He'd always worshiped women. "Let's find Alex," he chuckled.

"You go find her. And James, it wouldn't hurt to tell her how you feel."

It didn't take long for James to find Alexandra. He grabbed her hand and ran with her through the fields. The beautiful summer afternoon beckoned, and she had no choice but to run and frolic alongside her man. When she finally stopped him, panting and out of breath, he pulled her close and kissed her fiercely. Then he stepped back and held her at arms length. She looked into his clear blue eyes, saw the laughter, and the fear.

"Mother too much for you, yet? We can always send her back where she came from," he said in his soft lazy drawl. His lips nestled next to her ear, and the heat from his breath gave her other ideas. It wasn't his mother she wanted to think about. It was the heat curling in the pit of her stomach.

Overwhelming and powerful, the sensations left her weak with need. She wanted to bury her troubles in the depth of his arms.

"Promise?" she asked, pressing a soft kiss to his lips and pushing away. "Your mother might have something to say about that." She turned to run, playfully leading him on a chase through the trees and higher into the foothills above their property.

He caught her and they tumbled to the ground, laughing. "I'd promise you the moon if I could." His tone startled her. It was full of concern and sincerity. He had become her anchor and her strength, and she clung to the security he offered.

Alexandra knew instantly he meant his promise. "I don't want the moon or the stars. I only want to know where I'll be tomorrow and the next day. I want to tell everyone the truth, yet I know I can't. I want you to find Sean Cassidy and send him back where he belongs." She looked longingly into the distance then back to James. "Yes, I know I can't, and I know you've tried to find him. It's just that..." Tears welled in her eyes and she brushed them away.

Hold me. Just hold me until I can't forget what it feels like.

His body moved closer to her, and his hand slipped into her hair, holding her still. "She's been meddling then. What have you told her?" He soothed her as he would a child even while her body responded to his warmth. Her cheek lay against his chest. His heartbeat pounded close to her ear. James smelled of fresh air, sunshine, and hard work, and she wanted to taste him.

"Too much, nothing," she looked up, touched his cheek and traced his full lips lightly with the tip of her finger. "Yet I've told her more than I should have."

"Oh?" His voice sounded thready as if he strained for control. She leaned against him, hoping his strength would flow into her.

"It wasn't enough. I didn't tell her about the vortex," Alex assured him. "Told her to ask you. I don't want to keep the truth from her, but this all seems so impossible, so frighteningly unbelievable. The stories so incredibly bizarre, at times I don't believe them myself. How can I expect someone else too?"

"I don't know," His mouth came down to meet hers, silencing her then stopping to grin wickedly. "Why aren't you naked?" he asked with a chuckle that made her blood race through her veins. "When I catch a nymph flitting about in the fields, I expect her naked." He held her head between his hands, his thumb slowly caressing the pulse on her neck.

She pushed on his chest and laughed, pretending to deny him. "Get off me, you big oaf. Naked? Naked in the middle of the afternoon? You ought to be ashamed of yourself." She beat against him, struggling in his arms then willingly, almost urgently, surrendering. With his fingertips, he gently closed her eyes. With his lips, he left a gentle trail down her neck. Her arms wound around his broad shoulders, and her hands roamed beneath his shirt.

"I'm not." He groaned. "This is where you belong, darlin', in my arms. His tongue slipped into her mouth, demanding an answering response in Alex. Finally surfacing for air, they both appeared shocked by the intensity of the kiss. Her eyes fluttered open then closed almost immediately. The breeze rustled in the trees overhead.

"Oh, dear Lord, Alexandra, what you do to me. Do you have any idea?" he asked against her lips, his mouth hovering just inches from her.

"I think so," she gasped for air.

"You send me spinning."

"Just like the vortex."

"Yes." He kissed her forehead, her nose, before tracing her lips with his tongue, urging her to open for him.

"When you touch me, I can't think, James," she clung to him. Her fingers roamed the muscles of his back, his chest, his arms. He offered protection from her greatest fear, escape from a man who threatened her, security when she'd never thought to find it. Oh, how she loved him.

"What does my kiss do to you?" he prompted.

"It makes me hot. You make me so very hot. I can't think. Hold me. I need you."

His mouth moved down the column of her throat, farther to the soft mounds of her breasts. He teased her nipple, bringing the coral tip farther into his mouth, suckling. Even through the fabric of her dress, she felt the instant rise in temperature, and the strange shiver that went with it. "Anything else?"

"James," his name hovered in the air, lingered a moment then vanished.

"Alex, I want you now. I can't wait."

The sun and the wind silently applauded as he stripped them of their clothing, rushing headlong to the inevitable joining that mated them forever through all time and dimensions. James laughed and his kisses feathered across her body. He spread their clothes on the ground and lowered her to rest on them. Immediately, he covered her again, and his body hid her from the world. She clung to him, wrapping her arms and legs around him, bringing him to meet her. Then he entered her and that familiar heat he'd awakened her to pulsed between them. He moved within her, drawing them together until she touched the moon and the stars.

"Ah, sweet Alex, that was too soon, too fast, we'll do it better next time."

Alexandra relaxed beneath him. Too spent to move a way, she still clung to him. Her toes brushed his leg, and she marveled at the feeling. The hair on his leg tickled her and the hardness of his muscles thrilled her again, and when she felt the now familiar stirring so soon, she laughed at herself.

All I want is James.

Yet I still feel the call of home.

God, how she hated the fear of leaving, finding herself hurtling through that empty void to another time and place.

I need to know I won't be swept away. The niche I've made for myself feels comfortable and right. I belong with James and Jessie. I want to tell him I love him, would never leave, but I can't.

Sean Cassidy still threatened her, and the vortex still called to her. Sometimes at midnight she would wake up in a cold sweat, sick to her stomach, and feel the terrible call from the blackness beyond.

The beckoning she couldn't quell.

She resented that, begrudging every minute she'd worried about the future, envying James a place in time and the security she didn't have, never knowing if someday she'd find herself scooped up and shipped off to another century again. Just like boarding a plane for another destination, but in that there was a choice.

Alexandra groaned, suddenly realizing she was lying naked in a field of wildflowers. "Next time can we have a little privacy?" She looked into his clear blue eyes.

"No one's here." He watched the soft glow on her face deepen to a lovely red. "You blush very nicely."

"Why do I feel like we've been watched by a hundred prying eyes?" she motioned for him to look around. No less than two squirrels and a Blue Jay watched from perfect vantage points above them, and those were the animals she could see. The squirrel cocked his head to one side to get a better view. The Blue Jay cried out then flapped its wings, flying into the distance.

"Don't worry, love, it's my backside they see."

"I don't feel right." A cold chill slithered up her spine.

"I'll shoo them away." He wished she'd cuddle back in his arms.

"No, you won't. We aren't staying."

"Now that's where you're wrong. We're going to make love again, and this time I'm going to treat you to perfection. Before I'm finished, I'll have you begging."

Her body trembled. All her fear and doubts momentarily vanished. She tried to hold back the ripple of wanting; needed to tell him how much she wanted to stay, but the thought faltered and was lost in the surge of desire that followed his caress. Alexandra whispered against his neck, "James."

"One more time, angel girl, for perfection."

Good Lord, but it always felt like perfection with him. Something so perfect she'd never known it before, something she'd never forget.

"I won't live through this," she managed to say before his mouth slanted over her again with the expertise she knew so well. He tantalized her every sense. It was magical, yet it seemed so wicked.

He knew each secret sensitive part of her body by heart. She wanted him too much to be the least bit rational now that he kissed her again. She surrendered, a surrender complete and absolute.

When he feathered kisses down her body, across her stomach and back, fastening his lips on the tip of her breast, she succumbed to the fluttering within and the glorious sensations that would end all too soon.

She felt the heat of his kiss, the coolness of the spring breeze against her flesh. Covering one nipple with his mouth, he'd leave another exposed and vulnerable. Alternating heat and cold, her body responded with sweet harmony and pulsed with anticipation. He found every sensitive inch of her and loved each place with deliberate slowness.

Dusk had fallen. A summer planet hovered on the horizon, and the first stars glimmered in the darkening sky. By the time he finished loving her, she didn't want to move, wanted only to curl up with him for the entire night.

Alex's eyes fluttered closed while James fumbled with her clothes. Suddenly, strange voices seemed all too close. With impatience born of pending humiliation, her eyes opened and she tried desperately to dress herself. She managed in only a few short seconds to throw her dress over her head and fasten the buttons.

Chase stopped when he crested the hill, stood motionless before he turned and motioned the men that were following. James watched the men disappear from view, sighed and stretched.

She felt the heat of another blush steal across her face.

With a piece of grass stuck casually in his mouth, James lay comfortably beside her. One knee up with his hand resting carelessly on top of it, he arrogantly tapped the ground beside him. James was a picture of pure masculinity at its finest. His lips hinted at a smile, even as her eyes traced the length of his naked chest down to edge of his pants.

Chase and the men stayed at the top of the hill, seeming to wait for them.

"What will happen if I'm pregnant?" she asked.

"We'll have a baby to love," he said, cautiously weighing each word.

"But if I don't stay?"

The muscle in his neck suddenly pulsed. "I won't let you go."

"What if I don't have a choice?" her voice so low and soft he had to bend near to hear.

"You'd leave me then without a good-bye?"

"No," she said. "I didn't have a choice when I came here, what if..."

"Don't go near the vortex," he cut in harshly.

"But there could be other places. We know so little," she continued, paying little attention to the irritation that clouded his speech. She felt the hot rise of tears threaten.

"Do you want to go home?"

"I am homesick. I miss my mother and my friends. They must be worried."

"Alexandra..."

A little moan of understanding escaped her lips. She hadn't meant to give him that impression but everything she'd said was true. "No," she told him. "But--"

"No, what, Alex."

"I'm frightened."

He gathered her in his arms and held her. The night encompassed them, the moon rose over the hills, and she felt the chill of the unknown haunting her.

"If you trust in me, I won't let anything hurt you," he said and his finger brushed her cheek, tracing the line of her jaw. He stopped at her chin and lifted it.

"Some things are beyond our control. Haven't you learned that yet?" Her voice, hesitant at first grew stronger with each word. "I may not have a choice."

"I'm a slow learner," he said and bent to place a chaste kiss on her forehead. "C'mon, it's time we were getting back. Chase detoured the search party, but if we don't come over that hill soon, he won't be able to hold my men back."

"You mean they'd still come?"

"The men who work for me are loyal to a fault. And my sweet, they're loyal to me, not my father."

"Then what are we waiting for?" She moved to rise, but he held her back. Something in him prompted her to delay the moment. His answer was a doubting grin and a hand that came from nowhere to caress her cheek, moved down her arm possessively then rested at her waist pulling her closer.

"Not so fast?" he said. "Maybe..."

"Make up your mind," she said, exasperated with him. "One minute you want to leave, the next you hold back."

"I know but this has been a wonderful day and I just thought... I told mother about you."

She gasped, startled by his sudden revelation. "No."

"I'm not joking. We talked a long time. She doesn't believe, not yet anyway."

"They're going to have a great deal of questions. Are you ready for them?" she asked.

"As ready as you are."

"That's not what I wanted to hear."

He gave her a hand and helped her to her feet. They started down the hill, his arm around her waist. holding her close as if the gesture could keep her at his side forever.

"You asked a question. I answered."

"You don't do anything simple sweetheart," he said and leaned over to give her an unexpected kiss.

Alexandra touched her lips where his had just rested.

Chapter Twenty-four

Chase and Danielle did have questions, more than she'd ever thought possible, more than she wanted to hear. When it was over, nothing was settled. They simply found her story too hard to believe.

A shrill whinnying and the baying of hounds interrupted the fragile peace that had settled over the household. Horses hooves pounded through the night air. Rain thundered on the rooftop, lightening bombarding the skies. Gale force winds blew leaves from trees, catching anything that lay in its furious path. The weather reminded James of another night, not so long ago, a night where he had plucked Alexandra half naked from the frozen earth and brought her home.

Angel girl. My angel.

James knew it was Charles, had to be. Charles always came with the posse. He heard Charles booted feet as they pounded up the front steps. "James...James! Open the door." Charles banged on the solid oak and cursed, shouting orders.

Twelve men and six hounds waited. James turned from the window, a moment of foreboding haunting him. Alexandra opened the door, and Charles' huge shoulders filled the opening. He stood in the doorway for a moment. Unmoving. Light bathed his body, blocking out the darkness. The steady sound of the rain magnified in the unholy stillness, and wind rushed through the opening, the candle flickering ominously. A chill swept through the room.

"What's happened?" James asked. A muscle in his jaw ticked dangerously as he fought to tamp down his emotions. Angry with Charles and the posse, frustrated at the turn of events and the timing, he thought of the warm bed upstairs and the soft body that would fill his arms. Reluctantly, he turned his attention back to the matter at hand.

"Your man's been spotted."

James froze. Charles went on and the rest of his words faded into nothing. Suddenly, he felt an instant surge of energy.

"My man?" It really wasn't a question. James knew immediately Charles was speaking of Sean Cassidy, and this time he was more than eager to join these men and the hounds.

Charles was impatiently slapping his riding gloves against his leg. "Yes."

"James," Alexandra began, "Sean?" Instantly her face turned white and she swayed on her feet. She clutched at James' arm.

"God almighty, I know that but where?" he asked, adrenalin coursing through his blood.

Erase the fear in Alexandra's eyes.

Replace it with hope.

Bind her to me hard and fast, so thoroughly she won't ever want to leave.

"Stepped in for a drink at the Eldorado. One of the ladies caught his eye, and she recognized him from the drawing you had made. As soon as she had the chance, she slipped out the back door and found me."

"Good, where has he gone?" James voice was demanding and cold.

"Headed northeast. He's headed toward Gold Hill, Sardine Creek, the Forbidden Ground," Charles finished. Are you coming with us?" Charles asked.

"You sure he's left town?" James weighed each decision.

"Positive," Charles answered.

"Yes, I'm with you. I'll just be a second." He turned to Alex. "Lock the doors and windows when we leave. Don't let anyone in. This is important."

"I'm coming too." Chase said in the background.

~ * ~

They rode out that night in the midst of thundering hooves and pounding rain. Walking outside, Alexandra shivered. Darkness and despair ripped through her, and she felt cold within.

"I haven't told him. I haven't told him how much I love him," she closed her mind against the pain encompassing her.

I don't want to leave, but you won't be safe until I do.

Her focus swung to the north toward the vortex. It called and she felt a compelling need to answer. Her fingers gripped the railing that ran around the gazebo on the front porch. Looking toward Sardine Creek again, she forced her mind away from its drawing power.

"He'll believe the worst, but it's not true. I don't want to leave him."

The rain tuned into a constant gray drizzle. Alex watched the road. If the stars and moon existed, one would not know it by the blackness settling on the valley. No light penetrated the dense clouds that had brought the rain and now descended to hover near the ground.

She trembled, terrified of the future, fought back tears because she didn't have a chance to tell James how much she wanted to stay. She stared into the night. The sky was black, so dark, and so very dangerous.

It has come to this, just as I knew it would. No one ever really has a choice.

As the night wore on, she became more terrified. She looked to Danielle for answers.

"Alex, Alexandra dear, it's time to come in."

"I won't ever see him again." She turned to Danielle, but she felt as if a fist had just slammed into her heart. Tears welled in her eyes. "I have to go. The vortex is calling me. Don't you hear it?" Her voice wafted away on a breeze, ethereal and angelic.

"No, you don't. You don't have to go. It's not calling you. It doesn't exist. Listen to me. It doesn't exist." Danielle shook her hard.

"No, you're wrong. You don't understand."

"Go to bed, dear. This will all seem brighter in the morning when the day breaks, when sunlight can dispel all the fear and the nightmares," Danielle said.

"Tell him I love him." Alex stepped away from Danielle. Finally, she walked back into the house, saying nothing more as tears slid down her throat. The house was so very still, and Alexandra looked at every part every piece of furniture. Storing everything in her mind so she could remember her brief life with James. She was so very glad James wasn't here. She straightened, determined to find a way back to Sardine Creek.

The grandfather clock in the hallway struck once.

Now it was well past midnight.

She had one more day.

~ * ~

Danielle followed Alexandra inside, closing the door silently behind her. Alexandra paced nervously, watching Danielle, hoping against hope Danielle would retire for the night. Instead, Danielle sat in a stiff backed chair, nearly regal in her appearance, holding her hands in her lap. Danielle's eyes had a stubborn look, a look they always assumed when she decided on a course of action. They registered completely on her, and Danielle smiled knowingly at her daughter-in-law.

"Alex," Danielle's fingers drummed lightly against the armrest, "do you know the way to this vortex?"

"No, it's north of here, in the hills." Alexandra turned that direction as if answering a silent summons. The pull overpowered her, and she felt mindless and vulnerable, almost as if she was incapable of controlling her mind.

"Ignore the calling. You have to. If you want to stay here with James, you have to ignore it. Fight it, fight it with all your strength." Danielle's voice, urgent and commanding, penetrated Alexandra's wavering emotions.

"I'll try."

"Good, then I think we'll spend the night waiting up for our men. Play cards?"

"Solitaire."

"Poker?" Danielle asked.

"No."

"I'll teach you. Go get the box of matches."

"Whatever for?"

"To bet with, of course." Danielle grinned. "What did you think?"

Four hours later, Alexandra stifled a yawn then spread her cards in front of Danielle. The kettle boiled on the stove, and steam wafted into the air. The candle burned to nothing. Dawn followed midnight then vanished as well. Nothing happened. Kim's fresh baked bread they devoured around five in the morning and by the time Kim wandered into the parlor, she found the two ladies' heads bowed on the table, fast asleep.

~ * ~

The message came unexpectedly. Neither of them thought for a moment James would send a note instead of returning himself. Belinda Perkins brought it from town then drove her little buggy back to Jacksonville. Danielle had been sitting in the sunshine when the messenger arrived.

"Alexandra. Alex, come here." Danielle anxiously handed the telegram to her.

"What's this?"

"A telegram. The lady said it was for you."

For a long time Alexandra stared at the note. The paper shook so fiercely in Alexandra's hand she was forced to set the sheet on the railing behind her. The handwriting was unmistakable. Hated. The paper was dirty and the penmanship sloppy.

She reread the note carefully, word by word. "Alexandra. Meet me at the boulder. This afternoon at two. I have something you want. You're under my thumb, pretty lady."

"Jessica..." Alexandra felt the color slowly drain from her face. "Where's Jessie?" She crumpled the paper as she looked at the sun, willing it to move so she could hurry. She pressed her lips tightly together as she fought to push her fear away.

"I haven't seen her."

"Dear Lord," she murmured. The note wasn't from James. "Sean. Look in the house. Look everywhere. He's watching and now he must have Jessie. Get Kim, maybe she's seen her." She gripped the chair in front of her as waves of icy fear warred with a cold, iron rage.

Alexandra looked to the north. It wasn't to her the vortex beckoned, but she still felt the need to go, an irresistible pull to end this. "James, where are you? Don't be afraid, Jessie. I'm coming." Her voice shook with fear and confusion. "We'll find you."

Danielle nodded, her face set with grim determination.

"Two o'clock—at the boulder." Lord, she didn't think she could wait, but knew she had to. Patience, she told herself so many times she lost count and still the time drug by. They waited throughout the morning as helpless feelings surged to the forefront as hours passed and neither James nor Chase rode into view. Alex flitted from the garden to the kitchen to the upstairs rooms unable to sit still. She climbed the tree house with Danielle behind her to get a better view of the rolling landscape, but in truth she wanted to be the first to see the men returning.

As the morning wore away and the sun passed its zenith, she became frantic. Jessie was out there somewhere with a mad man. If only there were cell towers and she could call the men home. James was gone. She knew she had to do something, had to find Jessie. Everything was happening just as she'd feared so long ago, just as she'd thought the posse would find Sean.

This had nothing to do with the vortex or time traveling. It was all about a little girl's life and Sean Cassidy held the controlling card. She had to go. It was too late to tell James, too late to tell him she loved him. And it was too late to tell him she didn't want to leave. It had always seemed she'd have another day, another chance, but no longer.

"I want you to stay inside the house today," Alex said. "It's not safe out there. We don't know what Sean will do next."

"And you?" Danielle asked.

"I have to find Jessie, make sure she's protected." Her voice was soft, and it sounded so very strange, she thought. Again Alexandra looked to the vortex.

Danielle's breath caught on Alexandra's words. Her attention focused now on Alex. "I'm afraid I can't let you do that by yourself," Danielle said stubbornly. "Jessie is my granddaughter."

"I know, but it's not your battle. It's mine. I don't want you hurt, and I know Sean won't hurt Jessie unless I defy his orders. He's crazy, you know." Alex gripped her hands together. "It's my future, my destiny. I've been there before and understand what could happen. I don't think James or

Chase could protect me if I was supposed to leave. Another power, perhaps God, or the devil," she hesitated, "is directing the scene. I don't know why but I have to go," Alex told her, determined to see this through.

She would never have a future here, unless she met her fate head on and fought whatever demons dwelled on the mountain or in her soul.

Danielle grew silent, as if she was thinking over Alexandra's words. For a few seconds, her fingers drummed on the table. She paused then inadvertently wiped her hands on her dress. "If that's the way you want it. James won't like it and neither will Chase," she added. "But I'll go with you. I will not let you do this by yourself. You don't really know what Sean will do."

"James and Chase are no more in a position to question my judgment than they are to prevent me from riding into the hills. Unless they turn up in the next fifteen minutes."

Alexandra knew no one would follow. Every able-bodied man in the surrounding area was part of the posse, and they were chasing Sean Cassidy. Ironic, she thought. They weren't going to find him. Somehow Sean had outsmarted them once again.

Yet she knew in her heart she'd find peace tonight, and she felt strangely relieved this ordeal would finally end.

Exactly five minutes later, Danielle appeared, dressed in a pair of buckskin breeches and a white silk shirt. Danielle had two knives now. One tucked into its sheath at her waist and another within easy reach at the top of her knee-high moccasins. She held out a third one for Alexandra. She accepted it. "A girl should be able to defend herself," Danielle told her. "I'm ready whenever you are."

Within minutes, Danielle and Alex were mounted and riding.

Alex's breath was ragged. Her heart pounded. As they rode into the hills, the day turned a ghostly shade of gray, and the air became ominously still. Not even a breath of wind rustled the tall grass. They galloped, hooves pounding, and the sound echoed in the fog that had descended in a heavy veil.

They couldn't see beyond the next rise, but she knew Sean Cassidy was out there waiting for her.

Suddenly, the fog parted. She stopped, her horse dancing skittishly as if the animal expected demons to attack, Danielle reining in beside her. Alexandra tensed, staring transfixed at the apparition she saw in front of her, staring as if she was trying to convince herself.

"Jessie?" she gasped, stunned to see the little girl calmly astride her horse.

"Jessica." Danielle echoed Alex.

For a moment that felt like an eternity, all three stared at each other. Matilda shook her head then whinnied. Alexandra held fast to the horse. "Are you all right? Where's Sean?" she asked.

"Sean?"

"The man who took you. Did he hurt you?" Danielle's voice quivered as she spoke.

"I don't know where he is. I'm all right." Jessie grinned then looked sheepish as if she waited for the reprimand that should come the moment Alex caught her breath. "I didn't mean to wander off, really. It's just that he was so nice. He told me—told me his horse bolted and he'd give me money if I'd help him look."

"It's all right. No harm done, but Jessie, don't ever do that again," Alexandra warned.

"I won't. I don't know where he went. He told me he'd be right back, and I was to wait here for you." Jessie stared into the thick white clouds. Her gaze seemed to be concentrated on a patch of gray behind Alex. Nothing moved. "Is that him over there?" Jessie pointed. Her voice chattered on and she didn't wait for an answer.

Alex felt the chill of the damp air penetrate her body, and she wondered how Jessie could be so nonchalant. Jessie was acting as if nothing had happened, as if no one had kidnapped her.

"I certainly hope not. I don't ever want to see that man again. Come on, let's go home," Alex said firmly.

Jessie flashed her little white teeth at Alex. They suddenly heard movement.

Alex stifled a hysterical giggle.

"Go, Jessie," Danielle suddenly commanded.

Jessie didn't move. Instead, she peered into the fog-shrouded day just as Alex and Danielle were doing.

"Oh, no," Alex breathed. But even as Alex listened to Danielle, she knew something was terribly wrong. Alexandra suddenly sensed someone behind her. She froze, paralyzed with fear.

Danielle spun, knife unsheathed and ready.

Sean Cassidy stood before them.

"No!" Alex cried out again. "Go away, Sean. Go home, go to the vortex. There's nothing for you here." The horse whinnied and side stepped.

"Alex, I'm not leaving without you." Sean's evil voice hung on the air.

He held his gun on Danielle. They faced each other in a standoff, but it was no contest. He fired. Blood soaked the snow-white shirt that covered her.

"Danielle," Alex cried out, horrified. Ignoring Alex, he aimed at Jessie and fired again but the child had already reacted. Jessie raced past him into the fog. "Ride hard, Jessie. Get help!"

Then Alexandra threw her knife.

Even as the knife fell harmlessly to the ground, Sean turned on her. His face was contorted with unmasked fury, eyes narrowed to thin slits.

Alexandra opened her mouth to scream, but the sound never came. Sean spun so the gun pointed to her stomach.

"Angel eyes," he mocked. "I had thought to do this without this much company, but then you never make things easy do you?" His face, his words they all ran together and reminded her of that night on the hill.

"No, Sean. You'll regret this. Now I'm going to get off my horse and help Danielle."

"Ah...I won't regret a thing, and no, Alex, we don't have time to help anyone. We're going on another journey through time, sweetheart."

She defied him, dismounting and moving toward Danielle, but she kept talking, kept moving as if Sean posed no threat. "James won't allow it," she whispered. "You'll never get away with this. He'll follow us—forever."

His eyes threatened then danced with amusement. "That would be quite a feat, pretty lady."

"Nothing will stop him."

As the distant sound of voices floated through the fog, he stiffened, just as Alex did. Nothing tangible could be heard, but the sounds drew ever closer. And the hooves, it sounded as if hundreds of them came their way. They were coming for her. Now the hounds barked and she cringed in horror and relief. Chills ran the length of her spine.

Sean grabbed Alex around the waist and hauled her from the ground, holding her against his hip. "You're coming with me."

"Never!" she cried. "I won't. I can't go back there. I promised. Danielle, I can't leave her. And Jessie, I have to find her." She squirmed and struggled in his arm, but it was so useless.

"Be still." he thundered. To Alex's amazement, he holstered his gun. She opened her mouth to scream again, but his arms squeezed around her chest, the gesture smothering the sound and cutting off her air.

He was a strong man, yet she had fought him before and won, surely she could do it again, but, dear Lord, not without any air. She battled him madly, recklessly. It made no difference. She couldn't squirm from his arms.

He pitched her over his horse and she dangled precariously. He mounted behind her and they rode.

~ * ~

James had discovered the false trail after hours in the saddle. They were miles from home when the full implication hit him. They had been deceived. Cassidy had fooled the hounds and that amazed him even more. As a soldier, he'd been trained to be prepared for the unexpected, but this seemed to him as unreal as Alexandra's appearance in his century. The information came too easily. For months now, Sean Cassidy had kept to himself. Suddenly, without warning, he'd turned up in town. Incredible, James mused. The setup had been perfect, and like greenhorns, the posse had fallen for the ruse.

They had decided to trust the whore. She had sent them on a time wasting mission. Now they'd had to double back.

When they ran into Jessie, pale and trembling, he knew he was on the right track. For a brief moment, he allowed her to huddle in his lap. Tears flowed from her huge eyes, but she was able to blurt out what she knew. At the mention of Danielle and the gunshot, Chase turned and rode straight into the dense blanket of fog.

"The devil!" he'd roared, and they saw his back as he raced forward.

But when they reached the boulder, Alexandra had vanished and Danielle lay deathly pale on the ground. Her head lay on Chase's coat and he'd managed to stop the blood.

She was still alive. The bullet had only grazed her arm.

Panic overwhelmed James. He knew where they had gone. A vague place he'd never really located. Sardine Creek, a curious and foreboding place that terrified him. Anything could happen there, but the vortex might not open until midnight. He searched the ground for tracks, hoping he was wrong. But there were no clues. The path was too rocky. All that was left behind was a pearl button from Alexandra's dress. It lay on the hard granite rock.

A cougar screamed somewhere in the dark night.

The warm summer breeze that began clearing the fog filled him with hope and renewed his faith.

"Son of a bitch, he must know how to find the vortex, " James ran a hand through his hair and paced. His thoughts in shambles. His heart raced and his efforts to calm his nerves seemed futile.

He was terrified and angry with himself. Everything she had told him had been the truth. Sean. The endless black void. A place where the earth trembled and defied all laws of nature. Everything was out of the ordinary.

It would end soon. The man with the scar, Sean Cassidy, would not succeed. He'd meant to kill Danielle and failed. Now he would fail again.

I will protect Alexandra.

She is my life, my every reason to live.

Perhaps he thought to escape through the tunnel they had come through.

2015? Escape back to her time. Yes. It made sense but there were no guarantees. They could end up anywhere, anywhere at all. And what would happen to her?

He had Alexandra. She had rejected Sean and now he sought

revenge. Alex had inherited his fortune, and now he wanted the money back. It was the only reasonable explanation. But if Sean's plan didn't succeed and they ended up in the wrong place...

James agonized over that fear again just as he'd done so many times before. *Fight Alex, fight desperately. It's your only hope. Fight him until I can reach you.*

Crissakes, I can't think about it any longer. I'll go mad.

General Lee pranced nervously as if he knew as well. "Get moving, James," Chase urged. "Jessie's safe. I'll see Danielle home. And then I'll follow."

Danielle moaned and looked at her husband. "You have to go with him, please. I'll be fine. Let one of James's men take me home. James needs you more."

"If that's what you want," Chase said, gently brushing her hair from her eyes.

"Go. Don't waste any more time."

"Where to?" he asked tensely.

"Gold hill. His only escape is through the vortex. He won't make it. Son of a bitch, they won't make it," James said.

They rode and the fear inside him multiplied. He didn't know why, but he knew Alexandra wouldn't survive another journey through time.

They came to Sardine Creek and the old trail. Light from the moon, golden and strangely lined with silver, hovered in the hills above them, and as they moved closer it grew in brightness.

I will find the vortex.

Chapter Twenty-five

Do what thou wilt, thou shalt not so,
Dark Angel! triumph over me:

Lionel Johnson
"The Dark Angel"

    Besotted by memories and filled with desperation, James was momentarily stunned into silence. Vividly, he remembered the first time he set his eyes upon Alexandra. She was helpless, a stranger in a land she'd never known before. Yet courageously and by herself, she'd defied the freezing weather, surviving all that was thrust at her.

    Just as they had that night in February, the posse had galloped for hours along the old road that wound its way toward Sardine Creek. Now with their horses winded and heaving, the men of the posse waited further orders. The trail left the road and led into thick forest. Brambles, bushes, and fir trees crowded closely together and blocked the narrow path.

    Frustrated, Chase pushed his hat up with one finger. Without even looking up, he addressed James. "What do you make of this? I can't seem to find a path anywhere."

    A tiny scrap of material caught James eye. The blue calico dangled precariously from a bush. Chase reached out and plucked the fabric from its resting spot. He held it a moment before handing it to James.

    James cleared his throat then almost reverently touched the fabric, his eyes assuming a distant look. A soft breeze ruffled the needles on the fir trees surrounding them. He studied the signs, the subtle tale of Alexandra's passage. They were so clear and foreboding that he stifled a shiver, a twig broken here, a thread of cloth a little farther on, footprints no one bothered to hide. "I don't like this," James whispered. "I don't like this at all."

The trees reached out, the forest smelled musty and old, and the taste of death hung in the air.

"Is that from her dress?" Chase pointed to the torn and dirty blue calico scrap.

"A piece of her skirt," James said. He felt his muscles tightening with fear, warring with rage. Nervous energy slowly grew like ripples on a pond, changing to fierce anger then determination. Every second he lingered here, each minute he wasted in idle talk, Sean moved farther and farther away with Alex.

He'd hoped they would find Alexandra and Sean before it came to this, before they disappeared into the forest, before midnight.

A cloud slid across the moon and James felt a terrifying cold enter his body. This was the second day. How much longer?

"We should push on." Chase's voice sounded unsteady. "Don't want to waste any more time."

The posse waited, watching. Men sat their horses, staring at James as if they knew the verdict before he could voice it. The dogs whimpered, straining for freedom, for the chase. Charles dismounted and motioned for the others to do the same.

"We'll wait here for you unless you think you'll need us sooner."

"Two quick shots."

Charles nodded.

James moved swiftly, his fear pulsing within his heart, beating against his mind. He flashed Charles a quick smile and dismounted. Before he disappeared in the thick growth of the forest, Charles called to him. "Find the bastard."

James grunted, "Don't doubt it," and with Chase, turned to follow the overgrown trail, pushing and swearing softly at each obstacle. He understood the men of the posse wanted to go with them; understood, too, they couldn't. He stared into the thick forest and felt the ache and desolation, knew the emptiness he'd feel if he never saw Alexandra again.

All I want is to hold her, touch her. One more time. I'll give her a choice. If she wants to leave, I won't make her stay.

"She'll be all right." His fists clenched and he said the words again to convince himself. "She's a fighter. Hold on, Alexandra, please hold on. Don't give up the fiddle."

The wind whispered words that left eerie sensations and acute discomfort in his heart. He swiveled in an attempt to catch sight of the ghostly abstraction hovering in the night but could see nothing.

"Did you see that?"

"Shadows, only shadows," Chase said.

Sweat beaded above James' lip and on his forehead, trickling down the side of his face to his neck, slowly soaking into his shirt. James moved into the forest, Chase behind him, tree limbs reaching out to hold him, briars grabbing at his clothing. Sardine Creek rushed helter-skelter nearby, gurgling over rocks and under moss covered trees. Not a whisper of his movement sounded in the night. Cold enveloped him. The closer he came to the void and the blackness, the worse it became. Some unseen force beckoned him on, and he had no choice. No conscious effort could prevent him from reaching the spot as midnight approached. The witching hour, the hour where magic assumed control of the earth. The sky darkened and the stars evaporated from the sky. For a moment, only a vague suggestion of light existed before blackness reigned.

Sean would take Alexandra with him, willing or not; then what?

A cold sweat engulfed James from within and he hastened his step. A twig snapped and they both froze. Deep brown eyes stared back. A doe, foraging for food, and her two fawns stared at him. The deer, startled by the human presence, dashed into the night, taking all sound with her. James breathed deeply, hadn't realized he held it. It reminded him of the terrible peril that lay so close and a danger he felt so powerless to stop. He had to see her, touch her, taste her one more time. He could sense Alexandra's fear and ached to hold her.

~ * ~

Midnight had not arrived yet, and James understood nothing would happen until that hour. It amazed him Alexandra had come this way once before, braving the darkness and terror by herself.

Without warning, they entered a small clearing and a beam of moonlight filtered into the darkness. Instantly, the two men stepped back and skirted the edge of light, searching for Alex and her captor. Nothing moved and at that moment life seemed timeless. Then a whimper, a spoken word caught his attention.

"Alexandra," James whispered then lunged forward. Chase reached out, holding him back, cautioning him against any quick movements.

Alexandra struggled against Sean's hold, just as he struggled against his father's iron grip. "She's alive," Chase said. "She's fighting him."

"Over there, look, a hole is opening." James voice trembled and he moved forward even as he watched the transformation. He had thought he believed Alex all these months, but now, now he knew he'd only accepted Alexandra's story on faith. He had never truly believed.

"The devil," Chase said, as if he was awed by the alteration that was taking place.

A deep black hole, no bigger than a doorknob peered at them through the darkness. James was determined. He had to stop Sean Cassidy.

Yet with every minute the danger increased. Time moved forward, unconcerned and uncaring.

James willed his body to relax, but energy surged through his veins, and he felt ready to spring. Only Chase's innate calm and the restraining hand he placed on James' arm held him back.

"Don't jump in so fast. He might hurt her," Chase said.

James froze with his first step, knowing he hadn't thought, knowing he risked everything if he acted prematurely. "We wait for an opening and move slowly. Alex is distracting him. She knows we are here. Good girl."

"When?"

"We'll stay in the shadows and inch our way towards them." More time slipped away, and as it passed, the air grew heavier and the atmosphere bleaker.

Father and son moved, always closer, relentlessly silent, painstakingly staying at the edge of the shadows. Stopping for brief seconds to breathe, to gain their bearings then step again. Alexandra continued a desperate bid for freedom, keeping Sean occupied, making the noise James

341

and Chase couldn't afford. A cricket sung in the background, surprising James. The sound spoke of something foreign to this spot, and it spread a light of hopefulness in an all too depressing void. A frog bellowed to its mate and suddenly other noises interrupted the silence.

Yet as the dawn of hope crept into their hearts, the hole grew larger, Sean and Alexandra closer.

Midnight groped stealthily toward them. The air hummed and a breeze began as if in warning. They moved closer but not fast enough, because the hole had expanded more rapidly than expected.

James crept closer, Chase behind him, but as long as they wanted to remain unknown, there was little they could do except keep pace. In this space, this small secluded corner of the universe, good battled evil. Darkness transcended everything, enveloping the forest and snuffing out any light that dared to penetrate. He stared at the hole then the sky. The black hole grew steadily, and still no light penetrated the tiny glade. Instead the air hovered dense and heavy around them. When he looked ahead, the black void once more seemed to have shrunk in size.

He could no longer see Alexandra or Sean. Panicked, he turned to Chase. His heart leapt and ceased to beat in his chest. James felt as if steel bands wound around him, suffocating him.

"We have to move soon. Now. Before we loose them."

His body shuddered.

Alexandra, her name was branded in his heart and soul for all eternity. *Alex, fight him with every breath you have, he prayed. Don't let him take you with him.*

Fight, Alex fight.

I love you.

James battled the hand that held him back, warring with the blackness threatening to take over and looking to the beacon of hope above him. Once more as he moved in the shadows, the light increased, and James was filled with reassurance. The light warmed him, surrounding him with contentment, and he knew there was no reason to fear.

So he prayed, to a God he'd all but given up on.

And he held onto hope.

~ * ~

Her stomach rolled in violent waves of nausea. For the first few moments after Sean tugged her from the horse, little things penetrated her thoughts then she remembered Danielle and Jessie. Tears welled in the back of her throat, and she prayed, prayed with all her strength the two of them were safe.

She'd never told James she loved him or didn't want to leave him. Jessie would have to collect all the eggs, and she'd never dance in the rain with James again. Piggy would have no one to torment. Tears welled in her eyes for all the lost time, all the wasted minutes she'd allowed to vanish unappreciated.

James would survive. He and Jessie would be safe when she was gone.

When she saw the black hole, she understood immediately. The opening would grow and when they stepped inside, the vortex would toss them around and they'd land somewhere. Her fingers lay limp at her side, even as she struggled to push back the sickness threatening to overwhelm her. The sky unexpectedly cleared, a half-moon standing boldly in the darkness for all to see, and from this small beacon of light she took hope. Suddenly, she heard a voice reassuring her, telling her everything would be fine. It was James.

Alexandra tried to focus on Sean Cassidy, fought to stay away from the void, digging in her heels, but it was useless pitting her strength against Sean's. Her weakness frustrated her, and she swore under her breath.

The vortex, a place where nothing was as it seemed, and the odious scent of evil hung in the air.

Alexandra knew midnight closed in on them. Here in this little glade in the forest she'd meet her fate, her destiny. The hole pulsed, expanding more with each beat. Then it suddenly grew smaller. The light from the moon above grew brighter, giving her a wonderful new sensation, encouraging her to battle once more. So she prayed to the only God she knew, prayed James would come for her; find her and she'd have the strength to resist Sean. Because even as she prayed, she felt the endless pull of evil and it didn't give her a choice, just brought her ever closer to the blackness.

Oh, Lord, she felt doubt rip through her heart. What of James? He would believe she'd wanted to come because she'd never told him the truth. Danielle might have died, and Jessie didn't know the truth either; they didn't know how much she loved them. Sweet innocent Jessie, she didn't deserve this, to have her new mother ripped from her so soon.

Alexandra flexed her muscles, willing them to work. They had been so cramped and stiff, she could barely move. The hole was the size of a tire now, and she knew it wouldn't be long. Sean pulled her closer, and she struggled to stay away, but he was too strong. She wanted to scream but knew the effort would do no good. She clawed at his face even as she watched the black hole grow. Blood ran in streaks down his cheeks and he slapped her hard. Her head rocked back, the jolt stunning her for an instant. Bleary eyes focused on the light of hope that seemed to encircle them for a moment then vanished. Each time the light grew, the darkness shrank, and when the light shown about her, she garnered more strength to fight.

"Be still. This incessant struggling will do you no good. I'm taking you with me, see? The hole will be large enough in only a few minutes. You see, little Ice Maiden, we are going back, and I will have you. I'll have satisfaction."

She stared into Sean's leering eyes, shrinking back at the sight. The scar slicing across his face created a demonic look. Lank blond hair fell in his eyes. His grip tightened, and she nearly gasped with the pain. He'd stop at nothing. The bag of gold he carried weighted him down but not enough to allow her a victory over him. "You won't get away with this."

He laughed and Alex shivered as the evil sound sent chills spiraling within her.

"Who's going to stop me, sweetheart? You?" His laughter echoed between the trees.

"James," her voice wavered a moment then grew in strength. "James won't let anything happen to me."

"By the time he gets here," Sean shrugged, "we will have vanished."

"No." Alex struggled against his hold. "I'll tell everyone what you've done."

"You won't see anyone. I've a cabin in the hills not far from where we parked that night we both stepped into a different dimension. I'm taking you there."

"You're insane." She fought to loosen his hold, but his fingers tore into her arms and she heard his laugh again, diabolic and threatening. Her skin crawled. A breeze rustled her hair; the night sounds that had been so silent only a moment before started.

Whatever made me think I had no choice?

Her breath caught. "How can you know we'll go back to the twenty-first century?" she asked, confused by the change in the air.

"I don't," his voice was harsh and it held the slightest hesitation. "Nor do I care."

"Fool." she shouted at him. "Do you truly think that you can control that thing? You will never be able to find your way back, and if you take me with you, James will follow. I swear he'll kill you."

"You're wrong," he said, even as his smile widened and his hold upon her loosened. "I left a note. He'll believe that you came of your own free will. He will not follow us, Alex. After all, you don't love him."

"You left a note!" she echoed. "But he came upon us. We heard the hooves and the hounds and surely he'd listen to his mother. She knew I wouldn't come."

"But you did. I left a note for you, too, remember? And you came, knowing you'd meet me here. Even if she lives, she'll begin to doubt it herself. You were too eager, too proud."

"You watched," she let that sink in. She remembered now when she received the note. She watched him, her eyes on fire with hate and the deception. "You had no right. I'm not going with you. Never. I'd rather die first."

"You won't have a choice. I'll never give you the choice or the chance to hit me again."

She fought to hold back the words that lay on the tip of her tongue. He was a weak man and she'd win. Yes, Sean Cassidy would lose. The light instantly grew larger, and she knew James was close, but she didn't dare risk turning around. Didn't dare risk Sean would see him because she knew beyond any doubt she might have harbored he was there, waiting in the glade for the right moment.

Alex stilled, looking for a way to escape Sean. Her hair fell into her eyes cascading from the pins that had once held it in place. "You won't get my inheritance." She had to keep talking to him. "It's tied up in stocks. You'll need my signature. I'll never..." she had to make more noise, had to cover the approach of James. It was so important, but she couldn't think, and with her head spinning, this all seemed so desperate and impossible. "It's out of your reach." The thought of finding herself in that tunnel made her stomach roll. "No, don't. I won't go in there."

He breathed in her ear, threatening, demanding, his fingers threading into her hair to yank her head back. Their eyes met, "He can't follow us where we are going. We don't know," he said and his laughter echoed in her head. Still she tried so hard to hide her terror and her repulsion.

"He will. He'll never quit looking for me." But her voice wavered, her words tortured because she didn't know if he loved her enough to follow.

"Give it up, sweetheart. He doesn't care what happens to you. It was all for Jessie."

Alexandra ignored his taunting, pretending not to hear, feigning indifference, and she could hear herself but her voice sounded distant, "I'm going to be sick."

"Of course not."

"I can't go in there. I won't live. I know that now. You can't take me with you. You've got to let me go. I can't breathe." She did feel so very pale and her skin had turned cold.

"It makes no difference. I won't leave you here for him. At least not before I've tasted you, had you in my bed, not before I've had my fill."

"I'll never give you what you want," she warned, suddenly feeling the steady return of color to her face. "You'll always make me sick."

He paused and laughed. "You don't have a choice. Look, it is almost large enough for the two of us to step through."

"I won't." She wrenched from his grip, but his reach was too long and his reaction too swift. He gasped her wrist and spun her back into his embrace. She couldn't bear it when he reached out to touch her. Alexandra knew blood ran like ice in his veins, thought too she had to move quickly yet she stood paralyzed with fear. Her gasping breaths turned to sobs of despair. "Why?"

"Why indeed?" he responded. His hate showed clearly on his face. She knew he would never change his mind. She saw the determination in the set of his jaw and the tightening of his grip.

"You don't have to do this." The time to escape was now, before midnight came and there was no chance. But his hold was firm, and she couldn't wrench herself away from him.

His vacant eyes fastened on hers. "I've already explained myself. You appeal to me, sweetheart. I want the satisfaction of taming you. And you have the fortune that is rightfully mine. No woman has ever rejected me until you. Ah, pretty lady, I want satisfaction and revenge."

"That's not good enough. You have no right."

"It is for me and since I have the power to take you along, I will."

As if anticipating the step into the void, he moved closer to the enlarging tunnel, knowing from experience he'd have only a moment before it would close. He held Alex tightly around the waist with one arm, and his other arm held her wrists together. The bags of gold were slung over one shoulder. Still, she fought valiantly.

James moved closer.

He had but a moment as the hole gaped wide. Sean moved to step inside, and she tried to wrench loose.

His hold firm; he stumbled and they fell through the black void.

Chapter Twenty-six

"No! Alexandra!"

She heard James' voice, even as it echoed against the tunnel and bounced off invisible walls. He was too late. She was trapped. Panic seized her as she watched the hole begin to close around her and the blackness descend.

James will follow. I have to stop this.

Sean loosened his hold and he laughed. "Yes." He pumped one fist.

Chills twisted up her spine. "No," she whispered fiercely. Her body shook with fear, but she had to make her move now, this instant, because she could feel her body start to tumble and the sickness began to overtake her. She slammed her elbow into Sean's stomach and heard his groan of pain. With the disturbance, the void faltered and stopped spinning. She screamed, groping for the opening. "Help, James, I can't get out. God, help me."

Her legs trembled. Terrified and helpless, Alexandra reached deep within for the strength she needed. She set her mind, determined to get away from Sean Cassidy.

Sean's fingers gripped her hair and wrenched her back against his chest, forcing her compliance. She'd almost made it through. His gruesome face reeked of fury, and she smelled his anger, tasted his hatred. He would kill her now. But suddenly the tunnel stopped moving, peacefulness insinuated itself driving away the horrible fear. The tunnel shifted and the ground shook. Sean gripped her around the waist in a violent effort to keep her from leaping out and tossed her to the ground. Solid, hard earth existed beneath her. Nothing had changed, she was still in the tunnel, and now she heard cries echoing from outside. Moonlight found its way into the tunnel and a soft whisper of air caressed her cheek.

A cry from beyond shattered the darkness into a million tiny pieces. "Alex. Alexandra."

She rose on hands and knees, stretching one arm toward the voices, trying desperately to reach out to James. Incredibly he was there, so very close to her, almost touching her fingers as she reached for him, but he was in the forest and she was still in the tunnel. With astonishing speed, Alexandra leapt from the ground. The hole was growing smaller again, and the spinning had begun anew. She managed to reach the opening. She saw James. Helpless to stop the hole from closing, she prayed for the strength, the guidance and the courage to face the evil enclosing her within its tomb.

Once more James reached out for her with his arms extended, and she could see the frustration, the fury, too, etched deeply on every determined muscle, his handsome face lined and tensed. Alex wanted to be with him one more time.

She yelled out in pain and desperation. Sean had tightened his grip again. His hold around her chest wrenched the air from her lungs, cutting off her breath.

James ripped at the hole but it didn't widen and it was too small for him to get through. Alexandra again rammed her elbow into Sean's stomach. His hold relaxed for a brief moment, and she struggled from his hands.

"James, no. You can't make it. It might kill you too. Let it go. Take care. I love--"

Her words rumbled around the hollow swirling void as Sean yanked her back and the hole closed with a resounding snap. The clash reverberated over and over in her mind. He held her firmly against him. With the closing of the vortex, she had only her honor to live for so she fought him, sinking her teeth into his arm. He tightened his grip around her chest and she couldn't breathe. Her body slowly relaxed as no more oxygen pumped to her brain.

"I'll kill you, you little bitch. I don't need you alive." He moved his hands to her throat, squeezing, snuffing the life giving air from her.

Alexandra made one last conscious effort. She swung a fist,

connecting with his jaw, hard, but only hard enough to make him angrier. She kicked, clawed, flailed. He had stolen so much from her. She couldn't defeat him, and she knew it.

His fist connected at the side of her head and she slumped in his arms. Her breathing slowed then stopped.

She had died. She couldn't feel the beat of her heart and the blackness seemed darker, if that were possible. She should have felt the tumbling and the spinning, but instead the tunnel shook violently, and the roar in her ears thundered beyond endurance. The ground beneath her rolled in an undulating pattern that went on forever.

She had fought him every step; now she was dying, she knew it and she couldn't move. Soon she'd see the angels, the messengers of God.

The tunnel shook again, and she found herself catapulted through the air. Then a loud clap surrounded her as if bars on a jail cell had closed violently. The air reverberated with the sound then bleak, unrelenting darkness enclosed her.

~ * ~

James waited in the darkness as the forest slowly came back to life. At first he could see nothing then his eyes gradually adjusted, and he saw trees and bushes and even the grass. He thought he had been too late and Alexandra and Sean had vanished from his life forever, but something strange had happened. It had taken too long for the hole to close. He reached to his holster for his gun, convinced it was just a matter of time before he found himself facing Sean Cassidy.

The blackness slowly lifted. Sean wasn't in sight, but he could hear him, sense his presence, feel his pulse even as he felt his own, and he tasted his fear. A soft golden glow from the moon above shone down on the glade, focusing on him, and he stood out for all to see.

Mist rose around his legs, cold seeping trough his skin, penetrating to the bone. The night animals stopped their rituals and came to bear witness to the events yet to occur.

Then he saw Sean and a small form huddled on the ground near a wild lilac bush.

Oblivious to him, Sean was bending over Alexandra. James moved toward them, but he caught Sean's attention. "No." He let out a roar and raced for Sean.

James did so with such vengeance he reached Alexandra as Sean prepared to dash through the forest. James let him go, dropping down to cradle Alexandra in his lap. He searched her body for life, noticing the slow shallow breath, the weak but steady pulse. *Thank God, she's alive.* Letting his head fall forward and closing his eyes, he inhaled deeply several times. His father was standing over him then, bending down, checking with him. "I'll go after Sean," Chase said. "Don't worry, he won't get away. Not this time."

"No. That bastard's mine." James said venomously. "Stay with Alex. I'll be right back."

James heard Sean crashing through the forest, stumbling through the briars and the thick undergrowth. He chased after him, precious seconds turned into minutes, but he closed the distance. Sean scrambled over a huge dead tree that had fallen across the path. James reached him then grabbed him by the shoulder only to have Sean wrench away, but James was primed and ready to fight. He was prepared to follow Sean Cassidy into hell if he had to. Sean kicked out, hitting him squarely in the chest then fled into the forest again.

The long limbs of the trees and bushes reached out to hold Sean back as if in challenge. The growth was dense and nearly impassable. Sean stopped, slowly turning to face James. A mysterious smile touched his lips. Then he spoke.

"Do what you like to me. Then go to the pretty lady. She's dead, you know. I killed her."

Astonished, he stared at Cassidy.

Their gazes met. "Sean," he whispered furiously, "son of a bitch." Sean took advantage of James hesitation. He slipped away and was attempting to rush through the woods once more.

Nothing stood between them, but just as that thought flew from James' mind, Sean dashed through a clearing. He was getting away.

"No. By God, no." James tore after him, refusing to let Sean escape.

He raced forward. He did so with such determination and speed, he reached Sean as he ducked around a fir tree and prepared to jump across a rain-swollen creek. He spun Sean around, slamming him against a boulder.

James wanted nothing more than to pummel Sean until he begged for mercy, taking him back to hang. He wanted him to know how it felt to hurt deep inside, wanted to beat him so he surely thought he would die.

Coward that he was, Sean went limp, his fists hanging at his sides. He stared at James as if he wasn't there.

"Kill me, but you won't take pleasure in it. Your wife, is she alive?" He taunted James once more, believing he'd killed Alex with the blow to her head.

Hate filled him and James knew Sean spoke the truth. There would be no pleasure in Sean's death, but surely Alexandra would live. She had to. Yet even then he remembered when he'd bent over her the side of her head was horribly swollen and bruised.

"You've hurt her more than once. You better pray she lives. I'll skin you alive and leave you for the vultures," he threatened. Then determined to see Alexandra, he prodded Sean with his gun, forcing him to move back through the forest. The woods hummed with the sound of crickets and the chattering of squirrels. The bullfrogs near the creek bellowed and chanted.

After tying Sean's hands and feet, James ran to Alexandra. He found Charles bent over Alex, looking for a pulse. His men surrounded the body, and he pushed them aside.

He gazed down at her. Alexandra, still unconscious, slumped upon the damp earth. She wore a tattered and frayed blue calico skirt, and her white blouse reflected the moonlight that now shone brightly down on the little clearing. Her hair was loose and the fire of it framed her pale face.

"Alexandra." He whispered her name, ever so gently, beckoning her to return to him. He dropped to his knees and cradled her head in his lap. "Don't leave me now," he cried into the stillness that surrounded them. Somewhere, the screech of a cougar thrilled the air and water in the creek rushed by. Wind whistled above and a brilliant white light shone upon them in the glade. "Alexandra." he whispered again as if his call would keep her alive, would bring her back to consciousness.

Desperately, he gathered her into his arms and held her close to his heart. The heat from her body penetrated his soul and he prayed.

"Alexandra," he murmured next to her ear. "Don't leave me."

~ * ~

She felt his warmth, sensing his love and she tried to climb from the darkness embracing her, the blackness that held her so firmly in its grasp. Her head pounded but still she reached for the light, struggling to open her eyes.

He called to her and she wanted to come but didn't know the way. Her mind swam and still she groped through the blackness, the infinite universe that seemed to stretch on forever.

"Alexandra," he called her name again and she could feel the warmth of his breath on her skin and she felt alive, well and truly alive. He carried her now; she floated feather light as they traveled through the woods. The path was narrow, but James protected her, and she rested her head against his chest as she slowly regained her strength. So exhausted that even though she touched and heard James, she couldn't open her eyes. She hadn't strength to let him know she lived.

Finally, she did try to speak, a slight breath of air pushing from her lungs. She thought she whispered his name, but it was all an illusion. She rested again and felt the hazy mist enveloping her thoughts, felt his warm tears splash on her cheek.

Suddenly, Alexandra was alone again, yet she heard James' swearing as the echo bounced off trees and she heard him vow to kill Sean.

~ * ~

Chase strode through the woods, now leading Sean at gunpoint, Sean's wrists bound and tied behind his back. James lunged.

"Leave him alone, James. He'll pay for his crimes."

James gritted his teeth and knew he'd have to leave him to the law, but he couldn't let it go. He swung and knocked Sean to the ground with a single blow to his head. "You'll roast in hell for what you've done."

James gathered Alexandra in his arms and rested her in front of him on General Lee. So reminiscent of another night but it was so long ago, and now he was afraid for her, afraid she was dying. How could he live without her? He spurred the horse on and clung to her still warm body.

James tenderly wrapped her in his coat and held her next to his heart, hoping his warmth and life would seep inside her.

He felt the whisper of heat and a soft breath of air next to his skin and prayed she would keep breathing. The hair on his chest tickled as she caressed his skin with her fingers. He'd placed her hand on his chest, placed it there to keep her close, put it there so he'd know every slight movement she made. Still, he prayed for her to open her eyes, prayed she'd suffered no permanent damage from Sean's abuse then he heard his name.

"James?" So soft and so sweet, he couldn't believe he heard it, sure he dreamed.

He reined in and General Lee stopped quickly. The horse danced in a circle once, twice then stilled at his master's impatient command. James looked down and there she was. Alexandra, brought to consciousness by his prayers, staring into his eyes. White as death, but breathing, her eyes as clear and blue as he'd ever seen them. She was watching him intensely. He knew she had questions, but he didn't want to answer them, at least not right now. Instead he gathered her close and hugged her so fiercely he drove the breath from her lungs. When he released her, he couldn't help himself. He kissed her, her forehead and her cheeks and her fingers and he couldn't get enough of her. He wanted to keep her with him always. He vowed he'd never let her out of his sight again.

Thank God, she's alive.

"James, where are we?" Her hand touched the side of her head as if the pain was unbearable.

"We are going home, our home," he repeated.

"James? What happened to Sean?"

"Sean?"

"Where is he?"

"Chase is bringing him in to stand trial for murder." But then Chase also realized Sean Cassidy hadn't murdered anyone and Sean might still live.

"James." The cry thundered through the night, urgent and demanding. "James. For God's sakes stop."

James turned and saw Charles racing toward him. Charles drove his horse recklessly, racing furiously toward him as if the hounds of hell were after him. Now, when he'd stopped and listened, he could hear the dogs in the distance, the baying growing dimmer but still there.

"What do you want?" James asked.

Charles mouth fell open at the sight in front of him.

Alexandra was alive and breathing.

"Thank God," he said, hesitating only a moment before continuing. "Sean escaped. Chase went after him. The hounds will find him, and when they do, he'll wish he'd come back to stand trial."

"The devil," James said, his voice breaking with the news. He was tempted to leave. The revenge sweet, but he remembered the last time he'd left her alone. Tenderly, he brushed the fiery red hair from Alexandra's face. He would leave the task to his father.

She caught his hand in hers, imploring him silently to stay. "Please," her voice quivered and it seemed she wanted to say more.

"Please what, my love," he whispered next to her mouth, fanning it with his breath and teasing her. He touched her head and she winced even though the touch had been feather soft.

Time would ease the pain.

They had a lifetime together now and they would suffer no more.

"Bring me home," she said.

He bent to take her mouth in his in an urgent kiss. His tongue traced the outline of her lips, and she gave into the demand, kissing him back, opening herself to him. Warm gentle hands pulled her body closer to his, and he urged General Lee on. The air turned warm and the stars glittered. This summer night was so different from that cold icy winter's night he'd found her half naked and nearly frozen.

Now they belonged to each other and nothing would ever separate them.

They were alone now. Not even the sound of horses penetrated the night. Charles had returned to direct the men and restrain the dogs once they found their prey. General Lee carried them down the road.

"Did you mean it?" he asked her suddenly.

"Mean what?" she said, so tired now she could hardly keep her head from bouncing against his chest.

"I heard you call out of the hole. You said I love... Did you mean it?"

"Of course I did," she looked as if she wanted to tease him, to deny the words, but it had been so long and they'd been through so much. Perhaps, he thought, it was time to take the risk. After all, Alexandra belonged to him.

And he knew now, anything could happen to take away the happiness. A person had only so much time on this earth.

"Have I told you how much I love you?" he asked, tempting her with the sweet promise.

"No, you haven't, not once." Alexandra smiled at him moisture welling in her eyes.

"Not once?" He caressed her cheek then lifted her chin so their eyes met again. "Well, then I'll have to change that now, won't I?"

"I believe so."

"I love you, angel mine. You're here to stay, and I will cherish you forever, protect you with my life." His voice was tender, and she moved closer into his embrace, softly melding their bodies.

Beneath the stars and the moon and for the entire universe to witness, he kissed her again and held her close to his heart. He turned toward the vortex and smiled. After all, it had brought her to him.

Then he rode for home. The sun had risen from the east and sprinkled sunlight across the fields before they reached his house. When they did pull up near the front steps, it was so reminiscent of her first welcoming, it nearly captured his breath. Jessie catapulted from the steps to run into James' embrace, her arms flailing wildly and begging for hugs and kisses. Alex still sat on top General Lee, and Danielle followed behind Jessie instead of Kim.

"Thank God," Danielle breathed.

"Jessie, Danielle," came a soft tremulous voice. "You're both safe. Sean didn't--"

"Hush, love," James told her. "Save your strength."

"You'd never believe what happened, but she's safe and Chase should be home soon," James said. He turned to help Alex down. His hands wound around her waist and she melted into his arms. "We're home to stay."

Jessie flew into her arms and the tears flowed. She hugged Alex. "I'm so glad nothing happened to you," she cried, "I knew papa would save you from the bad man."

When James and Alex looked at each other, he saw the exhaustion in her eyes. He lifted Alexandra in his arms and carried her to the house. She didn't protest, couldn't. By the time they reached the doorway, she could hear the pounding of hooves as more riders approached, Chase in the lead and Charles close behind. The weary hounds, this time trailed behind with some of the other men.

James settled Alex in the parlor and returned to greet his father.

"James, good news."

Chase leapt from his mount and rushed up the steps. "He's dead. The hounds chased him, but he must have fallen. He hit his head on a rock and died instantly. Charles left some men to bury him. He'll cause you no more harm."

James breathed deeply, relieved it was indeed over. Then he grasped his father's hand in his. Their dark eyes met and twinkled affectionately, so much alike. James knew he gazed into his face thirty years hence. "Thank God it's over. Let's eat. I can smell it cooking from here." He clapped his father on the shoulder and led the way into the house.

Charles' men remained outside. The posse, ready to go home and seek their beds, waited for word. James hurried outside and bade them go.

James returned and steaming hot coffee sat on the table. He found Alex sound asleep on the couch with Jessie nestled in her arms. "Time for bed, sleepy head," he whispered to Jessie who blinked and smiled at him. She touched his arm, and he realized then how well she'd walked, no ran into his arms. A miracle he thought, but it was just one more to add to the ever growing collection of them.

"I didn't go to sleep all night," she blinked and her eyelids fluttered shut.

"I guessed, sweetheart," he kissed her on the forehead, gathered her in his arms and carried her upstairs to her room.

James ran down the steps, no longer hungry for food but hungry to hold his wife in his arms and tell her how much he did love her. He heard whispered voices from the guest room and knew his father had the same ideas, and he marveled he'd feel the same way in thirty years.

He crossed the floor to his sleeping wife but instead found her wonderfully awake and the passion in her eyes reflected off his own. He swept her gently into his arms and started for the steps. "My father and mother have beaten us again," he told her, staring into her eyes. "I want to make love to you, tell you that I love you more than life itself. Then I want to hold you all night long. I don't ever want to let you from my sight again."

She wrapped her arms around his neck and pulled him close. She brushed his lips with hers then deepened the kiss. "I want all that and a baby. Can you do that too?"

The sun had risen in the sky. The colors of dawn had vanished, but the blue sky of summer was a good sign. After he laid her on the bed, he opened the window and the fragrant smell of blooming flowers floated through the window. He vowed he would always keep flowers growing there as a reminder of their second chance and their new life, the new life he hoped they would create. "Now that I have you safe, I think I can do anything."

"Oh," she whispered. "I love you. Can we have a boy?"

"Anything you like."

"Braggart," she sighed and let her hands roam his broad back before they found their way beneath his shirt to the muscled planes of his stomach and his chest.

A gentle knock intruded on the spell she'd woven around them. "Papa? I heard," Jessie called from behind the closed door.

"Don't worry, Mr. James, I'll see Jessie to bed. By the way, Charles thought you'd want to know. Belinda left on the stage yesterday."

Kim must have come up behind Jessie just as she was knocking on the door.

James and Alex stared at each other then James rose to see Jessie to bed once more. Alex fell back on the bed, giggling.

He returned and grinned wickedly at Alex. "So, you think that was funny?" he strode to the bed and continued. "Now, there will be no more excuses and no more interruptions. I intend to make your every wish come true."

He gently caressed her cheek as he lowered himself to sit next to her. He loved the feel of it, soft as velvet against his fingertips.

"And I can hardly wait to hold the results of our loving," she promised him softly.

He proceeded to show her in more ways than one how much he loved her. They would create another miracle here this day, and they would take each other straight to heaven.

About the Author

achristay@aol.com

Born in Medford, Oregon, novelist Christine Young has lived in Oregon all of her life. After graduating from Oregon State University with a BS in science, she spent another year at Southern Oregon State University working on her teaching certificate, and a few years later received her Master's degree in secondary education and counseling. Now the long, hot days of summer provide the perfect setting for creating romance. She sold her first book, Dakota's Bride, the summer of 1998 and her second book, My Angel to Kensington. Her teaching and writing careers have intertwined with raising three children. Christine's newest venture is the creation of Rogue Phoenix Press. Christine is the founder, editor and co-owner with her husband. They live in Salem, Oregon.

Other books by Christine Young
Available at Rogue Phoenix Press

Catching Meara
Book One in the McKenna Clan Series

Meara Thorton was a feisty, world-class computer hacker—cornered by the FBI and shockingly given the chance to be their newly acquired technical analyst. Brilliant and intuitive, yet aching with the loss of everyone she has cared about, her restless heart led her to discover a love she fought and a world she didn't know could possibly exist.

Sweet Sexy Sadie
Book Two in the McKenna Clan Series

From the first time Sadie's eyes met those of Brody McKenna in the hot Sierra Madre Mountains, theirs was a potent attraction—not gentle, slow, and easy, but hot, hard, and all-consuming. The daughter of a dysfunctional family, Sadie had dreams no man could wrench from her with hot sex and an all-consuming passion. She'd challenge this alpha male with all the strength she possessed. But her red hair, fiery temperament, and indomitable spirit obsessed Brody...and he knew he had to find a way to show her he was more than he appeared and convince her to make a life with him.

Sweet Misbehavin'
Book Three in the McKenna Clan Series

Cast adrift after fleeing the home of Jokul, the ice demon, Atantsi, a firestarter, grew to womanhood as she moved through time to keep the demon from finding her. Though stubborn and courageous, she was ill prepared to use powers she had not been taught. Her first sight of the intoxicating Carr McKenna left her breathless, and her second encounter gave her hope for a future she never thought she had.

A playboy, a second son and a shifter, a man who thought his life would be carefree, Carr McKenna was shocked to discover the woman he'd paid as an escort is a firestarter who is running for her life. He is the leader of all the McKennas around the world and that he has multiple powers. His passion for Margo and the need to defend her might cost him his life as well as hers.

Sweet Talkin' Sugar
Book Four in the McKenna Clan Series

Lyonesse McKenna, was dreaming or was she? From the instant Lyn saw Deacon McClain across a black jack table in a crowed Las Vegas casino the unmistakable attraction sent Lyn's senses flying into overdrive. Her family of shapeshifters believed in soul mates. She'd always been skeptical yet she couldn't help but question the way her heart sped when he looked at her.

When Deacon appeared in Las Vegas he knew his first job was to save Lyn from a Sea Demon, but the next order of business was to convince her he would someday mean more to her than she'd ever expected. But her stubborn nature and unbendable spirit consumed Deacon...and he had to chase away all the demons real and imagined in order to win her heart.

Dakota's Bride
The first book in the Lakota/Pinkerton Series

When Emma St. John received her brother's letter imploring her to escape her stepfather's vengeful scheme and to trust Dakota Barringer with her life, she was willing to chance it. But the handsome, brooding riverboat owner Emma found in Natchez a danger of another kind. For Emma soon found herself surrendering to an unrelenting desire.

Raised by the Sioux when his parents were killed, Dakota had been betrayed once before by a white woman. He wasn't about to trust another, especially one claiming that her stepfather, a powerful U.S. senator, had framed her as a murderess. But he couldn't let Emma's intoxicating effect on him. Now Dakota would risk his very life to protect the innocent beauty who had seduced him with her tender love.

My Angel
The second book in the Lakota/Pinkerton Series

A BEAUTY IN BUCKSKINS
When her father decided to send her to a finishing school back East, Angela Chamberlain refused to be confined to stuffy drawing rooms. Instead, the daring spitfire who could shoot like a man and ride like the wind longed for a life of adventure and romance—and she knew exactly who could give it to her. Devil Blackmoor was a hired gun with a dangerous reputation. But Angela was willing to go to the ends of the earth to capture the handsome devil's heart.

A DEVIL IN DISGUISE
He'd come to America looking for excitement, but Devil Blackmoor got more than he bargained for when he encountered a beautiful rebel who answered his kisses with a wild innocence that touched his very soul. Yet standing between them were more obstacles than either ever dreamed. For

Devil had strapped on a gun for the wrong man. And that made Angela his enemy. Now he'll have to choose between his duty and the woman he loves more than life.

The Locket
The third book in the Lakota/Pinkerton Series

The year is 1894. Seeking revenge for crimes against his family, Misha Petrovich follows a path that leads straight to Ariel Cameron's boarding house in Mist Harbor, Oregon. A family heirloom in Ariel's possession leads Misha to believe she is guilty. The locket has been handed down to the oldest girl in the Petrovich family for generations. Ariel is innocent of wrong doing, but her father is not. Misha is torn by his feelings for Ariel and his need for restitution against her father. Knowing that the relationship between them is fragile, Misha does everything in his power to protect Ariel's father. His efforts are to no avail when her father is shot. Ariel comes to realize Misha's steadfast courage and determination to protect her and her father despite what has happened to his family. Ariel's love and devotion heals Misha's heart.

The Talisman
The fourth book in the Lakota/Pinkerton Series

Running from a marriage that lasted one night, Dr. Moriah McKeown discovers the land she has settled on is coveted by determined and lawless men. Yet the proud young woman who once vowed never to abandon her home has second thoughts when her adopted children are threatened. Her only recourse is to enlist the aid of a dark, dangerous gun for hire.

Haunted by the past and a betrayal he will never forgive, Ian Civanovich uses his fast gun and his reckless courage to forget the faithlessness of a woman in his past. He will trust no female—nor will he rest until the threat hovering over Moriah McKeown is put to rest.

Forever His
The fifth book in the Lakota/Pinkerton Series

Struggling to come to terms with the part she played in Jacob St. John's death, Etta Barringer resigns from Pinkerton Agency and seeks peace and solace in a Rocky Mountain Cabin.

Jacob has vowed to discover the reason Etta has betrayed him, sold him out to his enemy and left him for dead.

Isolated in their cabin, they discover their love for each other and learn to trust. But the trust is shattered when Jacob learns she is married to his sworn enemy; the man who left him in the desert to die.

Allura
The first book in the Twelve Dancing Princesses Series

Allura McClellan is horrified by her father's decision to take out an ad in the Times awarding her to the man strong enough and smart enough to win her hand and uncover her secrets. She's an intelligent young woman who takes great delight in the freedom allotted to her by her father. She's well aware that marriage would effectively curtail the adventures she's shared with her sisters and cousins.

Hunter Gray is nothing like the other men who've arrived to vie for Allura's hand in marriage and everything that goes along with it. However, he is the first to refuse to concede defeat and pursue her despite her attempts to disguise her true appearance. It's her temperament that is of more concern to him than her looks. Hunter has worked all his life with the hope of someday owning his own land. Now that it looks like there's a very real possibility that everything he's ever wanted is within reach nothing is going to deter him – including Miss Allura's disagreeable disposition.

The Wager
The second book in the Twelve Dancing Princesses Series

Amorica Hepburn was sent to London to find a husband. Finding a man was the last item on her agenda. With her two cousins, Amorica wagers she can dissuade her suitor before the others. Despite her efforts she discovers a chemistry that cannot be denied. Suddenly she is the arrogant man's wife, pledged to a marriage neither desire. But swept off to his ancestral home above the Dover cliffs and into his strong embrace, Amorica is soon possessed by a raging passion for the husband she had vowed to despise…

Damian Andrews couldn't afford to trust the emerald-eyed spitfire who happened upon his secret. Amorica's hatred of all men of his kind only inflames the war that rages between them. Still, he can not control the intense desire his stubborn bride inspires, or make her surrender to his will until he has conquered the headstrong beauty on the battlefield of love…

A Marriage of Inconvenience
The third book in the Twelve Dancing Princesses Series

A REGAL BEAUTY

When the duchess decides to wed her to a wastrel and a fop, Ravyn Grahm takes matters into her own hands and declares her engagement to another man. Instead of fessing up and telling her great aunt what she has done, she goes through with the pretense. Aric Lakeland is the bastard son of an earl and has a dangerous reputation. But Ravyn is willing to do most anything to keep the duchess from discovering the lie.

A DEVIL-MAY-CARE SMUGGLER

He'd bought land in America, looking to put down roots and end his life of adventure, but Aric Lakeland got more than he bargained for when he encountered a beautiful heiress who made a promise she didn't want to keep. But the promise could not be undone and standing between them were more obstacles than either ever dreamed. Aric had made plans to spend the rest of his life in America and that was at odds with Ravyn's plan of living in England and running her father's estate. Now, he'll have to choose between his dreams and the woman he loves more than life.

Highland Sunrise
The fourth book in the Twelve Dancing Princesses Series

HE MADE AND OFFER...

Life has thrown Christel McClellan some experiences that could have devastated a less determined woman. Beautiful, self-assured and fiercely independent, she is trying to forget the loss of her stillborn child. But is the child alive?

SHE COULDN'T DENY...

Life is carefree for Ryder MacLaren who loves to see what is on the other side of the sunrise. Laird of Clan MacLaren, he is wealthy, handsome and happily unencumbered...until stunning Christel McClellan enters his life. When he hears her story, he believes the child she thought dead has been sold to a wealthy buyer.

Storm's Passion
The fifth book in the Twelve Dancing Princesses Series

SHE MADE A PROPOSAL...

Life strikes Storm Graham a shattering blow when she learns her father has bartered her to a man she detests. Storm is beautiful, self–assured and fiercely independent, and refuses to be a pawn in her father's schemes, yet she can find no way out of this bargain made in hell. Going on the offensive she asks the wealthiest man on the eastern coast of England to marry her, never believing she might fall in love.

HE TRIED TO REFUSE...

For Hadden Johnston life has provided everything he ever wanted, including a sanctuary for homeless children. He is wealthy, handsome and happily unencumbered...until stunning Storm Graham marches into his life and proposes a marriage of convenience. Yet this type of marriage to a woman who inflames his senses is far from acceptable. If he's going to be tied down, he will move heaven and earth to have this woman warming his bed.

Rebel Heart

HER REBEL SPIRIT DEFIED HIS OUTSIDERS SOUL...She was velvet and silk, eyes the color of a summer storm and amber hair. Victoria DeMontville, because of a promise and a codicil to her father's will, was forced to marry one man to protect her from another. She hated Cameron Savage with a fierce passion. But to hold on to her genetic research and find a cure for the deadly Signe virus, she must pretend to love the enemy at her door, come with weapons of fire to melt her icy heart...

HIS OUTSIDERS TOUCH IGNITED RAGING PASSIONS...He wore a mask, disguised as the Phantom, a true legend come to life. Even as war and debate over new genetic research engulfed them all, he would find his greatest adversary in the beauty who'd branded him an outsider and barbarian, the woman he was born to possess, his soul mate.

A St. Patrick's Day Tale
by
Christine Young, C. L. Kraemer, Genene Valleau

Tumble through time…

…to Ireland in 1817, when tensions are high between Protestants and Catholics and faey people guide the fate of villagers. A lovely Catholic lass stumbles upon the weakly ritual fisticuffing between Irish lads. She falls into the lap of a handsome young Protestant. Family ties, grudges, and two conniving faeries threaten their budding love. But the faeries outsmart themselves when they hijack a time machine that has mysteriously appeared in their forest and are whisked to…

…Eugene, Oregon in the 20th century, amid a property feud between the local faeries and night elves. The conniving faeries from Olde Ireland try to stir up more mischief. However, a warrior gnome convinces the magic folk to control their own destiny, and forces the intruding faeries to take refuge in the time machine again, spinning their way toward…

…A modern day castle in western Oregon. An eccentric inventor is determined to reclaim his wayward time machine and save his beloved wife from her latest misadventure. If only they can travel safely past the black hole…

A Valentine's Anthology

The Lending Library-a fantasy by Christie L. Kraemer
Faeries try to fit into the human world when the forest where they make their home is destroyed by a mysterious enemy.

Chasing Rainbows-a contemporary romance by Genene Valleau
An eccentric aunt, an inventive uncle, a mother who wears poodle skirts, and a brother who wears pearls provide a hilarious backdrop for the courtship of a young woman who yearns for a "normal" family.

The Gift-an historical romance by Christine Young
A man and a woman on opposite sides of the Civil War get a second chance at love after one final battle returns soldiers to their war-torn homes to rebuild their lives.

Writing as AnnChristine

Safari Moon

Solo St. John, a wildlife photographer, is preparing for a trip to Alaska. Suddenly, Solo finds women of all sorts invading his privacy, his home and his office, all cooing nonsense words and blatantly throwing themselves at him. Solo doesn't know why, and he has no idea how to rid himself of the persistent women. He finally decides to beg a favor of his best buddy Nyssa Harrington.

In love with Solo for the past ten years and knowing he doesn't return her feelings Nyssa doesn't want to talk to Solo. She knows if she accepts his phone call, she will not be able to resist the temptation to hope again.

A Valentine's Anthology
Sharks by AnnChristine

Will Lily and Jacob, best friends forever, find love or will they discover friendship is not enough for a relationship to take the final step into marriage.

The House on Berkley Street by K. J. Dahlen

When Serenity is asked to find the truth in a forty-year old tragedy, someone in the town of White Oak, Texas doesn't want the truth told. Can they stop her before she finds out what they have kept hidden for so long?

The Placebo Effect by Solstice Stevens

First, there was the poison. Then, there was a four story jump and the basketball hoop. Jessamyn Hamhill's life has been one validation attempt after another . . . until now.

www.ingramcontent.com/pod-product-compliance
Lightning Source LLC
Chambersburg PA
CBHW070632180626
46817CB00006B/2104